BURN THE NEGATIVE

BURN THE NEGATIVE

JOSH WINNING

G. P. PUTNAM'S SONS
NEW YORK

PUTNAM
— EST. 1838 —

G. P. Putnam's Sons
Publishers Since 1838
An imprint of Penguin Random House LLC
penguinrandomhouse.com

Copyright © 2023 by Joshua Winning
Interior art: old abandoned house © Lukiyanova Natalia frenta / shutterstock.com

ISBN 9780593544662 (hardcover)
ISBN 9780593544679 (ebook)

Printed in the United States of America
1st Printing

Book design by Laura K. Corless

"When the legend becomes fact, print the legend."

—Maxwell Scott,
The Man Who Shot Liberty Valance (1962)

guesthouse
[gest-haus] noun

1 A modest hotel.

2 A domestic building, separate from a private residence, in which to host guests.

3 *The Guesthouse*, a gnarly goddamn 1993 horror movie set in a cursed hotel. Basically, everybody involved in making the film is dead so now you're 100% interested AMIRITE? Needle Man gon get you HAHAHAHAHAHAHAHAHAHAHAHA;)

ONE

By the time Laura Warren realized she was fucked, she was already halfway across the Atlantic Ocean.

The plane was full and she'd popped a sleeping pill thirty minutes ago, washed it down with a plastic cup of red wine. It dulled the drone of the engine and made the shapes of her fellow passengers pleasantly hazy. She could almost pretend they weren't there.

Travel was one of the few remaining perks of being a journalist. Her job had taken her all over the world: Tokyo, New York, Sofia. That last, an article about the city's booming film industry, earned her a lethal-looking award two years ago that ended up buried in the cupboard she called an office, along with a small forest's worth of *Zeppelin* magazine back issues. Awards weren't her thing. She just wanted to write words that mattered.

Los Angeles, though.

That made her want to take more sleeping pills.

The digital flight chart on the seat back in front of her showed a plane edging closer to California no matter how badly Laura willed it to turn around, and the pill wasn't working fast enough to numb the anxiety that razored her lungs. She wished the steward would circle back with the wine. He could leave the bottle if he liked.

Her neighbor grunted in his sleep, his knee pressing into hers.

Laura grimaced and shifted over. She wasn't a nervous traveler, had never been freaked out by the altitude or baby food, but she found planes to be *a lot*. The lack of space made her feel enormous. Like she was taking up more room than anybody else. More air.

She had caught the look from her neighbor when he sat down. Annoyance that his ability to manspread would be inhibited all the way from London to L.A. She could tell him to go to hell, of course. That she wanted to be there as little as he did.

Instead, she made a joke about how cozy the next eleven hours would be and, when he merely nodded, swallowed her frustration and opened her first mini-pack of pretzels.

Thirty-seven years old and she still filled every awkward silence with a joke.

Taking a breath, she resolved to keep her mind occupied until she passed out. She tapped the iPad propped on the tray table, opening the press release she'd started to read but neglected to finish in the lead-up to the trip. Everything was always so last-minute these days, and press documents gave her a headache. Their robotic enthusiasm was exhausting.

Begrudgingly, she scanned the first couple of pages, then scrolled to the "About the Production" section on page three. She read the first line—

Streaming mini-series *It Feeds* is a modern reinterpretation of '90s horror movie *The Guesthouse*.

—and every nerve in her body snapped.

Hair prickled on the back of her neck as if charged with electricity.

With numb hands, she dragged the iPad closer, convinced she was seeing things. She willed the sentence to change, to rearrange itself, but no matter how many times she read it, the words remained the same.

The Guesthouse.

THE GUESTHOUSE.

The goddamn motherfucking *Guesthouse.*

Her body suddenly felt distant, a concept rather than a physical object, as her mind went into overdrive. It buzzed with a single question like a wasp trapped in a glass.

How the hell did Mike find out about her past?

It was the only explanation for why her editor at *Zeppelin* magazine had signed her up for the gig. She'd refused more than a dozen times, but she might as well have been screaming into a hurricane. Mike was adamant that she take the job. He said again and again that she was the perfect writer for it.

Laura hadn't understood. It was just a routine visit to the set of *It Feeds*, a generic-sounding horror series and the kind of gig Laura had long outgrown after nearly two decades of journalism. Any graduate with a Dictaphone and a notepad could interview the cast, watch some filming, and write a "making of" to run prior to the series' debut.

But Mike had been immovable.

He'd wanted Laura for this assignment, practically put her on the plane himself, and she couldn't say no. She had already reassigned five articles to freelancers in the past two months, all of which she was supposed to write herself, and Mike wasn't happy. He'd begun questioning her dedication to *Zeppelin*. Even though he didn't state it outright, Laura knew the L.A. gig was a test. A chance for her to prove she wasn't getting picky about what she wrote. She was reliable. Enthusiastic. *L.A., baby! Sign me up!*

Of course, their past was an added complication. Even though Laura had dated Mike for only eleven months, had broken up with him by the time he became her boss, things were still weird between them. The professional line was forever blurred.

They both knew she was the reason it fell apart. Mike would've had to be an idiot not to notice the night terrors and the blackouts, or the nights Laura couldn't sleep at all. She lost count of the times he found her huddled on the sofa, wrapped in a throw blanket with *Heathers* or *Welcome Home, Roxy Carmichael* playing on the TV. And every time he brought it up, often over breakfast the next morning, giving her that half smile that said, *I care, please talk to me, nocturnal creature*, she found a way to shut him down. Keep that part of herself locked tight.

Now, somehow, he knew exactly what she'd kept from him. The splinter in their relationship that she'd refused to dig out was laid bare.

Wine burned the back of Laura's throat.

Did he know *The Guesthouse* was the reason for the nightmares?

No, Mike would have to be a psychopath to make that connection and still send her to L.A.

But how the hell had he figured it out? She'd spent the past thirty years eradicating any trace of her former life. She'd changed her name. Lost the American accent, developed a safely unspecific British one. She'd put on weight and her hair was wavy now, shoulder-length brown. She never wore yellow.

She looked nothing like the kid from the movie anymore.

Polly Tremaine, child actor, was as good as dead.

Yet here she was on a plane to L.A. with no choice but to see the job through.

"Shit," she whispered. "Shit shit *shit*."

She wished she hadn't booked the window seat. She wanted to get out. Move around the aisle. Escape the words on the tablet. But the guy next to her was already asleep and, besides, she couldn't feel her legs. Whether it was the pill or the shock, she couldn't tell.

She reached for her phone, then remembered she was on a plane. She reached for her wine, but only a trickle remained. The steward was a few rows ahead, a bottle in each hand, taking his sweet time as he poured and flirted with passengers. Laura couldn't wait. She hit the call button above her head and chewed her bottom lip as the steward came over.

"Hey, hi, fill her up?" Laura said, holding out her cup.

"Oh, I was just getting to this row." He nailed sounding simultaneously friendly and annoyed.

Laura didn't lower the hand. It trembled. "Sorry, I'm sort of a nervous flier." She tried for twitchy contrition. "Our little secret?"

The steward must've seen the anxiety written on her face, because he softened. He filled her cup to the brim and winked. "Don't worry, your secret's safe with me."

Laura managed a weak smile, waited for him to leave, then drained half the drink. The burn was immediate. She wasn't a drink-all-night journalist, rarely went to flashy events unless she was interviewing somebody, so the wine seared her throat like gasoline, then quickly smoothed the edges of her mind. She took a breath and her gaze found the press release again.

All she saw was that first line.

Streaming mini-series *It Feeds* is a modern reinterpretation of '90s horror movie *The Guesthouse*.

She should have seen it coming. Hollywood was all about rebooting. Remaking. *Regurgitating.* It was only a matter of time before somebody rediscovered that particular movie curio and gave it a fresh coat of paint.

She remembered the smell of dust burning as it hit the lighting equipment, the soft rustle of the paper fortune-teller in her hands. A single piece of paper folded into four conical points that you opened and closed with your fingers to predict the future.

She rarely permitted her mind to go there, pretended the memories had long since disintegrated like wind-parched leaves, but they were just waiting. Biding their time.

Sipping more wine, she attempted to build a mental wall, but the memories came regardless.

She was seven years old when she filmed *The Guesthouse* at Universal Studios. She was born Polly Tremaine and raised in L.A., and the first half decade of her life played out like a showbiz kid cliché. She was just six months old when her mom took her to an audition for Sparkleshine washing detergent. Everybody said Polly was the prettiest baby. The Sparkleshine people agreed. Within a month, Polly's chubby face and gap-toothed grin was on every carton of Sparkleshine. It was on every highway billboard, TV commercial, and cut-out-'n'-keep coupon. She was a household item a whole year before she took her first step.

The jobs kept coming after that. In L.A., success was a virus. As soon as one person caught your bug, everybody wanted it. Polly worked nonstop. Guest spot in a McDonald's commercial, a role in a Bon Jovi music video, two years as the sweet blond kid in the TV sitcom *All My Daughters*.

By the time she landed *The Guesthouse*, Polly had grown accustomed to smiling and nodding along with her mother. She agreed with everything the casting directors said, because it was what her mother wanted. She bit her tongue and pretended to listen, hypersensitive to her mother's heavy, watchful gaze.

One day, she dreamed, her mom would look at her the way the moms in the commercials did. The fake moms who smiled and brushed the bangs out of her eyes. The ones who laughed and pinched her cheeks and hugged her so tightly she held on even after the director yelled *cut*. She didn't want them to let go. She needed the closeness. The contact. The smiles.

Because nothing Polly did ever made her mother smile.

Polly had been living the Hollywood dream.

The only problem was that the dream wasn't hers.

"Nervous flier, hey?" the guy beside her asked. He had woken up and was looking at her, his eyes shaded by a baseball cap. Laura set her wine on the tray, confused for a second.

"Oh, that? The steward was too slow."

He laughed. Even his laugh sounded American. "I like your style. Cute accent, too. London, right?"

Oh God no.

He stretched and flexed his arms, which were thick with muscle. "Sorry about earlier, air travel makes me grouchy. So, what do you have planned for L.A.?"

"Just work."

"Oh yeah? What sort of business are you in?"

Laura tried not to engage. Tried to suggest with a look that just because she had the ability to speak didn't mean she wanted to speak to him. She noticed that the seat on his other side was empty. The third member of their row must be in the bathroom.

"I'm a journalist," she said.

The guy's eyebrows disappeared into his ball cap. "No shit. What kind?"

"Entertainment. TV shows, movies—"

"You know any famous people?" His gaze was too bright. "Do you know Emilia Clarke? I'm so into her."

Christ.

"Oh yeah, we're best pals," Laura said, reaching for her wine.

"Seriously? You've met her? Man, that British accent is such a turn—"

Laura knocked the wine over. Red liquid splashed up her neighbor's thigh and into his lap, soaking into the stonewashed denim. Laura feigned surprise.

"Oh God, I'm so sorry," she said, trying to hide her satisfaction as he yelled and bucked in his seat, held in place by the belt. "Here, let me get some napkins."

She slipped her iPad into the footwell, pushed up the tray, and forced her way past him, half knocking his legs into the aisle as she went.

"I'll be right back, promise."

You overfriendly douchebag.

In the bathroom, she closed the folding door and hit the lock.

The mirror showed her frazzled reflection. Heart-shaped face, mouth turned down at the corners, brown hair falling in uncombed curls to the shoulders of her khaki jacket. The only thing she liked about her appearance nowadays was her eyes, bottle green and too big for her face, which she felt made her look interested. Observant.

Now that she was alone in the cramped airplane bathroom, the reality of the situation solidified around her. It became a roaring in her ears.

She was on her way to L.A.

"Jesus," she whispered, seeing fear and anger on her own face.

When she was seven and got the *Guesthouse* gig, she was so anxious that she threw up on her dress. Her baby sister laughed like it was the funniest thing she'd ever seen, because Amy had a sick sense of humor, even when she was four. Her mom made her strip and scrubbed her angrily in the tub.

The unease filled her body like TV static.

They wanted her to play Tammy Manners. The star of the movie. The little girl who told people how they'd die.

If she'd known then how things would pan out, how the rest of her life would continue to pivot on that one moment, how her parents would uproot the family from L.A. and flee to London when she was eight years old, she'd have fought harder to ditch the *Guesthouse* gig.

But she couldn't have known. Nobody could have.

They called it "the most haunted film in Hollywood history."

So many people involved in *The Guesthouse* were dead or behind bars. Their lives ruined beyond repair. The last, in 1998, was Christopher Rosenthal, her onetime director. He was forty-six, found hanged in his home. No note. No history of mental illness. Just a noose and a staircase.

The Guesthouse: a synonym for *fucked-up.*

Somehow, Laura had evaded the tragedies that befell her '90s colleagues. She was the eye of the storm. The heart of the knot. She'd made a life for herself away from the spotlight and the speculation. Nobody aside from her family knew about her past and she intended to keep it that way. There was no alternative.

Hunching over the sink, Laura turned on the faucet and ran cold water over her wrists. She scooped it into her face, and the shock of it made her gasp. The cold brought her out of the past, back into her body.

She was going to be okay.

The past was in the past.

Not screaming toward her at five hundred miles per hour.

She frowned as her reflection juddered. The mirror was moving. The bathroom shook, looking as flimsy as a movie set, and the floor vibrated under her boots. The lights switched off and on, causing her pupils to dilate.

"Ladies and gentlemen, we're experiencing a little turbulence," a voice said as a seat belt sign pinged on above the mirror. *"Please return to your seats and make sure your seat belts are securely fastened."*

Laura ignored the voice. She grabbed a handful of paper towels and blotted her face as the bathroom trembled. The turbulence was oddly soothing. Maybe the plane would nose-dive before they reached L.A.

You should be so lucky.

After a second, she lowered the towels and stared at her reflection in the mirror. She almost screamed.

A shape stood behind her.

A figure in a black coat, its face bandaged beneath a black hat, clawed fingers raised to her shoulder, the blades glinting in the overhead lights.

A wheezing breath caressed her cheek.

With a cry, Laura spun on the spot, driving her elbow into the towel dispenser, then crashing against the back wall. She turned twice more, her heart racing, then finally stopped, grabbing hold of the sink, panting and feeling ridiculous.

She was alone.

Of course she was alone.

She was jumping at her own shadow.

"Get a grip," she told her reflection. She stood braced against the sink for a moment longer, wishing her heart would stop jackknifing in her chest, but it knew what she was thinking, no matter how hard she tried not to think it.

One way or another, this trip is going to kill me.

#1—*The Guesthouse* (1993)

Of all the films on this list, this is the Big Boy. It goes without
saying that this cult classic must categorically never, ever be
resurrected as a franchise. It's plain health and safety. Look
at the original: hardly anybody came out of that thing alive.
Besides, the film totally works as a stand-alone. The ending
doesn't leave much room for more, unless Tammy comes back
as a grown-up? She could be all badass and pissed off and . . .
NO! What am I saying? See how evil sequels are?! If you're
listening, Hollywood, here's some advice for free: just leave this
one the f**k alone.

COMMENTS

Candyham / *2 days ago*
The Guesthouse was a real-life tragedy. These were people's lives,
man. Quit shitting on stuff you don't understand.

🗨 41   🚩 87   ↻

AdrienneLove1980 / *4 days ago*
I'd KILL for a sequel to The Guesthouse.
We need more Needle Man!!!

🗨 211   🚩 16   ↻

PinheadsBoxOfTreats / *4 days ago*
Did you ever wonder what happened to that kid in The Guesthouse?
She must be so messed up. If she's alive, at least . . .

🗨 107   🚩 3   ↻

TWO

"Are you ready to be scared?"

Sitting in the back of the transit vehicle, Laura shifted her gaze to the woman beaming at her from the front seat. Madeleine looked more like a yoga instructor than an entertainment publicist—as polished and smooth as the iPhone that never left her hands. Sun-kissed, midtwenties, and with her blond hair tied up from her face, she was one hundred percent Hollywood. Just looking at her made Laura feel ancient.

The car window showed her weary face. After she had failed to sleep on the flight, her eyes looked wild and her skin itched. She felt bloated and full of plane snacks, disoriented by the L.A. sun that flashed through the windshield.

L.A.

Her first time here in almost thirty years.

A homecoming she never wanted.

Everything was moving too fast. Cars shot by either side of them, and their driver—a woman in a suit who remained professionally silent as she drove—wasn't exactly going easy on the accelerator.

"Do you *like* being scared?" Madeleine asked, still smiling.

Laura's jaw tensed and she heard herself say, "Nothing scarier than a bad remake, right?"

A single line creased the woman's forehead and Laura knew she had pushed too hard, too fast.

"Sorry, British humor, long flight."

The smile returned. "Oh, you'll just love *It Feeds*. It's going to make for a great article. Actually, FYI, we changed the title from *The Guesthouse* 'cause technically a 'guesthouse' in the U.S. is a private accommodation rather than a bed-and-breakfast. You know, British guesthouses are like hotels, right? I kind of like *It Feeds*, though. It—" Madeleine looked down at her phone. It hadn't stopped buzzing since they'd left the airport. She dismissed it, seemed unable to recall what she had been talking about, and continued regardless. "Trust me, this show is going to blow up. Do you think you'll want to interview the psychic?"

Laura wasn't sure she'd heard correctly. "The psychic?"

Madeleine grinned. "They hired one to keep an eye on the production. You know, in case anything *spooky* happens."

Laura managed to nod. She tried to look interested rather than appalled and said, "Okay."

"Did they say when your luggage would show up?"

Laura grimaced. "The guy on the desk said it'd take between twenty-four and forty-eight hours."

Of course the airline had lost her luggage, and of course it wouldn't arrive until she was due to leave. She was in L.A. for only two nights and she'd checked her suitcase after a plea from the airline to free up space in the overhead bins, an act of charity she knew she'd come to regret. "It happens," the man at LAX had said after the computer located her suitcase in Madrid. "A mix-up at Heathrow."

Laura couldn't help thinking this whole trip was a mix-up, something she should never have agreed to in the first place.

A fresh wave of anger almost overcame her. She had tried to call

Mike the moment she landed, wanted nothing more than to force-feed him a big piece of her mind. But he hadn't answered. She'd redialed, but then customs was hell, and there was the missing luggage, and then Madeleine appeared, chattering like an excitable teenager with barely a pause for breath. Mike would have to wait.

Maybe she'd quit *Zeppelin*, go freelance. She'd made a name for herself in the industry and her friends all said freelancing was the future.

Mike had acted like her friend even after the breakup.

"Just because we didn't work out as a couple doesn't mean I stopped caring about you."

Laura shuddered. He had a funny way of showing it.

"We could stop by a clothing store on the way to the studio," Madeleine suggested, tapping on her phone. "Or we could check into the hotel? Give you a chance to freshen up?"

"That's okay, I'll live," Laura said, even though her body ached with the need to shower off the plane residue. She just wanted to get their first visit to the set over with, and then maybe she could relax, hush up the demons in her mind.

She was grateful for the emergency underwear she'd packed in her hand luggage. Along with the Dictaphone and sleeping pills, they were all she needed to survive forty-eight hours in La La Land.

A good journalist is always prepared.

"You saw the original, right?" Madeleine asked, lowering her phone. "*The Guesthouse?*"

Christ, there was a question.

Technically, Laura hadn't seen it until she was fifteen. Her dad said it was too intense for a kid, even though Laura had snuck a copy of the full script and knew it backward and forward in time for the shoot.

She finally watched the film at a sleepover with her sister, Amy, years after they'd moved to the UK. She'd had no choice but to go along with the majority vote on that evening's scary movie, and as she withdrew into her sleeping bag, she couldn't get over how dated it looked. How fake. All the fuss people made and it was just a schlocky '90s horror movie about a cursed hotel.

Afterward, when their friends were asleep, Amy snuck into Laura's sleeping bag to ask if she was all right. She was three years younger than Laura but smart. Perceptive. Maybe that was what happened when your family plucked you from your home and dumped you in a new country. You got good at spotting when things were off.

Their father was British, had immigrated to the United States in his twenties, which made moving to the UK straightforward enough. But England hadn't been home to the girls or their mother, and the change affected them all.

Amy and Laura never spoke about *The Guesthouse*, and Laura hadn't wanted to talk about it that night at the sleepover. They both knew it was the reason their parents fled L.A. Amy had almost no memory of America, but she knew *The Guesthouse* was the reason their lives were upended.

Remade, Laura thought.

It was better to pretend the film didn't exist.

"Yep," Laura told Madeleine. "Love it."

"Right? There's something about it that still slays." Madeleine rested the phone in her lap. "So many horror movies feel safe, like you can see they put a filter on it. But *The Guesthouse* is bitchin' even now."

Laura nodded, her back stiff. Even for a writer, sitting for over twelve hours straight wasn't healthy, and she felt the need to move. Shake off the wooziness of the sleeping pill. Get some feeling back in her body.

She looked out the window and tried not to think about how much she wanted to tell Madeleine to turn the car around and put her on the next plane home. The industry was small and people talked. A lot of money had been spent on this trip and Laura couldn't ditch it without putting her reputation on the line. Just one more thing to thank Mike for.

She cursed the day she decided to train as a journalist. Writing had saved her as a teenager. It provided an escape from her mother's snide comments, the pressure of her studies, and the nightmares that waited for her to put her head on a pillow. Her journals were a safe space. She could be entirely herself, and there was no doubt in her mind that she wouldn't be here today without them.

Though she hadn't set out to turn her fondness for writing into a job in the media, she gravitated toward their stories. She loved stories in every form. News features, web articles, books, TV, even films. Stories were magical. Done well, they lit you up. Set your brain on fire.

Her path to journalism may have been unconventional, but it had been the making of her.

Until today.

On the horizon, downtown L.A. rose like a fortress, a distant collection of smog-blurred skyscrapers. Heat prickled the inside of Laura's chest. She had forgotten how immense L.A. was. How it always seemed to be about to swallow you up. She had a hard time believing she used to call it home.

A bridge came into view, spanning the highway.

Laura was about to take out her phone and check her emails when she spotted somebody standing high up in the middle of the bridge. It looked like a man.

He was motionless, watching the traffic as it streamed beneath him. Something about his silhouette, so black against the bright L.A. sky, caused her arm hair to rise. Though she couldn't explain why, she got the sense the man wasn't idly observing the vehicles as they whizzed by. He was watching one vehicle in particular.

Hers.

She craned forward in her seat, attempting to get a better look through the windshield. She tried to bring the man's face into focus, but it was a shadowy blur. He could be laughing or screaming for all she could tell. What was he doing?

The interior of the car blackened as they passed beneath the bridge.

When they came out the other side, Laura turned and looked through the back window, just in time to see the man jump.

It was over in an instant.

One second he was falling, and then he was on the road, cars swerving around him, horns blaring. A number of vehicles rocked to a standstill at the roadside, forcing those behind to brake.

Laura didn't make a sound.

In the front seat, Madeleine was still talking. Neither she nor the driver had seen. But Laura had.

She turned back around, numb to what she'd witnessed, and tried to crush the thought worming up from the depths of her mind.

Here we go.

It's started.

B/W photograph of VINCE MADSEN (white, 30s) on the set of
The Guesthouse.

                    CHRISTOPHER ROSENTHAL (director)
                              (v.o)
        He was a regular guy. Loved movies. Loved making
        movies. There was no job too big or small. He was
        the perfect construction foreman--that was his
        title but he did plenty other jobs too.
        Adaptable. Dependable. Exactly the kind of guy
        you want on your crew.

B/W photograph of a stretcher covered in a white sheet
being loaded into the back of an ambulance.

                        YVONNE LINCOLN (writer)
        That was a hard day.
                              (pause)
        A really hard day.

COLOR FOOTAGE: Grainy 8mm footage of the Universal set.
We move through working crew and actors, past POLLY
TREMAINE (seven) in her yellow dress, then maneuver to look
up at the Cricklewood Guesthouse.

                        CHRISTOPHER ROSENTHAL
        Vince was working on the roof. The rest of us had
        broken for lunch and while we ate in the canteen,
        he was securing some tiles that had come off
        overnight. The lights get so hot in the studio,
        they melt everything.

                        YVONNE LINCOLN
        I remember I was eating lunch in the canteen,
        talking through some of the dialogue in the next
        scene with Chris.

                        CHRISTOPHER ROSENTHAL
        I returned to set before everybody else. Wanted
        to check on Vince and make sure everything was
        ready for the next scene. It was oddly quiet when
        I reached the soundstage. Even then, I just had
        this feeling we were in trouble. I've had that
        feeling ever since.
                              (shakes his head)
        And I'll never forget the moment I found him.

AUDIO: 911 recording.

> CHRISTOPHER ROSENTHAL
> He's not moving. I think he fell. He's not
> moving.

> OPERATOR
> Sir, an ambulance has been dispatched. I'm
> going to ask a couple of questions to help--

> CHRISTOPHER ROSENTHAL
> No no no. I think he's dead.

Cut to: Yvonne Lincoln interview.

> YVONNE LINCOLN
> It's a big drop. About 50 feet from the roof of
> the guesthouse to the soundstage floor. He
> must have lost his footing or tripped. Nobody
> saw a thing.

Cut to: Christopher Rosenthal interview.

> CHRISTOPHER ROSENTHAL
> (emotional)
> Yeah, that was a really tough day.

He tears up, waves a hand that signals he wants to stop
the interview.

Cut to: B/W photograph of Vince smiling into the camera
while hugging Polly Tremaine.

> NARRATOR
> The coroner's report states Vince Madsen died
> from a broken neck. He would most likely have
> died on impact. He was just thirty years old,
> the first member of the *Guesthouse* crew to
> lose his life. Sadly, he wouldn't be the last.

THREE

The Universal Studios lot was bigger than she remembered. Off-white warehouses lined the wide avenues and their reflected light blinded her. The trapped heat felt like a physical presence Laura had to push against just to keep up with Madeleine as she skipped down the middle of the avenue.

"They're shooting on stage five," the PR said, shades on. "It's where they shot *The Guesthouse*, plus *Weirded Out* and *I Know Something You Don't Know*, so it has horror continuity. You know, people go nuts over stuff like that."

Laura said nothing, which didn't seem to bother Madeleine.

She was still shaken by the sight of the man.

"Jumpers" they called them over here in the States. Except the man hadn't jumped, he'd dropped. Like a bag of bones. She kept seeing him suspended over the highway, his limbs hanging limp, head pointed toward the tarmac. Then the impact, his body crumpling.

"Laura?" Madeleine's voice scattered her thoughts. She saw the publicist holding open a door in the side of one of the soundstages. It led into a rectangle of darkness.

"Sorry, jet lag's killed my few remaining brain cells," Laura said. Only half a lie. She felt dried out from the plane, hungover from the wine, and frazzled by the sleeping pill that had failed to do its job.

"We'll get you coffee," Madeleine said. She stepped through the door and Laura followed. "Or tea, if you prefer. Brits go gaga for it, right?"

"Coffee's fine."

It took a moment for Laura's eyes to adjust to the change in light.

The air was cooler in the soundstage, nipping at her cheeks, and she heard a hum of activity ahead, people talking, someone hammering. As her vision adjusted, the darkness receded and a large structure materialized at the center of the space, as if emerging from fog. It solidified with every passing second until Laura recognized the bulk of a house.

A tremor traveled through her.

She felt sure her skull had cracked open and emptied the guesthouse onto the floor.

It was a complete build. A full house, its windows lit from within, the roof nearly touching the vaulted ceiling. It looked as if it had been airdropped in from another time. An imposing artifact, all angles, painted wood, and cold glass.

For a moment, she was back in 1993, making *The Guesthouse.*

She felt the past clutching for her and stepped out of its grasp.

"Impressive, right?" Madeleine pushed her shades into her hair as she led Laura farther into the soundstage.

"They built the whole thing," Laura murmured.

Her head started to pound as they drew nearer to the set. A sick sensation settled below her rib cage. She thought she might vomit.

But she knew the feeling.

It was the kind that comes with a memory long buried. A memory that wants out.

She realized she was really going to have to do this. She was going to have to talk about the one thing she always refused to discuss.

Years ago, in a moment of morbid curiosity, she'd read a couple of articles about the film online and felt sickened by what she found. They all wanted to know one thing: How had the movie fucked her up? What scars remained? Was that why she retreated from the limelight, never to be seen again? All in order to escape the shadow of *The Guesthouse?*

Looking at the set, Laura tasted blood. She'd chewed a strip of skin from her bottom lip. She bit down on it, forced herself to swallow.

"Hey, Kyle," Madeleine said to an immaculate blond woman walking past in a white bathrobe, escorted by a couple of workers in black T-shirts.

"Maddy!" the woman said, waving but not stopping. "I'm off to get gory. Speak later?"

"Sure thing." The publicist turned to Laura. "That's Kyle Williamson, one of our stars. She's a doll. We'll get time with her later. Oh, hey, there's Todd." She gestured at a skinny guy in a John Carpenter T-shirt who was talking to a woman wearing a headset. He noticed Madeleine, said something else to the woman, then strolled over.

"Hey, hi, welcome to Cricklewood!" He looked even younger up close, twentysomething with a boyish grin and wavy black hair that belonged on a catwalk. Laura doubted he shaved more than twice a month.

"Todd, this is Laura from *Zeppelin* magazine," Madeleine said. "Laura, this is Todd Terror."

"Director and showrunner," he said without a hint of embarrassment, shaking her hand.

He was the showrunner? Jesus, where were the adults in Hollywood?

"Laura Warren, hack writer."

He laughed. "Right! I love the magazine, big fan. Did you have anything to do with the Bob Corman piece last year?"

Laura blinked. "Actually, yes. That was one of mine."

"All right! What a guy. You really captured him. Hell of an article."

She couldn't tell if it was Hollywood spiel or genuine enthusiasm. Americans had customer-service politeness down to an art. She suppressed a scowl.

"Hey, we're resetting for lunch, want to come inside? Check in to the Cricklewood?"

"Great," Laura said, even though her stomach had started eating itself and she was aware of the exit behind her, forty feet away, so close she could turn and run for it.

But then Madeleine said she'd circle back in a few minutes and vanished, and Todd started talking, leading her past a snack table against one wall, then past another table laid with props. He went up the wooden steps to the front door of the guesthouse, and even though Laura wanted to take a minute, delay the inevitable, her feet followed.

She was doing this.

She remembered to take out her Dictaphone and hit record, clenching it tight to stop her hand shaking.

They stood in the entrance hall.

"Our production designer is a genius," Todd said. "She looked at real turn-of-the-century British guesthouses, soaked up their vibes. Not bad, huh?"

Laura surveyed the hall, the noise of the soundstage muffled by the walls. Something about it made her uneasy. The house appeared distorted. It looked almost Victorian but too big, too ornate. The surface vibe was kitschy British, which didn't fit with the all-American size of the place, and every light fixture and picture frame was gaudy to the point of comical. It was as if somebody had cannibalized a dozen guesthouses from around the world and pieced together a Frankenstein's monster of a hotel.

"You're British, right?" Todd said, and Laura didn't correct him.

Aside from the odd word, she had entirely lost her American accent. She could be a native Londoner. "We were really inspired by British design. Have you ever stayed in guesthouses over there?"

"Yeah, but they don't look like this."

Todd's grin slipped.

Shit.

"I mean, this kind of bed-and-breakfast is usually outside of my budget."

"Right right right. Why don't we sit and you can ask some questions?" Todd led her through a doorless archway into a lounge that hadn't been told the 1970s were over. Dark wood and floral wallpaper gave the room a heavy feel, the decadence brooding and obvious. The ceiling was glossed tree-bark brown. The plush carpet sucked at Laura's boots.

Todd gestured to an oversized chair and Laura sat. Todd perched on the sofa. Behind him, bay windows gave a view of the soundstage, the shapes of workers moving in the dim environment like deep-sea creatures.

Laura tried to gather her thoughts.

Act professional.

But her brain felt like it was being stretched in ten different directions. Memories she'd kept under wraps for decades jostled to be acknowledged. She cleared her throat, considered taking out her notebook just to have something to look at, but it was buried in her bag and if she started rooting around for it, she'd lose her cool.

"So, uh, let's start at the beginning," she said. "What drew you to *It Feeds?*"

Todd grew serious. "It started with the original film, right? Everybody knows *The Guesthouse.* It was part of my final thesis at film school. I was nuts for it. Still am. I actually own the original print. I won it at an auction a few years back after the distributor went bust."

He looked so proud.

"You own the negative?" she asked.

"Yeah. Well, it's not a negative. Technically, it's an Answer Print, but I guess 'negative' sounds cooler. It's locked in my office on the lot. Anyway, when my agent heard Netflix had bought the rights to the property, I hassled her for months to get me a meeting. Nobody loves that film more than me, so I couldn't let *anybody* fuck it up but me."

He paused as if waiting for her to laugh. Laura wasn't in the mood.

"If the show's a reboot—" she began, but Todd cut her off.

"A *reinterpretation*." He grinned. "Corny, right? But it's true. I hate remakes that follow the road map without doing something different. I think it's possible to retain the spirit of a film without tracing over the blueprint. That's why we're calling it a reinterpretation. Like Burton's *Apes*, only hopefully better."

He looked around the living room. "There's stuff that people will never expect, but at the same time, it has to *feel* like *The Guesthouse*. It has to tap into that same fear of staying someplace unfamiliar and being consumed by it."

Laura felt like somebody else was nodding and holding out the Dictaphone. She wasn't in her body. Her mind circled the ceiling, seeking cracks through which to escape.

It's just a set. Just a set.

"Did Madeleine tell you about the psychic?" Todd asked.

"She mentioned it."

"It's not a stunt. I'm taking the curse shit seriously. You know the stories, right? All the stuff that happened after *The Guesthouse* came out?"

Laura nodded, surprised he'd brought it up. She'd assumed he would want to distance his production from the controversy, but Todd seemed to be running right into it.

Then again, she supposed it was unavoidable. Eight people had died both during and after the making of the film. The first was a horrible accident, the crew member falling from the roof of the set in '93. The second was her on-screen sister who, two months after the movie came out, burned alive in her bathroom after an electrical fault. The third, her on-screen mom, was the victim of a freak spider bite incident in 1994.

All of their deaths oddly mirrored events from the film, which naturally drew the ghoulish attention of movie lovers who read more into it than they should have. And they all conveniently failed to notice that the deaths stopped in 1998.

Laura reminded herself to breathe. Todd was still talking.

"The last thing we want is for anybody to get hurt," he said. "I know there are skeptics who say the curse isn't real, but if church has taught me anything, it's that there are things around us that we don't—and shouldn't be able to—understand."

He sat forward, rested his elbows on his knees. "Did you know they brought an exorcist to the studio a year after the film came out? Some people said this soundstage was cursed. Others said the script itself was an elaborate hex designed to harm everybody involved, but I figure that's just sexist bullshit spouted by people who hate that a woman wrote the screenplay."

He shook his head. "I guess what I'm trying to say is that there isn't always a hard-and-fast truth about these things."

"People who think that are usually too lazy to dig for the truth," Laura said.

Todd looked at her as if he couldn't tell if she was joking.

She wasn't. Getting to the heart of a story was the thing she prided herself on. There were plenty of hack journalists out there but she wasn't one of them. Hunting for the truth was as essential to her life as was her Winona Ryder DVD collection and Swedish rock on her Spotify.

And here Todd talked about the "curse" like it was a marketing angle. A selling point for his shitty reboot series. A hot topic on which to hang her article.

Laura didn't believe in curses, and she didn't believe in coincidences.

People had died.

She still had nightmares.

And this dipshit wouldn't know trauma if it hacked off his arm.

She took a breath, wondering if she'd sabotaged her own interview, when a woman wearing a headset appeared at the door.

"Todd? We're all set."

Todd nodded. Laura stood with him. "Let's catch up later," he said, his tone more guarded than it had been. "You're here a couple days, right? I want you to get everything you need."

"Thanks."

"Later."

He hurried off into the depths of the house with his colleague, their voices growing distant. Laura found herself alone. The sudden quiet was unnerving.

An empty film set was like an empty school. Drained of purpose, which made it feel like anything could happen.

She peered around the lounge, taking in the scent of new carpet, wallpaper paste, and air freshener, wondering what kind of horror Todd had planned for it.

A groan resounded through the room.

It sounded like the creak of wood joists and plaster. She saw dark whorls like eyes in the wood, gleaming brass screws, and flowers like faces in the wallpaper.

It almost felt like the room was looking at her.

"Fuck's sake," Laura said.

She was exhausted. She had to get out.

Going into the hall, she cast about for the front door and found the stairs leading up to the second floor. Her breath caught.

She was sure she'd seen a flash of yellow as somebody ran up the stairs. A little girl.

A singsong voice echoed down to her.

"One for sorrow, two for mirth . . ."

Darkness crowded her vision.

Laura started counting—*one, three, six, nine*—trying to match her breathing to the numbers, an old coping mechanism that curbed her anxiety. But the bubbling voice intruded, breaking her concentration.

"Three for a funeral, four for birth . . ."

Laura turned on the spot, nearly lost her balance. She couldn't tell where the voice came from. One second it was to her left, and then it seemed to echo from the lounge.

She turned again and froze when she saw movement in a dark doorway.

A gargling breath wheezed.

Five needlelike claws wrapped around the doorframe. Beyond them, something shifted in the darkness, and Laura heard it whispering.

"pollllllllyyyyyyyyyyyyyyyshhhhhh."

She ran for the front door and dashed down the steps onto the soundstage floor, heart thumping in her throat. She saw the exit ahead, a rectangle of light at the far side of the warehouse. Outside.

But she'd stopped. She wasn't running anymore.

She didn't want to turn back, resisted with every fiber of her being, but she felt powerless against the force that turned her body.

She looked up at the guesthouse and saw the man fall. He dropped from the roof like a dead weight and thudded against the floor, spraying blood in the air.

Nausea pinched Laura's throat, flooding her mouth with saliva.

"Laura?" Madeleine's voice pushed through the static in her ears. The PR had appeared at her side, that single line creasing her forehead again, but Laura ignored her.

She scanned the floor, searching for the man who just fell, but he was gone.

"Did you see anybody just now?" she asked Madeleine, breathless. "On the roof?"

Madeleine went still. "No. Why?"

"Did you hear anything?" Laura looked up at the façade, then the warehouse floor again, looking for a sign that the man had been there. The thump of impact and the splash of blood had been so real. But there was nothing. No blood. No body.

"Are you all right?" Madeleine asked.

Laura barely heard her. Doubt dulled the panic that had gripped her, but the doubt felt almost worse, because she was so sure she'd seen the man fall. Her throat burned and she realized she really was going to throw up.

"Where's the toilet?" she asked. "I mean the bathroom."

Madeleine's eyes got big. "Through those doors. Want me to show you?"

"No, I'm fine."

She made it to the stall just in time to flip the seat up and vomit into the bowl.

The man from the highway cycled through her mind, falling over and over, and she heaved, her back aching as she emptied the contents of her stomach.

When the retching ended, she rested back on her heels, wrung out. She flushed, put down the seat, and sat looking at her hands. She willed them to stop trembling. She took a breath and released it slowly, tasting vomit and plane pretzels.

It's just a show. A shitty mini-series that'll end up canceled after its first season and quickly forgotten.

This was no different than any of the other junkets or set visits she'd done over the years. It was just a few days. That was all. This time next week she'd be back in London working on a different feature, something safe and impersonal, and she wouldn't have to think about *It Feeds* or Todd Terror or *The Guesthouse* ever again.

She peed, checked she hadn't gotten upchuck on her khaki jacket, and left the stall.

A woman stood at the sink washing her hands.

Laura went to the next sink, trying to ignore her puffy reflection. The other woman looked malnourished, her face narrow and skeletal, and Laura wondered if everybody in L.A. was on a diet. She guessed the woman was in her fifties. She looked like she belonged in a biker bar, wearing a loose blue shirt and torn jeans, fingertips nicotine-stained. No visible audio pack or personnel badge. Her brown hair was scraped back into a ponytail, which had the alarming effect of accentuating her dark eyes. They were almost all black.

Laura had a feeling the woman knew she had been freaking out in the stall. Maybe she'd heard her vomiting. Either way, her gaze in the mirror made her tense up. It was almost as if the woman recognized her, even though they'd never met before.

"Are you working on *It Feeds*?" Laura asked. She didn't usually interact with movie people when a PR wasn't there to monitor, but she couldn't help feeling curious. Plus, it was a good distraction from her spiraling thoughts.

"If you can call it work." Her voice was low, bored.

The woman looked away and the tension in Laura's shoulders eased. She watched her go to the paper dispenser and dry her hands. A cigarette pack was stuffed in her back pocket. As she approached the exit, the door opened and Madeleine appeared, only just avoiding bumping into her.

"Oh, hey, Beverly," Madeleine said, moving to one side. "Sorry 'bout that."

Beverly didn't respond. The door closed behind her as she left.

Madeleine wiggled her eyebrows at Laura.

"Looks like you just met our psychic."

Excerpt from The Guesthouse *screenplay, dated October 16, 1992, written by Yvonne Lincoln*

INT. CRICKLEWOOD GUESTHOUSE BREAKFAST ROOM--MORNING

TAMMY, 7, an angelic blond girl wearing a yellow dress, makes her way between the tables, where guests eat their breakfast.

Tammy approaches an ELDERLY WOMAN sitting by herself at the window.

                    TAMMY
     Want to play?

She holds up a paper fortune-teller.

                         ELDERLY WOMAN
          How delightful, I'd love to.

                         TAMMY
          You have to pick a number.

                              ELDERLY WOMAN
               Okay, let's say five.

Tammy CHANTS while moving the fortune-teller between her fingers.

                              TAMMY
               One for sorrow,
               Two for mirth,
               Three for a funeral,
               Four for birth,
               Five for Heaven,
               Six for Hell,
               Seven for the Devil, his own self.
               One, two, three, four, five.

She shows the woman the new selection of numbers revealed.

TAMMY

You have to choose another number.

ELDERLY WOMAN

Two.

Tammy unfolds the fortune-teller to read out the words
written beneath number two.

FOCUS ON: the writing, as Tammy reads.

TAMMY

"In the bath."

ELDERLY WOMAN

In the bath? What does that mean?

TAMMY

That's where you're going to die.

ELDERLY WOMAN

That's not very nice.

Tammy SHRUGS.

TAMMY

I don't make up the rules, the Needle Man does.

FOUR

H ow long have you known?" Laura demanded.

On her phone screen, Mike sat in a high-backed desk chair. He was on the youthful side of forty, bald, dark-skinned, and handsome in a fitted yellow shirt that showed off his muscular shoulders. He had the kind of face that, in the five years they'd known each other, was usually difficult to stay angry at. His laugh was infectious. It was one of the things that had attracted her to him. His sense of humor, his ambition, his love of Korean food and Tori Amos. It helped that he wasn't big on horror. Had never heard of *The Guesthouse*.

Today, though, her editor-slash-ex's open smile made Laura want to claw the screen, the same words buzzing on the tip of her tongue: *you set me up you set me up you set me up.*

Mike ignored her question. "Have you slept? You look exhausted."

"As a matter of fact, no, I haven't slept since London."

Madeleine the PR had dropped her at the Loft Hotel twenty minutes ago. After Laura's encounter with the so-called psychic,

Madeleine had insisted that Laura check in, take a load off, and get her bearings. Laura understood that was L.A.-speak for *You look like hell, hon.*

The hotel was rustic with an industrial edge. Faux exposed beams, plants, metal finishings, shag rugs, and mirrored glass. Not a place Laura would have chosen for herself.

If she'd made the call to Mike in her room, she'd have been unconscious in two seconds, so she found a table at the hotel bar. It was only five p.m. but she felt the jet lag like a physical entity sharing her body. It was one a.m. in London and she begrudged the fact that Mike was awake when she called; she knew he was a night owl but had hoped to outlast him. To wake him up, yell at him while he was half-asleep and defenseless.

Not for the first time, she wished he'd stop being so freaking perfect.

"Laura—" Mike began, his voice coming through her earphones, but Laura cut him off.

"How *long* have you known, Mike?"

He sighed, rubbed the back of his neck. "Six months."

Laura felt a punch to her gut. Six months. Mike had carried on calling her Laura for six months and she hadn't suspected a thing.

"I wanted to tell you but I couldn't find the right time."

"How?" she asked, her voice flat. "How did you find out?"

"Amy told me." Quickly, he added, "Look, it's not her fault, she didn't go into any detail. Just enough that I made the connection."

"Fuck." Laura's free hand tangled in her earphones' cord, yanking them out. The sounds of the bar rushed into her ears, a deafening hiss of voices and coffee-machine steam.

Amy. Of course.

Laura had introduced her sister to Mike when they were dating, and she knew they'd stayed in touch in the four years since the breakup.

They were close. Friends-ish. She didn't think anything romantic was going on there—Amy had better taste than that—but Laura resented the alternative: they talked about her.

I'm going to kill her.

She stuffed the earphones back in. "Rebook my flight for tonight. I've spoken to the showrunner, been to the set. I have enough material—"

"Laura—"

"You knew and you sent me here anyway. Do you know how fucked-up that is? It's not like that film is even big outside the cult crowd—"

"I'm sorry," Mike broke in, "but you wouldn't have gone if I told you the truth."

"Damn fucking right I wouldn't have."

The woman at the next table looked at her. Laura didn't care.

"They have a psychic, for God's sake," she said. "This whole production's a joke."

"Really? Can you get time with them? A psychic would make for great color!"

Facing her dead-eyed stare, Mike deflated. His voice softened as he continued. "I really am sorry, but it was the only way I could get you on the trip. I figured once you got there, you'd be okay. It had to be you, Laura, because you're right, nobody really cares about a cult horror film, but they will care about you. How could they not?" He looked right at her through the screen. "*You're* the story, Laura."

"What?" Her lower back pinched against the back of the chair as she shifted her weight.

"Think about it from a reader's perspective. The press-shy star of the original *Guesthouse* comes out of hiding, reports on the remake, and finally tells her story to the world. It's got it all. Emotion, redemption, hope for the future. Don't you want people to know the truth?"

Any final reserves of energy left her body.

The phone was heavy in her hand.

And Mike was out of his mind.

Laura told other people's stories, not her own. That was the deal she'd made. Tell a stranger's story and nobody would care about hers. She was invisible. A conduit. Words on a page. There was no way in hell that would change.

When she failed to answer his question, Mike sat back in his chair. He released a breath. "You've been so busy since your dad died, and I know your mom—"

"I've been *working*," Laura snapped. "Working for *you*."

She couldn't think about her parents. Her head already felt swollen with jet lag and the knowledge that her sister had sold her out.

When she finally met Mike's gaze, he had his "editor face" on.

"I didn't want to bring this up, but whatever you're going through, it's affected your work. I've tried talking to you, but things keep getting in the way. When this trip came along, I figured a few days in the sun writing about a glossy streaming series could help you get your mojo back. Remind you how far you've come since the movie. Make your stuff less tired and distracted."

Laura's insides twisted. *Tired? Distracted?* Editors often gave feedback on copy, suggesting word changes or asking for clarification on certain sentences, but this was the first she'd heard Mike complain about the quality of her work. It stung because Laura was the more experienced of the two, in just about every area of her life. She'd given him her own performance review after their first night together. Verdict: room for improvement.

And it didn't feel like he was speaking to her as an editor. It felt like he was speaking as a guy who had no idea why they weren't still together.

"You're a different person now, right?" Mike said. "The movie's in the past."

Her grip tightened on the phone. She suddenly felt justified in keeping her Hollywood history from him. She'd had a feeling even then he wouldn't be able to handle it. Her voice emerged throaty and raw.

"You have no idea what you've done."

Mike frowned, searching her face, looked like he was about to ask a question, then suddenly stopped moving.

"Wait," he said. "Shit. Is this what was going on when we were together? The sleep problems? All of that? It was about the movie?"

She couldn't speak. Her thoughts were elsewhere. She'd met Mike's parents at a summer barbecue six months into their relationship, and she couldn't believe families like his really existed outside of infomercials and Hallmark. Mike's father was funny and kind, his mother warm and loud. When it rained, the day only got more fun as they all piled into the kitchen laughing and drying off, their dogs tracking mud everywhere. Laura had felt a part of something. Something alien but *good*. They were a family. Their lives full of light and color. Their love unconditional.

Laura chewed the inside of her cheek.

Mike would never get it.

He wanted her to write about her life, but she couldn't open that floodgate. She knew what kind of people were out there. She could still smell the woman in the supermarket parking lot, the one who sparked their relocation to the UK when she was eight years old. It was one of the few things she remembered about her. The smell of washing detergent and cigarettes and the sound of that shrill voice.

"We'll go for a ride! It'll be so fun!"

"Laura?"

Mike's voice made her jump. She tried to focus.

"It is, isn't it? Shit, Laura, I had no idea. God, I'm such an idiot. I would never have sent you if I thought this was anything to do with that."

He looked genuinely upset, but Laura was tired of trying to make people understand.

"You can have my audio files," she said coldly. "I'll do the interviews, get your access, but you can commission somebody else to write the fucking thing because I'm fucking done."

She hung up before Mike could say another word.

News | **Entertainment** | **Style** | **Royals** | **Stream** | **More**

The Secret to Raising a Child Star

Fame can come at a price, but Hollywood mom Pamela Tremaine tells us the key to raising a happy child actor, and how to avoid the pitfalls of stardom . . .

BY PATTY KING

"We just play make believe," says Pamela Tremaine when *Ours! Weekly* meets her for coffee on Melrose Avenue. "Every day is a game. Honestly, it's a dream, and I'm so proud of Polly and everything she's accomplished."

As glamorous as she is warm, Pamela Tremaine almost looks like a star herself. Blond and trim, she is immaculate in a baby-blue pantsuit that matches her eyes, which light up with pride whenever she talks about her talented daughter.

Pamela is, of course, the mother of Polly Tremaine, the star of horror movie *The Guesthouse*, in theaters this week. It's the younger Tremaine's first movie role, and looks set to shatter her image as the "Sparkleshine baby" once and for all.

According to Pamela, Polly didn't balk at the *spooky* subject matter: "Oh, she doesn't scare easy. She loved the script! This is all Polly wants to do. If she told me tomorrow that she didn't want to act anymore, we'd bid farewell to Hollywood. But she loves it. She was born to be a star."

Clearly, Pamela knows what she's talking about. So what's the secret to raising a well-rounded and happy child star? "To start off," she says, "you must . . .

Subscribe for just $15 a month to read the rest of this article!

FIVE

n her room, Laura looked around the beige suite, feeling lost. Hotels were meant to make strangers feel at home, but the comforts on offer here felt artificial. Unloving.

She had no luggage, just her travel bag and a throat full of emotion she had no idea what to do with.

Her mind hopped between anger and irritation. And fear. She felt hot all over but frozen at her core.

Even after everything, she'd thought Mike was on her side. More than just an editor or an ex-boyfriend. A friend. But she'd forgotten that all he really cared about was the magazine. He was obsessed with circulation, ABCs, and print costs. He didn't give a damn what she'd been through or what this trip was already doing to her.

She'd spent ten minutes on the set of *It Feeds* and that had been enough for her mind to inflame. Imagine things that weren't there.

She shuddered at the memory of the claws curling around the doorframe.

Not a memory. A trick of the light. A hallucination brought on by lack of sleep and a good meal.

She showered, lathering herself in expensive hotel products that smelled of mango, and pulled on the fluffy white bathrobe hanging on the back of the door. The suite of rooms was impressive and the production company had given her a higher-than-average per diem to spend on food and drink. Being a journalist wasn't always a kick in the teeth.

Laura wished she could feel grateful, but all she felt was ill. The comforts of her London flat were so far away she might as well be on a different planet. The life she'd built could be a dream, and she didn't want to wake up from it.

On the bed, she cycled through TV stations, praying for a Winona Ryder movie. Back home, when she was in this kind of headspace, she put on *Heathers, Mermaids, Beetlejuice,* or *Girl, Interrupted* and escaped into their tales of kooky outsiders attempting to make sense of the world. They reassured her that reality did, in fact, bite, and she could quote them verbatim. Even *Alien Resurrection* offered a deep-space spin on the weirdo loner fighting to survive.

Nobody did it for her like Winona. Nobody was as intelligent yet fragile, like a peppered moth that fluttered knowing the world could crush it in a breath. Nobody knew about the darkness within the way Winona did. And nobody pulled off a pixie cut like her. Not Mia Farrow, not nobody.

The TV failed her. Laura shut it off, trying not to think about the highway man, nor the psychic in the bathroom, nor how strange it was that she'd seen a jumper the moment she set down in L.A.

Her jaw creaked.

If Mike knew about her past, who else did?

Who else had Amy told?

Laura picked her cuticles.

Amy of all people should understand what could happen if people found out. The supermarket incident was just nine months after *The Guesthouse* came out, and it changed their lives forever.

The week before they moved, her mother made her cut her hair. Then her mom fired her agent.

She dressed Polly in baggy jeans and T-shirts: the kind of clothes Tammy would never wear.

She made it seem like she was protecting Polly, trying to make sure that what happened at the supermarket never happened again, but even then Polly saw it for what it really was.

Punishment.

Eight years old and she knew punishment as well as anybody. Punishment for not memorizing her lines. Punishment for putting on three pounds. For playing outside and getting tan, messing with the show's continuity. For telling her father that she didn't want to act anymore, because please, please, she just wanted to be normal. Not on TV. Not in people's living rooms. Not something to be owned and scrutinized and talked about by strangers.

Pamela Tremaine had punishment down to an art.

"You don't want to be . . . boring, *do you, Polly?"*

To her mother, being boring was the worst crime a person could commit.

Sometimes, if they'd signed a new contract or aced a chemistry read, Polly would hear her mom singing in the bathroom. She hit every note of "California Dreamin'" and her voice was so beautiful it gave Polly goose bumps. She wished her mother's personality matched her voice.

But her mother knew exactly how to get what she wanted. She would confiscate Polly's Funshine Care Bear or send her to bed hungry.

And then there was the "match game."

The day the playroom went up in flames was as fresh now in Laura's mind as it was the day it happened.

It was a week after her *Guesthouse* audition, and they'd heard nothing. Pamela was convinced Polly had blown it. The gig would go to somebody else. Her mother hadn't left the house in days. She stayed close to the kitchen, waiting for the phone to ring, and she couldn't look at Polly.

Then she heard about another audition, this time for a blockbuster with Arnold Schwarzenegger, and the color returned to her cheeks. Her gaze became hungry once more.

"This could be huge for us! This could be the start of an amazing new chapter for our family!"

Polly hadn't wanted to learn the lines. Her father was at work—he always seemed to be at work—and Amy was on a playdate. Polly refused to wear the pink dress her mother made for her. She didn't want to go into rooms full of strangers anymore. She wanted to play with Funshine and pretend she was in the faraway world of Care-a-Lot.

Eventually, Pamela dragged her into the playroom. She wrestled the dress over Polly's head and stood her in the center of the play mat with a tin bucket at her feet. She produced a box of matches, shaking one out and striking it. Then she handed it to Polly, forced her to hold it between her thumb and forefinger, and stepped back with her hands on her hips.

"Say the line, Polly, and you can put the match in the bucket, but not a moment sooner." Her tone was encouraging but threaded with danger. "If you put it out early, we'll start again. Now say the line. *Please don't hurt my daddy.* Say it and mean it."

The flame flickered, blackening the matchstick, and warmth licked Polly's thumb and finger. She held the match away from her body. She didn't want to say the line, but she didn't want to burn herself, either.

In a small voice, she said, "Please don't hurt my daddy."

"No!" Her mother paced, bracelets jangling. "Say it like you mean it, Polly! 'Please! Don't hurt my daddy!'"

Heat spread to Polly's fingertips, buzzing and stinging. She desperately wanted to toss the match, but her mother's glare froze her where she stood, and she knew that if she dropped it before she'd said the line right, she'd have to start all over again.

"Please don't hurt my daddy."

"No!"

"Please! Don't hurt my daddy!"

"I don't believe you!"

Her fingertips throbbed and her belly quivered with fear as she saw that the flame had eaten up most of the match, almost reaching her nails.

"Please! Don't hurt my daddy!"

She tossed the match just in time and jammed her fingers in her mouth.

The match dinged off the rim of the bucket and landed on the mat. Instantly, fresh flames caught, withering the woolly fabric. They burned bright and quick.

"I still don't believe you," Pamela said. She stood rigidly, the firelight reflected in her eyes. "Say the line again."

"But, Mommy, the fire—"

"Say the line."

"Mommy—"

"Say the line!"

Tears stung Polly's eyes. For a moment she wished the fire would consume her as it did the mat, if only so she could escape her mother's pitiless stare.

"Please," she whispered, her vision wobbling, her voice breaking, "please don't hurt my daddy."

A slow smile spread across her mother's lips. Her eyes sparkled as she beheld her daughter, her star, with something akin to love. A moment later, Pamela took the bucket and upended it over the fire, extinguishing it. In the silence that followed, they stared at each other, Pamela flushed with triumph, Polly trembling and wishing she were anywhere other than in this room with her mother.

The phone rang. Pamela ran to answer it and Polly heard her breathlessly conversing.

Even before her mother returned, she knew what the call was about.

She'd gotten the *Guesthouse* gig.

She was going to be Tammy Manners.

Polly wanted to scream, but her mother was happy. Then Polly thought that maybe, just for a little while, things would be okay.

If anything, they got worse.

When everything went wrong after *The Guesthouse*, Pamela never forgave Polly for taking the dream away from her.

For ruining their lives.

And now here she was. In Hollywood. People usually came here to pretend they were somebody else, and yet the opposite was true for her. She was being confronted with the person she used to be.

Laura looked down. Her nail was bleeding. The skin around the cuticle was red and irritated where she'd picked it.

Sucking on the blood, she attempted to disconnect her mind from the whirlpool in her chest.

She'd get through this.

It was just two days, and then she'd be home again. She was Laura goddamn Warren! The woman who had pacified prissy actors, temperamental chefs, and leering jailbirds, all in a day's work. She could do this. She'd been through worse. Right?

She checked her phone. It was seven p.m., which made it three a.m. in the UK. There was no point attempting to reset her body clock when she was leaving in just over a day. She'd sleep now and worry about waking up groggy at two a.m. later.

She rummaged in her bag, searching for the bottle of sleeping pills, and winced as something snagged her finger. Withdrawing her hand, she inspected a cut on her index finger. She foraged some more, looking for what it could be, and stopped when she glimpsed something white in the dark of the bag.

Slowly, she extracted an object that shouldn't be there.

A paper fortune-teller.

It was a little crumpled, the paper soft with age, the edges still sharp.

How had it gotten there?

She turned it over in her hands, resisting the urge to crush it into a ball and toss it in the trash. Her fingers almost slipped into the conical compartments, muscle memory urging her to start counting. It was almost identical to the one she had used in *The Guesthouse*, so familiar it made her body heavy with memory.

One for sorrow, two for mirth . . .

She frowned. Faint black marks blotted some parts of the paper, as if something had bled through from the other side.

Curious, she unfolded one flap at a time, until it was nothing more than a creased A4 sheet of paper.

She saw what had made the black marks and her fingertips went cold.

Three words were scrawled in marker pen.

Welcome Home Polly

FACT VS. FICTION:

The Guesthouse Deaths

Now here's something to keep you awake at night!
If you've heard of *The Guesthouse*, you'll know all about the spooky happenings on and off the movie set. Eight people died, some during the making of the movie and some in the years after, and the real-life deaths were creepily similar. Let's take a look at the evidence . . .

IN THE MOVIE	IRL
Victim #1: Ted Adair **Death:** Falls downstairs	**Victim #1:** Vince Madsen (set crew) **Death:** Fell off set roof **Year:** 1993
Victim #2: Una Travers **Death:** Burns alive in the shower of room 305	**Victim #2:** Ashley Young (actor) **Death:** Electrical fault in bathroom **Year:** 1993
Victim #3: Dudley Lane **Death:** Bitten by spider in room 204	**Victim #3:** Julia Barker (actor) **Death:** Bitten by tropical spider **Year:** 1994
Victim #4: Elderly Woman **Death:** Drowns in bathtub in room 103	**Victim #4:** Terrence Hodges (actor) **Death:** Drowned in local pool **Year:** 1994
Victim #5: Maintenance Man **Death:** Decapitated by Needle Man in basement	**Victim #5:** Victor Hooper (producer) **Death:** Decapitated by fairground ride **Year:** 1995
Victim #6: Mrs. Manners **Death:** Buried alive in basement	**Victim #6:** Isabelle Plummer (actor) **Death:** Vanished without a trace **Year:** 1995
Victim #7: D'Arcy Carradine **Death:** Stabbed to death by Needle Man in room 205	**Victim #7:** Kenny Lincoln **Death:** Stabbed to death by wife, Yvonne Lincoln (writer) **Year:** 1997
Victim #8: Mr. Manners **Death:** Hanged in stairwell	**Victim #8:** Christopher Rosenthal (director) **Death:** Hanged at home **Year:** 1998

SIX

People in Hollywood must drink different water from the rest of the world. It was the only way to explain their glow, the way they seemed to be lit up from within.

When Laura entered the dull meeting room on the Universal lot at ten a.m. the next morning, haggard and half-asleep after a restless night, she felt blinded by Kyle Williamson.

The twentysomething star of *It Feeds* wasn't wearing any makeup and her beach-bronzed skin looked radiant. Her blond hair was loosely tied back, her sea-spray blue eyes framed by high cheekbones. As she bounced up out of her brown chair in welcome, she swirled with color, wearing a blue tank top and a rainbow skirt.

"Hi, welcome! I'm Kyle!"

Laura felt the softness of her palm and smelled a floral perfume. Kyle had lit an incense burner on the coffee table. Instead of softening the meeting room, it made it stranger. Like somebody had booked the office for a spiritual retreat.

"Laura," she said.

"Oh wow, my mom's name is Laura! What are the odds?"

Kyle looked thrilled by the coincidence. She gestured to a bowl of chips by the incense burner.

"Want snacks? They're so *good*. I can't stop eating them."

"Thanks, I just had breakfast." Laura heard the edge in her voice and tried to soften it. It wasn't Kyle's fault that she'd woken up irritated, or that her irritation had only grown since she left the hotel. She kept hearing Mike telling her that her work was tired, that she needed to rediscover her mojo, that he was an idiot. She agreed with that last one, but that didn't make her any less annoyed.

More seriously, she wondered if her job was on the line. Mike had let writers go before, when he felt they'd lost the love for *Zeppelin*. He liked to cut off the limb before it poisoned the body. Laura had found his ability to dismiss talent unnerving. Would he do the same to her?

She pushed the thought away. Screw him. And screw whoever thought it was funny to slip the fortune-teller in her bag.

This was just a job. The past was in the past. She'd complete the interviews, fly the hell home, and prove them all wrong.

She clicked on her Dictaphone.

"Want to put it by me?" Kyle took the device and rested it on the arm of her chair, leaning in to say, "Howdy and hello, this is Kyle Williamson speaking. Please don't quote me on anything that makes me sound stupid or lazy?"

Laura's mouth twitched with a near smile.

"I'll try not to," she said.

"Oh, I was only kidding. You seem nice. Some journalists are sort of shady, they ask crazy things. But we're good, right? Just us girls?"

Laura nodded. Actors would make good journalists if they didn't spend their whole time pretending to be other people. Most were naturally personable. But then, when you're rich and beautiful, why wouldn't you be?

"Are you filming today?" Laura asked.

"Not till later, they're setting up the bathroom for a big set piece, but *spoilers*, they'll kill me if I say any more."

"Got it. Let's talk about your role, then. Is she a different kind of character for you?"

Laura had no idea who Kyle was playing. With the shock of the jumper on the bridge and her call with Mike, she'd forgotten to read the rest of the press release. Her brain felt thick and slow with jet lag.

"Oh, she's nothing like the girl I played on *All My Granddaughters*. Tammy's sort of bookish by comparison. Kind of a nerd."

Laura frowned. "I'm sorry, did you say Tammy?"

Kyle nodded. "Right. That's the fun part of rebooting a film. Shit, not rebooting . . . *reinterpreting*. Don't tell Todd I said that. But yeah, they decided to age Tammy up for the show . . ."

She kept talking but Laura wasn't listening. She was dumbstruck.

They'd turned Tammy from a sweet little blond kid into the kind of woman who sold probiotic yogurt by flashing her perfect stomach on TV.

She'd laugh at the absurdity if it weren't so insidious.

Looking at Kyle, Laura couldn't help seeing everything that was calculating and creepy about Hollywood. The way that aging up the character not only bypassed all kinds of child labor laws but also injected the show with S-E-X.

The stuff Hollywood was made of.

Not that it was Kyle's fault. She was just the face on the billboard. And she seemed so excited by it all. Laura almost pitied her.

"Sorry, I'm babbling." Kyle fanned herself with her hands. "I guess I'm just trying to say that my Tammy is different than the old Tammy. There are a few nods to the original, but I'm a whole new model."

"Model" is right.

Laura blinked and tried to look interested. She cleared her throat.

This was usually the point in the interview where she'd ask about working with Todd, or what Kyle's favorite scary movie was, but she thought about what Mike had said about telling her own story. That was off the table, but maybe she could get the cast and crew to debunk the bullshit movie myth for her.

"I'm sorry if this is insensitive, but can you talk about the curse?" she asked. "Has anything weird happened on set?"

She managed a crooked grin, expecting Kyle to laugh and make a joke about bats flying out of her dressing room.

Instead, Kyle went still. Laura noticed tension creep into her jaw.

"I'm sorry," she said, "I guess that was sort of poor taste."

"No, it's not you." Kyle spoke softly. She looked over her shoulder at the door, as if expecting to find somebody watching them. Laura felt a chill and couldn't help picturing her old co-stars. Her on-screen mom and dad were so funny and warm she sometimes forgot she was acting, wished she was living that life for real. Both were dead before they could ring in the millennium.

She pinched the back of her hand, bringing herself back to reality.

Kyle leaned closer, speaking in little more than a whisper.

"At first, I thought I was imagining it. Stuff kept going missing from my trailer. My phone charger, my favorite lipstick. I figured I was just tired. We shoot long days and they can get intense."

She paused, seeming to wrestle with herself. "My second day on set, I found a message on my dressing room mirror. Somebody had stuck up one of my headshots and written the word *IMPOSTER* across it in lipstick. My missing lipstick. Then last week, I found a dead rat in my bathroom. Not just dead but torn open, like in a horror movie. There was blood everywhere."

Despite herself, Laura felt a twinge of sympathy. Kyle really looked upset.

"Did you report it?" she asked.

"Sure, but nothing changed, even when I moved trailers. Security got tightened and I'm escorted basically everywhere now, but nobody's been caught. Todd's so busy with the show, he doesn't have much time for anything else. And that wasn't everything."

She swallowed, taking out her phone. "Just yesterday there was this."

She showed Laura a photo of a messy trailer.

On the wall above the couch, somebody had carved the words *SHE'S HERE*.

An icy nail ran down Laura's spine.

Her gaze went to the window behind Kyle. She was sure a shadow had crossed it, but when she ran over to look, nobody was outside.

"Is everything okay?" Kyle asked as Laura returned to her seat, feeling flustered.

"Sorry, I thought I saw Meryl Streep," she said, mustering a smirk as she shook off the chill. Kyle didn't need to know the photo had rattled her. She tried to focus on the woman on the couch. There were always pranks on movie sets. George Clooney once tasked a whole costume department with altering Matt Damon's wardrobe over a period of weeks to convince him he was putting on weight.

This was a horror show. Of course the pranks were meaner.

"Do you have any idea who could have written that on your wall?" she asked.

Kyle thought for a moment, then sighed.

"To be honest, it's probably just Todd trying to help me get into character. Horror directors, right? Maybe don't mention it in your article? I wouldn't want to get anybody in trouble."

She smiled, and it was so dazzling Laura found herself smiling back. Laura's mouth tensed, though, when she thought about the words on Kyle's wall.

She's here.

The message appeared yesterday.

The same day Laura arrived in L.A.

Although she knew it was absurd, hated herself for evening thinking it, Laura couldn't help wondering if the message was about her.

Back on soundstage five after the interview, Laura helped herself to coffee from the craft services table while Madeleine the PR checked who else was available to chat.

Laura would have happily retired to the hotel. Just the thought of another ten minutes with Todd Terror made her want to fake a fit. But the coffee perked her up and the couple of Snickers bars from the craft table she'd slipped into her bag would come in handy when she needed a sugar boost.

She took out her journal. Simple, black-lined, own-brand WH-Smith. She'd bought the same one since she was fifteen and had boxes full of them. Years' worth of thoughts and memories. Some pages were neat, ordered. Others looked like they'd been attacked by a kid on a candy high.

The therapist she saw as a teenager was the one who got her into writing. He was patient and thoughtful and looked like Bruce Willis in *The Sixth Sense*. He told her to exorcise every thought and fear by putting it into words. *"Burn the negative,"* he said, *"unleash the positive."* And she had. She developed a love for words, became a destroyer of notebooks. At least five a year every year of her life, just getting it all out of her head and onto the page.

"A waste of paper," her mom would say, looking like she'd tasted something foul, but that only spurred Laura on. The journals were hers. Only hers. Nobody could take them away from her.

She had no intention of writing about the set visit, but her hand ached to hold a pen. The habit was ingrained. She scrawled a few lines, but the never-ending stream of crew members moving about the soundstage was distracting. Beyond them, raised voices echoed from the guesthouse set. Laura forced herself to look at it. Silhouettes moved behind an upstairs window and Laura wondered which scene they were prepping, if the bathroom set piece Kyle had mentioned would be anything like the one in *The Guesthouse*.

Kyle had looked so unsettled when she talked about the message on the mirror. It was clear that she thought something was going on. But was it all for publicity, just like Todd's hiring of the psychic?

The psychic was another misshapen piece of the *It Feeds* jigsaw. She recalled the woman's reflection in the bathroom mirror, the gaunt face and scraped-back hair, the pack of cigarettes in her pocket. She hadn't looked anything like the psychics Laura had read about or seen in movies. There were no oversized rings, no tassels, no heavy eyeliner.

She'd looked more like an addict than a spiritualist.

And the way she had glowered at her in the restroom mirror sent a shiver down Laura's arms even now.

She had to get time with her. If nothing else, it would make her article pop.

Not your article, remember?

As she stuffed her journal back into her bag with one hand, holding her coffee in the other, a sound came behind her. A gurgling breath. Laura turned just in time to dodge a set of claws.

She dropped her coffee as a man in a trench coat lunged for her, growling. His face and hands were mummified in stained bandages and his fingernails sprouted long, needle-like claws that flashed in the studio lights.

Laura staggered backward, a shout catching in her throat as the stranger slashed the air between them.

"Gotcha!"

Madeleine popped up behind the figure, grinning as the clawed figure went still. Beside her, Todd Terror laughed and slapped the monster on the back.

"Sorry, we couldn't resist," he said, getting his laughter under control. "Brad's made up for the next sequence. We thought you'd get a kick out of seeing him in the Needle Man getup."

The figure wiggled his needle-claws at her and curtsied, a light voice emerging from behind the mask.

"Sorry if I scared ya."

"Did we get you?" Todd asked. His T-shirt read *BE MY VICTIM*. "We got you, right?"

Laura tried to smile, but her pulse thumped in her ears and she smelled spilled coffee. She didn't want to admit that, just for a second, she'd thought her nightmares had crossed over into reality.

"You're lucky I don't have my Taser on me," she said.

Todd and Madeleine laughed, but Laura wasn't amused. She remembered the claws coming around the doorframe the previous day. The hissing voice calling out to her.

Welcome home, Polly.

"Were you on set yesterday?" she asked the guy in the Needle Man costume, forcing her gaze to meet his pure black eyes. Contacts.

He shook his head.

"We didn't shoot any Needle Man yesterday," Todd said. "Why'd you ask?"

"No reason." Laura found it difficult to look away from the movie monster, taking in every nightmare inch of him. They'd stayed true to the original. The black trench was scuffed around the collar but sort of stylish, as if marketing were planning a Tom Ford tie-in collection, and the dusty black Stetson rested at an angle. Only the claws were different. Larger, sharper, and so clean you could eat dinner with them.

"We better get back," Todd said. "Catch you later, Laura."

She nodded and watched Todd and Brad-the-Needle-Man walk to the Cricklewood set and climb the steps to the front door. In the brief moment before they entered the guesthouse, Todd turned his head to flash her a look across the soundstage, his eyes catching the studio fluorescents. A shiver trickled down Laura's spine.

He'd enjoyed scaring her.

aura sat in the shade of the soundstage with Beverly the psychic. Madeleine had suggested they enjoy the fresh air and fetched a couple of fold-out chairs, but Laura still felt on edge after the Needle Man prank, and the air did nothing to defrost the psychic. Beverly looked as sour as Laura remembered, her face makeup free, her yellowed fingertips knitted together in her lap. Laura struggled to think through the persistent sense of unreality that infused this whole visit.

"Thanks for giving me some time to chat," she said, holding out her Dictaphone. There was nowhere to set it down. "My name's Laura, I'm from *Zeppelin* magazine."

Beverly's lips pinched together in response and she watched a golf cart drive by carrying a man in a bathrobe. Again Laura noticed that the woman's eyes were so dark they were almost all black—

Like the Needle Man's

—and she was so thin that her denim shirt and white jeans bunched at her elbows and knees.

"I guess to start," Laura said, "would it be all right if I asked your official title?"

"I'm a psychic medium." There was an unusual quality to her voice. A smokiness that made it seem like speaking was uncomfortable.

"Is that different than a psychic large?" Laura heard herself say, and winced. *Dial it down, Tina Fey.* "Sorry, bad joke. I just meant, can you define that for me?"

"It's somebody who can see bad jokes coming a mile away."

Laura couldn't tell if she was kidding. Sighing, Beverly added, "Some people call us sensitives, which works. Doesn't matter what you call it, life beyond death or quantum realms, it's all 'other,' and that's what we specialize in. Other."

Laura nodded. So far so vague.

She had read too many articles about fraudulent mediums to accept that Beverly really was gifted, but she was intrigued. Behind every psychic was a story, the reason they saw the profession as their only way to make money. Some truly believed they had the "sight"; others were hard-and-fast cons. Beverly seemed more like the former, but there was something off about her. Something arrogant. It was almost as if she didn't believe her own words.

A skeptic psychic? That was new.

"Can you tell me about yourself? Your history?"

Beverly's eyes narrowed. She scratched her knee with her index finger, then stopped, as if she'd only just become aware she was moving.

"I've been doing this a long time, let's just leave it at that."

"By 'this' do you mean working on TV shows?"

A crack appeared in Beverly's expression and Laura couldn't tell if she was suppressing a laugh or grimacing.

"This is my tenth," she said. "Pay's good. That's about it."

It had been a while since Laura had interviewed somebody with no interest in answering questions. She wondered what Beverly's deal was. A couple of years ago, Laura wrote an article for *Zeppelin* about scam artists. Though the magazine prioritized entertainment features, it often branched out into investigative journalism. She interviewed victims of scammers and ex-cons, uncovering a world of subterfuge and exploitation. Of them all, though, she found scam psychics the most unnerving. They had an uncanny ability to zero in on vulnerable people, read them, and exploit them for financial gain.

That fact only spurred her on. If Laura had learned anything from having a mother like hers, it was that an icy exterior was merely a mask.

"It's still sort of unusual for a show to hire somebody in your line of work, though. Do you know why you were brought in?"

"To keep an eye on things. Keep people safe."

"And have you sensed anything unsafe?"

Beverly looked unsure how to answer. Her gaze went to the press pass around Laura's neck.

"Sure," she said, her tone bored. "So much history here, it'd be impossible not to."

"What do you think about stories regarding the curse?"

"What do I think about them?"

Laura nodded. "Do you believe in it?"

Beverly considered her. She looked tired. "When you spend your whole life not being believed, you sort of stop caring about the truth." The corner of her mouth creased ever so slightly. "It's not like one of those paper fortune-tellers. You never get just one answer to your question. There are infinite possibilities."

Something about the way she spoke made Laura frown.

Beverly had been on set yesterday.

She'd been in the bathroom, within coughing distance of Laura's bag.

What if she was the one who had slipped the prop in?

"It's funny you mention the fortune-teller," Laura said, but then stopped. Beverly had stood up.

"I have to go." She paused, then added, "Nice meeting you, *Laura*."

Laura stood, too. "Okay, well, thank—"

Beverly had already disappeared back into the soundstage.

Unsure if she was annoyed or relieved, Laura clicked off her Dictaphone. Hot air buffeted her, squeezed between the soundstages, but she barely noticed it. Her mind hummed as she thought about the way Beverly had said her name.

Laura.

She'd said it so pointedly.

Like it was a joke.

Like it wasn't Laura's name at all.

Which was crazy, because she'd been Laura for longer than she was ever Polly. Aged sixteen, she'd legally changed her name by filling in a government form. It had been so easy, it felt like a trick. Mail a piece of paper, pay the fee and—*voilà!*—two months later, you're a brand-new you. She'd finally shed the identity that meant pain and paranoia and night sweats.

The way Beverly spoke, though, it was almost as if she needn't have bothered.

Underneath it all, she was still Polly.

At the hotel, Laura was still thinking about Beverly when the concierge informed her that her luggage had arrived. Laura thanked him, though she was too distracted to be properly relieved. Her head was still at the Universal lot, her mind swirling with sound bites and sentence fragments, potential lines for an article she had no intention of writing.

Up in her room, she ordered room service, showered, and got into her robe, then laid out her burger, fries, and bowl of ice cream on the bed.

As she dunked fries in ice cream, one of the few good habits she'd inherited from her American mother, she saw she had a missed call on her phone.

Amy.

She must have found out that Laura knew she'd blabbed to Mike. She probably wanted to try to talk Laura into forgiveness, but Laura wasn't ready for that. She wanted to stay angry for longer. She knew Amy would try to subdue her with an apology. She'd call her "Pill" like she had since they were kids and she couldn't pronounce "Polly," and she'd remind her of the time Amy took the fall when they had a pink hair-dye disaster. It had been Laura's idea but they both knew their parents would go easier on Amy.

Nobody ever stayed mad at her.

Their dad called her "Miss Happy-pants" because she was the most unflappable child you could ever hope to meet. She drew pictures of butterflies and smiling children. Her "difficult teenage phase" never amounted to anything more than a sick sense of humor.

There were times when Laura hated it. Even though their father never verbalized it, she could see the question in his eyes. Why wasn't she more like Amy? Couldn't she just *try* to be more like Amy? What if she smiled more? Thought positively? She knew he'd never understand the answer. No. No, she fucking couldn't.

Laura loved her sister, but she hated her sometimes, too, because merely by existing, Amy showed Laura all the ways she failed as a daughter. As a sister. As a human goddamn person.

Amy was light, fun, and quick to laugh. Laura brooded and liked her own company.

But she could never stay angry at her sister. The one thing they shared was the one thing that nearly broke them both: their mother.

When Amy was born, their mother tried to get her into the family business. She took her to audition after audition, hoping to have *two* showbiz daughters, practically a dynasty. But Amy failed to land a single job. They heard the same thing over and over.

"Amy just doesn't have the look *we're going for."*

She even went for a small role in *The Guesthouse*. But the part of Child Guest #3 went to another girl who was better at memorizing her lines.

As a baby, Amy was happy, round, and doughy, like prebaked pastry.

When she grew up, she emerged from the baby fat as a natural beauty. She could have used her looks for any number of careers, but she wanted to act, more than anything in the world. And yet acting jobs eluded her. Casting directors loved her headshots, but then she flubbed lines, got nervous in chemistry reads, and fumbled props when she was asked to use them on camera.

It broke Laura's heart to see her fail.

Rejection was the worst part of the industry, and Amy had had nothing but.

"You had fame and you threw it away," Amy said once, when they were teenagers and Laura had tried to convince her to think about a backup career.

Amy had never understood. Laura hoped she never would. She ignored the call and set her phone to charge on the nightstand.

Full and sleepy, she was just sinking into her pillows when she heard movement. A wooden creak. A sound like a floorboard warping under the weight of a boot.

She sat up, instantly alert.

She was sure the sound had come from the corner of the room, where a high-back chair rested, angled toward the bed. On the table by the chair rested the paper fortune-teller. In the dark, it looked like a crouched spider. Watching her.

Had she refolded it last night?

She'd pulled the fortune-teller apart to read the message inside, but she struggled to remember what happened after that. She was sure she'd thrown it in the trash. Hadn't she?

Either way, it now sat on the table, refolded, its edges crisp, as if she had never touched it.

If she unfolded it again, would the message still be there?

Don't you dare look, she told herself. *Just get through one more night without losing your mind.* Tomorrow, she was flying home. She'd be home free, literally. There was no point getting hung up on a stupid movie prank, no matter how much it unsettled her.

And it had unsettled her.

The fortune-teller had been meant for her.

She took a sleeping pill and lay in the dark, waiting for the melatonin in her brain to kick her into blissful oblivion. The only light in the room came from the AC panel, which gave the walls a witch-green glow.

Laura's eyelids grew heavy. The room blurred and she felt sleep reaching for her, but then she noticed that the chair in the corner had moved.

The AC light only just reached it and Laura tried to remember if it had always been pushed up against the window like that. The more she thought about it, the less it looked like a chair. The shape by the window was too tall and so dark it was like a black hole, slowly drawing everything toward it.

A rasping sigh slipped through the quiet.

And Laura realized the shape wasn't a chair but a person.

Somebody standing in the corner, watching her.

"polllyyyyyyyysshhhh . . ."

She struggled to focus, making out a hat and stained bandages. She was just thinking it looked kind of like the Needle Man when the pill overpowered her and she fell into darkness.

Excerpt from The '90s Horror Files *by Matt Glasby*
(Goliath Publishing)

KILLER PROFILE: THE NEEDLE MAN

"If you want to make a horror villain scary, arm them with some-thing pointy," says Yvonne Lincoln, writer of 1993 spook-flick *The Guesthouse*. "If you want to make them terrifying, make them human."

That's certainly the case with this bandaged baddie, whom we glimpse only in shadow for much of the film's run time before he reveals himself in all his trench-coat-wearing, needle-stabbing glory.

Before he became the Needle Man, Claude Cranley ran the Cricklewood Guesthouse in the fictional town of Orville in 1930s England. After succumbing to a terrible wasting disease, Cranley lost his fingers and toes, and fitted needles to his finger stubs in order to eat. But Cranley was demonized by the town and eventu-ally threw himself off the roof of the Cricklewood. A year later, townspeople started to die in mysterious ways, and the legend of the Needle Man was born.

Recalling past horror greats like Frankenstein's monster, Count Orlok, and, naturally, Freddy Krueger, the Needle Man is a tragic figure whose motivation is clear: he will kill anybody who enters his guesthouse.

"Freddy was an inspiration, but Freddy's a joker," Lincoln says. "The Needle Man is fueled by pure rage. He was wronged in life, and that kind of torment is everlasting. If you ask me, he's still out there now."

SEVEN

The first thing Laura felt was heat.

It crackled against her skin and she tried to inhale, but the air burned her throat and she choked. She tried to inhale again and it was like trying to breathe through a gag, suffocating and panic-making and fused to her mouth.

She opened her eyes, which immediately pricked with moisture, smudging her vision. She rubbed them with balled hands, fighting panic, taking shallow breaths as she sat up and attempted to comprehend the smear of fire and black smoke before her.

The bed was solid beneath her and cold as stone, and it took her a second to realize it wasn't the bed at all. It was the floor.

A tiled floor.

To her left rested a white toilet, beside it a pristine sink beneath a mirror. In the corner of the room stood a shower cubicle. All around her, shadows flickered and stretched, the walls writhing, as if the room itself sought to shake off the flames that spat across the ceiling, spreading like oil, so loud it was all she could hear. The sound of fire chewing and snapping everything it got its teeth into, the air hissing and cracking and sticking in her throat. A line from *The Guesthouse* leaped forward in her mind.

"Fire is always hungry and it doesn't care what it eats."

As she covered her mouth with her hand and tried to find a way to breathe that didn't scar her lungs, she realized this wasn't her hotel bathroom.

She wasn't at the Loft.

She didn't recognize the blackening room.

Her chest hurt.

She was dreaming.

She *had* to be dreaming.

But heat pressed around her, baking her skin, and she knew this was too real to be a dream. Too unbearably hot and loud and she had to get out. Right now.

Laura struggled to her feet, which made her pant, robbing her of what precious oxygen remained. She crouched low as the heat intensified above her head, becoming a solid wall, and her eyes stung, still watering, making it difficult to see.

She fumbled for the door, relieved when her fingers met an over-warm handle.

She stopped.

For a second, she was sure she'd heard something above the roar of the fire. A sharp sound like metal scraping metal.

It had come from the shower stall. That was where the fire burned brightest. It beat the inside of the glass, singeing it black, and despite the unbearable heat, Laura flushed cold with shock when she glimpsed a shape inside, slumped against the glass.

Somebody was in there. In the shower.

They weren't moving.

But their palm was burned into the glass. Five blackened fingers.

The walls groaned and Laura coughed, wanted to keep coughing until her lungs cleared. Dizziness contorted the room as she tried to draw breath, but it wouldn't enter her throat. There was no air and she knew she couldn't delay. Whoever was in the shower was dead. They weren't moving, their fingers stiff behind the glass.

Tugging her T-shirt over her mouth, Laura opened the door, battling into the old-fashioned hallway, which was already smoke-clogged. Her lungs screamed for fresh air. She went down a set of stairs, not caring where she was anymore, just wanting to get out. She hurried for what she assumed was the front door and burst outside.

Except she didn't find herself outside.

Blackness reared up around her, reaching high above her head, closing her in, even though she was sure she'd run out the front door. As she coughed and tried to clear her head, she realized what the blackness was, *where* she was.

The soundstage.

She was at the Universal lot, on the set of *It Feeds*.

Looking down at herself, she saw she was still in her sleepwear. A crunching sound demanded her attention and she turned to look at the guesthouse.

It had become a pyre. The roof was ablaze and fire danced behind the windows, making the house appear demonic. As if it were furious she'd escaped.

Its death groans were accompanied by a mechanical wail. An alarm.

Laura pressed her hands to her ears. Yellow lights spun and flashed as the building's emergency systems triggered and their screams spoke for her, vocalizing her own distress.

What the fuck am I doing here?

A hand seized her, and Laura stared into a panicked face. The man wore a security uniform and his mouth moved, but she couldn't hear him over the noise. He looked young and afraid as he pulled her away from the guesthouse, escorting her outside, and Laura finally took a deep breath of nighttime air as she left the soundstage. Her ribs cramped and she coughed, tasting smoke, her throat raw. She managed not to vomit.

The guard talked into his phone, but in the dark of the avenue, Laura only heard one thought repeating in her mind, as persistent as the flames.

Somebody died in there.

Somebody's dead.

But who had burned in the shower?

And how had Laura got there?

Two hours later, she was still being questioned. The police had shown up along with three fire trucks and an ambulance. Once Laura got the all-clear from the medic, two detectives took her into a meeting room just off the main avenue, and Laura sagged into a chair, tugging the blanket the medic had given her around her shoulders, still trying to process what was going on.

"Ms. Warren, can you tell us what happened here tonight?" asked Detective Lang.

He was everything you'd want in a cop. Tall, solid in his uniform, jaw like a tire iron. By his side on the sofa, Detective Fernandez gave nothing away, her hair buzzed short, back straight. Her pencil was poised over a notebook.

Laura couldn't help thinking this was a parody of her interview with Kyle Williamson. The stale room was identical, but now she was the one being questioned.

"Ms. Warren?" Detective Lang said.

Clearing her throat, she told them about waking up on the set, finding it on fire, and then fighting her way outside, being found by security.

"You were in the bathroom?" asked Detective Lang.

She nodded. "I don't know how. I just woke up there."

The detectives didn't look at each other, but they didn't blink.

Laura shivered. Somebody had moved her. In her sleep. It was the only explanation for how she had found herself back at Universal Studios in the middle of the night.

"Have you been here before?" asked Detective Lang.

"Yes. I'm a journalist. I'm on assignment covering one of the shows shooting here."

"So you've been to the set before?"

She nodded. "Yesterday, and the day before that." She coughed. A fine layer of skin had been stripped from her throat. She was desperately thirsty, but she knew if she drank, she'd throw up.

"And you have no memory of leaving the hotel and coming here?" Detective Lang asked.

"No. I don't remember."

"What's the last thing you do remember?"

She twisted her fingers together. "I remember falling asleep in my hotel, the Loft, and waking up on set. That's it."

"Did you see anybody acting strangely at the hotel?"

Laura went to shake her head, then stopped as cold bristled the backs of her arms. She had seen somebody. Right before she fell asleep.

"I think somebody was in my room last night," she said, both troubled and energized by the memory.

Detective Fernandez's gaze sharpened. "You saw somebody?"

"Yes. Well, I think I did. They were standing in the corner, watching me."

"Did you phone security or the police?"

"No, I . . ." She knew it sounded ridiculous. "I fell asleep."

The detectives looked at her in a way that caused a stab of anxiety in her sternum.

She struggled to remember what she'd seen. She'd taken a pill to help her pass out and, in her sleepiness, she'd seen the Needle Man standing by the window, unmoving. Observing her. She'd heard his wheezing in her dreams.

"I took a sleeping pill," she said. "It sort of knocked me out."

Detective Fernandez wrote something in her notepad.

"Are you taking any other medication?" Lang asked. "Prescription or otherwise?"

"No."

She saw their looks. Guarded and alert.

She thought of her secret tattoo, inked on the inside of her left knee.

WWWD?

What Would Winona Do?

Stay quiet.

No, never stay quiet.

Ask the right questions.

"Have you gotten them out of the shower?" she asked.

"The shower?"

"There was somebody in there. Burning."

"We're working on it."

Laura saw the shape in the flames. The anxiety she'd kept a lid on ever since she landed was beginning to seep out like air from a tire. She had to keep it under control.

Welcome home, Polly.

The falling man.

She's here.

"Can I go now? I need to pack."

Detective Fernandez stopped writing. "Pack?"

"I'm leaving. Going home to London today."

The detectives shared a look.

"Ma'am, we can't let you leave the country. Not until we've investigated this further. We may need to speak to you again."

She heard his words, but they didn't compute.

"I have a deadline at work and my flight's at midday," she said. "I have to get to the airport."

"The airline can reschedule your flight," Lang said. "Look, we're not going to keep you here indefinitely, but you can't leave today. You're the material witness in a major crime."

The anxiety glowed like hot coal and Laura tried to breathe, stop it from burning her up.

What were they telling her?

She couldn't leave.

She was grounded.

Trapped in L.A.

"Ma'am, are you okay?" Detective Lang was looking at her hand. Laura had been pinching the flesh so tightly the skin was white and she was sweating. She forced herself to stop.

"How long?" she asked. "How long am I stuck here?"

"A couple days, maybe a week. We'll let you know. And it would be advisable to stay away from anybody involved in the production of the show. For their safety as well as your own."

Laura felt like she was made of ash. A single gust of wind could scatter her across the studio.

Not okay, she thought.

"Okay," she said.

CITY OF LOS ANGELES
POLICE DEPARTMENT

Case Number: 0092055   **Date:** 11/13/1993

Reporting Officer: Bill Landis

Incident: Suspected death by misadventure

Detail of Event:

ASHLEY YOUNG was found dead in her bathroom on the evening
of November 13, 1993. The incident was called in by her neighbor,
LESLIE HODDER, who reported a sound like a small explosion,
followed by smoke coming from under Ms. Young's apartment door.

Ms. Young was discovered half-in and half-out of the empty bathtub.
It is unclear if she was thrown into the tub by the blast or had
crawled into it attempting to escape the fire. She was covered in
burns and half her hair was missing. She wore a burned robe.
Firefighters were able to control the blaze before it went beyond the
bathroom and identified a ruined power outlet by the sink as a
probable source of the fire. A melted hair dryer was found near the
body, and the mirror above the sink was cracked. A pair of footprints
burned into the floor remain unidentified and appear too large to
belong to the victim.

EIGHT

Detective Fernandez escorted her back to the hotel. They went up to Laura's room and the detective told her to wait outside while she checked it over. Laura heard her moving around inside and knew she wouldn't find anything. That didn't stop her from counting the seconds, her pulse ticking in her ears, wondering if a dark shape would suddenly burst out into the hallway.

Reality had frayed around her. She kept trying to grab hold of it, but it was like the smoke that had poured from the Cricklewood set, impossible to grasp onto. The past few hours replayed on a loop in her mind, and she scrolled between mental snapshots of fire, blackened fingers, and strobing lights, trying to make sense of it all. She failed at that, too.

The detective appeared at the door and Laura jumped. She had almost forgotten why she was standing in the hall. Fernandez gave the lock a cursory check to see if it had been tampered with, then dismissed it.

"All clear," she said.

Laura looked past her. Her journal was still on the nightstand by her phone, her suitcase against the wall. Nobody was hiding under the bed, as far as she could tell. She felt foolish for checking, but she was nothing if not thorough.

Fernandez seemed less interested in the room than she was in Laura. Her gaze hovered on Laura's face, as if watching for a slip. Some kind of sign.

There was no mention of dusting for prints or calling in the CSIs, and Laura realized that they didn't believe her, at least not the part about somebody breaking in here.

"What are you going to do now?" she asked.

"We'll continue our investigation. If you're worried about security, you could have a new key card made or request a room change." Her expression said, *But we both know that won't be necessary, right?*

"We'll be in touch if we need to ask you more questions," the detective added. "I'd advise you to restrict your movements to the hotel and the surrounding area."

Laura stared at her.

That was it? She'd been abducted and nearly incinerated, and they were filing her away for later?

In that moment, she knew they suspected her.

If a body turned up in the shower, there was a high probability she'd be charged with murder, or at the very least manslaughter.

She couldn't breathe.

There had to be a way to prove this had nothing to do with her.

"What about CCTV?" she said. "The hotel security cameras must have picked something up."

Like the Needle Man snatching me in my sleep.

"I'll check with hotel security on my way out," the detective said.

"I'm coming with you."

Detective Fernandez gave her a look that said, *Back off, suspected arsonist,* but Laura refused to give in.

"If somebody broke into my room last night, I want to see it for myself."

The detective's gaze lowered, and Laura remembered she was still wearing her nightclothes.

"If you'd like to change first," Fernandez said, "I'll wait outside."

Feeling embarrassed and annoyed, Laura went into her room and quickly changed into the same T-shirt and jeans she'd worn since leaving London, too wound up to care that they were starting to smell. She tugged on her khaki jacket and felt something in the pocket. Her visitors' pass from the studio. She shoved it back in her pocket, took her phone and bag, and left the room.

Down in the lobby, she stood by as Detective Fernandez requested access to the hotel's surveillance footage, explaining that it was an urgent police matter. She almost sounded sarcastic as she said it.

Laura was sure she needed a warrant, but the hotel manager took one look at Laura and agreed. She must look worse than she thought.

A security guard showed them into the office and loaded the digital files for a couple of cameras, including one in the lobby and one on Laura's floor.

Laura held her breath as the guard scrubbed through hours of footage, fast-forwarding through mostly static black-and-white images that resembled an uninspired found-footage film.

The files showed nothing suspicious.

No dark figure breaking into her room.

Nobody carrying her unconscious body down the hall and into the street. Just a static hotel hallway.

Then, at 2:05 a.m., her bedroom door opened.

Laura watched as her on-screen self walked down the hall. She looked pale, washed out by the monochrome recording, and it was impossible to tell if her eyes were open. The footage showed her getting into the elevator, the doors closing.

Fernandez straightened.

"The lobby camera?" she said, and the guard clicked over to a different feed.

Laura's temple throbbed as she watched herself walk out of the elevator, cross the lobby, and pass through the hotel doors. She vanished into the night.

"That's . . . that's . . ." she stammered, but words eluded her.

The footage made no sense.

How could she have just walked out of the hotel like that?

Except, said a quiet voice in her ear, this wasn't the first time she'd done something in her sleep that her conscious mind had no recollection of.

Fernandez thanked the security guard and went back into the lobby. Laura followed, her head heavy. She felt the urge to talk, make a joke, convince Fernandez that she had no idea what was going on and, say, didn't journalists get enough of a bad rap without being fingered for arson?

For once, she held her tongue.

"You said you had no memory of leaving the hotel," Fernandez said.

"I don't."

The detective remained silent. She must do this a lot. Spend time with liars and weirdos. She had the look of somebody who could out-wait anything.

"I sleepwalk," Laura said. "Or I used to."

As far as she knew, she hadn't sleepwalked in years. It wasn't like she'd had anybody around to confirm it. Not since Mike.

Fernandez looked like she was holding something back. An exclamation, maybe. Or an accusation.

Finally, she dug in her pocket and handed over her card. Her expression was stiff, restrained, and Laura was sick of her looking at her like that.

"Get some rest. We'll be in touch. And call this number if you remember anything."

She turned and left.

Instead of feeling relieved, Laura felt hollowed out.

She found herself alone, clutching the card in one hand and her bag in the other. The lobby wheeled around her and the footage replayed in her mind. She willed herself to remember leaving her hotel room, but it was no good. The train had moved, but the engine had no memory of it.

She sank into one of the enormous hotel sofas, held upright only by the tension in her muscles.

She felt exhausted but completely awake, brain-fried and confused by the world she had found herself in. She didn't even know what day it was. Taking out her phone, she saw it was Thursday, and she had a couple of notifications.

Five missed calls from Amy.

Two from Mike.

She hit call for Mike, then remembered she was angry with him and hung up. She lowered the phone into her lap and tried to order her thoughts.

The Needle Man had been in her room.

She'd recognize that silhouette anywhere.

It was imprinted on her mind like a tattoo, along with the character's sinister backstory. The Cricklewood Guesthouse, the wasting illness, the townspeople whose cruelty birthed the Needle Man.

And a year after he died, people started to go missing.

That was all origin stuff, of course, learned in pieces over the course of *The Guesthouse*. The real story focused on the Manners family, who bought the hotel in 1970 and attempted to turn it around. Everything seemed fine for a while, but then their youngest daughter, Tammy, started seeing a man in the hotel. She called him the "Needle Man" because of his claws.

Soon after, the guests started dying.

It was a ghost story and a slasher movie rolled into one. The tale of a wronged man turned monstrous, exacting his revenge from beyond the grave.

Laura picked her nails.

There was one thing she hadn't told the detectives, aside from her personal connection to the production, and it was surely only a matter of time before the public pieced it together.

In *The Guesthouse*, each of the guests staying at the Cricklewood died in horrific ways. Spider bites, hanging, drowning in the bath.

But one of the first characters to die burned alive in the shower.

She didn't know what to do with that information. It stuck in her mind like a thorn and it was too much of a coincidence to be irrelevant. Had somebody staged the death in homage to the film? Or had this been just another prank, this time gone horribly wrong?

An even more disturbing thought occurred to her.

She'd arrived in L.A. two days ago and now somebody was dead.

Because of her?

She's here.

The words on Kyle's wall resurfaced in Laura's mind and she wiped her face, rubbing her eyes, again seeing the Needle Man in the corner of her room.

Had she imagined it? Or had somebody really been watching her sleep?

She couldn't just sit around waiting for Detective Fernandez to call. What if she came with handcuffs and an arrest warrant?

She couldn't let them pin this on her. She'd worked too hard to make a life away from all of this.

She stood and was about to head back up to her room when a voice spoke behind her.

"Laura?"

Laura turned, seeing a rail-thin woman approaching from the

hotel entrance. Her hair was pulled back from an unsmiling face and it took Laura a second to recognize her, she looked so out of place in the Loft.

"Beverly?" she said. "What are you doing here?"

The so-called psychic looked on edge.

"Can we talk?" she asked.

I dreamt about the house again. It's a proper horror movie house. The kind that squats and looks hungry, like it wants to open its mouth and eat me up.

There are plenty of houses like it in the movies, but none of them make me feel the way this one does. It's like it knows everything about me. Every secret and bad thought that's ever crossed my mind. It's storing them up in its rooms and hallways, feeding them, making them grow; making them strong enough to hunt me down one day and drag me over the threshold, never to see daylight again.

Yeah, hi melodrama, it's Laura here, miss me? Honestly, the fact that I keep dreaming about this place is starting to piss me off. And freak me out.

I've read the WebMD crap about recurring dreams simply voicing your unconscious mind. The house is representative of something and it doesn't take a genius to figure out what. But if it's that straightforward, why do I keep seeing it? Why won't it leave me alone? And why do I still feel it watching me, even when I'm awake?

NINE

How did you know where I'm staying?" Laura asked.

"You're really going to ask a psychic how she knows stuff?" Beverly didn't smile. She waved a hand. "They put everybody up here. Press always stay at the Loft."

A little tension eased in Laura's shoulders, but Beverly's presence made her nervous. She had made her feelings about Laura quite clear during their aborted interview. What was she doing at the hotel?

"It's about last night," Beverly said. "I know about the fire, and you. Are you okay?"

There was no tenderness to her tone. Laura didn't know what to think. Beverly had been aloof and guarded during their previous interactions.

Now her eyes were bright and intense. She looked like she was running a fever. The transformation was unsettling.

And how did she know Laura was involved in the fire?

"I'm fine," Laura said. She could be monosyllabic, too.

"They're going to say it's the curse," Beverly said. "The media, people online. They're going to say the *Guesthouse* curse has infected *It Feeds*. The fire will only fuel that whole mythology."

"I know." Just the thought tired her.

"It's bullshit," Beverly said. "There's no such thing as a cursed film. It's Hollywood spin. A curse didn't set fire to the guesthouse, a human being did."

Laura blinked in surprise. She had assumed that Beverly bought every bit of the *Guesthouse* legend. It sort of came with her territory, she figured.

"Are you saying you know who set the fire?" she asked.

Beverly shook her head. "No, but I know it's got something to do with you."

Laura felt like she'd been punched in the abdomen.

"Me?"

"I felt it the moment we met. There's something different about you. I couldn't put my finger on it before, but I think it's the reason the set burned down."

No.

Laura remembered the way Beverly had said her name before. Like it was a joke.

But there was no way this rent-a-psychic knew about her past.

"It's got nothing to do with me," she snapped. "Somebody's been pulling pranks on set. One of them got out of hand. End of story."

"And you're the one who woke up in a burning soundstage. Why?"

Laura's neck pinched. She couldn't go there.

"People will do anything for a headline," she said.

For a second, she felt guilty withholding her identity from the police. Somebody had lost their life on the soundstage. They deserved justice. But she felt certain that telling the detectives about her personal connection to *It Feeds* wouldn't make that happen any faster. It might even complicate things more than necessary. If the cops knew she was the kid from *The Guesthouse*, they might see motive where there was none.

It was better if she stayed silent.

Let them figure it out for themselves.

Beverly frowned and, for a moment, her usual stoicism returned, her face becoming unreadable. But then her dark eyes filled with certainty.

"You can deny it all you like, but something's going on with you," she said. "And I want to help."

Laura felt her mind threatening to splinter.

First the police, now Beverly. Couldn't they see this was bullshit?

She couldn't let them do this to her. There had to be a way to uncover the real culprit.

The one thing she knew for sure was that somebody who looked like the Needle Man was in her room last night, and it wasn't the first time she'd seen somebody dressed up in that costume.

"You want to help me?" she said. "Get me back into the studio."

Laura took a gulp of the coffee they'd picked up from Starbucks and tried to stop her leg from shaking. The caffeine perked her up, but it also made her antsy. She should be on a plane right now, cramped into a seat safely heading back to London. Not sitting in Beverly's Volvo as they drove down Wilshire Boulevard, one of L.A.'s main arteries.

"Do you know who died?" Laura asked, suppressing a shudder at the memory of the shape in the shower. "Has the studio said anything?"

Beverly shook her head. "All the studio said is that production's suspended. Indefinitely. I'm supposed to go in to be questioned this afternoon."

Suspended. Laura almost felt relieved. The feeling was quickly followed by more guilt, because even if *It Feeds* had been shelved, maybe never to see the light of day, somebody had died in the process. The press furor might end up being forgotten in a couple of days, but at what cost?

"And you don't sense anything?" she asked, trying for a poker face. It felt strained.

"If you knew who died, I could read it in you. But you don't."

Convenient.

Uneasily, Laura wondered if Beverly was wrong, if she *had* seen who died. She could even have seen who set the fire. The security footage suggested she'd sleepwalked to the studio, and yet she had no memory of it. What if she'd seen the arsonist but their identity was shut away in the vault of her mind?

She silenced the thought. This wasn't like before. It wasn't anything like the blackouts she'd suffered as a teenager.

"Did you ever see anything weird during filming?" she asked. "Anything suspicious?"

Beverly emitted a clipped laugh. "Every goddamn day. People in movies are insane." She paused before adding, "Todd loves fake blood. He keeps a vial of it around his neck, says it's from the '70s version of *Carrie.* Doesn't make him a killer, though."

"Right. But you never *sensed* anything?"

She felt ridiculous just asking.

"Oh, plenty. That studio's a hundred years old, the place is giddy with psychic energy. It's got bad vibes coming out of every crevice, especially those meeting rooms. But no, I never sensed anything on the set of the show."

Because there's no such thing as curses.

"I'm not saying curses don't exist," Beverly said, and Laura looked at her. She almost seemed to have read her mind.

"I'm saying *this* curse doesn't exist," Beverly continued. "It's like the story about the Munchkin's suicide making it into the final cut of

The Wizard of Oz. Not a grain of truth in it, no matter how many blog posts are written about it."

Laura was sort of impressed. She'd met so few people who didn't believe in the *Guesthouse* curse. It was refreshing.

She couldn't relax, though. A part of her was grateful for Beverly's help, but she couldn't let her guard down. She still had no idea *why* Beverly was helping her.

At the studio entrance, Laura gripped her seat as a security guard approached Beverly's window. Beverly showed him her staff badge, and then Laura pried her fingers free to flash her visitors' pass. The guard waved them through without so much as a suspicious glance, and Laura released a slow breath.

They drove through the back lot and she scooted down as they passed soundstage five. Cop cars and uniformed police were stationed outside, and a barrier had been erected to prevent anybody getting in.

Laura expected to feel a chill being back there, or at least an expanding wave of anxiety, but she felt nothing. It was all so unreal.

Beverly parked outside a smaller building that looked like a regular office.

"Here," she said, tossing Laura a ball cap as she got out of the car. "Figure you want to go incognito."

"Thanks." Laura tugged it on. If nothing else, it would hide her unwashed hair.

"Production office is this way. *It Feeds* has the whole second floor."

Beverly led her into a wood-paneled reception area that smelled of Turtle Wax and cherry air freshener. Framed movie posters hung on the walls, most of them Spielberg classics, and a couple of ficus plants completed the retro look. The place couldn't have been renovated since the '90s.

Now that she was inside, Laura felt jittery. She half expected a cop to appear and yell at her to freeze, or Todd Terror to pop out and accuse her of ruining his show. When neither of those things happened, she told herself to chill and followed Beverly into an elevator.

As the doors closed and they started moving, she wondered what Beverly really wanted. The scam psychics Laura researched for her article a couple years ago were great at spotting a victim: a person who was so desperate for human contact that they accepted any kind of help, no matter how absurd. Was that how Beverly saw her? As some kind of meal ticket? Laura hugged her bag to her like a shield and decided to ditch her the first chance she got.

"Where would Brad be?" she asked. "The guy playing the Needle Man." Might as well start with the employee who had spooked her on set yesterday.

"If he's in today, he'll be around. You want to talk to him?"

Laura nodded as the doors opened.

The second floor was quiet. A few people milled down the gray hall, talking in hushed voices before disappearing into side rooms. Most of the crew must've been dismissed and only a few remained, probably the senior producers and publicists dealing with the press.

At the far end of the hall, Detective Fernandez stood by an open door, talking to somebody she couldn't see.

Laura tensed and tugged at her cap.

"They're outside Todd's office," Beverly said. She seemed to notice Laura's discomfort and gestured at a door to Laura's right. "Go in there, I'll look for Brad."

She strode off down the hall and Laura went into a room plastered with black-and-white drawings. Storyboards. They covered every surface, giving the room the impression of an artist's studio run wild.

Laura was impressed until she realized the illustrations showed the entire plot of the show. *It Feeds*, broken down into a series of episodes and scenes, all rendered in scratchy black ink. One showed grown-up Tammy playing with a fortune-teller app on her phone;

another featured the Needle Man lurking in the shadows of a bedroom closet.

She paused by one board and moved in closer, examining a sketch of a bathroom.

The storyboard showed a woman getting into the shower, then the shower erupting in flames, the woman screaming, her palms against the glass. A handwritten note next to the panel read *DOOR WELDED SHUT.*

Laura frowned, moved in. The final panel showed the bathroom from above. A scribble of black lines denoted a person crouched by the door, watching the shower burn.

A woman.

Hair prickled the backs of her arms.

The woman looked a little like her.

"Laura," Beverly said, and Laura jumped.

She turned to see a nervous guy who must be Brad standing by the door, scratching a thick mane of strawberry-blond hair. She barely recognized him out of costume. He was so thin an autumn breeze could push him over, and he was younger than she'd imagined, probably early twenties.

"Hey?" he said cautiously.

"Hi."

"Okay, um, Beverly said you had some questions or something?"

Laura tried not to picture him creeping into her room while she slept, and reminded herself to warm him up before getting to the difficult questions.

"Were you at my hotel last night?" she asked, throwing her strategy out the window.

Brad offered a bemused look.

"Is this a joke?" he asked.

"No."

"Okay, uh, I don't know what this is about, but I was with my boy-friend last night, out in the Valley."

Easily verifiable, although it wouldn't be the first time somebody provided a false alibi for their partner.

"Do you ever take your costume home after filming?" Laura asked.

"What's this about?" Brad asked. At her stare, he blushed and added, "No, of course not. The costume department would kill me if I took anything off-site."

"Could anybody else have taken your costume?"

"Sure, I guess. I don't see why they'd want to, though. It sort of stinks."

Laura held his gaze a moment longer, noting the color creeping up his neck and the worried look in his eyes, and she knew she was clutch-ing at straws.

What did she really hope Brad would say? That yes, his costume had gone missing and, oh, by the way, did he mention Todd was a se-cret arsonist who hated his own show?

"Thanks," Laura said, feeling foolish.

"Okay, well, see ya, I guess." Brad left and Laura released a breath, at a loss.

"You want costumes?" Beverly asked. "Come with me."

Beverly went back out into the hall. Laura paused by the door, noticing a stack of scripts. She checked that Beverly wasn't looking, then grabbed a handful and slipped them into her bag. It was a long shot, but they could hold some clue.

Out in the hall, Beverly led her around a corner into a hallway lined with clothes racks. A lifetime's worth of jackets and trousers and shirts, just for one show. Laura's mind boggled.

They went into a room that was little more than a cupboard, and Laura stopped short.

The room was full of black coats.

At least fifty hung on hangers, aged and beaten to look the same.

There were hats, too, and shoes. Everything you could want to transform into the Needle Man. The only things missing were the claws. Laura assumed they were elsewhere, the armory maybe, under lock and key.

She found Beverly studying her.

"What are you really looking for?" Beverly asked.

Her dark gaze was penetrating, and Laura felt heat building in her chest.

"I don't know," she admitted.

She was chasing shadows.

The same shadows that had gathered around her since she read the press release on the flight from London.

Trying to gain control of a situation that was completely beyond her control.

Anybody could have dressed up as the Needle Man and broken into her hotel room.

Assuming she hadn't imagined the whole thing.

"Let's go," she said.

They caught the elevator downstairs and went back to Beverly's car.

"You don't have to drive me back to the hotel," Laura said. "I can get a taxi or walk."

Beverly dead-eyed her. "Nobody does either of those things in L.A. Get in."

They didn't talk much on the drive back. Laura still didn't understand what Beverly's deal was, and the psychic was so cagey there was no point asking any questions. They'd only be ignored or spat back at her.

The only piece of information Laura got out of her was that Beverly wasn't born in L.A. Then again, who was? She moved there over a decade ago and even though she seemed to hate it, she didn't say anything about leaving. Laura wondered if that was why Beverly was so morose. She had run away from something. Somewhere.

Beverly dropped her off curbside at the Loft Hotel, and as Laura stood shielding her eyes from the sun, the psychic leaned across the seat to talk through the passenger window.

"I have this police chat at the studio now, but we could meet here later? Regroup?"

Laura merely nodded. The thought of spending more time with Beverly wasn't a welcome one, but she didn't have the energy to argue.

She watched Beverly perform a U-turn across traffic, then turn off at the lights, vanishing from sight.

Relieved to be alone, she stepped into the hotel parking lot.

The moment she did, a flash of light blinded her. Somebody called her name.

Laura stumbled, righted herself, and found herself staring down the barrel of a camera lens. The thick-set man holding it wore a ball cap and shades, hairy forearms poking from his T-shirt.

"Hey, Laura, give us a shot?" His voice was husky and overly friendly.

Others quickly crowded around her, camera shutters snapping like teeth, their flashes making lights pop in her eyes.

"Hey, Laura," the paparazzo said again, "tell us what happened. You were there, right? You saw?"

Snap-snap-snap.

Somebody must have tipped them off.

She tried to push past, tried to head for the hotel entrance, but they barred her way.

"Right, Laura? You saw who set the fire? Was it a ghost?"

Snap-snap-snap.

"Get the fuck away from me," she said, attempting to elbow past.

"Nice!" the paparazzo said, snapping. "Look at me? Come on, just give me the shot, Laura."

Another man appeared, shoving the pap back. "She said to get the fuck away from her!"

"Quit it, man," the paparazzo complained. "I'm just doing my job."

The newcomer wasn't listening. He was tall and wore a *Demons* T-shirt and an earnest expression on his round face. Black hair tufted over his ears, falling to his shoulders.

"Laura," he said, as if he knew her. "My car's right over there. Need a ride out of here?"

For a second, she was back in the supermarket lot. The woman taking her to the car, the smell of cigarettes and perfume. She knew a *Guesthouse* fan when she saw one, and this guy was giving off uber-fan vibes.

She managed to free herself from the scrum and ran into the lobby.

Breathlessly, she hurried for the elevators, hearing her name being shouted over and over like a threat.

As the doors opened and she rushed inside, she was sure she heard somebody say, "Polly."

Closing credits of **The Guesthouse** *(1993)*

C A S T

Tammy Manners	POLLY TREMAINE
George Manners	TERRENCE HODGES
Margaret Manners	JULIA BARKER
Melanie Manners	ASHLEY YOUNG
Elderly Woman	ISABELLE PLUMMER
Maintenance Man	RAY HEWITT
Andy	BRIAN ARENBERG
The Needle Man	HIMSELF

TEN

Polly was shopping with her mom, nine months after *The Guest-house* was released, when the woman in the supermarket recognized her. They were at their local Walmart, playing their usual game of find-and-seek. Her mom would look over her list and tell Polly to fetch something from the other end of the aisle, and then Polly would run off to get it, sneaking in Push Pops and soda along the way.

While Amy whispered with her toy doll, their mom checked her shopping list and sent Polly to get yogurt.

Polly was at the dairy section, carefully selecting the right Yoplait Trix, when a woman cried out behind her.

"Tammy! Oh my God, you're *Tammy*!"

Polly stared up at a woman with cotton-candy hair and a face stretched tight with excitement.

"Oh, we just love you!" The woman's acrylic orange nails flashed, clashing with her leopard-print shirt. "We went to your movie five times! I can't believe you're here!"

Polly looked down the aisle, seeing her mom at the cheese counter with her back turned, Amy by her side.

"We're calling her Tammy, just like you," the woman said, stroking her swollen belly in a way that told Polly she was pregnant. "Oh, Mark will hate that he didn't see you! He's putting gas in the car. Hey, why don't you come say hi? Here, want this?"

The woman took something brightly colored from her basket and held it out. A Push Pop.

Polly smiled.

It was only when they were outside that she became uncomfortable. The woman's voice was so shrill, it made her nervous, and she kept calling her "Tammy," talking about *The Guesthouse* like it was real. Only, Polly knew it wasn't real, because she'd seen how it all was done.

"It was so sad, that man dying," the woman said. "Did you see it? Did you see what happened?"

"I think I should—" Polly began, but then the woman's hand was on her shoulder, squeezing, her nails like claws, and Polly was hurried along, farther into the parking lot so that she couldn't see anything but cars.

"Oh, there he is," the woman said, and she was so close that Polly smelled her. Detergent and cigarettes. It made Polly's nose itch.

The next few minutes were a blur, but Polly remembered the woman saying, "Mark, look who I found!" and "Our friends love the movie, too. Oh, they'd just *love* to meet you. Why don't you climb in the back? We'll go for a ride! It'll be so fun!"

Polly didn't like the look of Mark's greasy, shoulder-length hair, the cigarette between his lips, and she didn't want to get in the car. She started to cry, and the woman's voice became treacly. She tried to give her more candy, tried to get her into the car, but then a voice shouted, *"What the fuck are you doing!"* and it took Polly a moment to realize it was her mom. Her voice was so different. She looked chalk white, her eyes bright, Amy wriggling in her too-tight grasp. Her mom panted as she snatched Polly away, yelling something about alerting security.

The woman's smile dropped. She jumped in the car and sped out of the parking lot.

Her mother crushed Polly in a hug, yelling and crying.

And then she laid into her.

In the elevator, Laura video-called Mike.

"Jesus, Laura, are you okay?" He sat in the kitchen in his London flat, the phone propped up to show him wearing a white T-shirt, a *Towering Inferno* poster on the wall behind him. It was ten p.m. on the other side of the Atlantic, and Laura remembered being in that same kitchen five years ago, drunk on wine and laughing at Mike lip-syncing to Tori Amos's "Crucify." Suddenly, she couldn't remember why it had gone so wrong between them.

"Have you heard?" she asked, attempting to focus on the now while calming her heart rate after her dash from the paparazzi.

"Yeah, just now. Are you okay?"

"Oh, great. I love being on a flight ban in the craziest city in the Western Hemisphere."

"Right." He played with a coaster from the coffee table, the guilt clear on his face. "I'm so sorry. I should never have put you in this position."

"It's fine. Talk to the police for me. Get them to lift the ban."

"I can try, but—"

"Just get me out of here," Laura said, and she heard the edge in her voice, the raw fear. Her nerves felt pulled tight.

The elevator doors opened and she walked down the hall.

"Do you want to talk about it?" Mike asked. "What happened?"

"No."

"You can tell me," he said, and she almost laughed, the conversation was so familiar.

"What do you see?" he'd asked when they were dating. *"When you're asleep?"* He was sleeping over enough to notice when she had night terrors, and even if she'd wanted to tell him what came to her in the nighttime hours, the words would never form properly. They thickened in her throat, lodged there, immovable.

When they first started dating, Mike had welcomed Laura into his life so effortlessly, it was as if the space had been made just for her. He involved her in parties, get-togethers, and weekends away, and he made it look so easy, like it was no great thing to open yourself up entirely to another person.

She had found his honesty charming. After two months, he told her that he loved her, and she'd found it easier than she'd expected to admit she felt the same. He'd grinned like a teenager and scooped her into his arms, and she'd laughed and called him a goofy idiot, but affectionately, because he was a goofy idiot that she loved.

"It might help to talk about it," he'd say in the middle of the night, and he'd stroke her arm, and though she knew he meant well, the contact made her skin crawl, because the images were ever-present in her mind.

For the briefest period, she'd thought maybe she could do this.

If she could let *anybody* in, it would be Mike.

But she'd been wrong.

"Is it your mom?" he asked one night when he found her splashing water on her face in the bathroom at two a.m., and that was when she pulled away for good. Knew she was ending it with him. Because she wasn't broken. She'd dealt with her shit. Had years of therapy. But Mike always made her feel like she was fundamentally damaged.

She could never be as open and unguarded as him.

And a part of her resented him for that.

On-screen, Mike rubbed the back of his neck and sat forward.

"Look, don't hang up on me," he said, "but I've been thinking about this a lot. It's possible you have more power than you think, especially when it comes to the ban. If you go public—"

"I'm not doing that."

"Just hear me out. If you go public, tell your side of the story, foster a little public sympathy, this could go away. You could be home in a couple of days."

Laura saw the logic in his reasoning, but she had purposefully hidden her identity from the cops. She'd lied about having no connection to *It Feeds*, other than as a journalist. And the media hook was so strong she could practically write the headline herself.

EX–CHILD STAR WANTED FOR MURDER.

The papers would eat her alive.

But what if Mike was right? There was nothing like bad press to speed up the authorities, force their hand. Could she pull off the role of victim if her freedom depended on it?

"I'll think about it," she said, then ended the call.

She couldn't bear Mike looking at her in that infuriating way he did. He always seemed to know how she was feeling no matter how hard she tried to conceal it, and he never bought her tough act. She supposed that seeing somebody in the grip of a midnight anxiety attack humanized them pretty quickly.

She wondered if he was already making calls on her behalf. Even after the breakup, Mike had looked out for her. Two years ago, a freelancer whose work Laura had rejected filed a lawsuit against *Zeppelin*, claiming Laura had plagiarized a series of articles from his website. Laura had been incensed. She'd wanted to confront the writer, slap him with a countersuit, then slap him *in the goddamn face.*

Mike talked her down. He didn't believe for a second that she had stolen some hack's work. Once he'd made sure she wouldn't do anything rash, he told her to leave it with him.

A week later, the lawsuit was dropped.

Laura still didn't know the specifics, but she knew Mike was responsible. She didn't press him for details and he never mentioned it again. And even though his actions made her feel like a women's lib failure, she was grateful. She'd only have made the situation worse.

L.A. was different, though. This was her shitstorm. Her past. She couldn't rely on Mike to make it go away. She didn't *want* him to. This was on her.

Her phone said it was two-thirty p.m., which she found difficult to believe. Where had the day gone? The world was moving around her, but she was stuck still, like a bug on a pin. She had to do something to free herself.

She went to her room and used the key card to open the door. She stopped on the threshold, stunned by what lay waiting for her.

The room had been wrecked.

The TV hung off the wall and the bed had moved halfway across the room, sheets and pillows scattered all over. The curtains had been ribboned, light showing through long gouges in the fabric, and the mirror was spider-webbed with cracks.

Laura listened but didn't hear anything. Whoever had done this was no longer there.

She stepped inside, the door clicking shut behind her, and went quickly to the nightstand, then searched the floor around it, releasing a frustrated cry.

Her journal was missing.

She kept searching in case it was simply lost under the mess, but it wasn't there.

"Fuck!" She paced, hands in her hair.

One, two, five, nine . . .

The counting helped. It started when she was thirteen. Whenever she felt stressed or trapped, she'd count. She'd keep counting until all she heard were numbers. They drowned out the shrieking drill of anxiety. It was months before her therapist pointed out that Tammy Manners counted, too. Counted the numbers in the paper fortune-teller.

Laura could never shake the compulsion.

She stilled as she noticed her suitcase on its side by the wall. It was unzipped, contents threatening to spill out. And on top of the case rested the paper fortune-teller.

The sight of it caused her tongue to swell in her mouth.

There was no way the fortune-teller had fallen there by chance while her room was ransacked.

Somebody had placed it on top of the case, almost ceremonially.

Right where she'd find it.

Shaking, she approached the luggage, dreading what she'd find inside. She crouched down, feeling ill at the thought that somebody had been through her possessions. It was as if somebody had put their hands on her body as well as her belongings.

Kneeling, she brushed the fortune-teller onto the carpet, then flipped the lid and stared at the interior.

The case was filled with shredded fabric.

Struggling to process what she saw, Laura reached in and sifted through the case. Her favorite pair of jeans, her black I-mean-business shirt, the oversized *Heathers* T-shirt that she slept in.

All shredded.

Ruined.

She pushed the fabric around, trying to find just one intact article of clothing, unable to comprehend that everything had been destroyed.

She stopped.

Yellow cotton nestled amid the tatters.

She never wore yellow. And definitely not this sunflower shade.

Trembling, Laura tugged the yellow fabric up out of the suitcase, already knowing what it would be but not wanting to believe it, not even when she held it up in front of herself.

A dress.

It was just like Tammy's, the costume she'd worn as a kid. The one she wore in the poster, which showed her going into room 205, the door aglow, her shadow stretching behind her across the hall floor.

This dress was adult-sized, and Laura knew it would fit her if she put it on.

She dropped it into the suitcase, her fingertips itching where they had made contact with the fabric. Her chest juddered, spitting embers, and she felt light-headed, the room whirling around her.

Somebody had messed with her luggage.

Somebody had gone through her belongings, systematically destroyed them, and planted the dress. They might have even *made* the dress. Her mom was the only person who had ever created clothing for her, and that thought made her shake more than ever.

The paper fortune-teller was one thing—there were a hundred ways it could've ended up in her bag, not all of them sinister.

But this? This was somebody fucking with her.

It finally made sense.

Somebody knew who she was, and they wanted to torture her. It was the only way to explain everything that had happened in the two days since she arrived in L.A.

Somebody knew her, but who?

And why did they care?

She got up from the floor and went to the door. What if it was one of the paparazzi outside? The weirdo in the *Demons* T-shirt?

They were probably still downstairs, waiting for her.

Shaking with anger, she opened the door and cried out in shock. A woman stood waiting, her hand raised to knock. Laura felt the final remnants of rational thought crumble.

"Amy," she said.

Mom lost her shit at me today. BIG TIME. The last time she blew up like this was when Dad bought a new car we can't afford. I thought they were going to divorce but then Dad sold his golf clubs and said something about working overtime and Mom seemed to forgive him.

I was in my room reading (IN COLD BLOOD, so good and so horrible) when Mom came in and started yelling. She had a mostly full bottle of Jack Daniel's and kept asking when I drank it, what I was thinking, how I could be so stupid. I didn't understand and she asked if I thought I was clever, topping the bottle off with water to make it look like it hadn't been drunk. But if I was REALLY clever, I'd only have topped it up a little.

Anyway, she refused to believe I hadn't touched the stuff and I'm grounded for a month. Which is fine because there's fuck all to do here anyway, especially for teenagers. I'd stay in my room forever if Mom wasn't always telling me to get up, go to school, go grocery shopping with Dad. But it's not fair. I didn't drink. Why would I? Alcohol's for losers.

Amy came in a little later. I was on the bed and she knew I'd been crying because I didn't shout at her to get out. She curled up around me smelling of strawberry gummy bears.
Fourteen and she's still obsessed with them.

She said, "I believe you, Pill. I'll always believe you."

It felt nice that someone did.

ELEVEN

Wow, I knew you were messy, but this is another level," Amy said, flicking a look around the hotel room as she wheeled a mini-suitcase inside. "Did somebody let a gremlin loose in here?"

Laura stood by the door, too stunned to speak.

Amy looked like she'd stepped out of a TV commercial for beachwear. She always did.

Her sunshine-blond hair pooled over her bare shoulders, and her sparing makeup was immaculate, just enough to accentuate her chocolate-brown eyes. It didn't take much for Amy to look good. There was nothing posed or calculated about her. Her social media posts usually showed her laughing in a heap or eating messily. Somehow, she always pulled it off. Today, she wore a blue halter top and designer jeans, an Armani bag slung over her shoulder, and Laura blinked a couple of times, half expecting her to be a mirage.

Too many questions collided in her mind. In the end, she settled for "What are you doing here?"

"Now, there's a rock star welcome." Amy smiled, then dropped the act. "Mike called me yesterday morning. I was in New York on assignment for Charles-Edward."

"You were in New York?"

"For work. I knew you'd be freaking out being back in L.A., so I caught an afternoon flight. I figured I'd surprise you, but when I landed last night, you weren't answering your phone. I checked in to a place down the street, and then I saw the news this morning, and you still weren't answering your phone, and . . ." She stops, takes a breath. "Are you okay?"

"I'm fine."

"Yeah, your room agrees."

Laura shook her head to disperse the remnants of surprise. She hadn't been in the same room as Amy for a couple of months, not since Amy relocated to Manchester to subsidize her acting dream by part-timing as an assistant to fashion guru Charles-Edward. The distance didn't matter. They were close in a way that bent time. They texted most days, FaceTimed every week or so, but now Amy was here, in the flesh. It didn't make any sense.

Amy had been in New York? How hadn't Laura known that?

She eyed the wrecked room, her temples buzzing.

"I just found it like this."

Amy frowned. "Somebody trashed your room?"

"Looks that way. What are you doing?"

Amy had taken out her phone and was snapping pictures. "For when you report it," she said. "Photographic evidence."

"Stop it."

Amy ignored her, taking shots of the bed and the suitcase. Laura went over and pushed the camera down. "I said stop."

Amy looked annoyed, then blinked and threw her arms around Laura's shoulders.

"I'm so glad you're okay. I was so worried. The motel last night was disgusting. You're glad I came, right?"

Laura squeezed her back, feeling how solid she was. Not a figment of her imagination. Her sister, right here in her hotel room. She forgot she was angry with her. Forgot to scream with fury and demand to know just when exactly Amy told Mike about Laura's past. She had every right to do so, but something stopped her. Though they were close, Laura often sensed a hairline fracture in their relationship. A crack threaded with all the things they didn't say to each other.

For now, though, she didn't care.

Her sister was here. Amy had come for her. And Laura was more grateful than she could admit.

"We have to get out of here," she said. "It's not safe."

"Pill," Amy began—the nickname had stuck even after Laura filed the legal document that eradicated Polly Tremaine forever—but Laura shut her down.

"Somebody's been in here. At least once, probably twice. We have to find somewhere else to stay. Now."

Amy didn't argue. Laura threw the remnants of her belongings into the suitcase, and then they caught the elevator downstairs. She didn't check out at the front desk. Whoever had broken into her room could have access to their information. Better to let them think she was still at the Loft in case they made another move.

They went out into the humid afternoon and Laura scanned for paparazzi. As she approached the taxi line, she saw a couple of guys smoking by a Prius, cameras slung around their necks. They were laughing and their cigarettes glowed. Laura got into the taxi before they could spot her.

The driver looked confused when Laura asked to be taken to a motel, *any* motel. Amy leaned forward and gave her the name of the motel she stayed at the night before, and they drove twenty minutes away to a place called Fifty Winks. It was a two-story building shaped like an L, identical to any one of the motels Laura had seen in movies.

She pictured Thelma and Louise standing behind the railings along the top level, Guy Pearce in *Memento* hunched behind one of the mustard-yellow doors, Norman Bates on desk duty.

It looked quiet, though, practically deserted.

Laura checked in using some of Amy's cash and they went to their room on the upper level. The door creaked when they entered and Laura surveyed the two rumpled beds, the threadbare carpet, and the dated wallpaper. It looked a little too similar to the *It Feeds* set, but it would do. Already, she felt she could breathe a little easier knowing that nobody had any idea they were here.

"Okay, we're in," Amy said, sitting on the bed and patting the space beside her. "Now tell me everything."

Laura rubbed her forehead, took a breath, and sat against the wall, her knees drawn up. She started with the set visit, meeting the psychic, then finding the paper fortune-teller and, later, the dress, waking up in the burning guesthouse, and being interrogated by the police.

"Somebody knows who you are," Amy said.

Laura's reply shot from her mouth: "Have you blabbed that to anybody else lately?"

Amy's face crumpled.

"Pill, I'm so sorry. I barely even remember what I said to Mike. We'd been drinking. It was after you bailed on my birthday for that interview. I was angry with you. It just sort of came out."

Laura remembered that night. She'd been heading out the door for Amy's party when a PR called saying rock god Raiden Greene was free for a Skype chat. Laura had been trying to get time with him for months, and the PR promised he'd call direct in thirty minutes. An hour went by, then another, until it was past midnight and the interview never happened. Laura didn't make it to the party and was still waiting for Raiden Greene to call.

She didn't blame Amy for being angry. And she knew Amy wasn't the reason Laura was in L.A. Mike was.

The way Amy hunched on the bed, sitting on her hands, sent an involuntary tremor down Laura's spine. In her mind, Amy was still the pudgy baby who never landed any roles. Still the teenager who smiled through every rejection. Even through their mother's repeated dismissal of her.

Amy was a trier. A doer. And something about that always made Laura feel sort of sad.

"Forgive me?" Amy asked.

Laura realized her sister had accepted everything she had just said, carte blanche. It felt good that somebody believed her.

"I'll think about it." Laura shook her head. "Let's just look at this for a minute. Okay, somebody knows who I am, but why are they messing with me?"

"Is anybody on the show connected to the original movie?"

"I don't think so. It's a whole new crew."

Because there's nobody left alive from The Guesthouse.

"I guess that rules out somebody with a grudge. You really have no memory of going to the studio last night?"

"None."

"Jesus." Amy started chewing her nails, a habit she'd shared with their dad. "You were at the crime scene, though, which means the cops probably think you set the fire."

Hearing Amy say it made it sound so much worse than it had in Laura's head.

"The question is why," Laura said.

"And who. And *what!*"

"All right, Tim Curry." They'd worn out their *Clue* VHS years ago.

Amy stopped chewing. "We're going to figure it out, Pill. You're innocent. We just have to find a way to prove it."

"Thanks." Laura tried to smile, but it snagged at the corners of her mouth.

"You should call Mom, in case it made the papers."

Laura shuddered. "I will."

"I've been going through Dad's vinyls. There's some cool stuff in there."

"Cool."

Amy was always closer to their father. She spent more time with him as a kid because Laura was always at a job with their mother, and even though Laura knew her dad had loved her, sometimes she'd caught him looking at her so deeply, it made her breath hitch, because it almost looked like pity. Did he think Hollywood had broken her? That their mother had? Maybe he thought he'd failed her. He was the one who got them out of L.A., finally said enough was enough, but by then the damage was done. Laura was already a mess, permanently bruised by her time in L.A.

His death a year ago hit them hard. Cancer. Quick and ruthless. Just six months from diagnosis to dead. Laura was still recovering from the whiplash.

She hadn't cried at the funeral. She simply couldn't believe he was gone. Their father had been the opposite of their mother. Bright and talkative with no hidden agenda. He adored his girls and Laura wasn't sure what she'd have done without him.

When they lived in L.A., his job at the record company kept him out at all hours, and she doubted he knew half of what she went through. But when they moved to the UK, he was there for her in a way that he hadn't been before. Laura had vivid memories of waking up with night terrors, wrapped in her father's arms. She'd claw at him and pull him close, a wild thing, oblivious to where she was, what was happening, trapped in that runaway feeling of fear.

"Come back to me," her father would murmur, holding her tight while she fought off the nightmares. *"Wherever you are, my love, just find your way back to me."*

And now he was gone.

Amy jumped up and went to the bathroom. "I'm going to run you a bath and see if I can find a take-out menu. Then we'll work through a list of suspects and get this show on the road."

She rarely took charge, but Laura was so tired, she was happy to defer decision making to her baby sister. She would have cried if she weren't so dehydrated.

An hour later, she sat in one of Amy's oversized nightshirts, hair air-drying. In the bathroom, Laura had given her reflection a cursory glance and was shocked at how enormous her eyes looked, perpetually startled in a face that was deathly pale. The bath hadn't soothed any of her anxiety, but it had made her feel more human. Or maybe that was just Amy.

They ordered Chinese and sat at the table by the window, looking out at the L.A. street, the sky a ragged blend of blue and orange. Amy scrolled through her phone while she picked at a tray of steamed vegetables and noodles.

"Looks like the shower victim was a guy named Todd Terror," she said.

A bolt of surprise shot from Laura's sternum into her fingers, which tightened around the chopsticks. "Shit, Todd?"

"You know him?"

"I interviewed him two days ago. He's the showrunner."

She stared into her chicken chow mein, the smell of food making her nauseated as she remembered the blackened hand pressed against the shower glass. It hadn't felt real at the time and she'd been so caught up in her own turmoil, she hadn't thought much about who had lost their life on the set.

But now she knew.

Todd was dead.

"They've confirmed it's him?" She hadn't expected them to ID the body so quickly.

Amy shook her head. "'Unconfirmed reports,' but it's looking likely."

"Shit." Laura pushed away the food, recalling how young Todd was, how excited he had been about the show, so much so that he hired a psychic to protect it. He had been kind of a moron, but he was a human moron. A moron who didn't deserve to die.

On her phone, she navigated to Todd's Instagram. It was a bloodbath. There were behind-the-scenes shots of gory chaos, one showing him kissing a decapitated head, and a video of him being doused in fake blood to celebrate wrapping a short film called *Get Some Guts!* Another photo showed him grinning and holding a silver film canister with a label reading *The Guesthouse.*

He hadn't been lying about owning the original negative.

Not negative. Answer Print, or whatever the hell he'd called it.

There was a post of Todd with Kyle Williamson, and Laura followed the link to Kyle's profile, losing herself in the grid of photos.

Something about Kyle was weirdly compelling. She was so perfect she was almost hideous. Grew up in Kentucky, a child pageant queen whose mother had dreams of stardom and made all the right moves until Kyle got her own Disney show. Her upbringing eerily mirrored Laura's, and she wondered how Kyle had survived so many years in a business that sucked the life out of people like Arnold Vosloo in *The Mummy.*

Maybe Kyle's mom was kind.

"Who else did you speak to?" Amy asked. She had a notes file open on her phone and Laura saw her compiling a list of names and theories.

Laura went over meeting Kyle Williamson and Beverly the psychic, adding in her embarrassing attempt to cross-examine Needle Man Brad.

"And you didn't speak to anybody else?"

"Just Madeleine the PR, but trust me, she's not the killing type."

"I'm putting her on the list anyway. Everybody thought Emma

Roberts was apple pie and ice cream until she threw herself on a glass table."

Laura felt a sudden swell of love for her sister. She nudged her with her knee.

"I'm glad you're here."

Amy kneed her back. "Me too, even if it's because you're a murder suspect."

Laura managed a smile. "How's auditioning going? Getting any gigs?"

Amy gave her a look as if checking the legitimacy of the question. Ever since they were teenagers, whenever Amy talked about acting in front of their parents, their mother would go still and say nothing, her face a mask that barely concealed her bitterness. Their father convinced Amy to study business as a fail-safe, so she interned at Dior, jumped through all the hoops.

But Laura knew Amy dreamed of her name in lights. She tried to support her, because even though she'd seen the dark side of fame, and even though Amy's optimism seemed endless, Laura sensed that she needed somebody to believe in her, too.

"I was down to the final two girls for a car insurance commercial," Amy said, dipping a spring roll in soy sauce, "but they said the other girl was more believably into car insurance."

"That's probably a good thing."

Amy shrugged, looking at her screen.

"*The Guesthouse* turns thirty this year," she said.

"Fuck, I feel old."

"The anniversary, though. Could that be a part of this?"

"Sometimes a coincidence is just a coincidence."

"And sometimes murderers are excellent timekeepers. They live for anniversaries."

Laura nodded. "So do movie studios."

She saw that Amy was compiling a new list. "What's that?"

Amy turned her screen away, then noted Laura's suspicious expression and showed her.

1. Falling
2. Burning
3. Spider bites
4. Drowning
5. Decapitated
6. Buried alive
7. Stabbed
8. Hanged

"It's the order people died in *The Guesthouse*," Amy said. "And, I guess, real life, mostly. When you look at it, it really does look weird. The deaths were so similar to what happened in the movie."

"Statistically, those are all pretty common ways to die."

"True, but in that exact order? And now Todd's dead, too . . ." She trailed off, thinking. "But he's broken the order. The burning wasn't first in the movie. What if the streaming show restarted the whole thing?"

The man who fell from the highway.

As far as Laura knew, he wasn't connected to the show.

She took out the scripts she stole from the production office.

"What are those?"

"*It Feeds* episodes," Laura said, flipping open the first script. "The pilot episode opens with spider bites."

"I always thought that was a weird one."

Laura kept flipping until she found another death sequence. "The second is hanging." She looked up. "They changed the order."

"Remakes, am I right?"

"No, listen. That means we have no idea what's next," Laura said. "At least if somebody was following the order of the series, we'd know what to look out for."

Amy sighed. "It's a shame Todd's dead, because that guy screams suspect."

Laura abandoned the scripts. "There's something off about Beverly."

"The psychic?"

"She said she wants to help me, but I don't know why. I think she knows more than she's saying."

"Let's stick to reality," Amy said. "What if somebody was trying to shut down production?"

"Who would benefit from that, though?"

"Somebody who's mad the show's being made? Somebody who wishes the past would stay buried?"

"You just described me," Laura said.

Amy dug into her noodles and said nothing.

When they'd worn themselves out googling their tiny list of suspects, Laura suppressed a yawn. It was eight p.m. and she felt a hundred years old. Haggard and so tired she could sleep for a week, but the thought of sleep sent panicky spasms shooting down her arms and legs. What if she saw the man in the corner? What if he took her again?

No. They'd moved locations. Nobody knew she was there except for Amy.

She cleaned her teeth, switched her phone to silent, and checked that the door was locked. Then she went to the bed. Amy was curled up in the middle of her mattress, eyes closed, breathing softly. Asleep already. Another reason Laura hated but loved her. Amy never had any trouble sleeping.

She climbed onto the bed and curled up facing her sister.

"Amy?" she whispered.

Amy's head moved but she didn't reply.

"What if . . ." She swallowed, sought the courage to say the words. "What if I did set the fire and I just don't remember?"

No reply.

Laura snuggled in closer, breathing in her sister's musky scent and succumbing to sleep.

THE HORROR ENCYCLOPEDIA

If you've accidentally checked in to the Cricklewood Guesthouse, here are 10 top tips to help you stay alive . . .

1. Avoid room 205.

2. If you come across a spider, RUN FOR YOUR FREAKIN' LIFE.

3. The color yellow = death.

4. Seen the Needle Man? That's no hallucination! See tip #2.

5. Consider the basement off-limits if you don't fancy taking a dirt nap.

6. Actually, bathrooms are off the menu, too. It's better to be stinky than a stiff.

7. A little girl asks you to play a fortune-teller game? *Get outta there.*

8. Don't poke around in the history of the Needle Man; some things should be left buried.

9. Trust *no one.*

10. If all else fails, sorry, we should've mentioned it's basically impossible to survive a stay at the Cricklewood. Best you can do now is say your goodbyes, get comfy, and pray it's quick. Bye!

TWELVE

The next morning, Laura left Amy asleep in bed and called home. She stood on the terrace outside the room, breathing in early-morning smog and hoping nobody would pick up on the other end. It was around four p.m. in the UK and her mother ate dinner early.

Her heart sank when the line clicked after two rings.

"Hello?" A male voice, pleasant but professional.

"Hi, Colin, it's Laura."

She'd only met Colin a couple of times, but he seemed like a good fit for her mother. He was patient and difficult to offend, and he didn't patronize Pamela the way some of the nurses did. After their father died, Pamela refused to leave her home, and she had enough savings to justify it. The money Laura had made during her childhood in the spotlight was now paying for her mother's live-in carer.

At least it meant Laura didn't have to take on the role herself.

"Oh, Laura, hi," Colin said, and she could tell from his strained tone that he'd seen the news. "Your mom is in the living room. I'll take the phone through to her."

"Thanks."

She heard a noise, something too far away from the phone for her to identify, then Colin talking to somebody. She fought the urge to hang up, already knew this was a mistake, but then Colin said, "Here she is."

"Hello?"

Laura gripped the rail, willed herself to speak.

"Hi, Mom."

"Amy?"

"It's Laura, Mom."

"Laura." It didn't sound like a question, but it was.

Laura closed her eyes.

It was one of those days, then. Sometimes her mother remembered her, sometimes she didn't. Neither was easy to deal with. She pictured her mother's confused face, the lines around her downturned mouth, her dark blond curls thin and wispy. Pamela Tremaine would hate what she had become.

"Polly," Laura said, her jaw creaking with the effort of saying her old name.

"Polly." She could tell her mother was smiling now. "Yes, of course. Where are you?"

"I'm in L.A."

"That's nice. When are you coming to see me?"

Her voice was so different now. When Laura was a child, her mother's tone had been sharp and certain. Habitually set to a couple degrees below zero. Now it was worn smooth, lilting, and warm as microwave-fresh popcorn. So different, it was like speaking to a different person.

"I'll come see you soon, Mom," Laura said. "I was just calling to let you know I'm okay."

"There was a fire?" her mom said.

"Yes, but I'm fine. Amy's fine, too. She's with me."

"It's so lucky she was in L.A."

Laura rubbed her forehead. "Yeah, she flew in yesterday. Look—"

"No, she's been there a while. A couple of weeks. She said she'd bring me back saltwater taffy."

Laura stilled. Her mom often got confused. It was the first sign they'd had that something was wrong with her. One weekend five years ago, Laura came home for her dad's sixtieth birthday. When she walked in the front door, her mother startled and gave her a terrified look. She shouted at Laura to get out, her voice high and thin, her eyes shimmering with fear. As if she had no idea who Laura was. As if she were a stranger.

It took her mom a whole minute before it clicked, and afterward she had no memory of not knowing her elder daughter.

But Laura remembered.

She pushed a hand into her hair, clasped her scalp. Her mom must be mistaken about Amy and L.A. Amy had put on a good show of flying in from New York for Laura, her knight in shining Armani.

Why would she lie?

"I've got to go, Mom."

"Okay, Polly. I love you."

The words came so naturally, it was as if her mother really meant them. But Laura knew they were just another symptom of her dementia. In the past, when Pamela told somebody she loved them, it was to pacify or manipulate them. Her affection was always a front for something else.

"Me too," Laura said. "Bye."

She hung up and stared down at the pool for a while, her mind filled with her mother. She always felt nervy after hearing her voice. As much as she hated to admit it, there was a part of her that wondered if the dementia was a trick. Another version of the "match game." Just another way for her mother to torture her. Laura wished it were, because the reality was even more difficult to accept.

The woman she'd known was gone.

All that spite and nastiness disappeared practically overnight.

And it made Laura so angry sometimes, she wanted to tear the world to pieces with her bare hands.

Back in the room, she found Amy sitting up in bed, reaching for a bottle from the nightstand. She unscrewed the cap and gulped down water.

"How's the jet lag?" Laura asked.

"Just gotta stay hydrated. Wait for my body to figure itself out."

She didn't look tired, but then Amy rarely did. When they argued as teenagers, it had been easy for Amy to pretend they weren't related. They were so different in every way; people were often shocked that they were sisters.

Laura watched her sister and squinted.

Maybe their mom was confused. It was just another sign that she wasn't the woman she used to be. But what if she was right and Amy *was* already in L.A.? Why cover that up?

Before Laura could ask, Amy screwed the cap onto the bottle and slid her legs off the mattress.

"I have an idea," she said, "and you're going to hate it. But hear me out."

"Go on."

"Everybody thinks you're either involved in the fire at the studio, or you're this Christ-like survivor who's somehow evaded a film curse."

"Fair assessment."

"People keep telling your story for you," Amy said. "They have been for years. Isn't it time you told it yourself? I can be your film crew. We document the truth. Show you getting to the bottom of this, the fire but also *The Guesthouse*, once and for all."

Laura's eyes narrowed. "Did Mike put you up to this?"

"What? No."

Amy was serious about shooting the video.

Just a few days ago, Laura would have jumped down her sister's throat at the mere suggestion that she expose herself as the kid from *The Guesthouse*. But Amy was making sense. Maybe it was Todd's death, or maybe L.A. was rubbing off on her, but Laura now felt differently about the whole thing.

Why not weaponize the truth? Use it to her benefit?

They'd hold back the footage, store it up for later. By the time anybody saw it, Laura would have helped close the case.

"Fine," she sighed.

Amy hopped on the spot. "Really?"

"But you can't release any footage until this is over. Recording only."

Her sister beamed and took out her phone. Just the sight of it made Laura's jaw tighten.

"We're starting now?" she asked, staring into the black eye of the lens.

"Of course. Candid footage is essential, it gives the feeling of a journey."

"Wow, five seasons of *The Simple Life* finally paid off."

Amy tapped her phone screen. "Okay, recording. Tell us what we're doing. And try not to look so stiff. Just be natural."

Nothing's natural in L.A.

They shot some footage of Laura talking about traveling to L.A. to cover *It Feeds*. Then she brought out the paper fortune-teller and the yellow dress, along with the shredded contents of her suitcase. She felt awkward and self-conscious the whole time, tripping over her words and trembling.

When Amy stopped recording, though, Laura realized it had helped. She felt a little more in control of the past few days. She had a record of what had happened, in her words, with evidence to back it up.

Through it all, though, she couldn't help picturing the Needle Man standing in the corner watching her, and the thought caused a dull pain to throb in her solar plexus.

While Amy showered, Laura opened Instagram, the perfect distraction from unwanted thoughts, and saw that she had five hundred notifications. There were usually zero and she only had two hundred followers.

Now the follower count said 1,103. It ticked up before her eyes. 1,104, then 1,124 . . .

"Instagram's gone weird," she said as Amy emerged from the bathroom in a cloud of steam, towel fastened around her torso.

"Let me see." Amy took the phone from her. "Wow, Pill, your feed is horse shit. You've posted how many pictures of the London Underground?"

"I was trying to document the old architecture for—never mind." It seemed stupid now.

"Here, you were tagged in a bunch of posts." She looked at Laura. "A load of people seem to know you're Polly."

"What?"

Laura went to her side and watched as Amy scrolled through the posts Laura had been tagged in. Some were stills from *The Guesthouse* showing her holding the paper fortune-teller; others showed horror collectors posing in their memorabilia cupboards, surrounded by shelves of VHS tapes and Freddy figurines.

None of the people looked familiar.

"How did they figure out I'm her?" Laura asked.

"We could message them," Amy suggested. "One of them could be—"

"No." Laura snatched back the phone.

"Use your kind hands," Amy said, something their dad told them when they were young. "They could know something."

"Never feed the trolls. How do I block them?" Laura tapped through pages, looking for the block option, but somehow ended up back in her notifications log. She stopped tapping. Frowned.

"What?" Amy asked.

Laura looked up. "Kyle Williamson just followed me."

"The actor? Why would she follow you?"

"I don't know. Maybe she follows all the journalists who interview her. Keep your enemies close."

Or maybe she'd seen that Instagram had figured out she was Polly. Either way, Laura felt unnerved.

Kyle's most recent post was a close-up selfie looking into the camera, face expressionless, big eyes refracting light. Beautiful and fragile and oh-so-Hollywood. She'd posted it an hour ago.

RIP Todd.

"She was scared," Laura said, thinking over Kyle's prank story. At the time, she'd dismissed the prank as typical movie high jinks, but now she wasn't so sure.

She's here.

"She could know something," she said. "I'm messaging her."

"Oh, sure," Amy said, toweling her hair dry. "Message the airhead actor but ignore the creeps who could be killing people."

She had a reply from Kyle within five minutes.

Sure, I'd love to talk. Come to me? This is my address.

Laura was stunned. She hadn't expected it to be that easy. Maybe Kyle liked her. It was the only reason she had for why a TV-slash-movie-star would hand over her address on Instagram, especially to a journalist.

She reread Kyle's message. Her place was in the Hollywood Hills, because of course it was. Before she could consider going there, though, she had to know what Amy's deal was.

"Ame, when did you say you flew in?" she asked.

"Two nights ago. The night before I came to your hotel."

There was a slight question in Amy's eyes, though her face remained expressionless.

"Mom said you've been in L.A. for weeks."

"Really?"

"Amy."

"What?"

"Don't make me ask again."

Amy shook her head. "Mom got it wrong. Why would I lie about something like that?"

Laura held her gaze. "I don't know."

Their mom hadn't sounded confused on the phone, but then, their mom often sounded lucid when she wasn't. It was one of the worst parts of the illness. She sounded caring and loving and light, all the things she wasn't before the dementia took hold.

Laura knew that she should be grateful. Her mother's changed personality made it easier to get along with her. When she had her good spells, she was even fun. But Laura felt like a fraud. Overnight, she'd had to bury thirty years' worth of resentment. She'd never confronted her mother about their years in Hollywood. Never said all the things that prickled her tongue, desperate to be spoken.

How awful her mother had been.

How nowadays it would be considered abuse.

How Laura hadn't cared what anybody else thought, she just wanted her mom to love her.

But now it was too late.

How could she hold accountable a woman who barely knew what day it was?

She'd waited too long. Held on to the pain for too many years.

Across the room, Amy began to dress. "Come on, let's go meet your new showbiz pal."

Laura didn't have the energy to argue. Whatever Amy was hiding, it could wait.

Everybody agrees that Hollywood is no place for children. This town is strewn with the ghosts of child stars gone AWOL. Sure, there's the odd happy ending. But for every Drew Barrymore—who outgrew her wild-child phase to become America's goofy sweetheart—there's a Lindsay. A River. A Corey.

Here are the uncomfortable questions that Hollywood doesn't want us to ask: What are the long-term effects of growing up in front of the camera? Where does free will come into this? Is it really appropriate for a child's parent or guardian to give permission for their young charge to perform? And most importantly: What more could be done to protect these vulnerable young people?

Far be it for me to cry, "Won't somebody think of the children?" However, it seems that as long as somebody is getting rich off the exploitation of the naive and the impressionable, those around them are more than happy to turn a blind eye. And what of the children? Well, they sure sell papers, now, don't they?

THIRTEEN

little over an hour after Kyle's message, they pulled up outside a set of iron gates. The taxi had driven them out of the smog and congestion of L.A. and up into the winding green avenues of the Hollywood Hills. Laura swore it was brighter up there, the houses tucked behind tall trees and taller walls, appearing as flashes of white like rabbits hiding amid the foliage.

They had stopped at a cell phone store along the way. Amy insisted Laura change her SIM card just in case somebody was tracking her. Amy changed hers, too, for good measure.

Laura felt a little less hunted afterward. The thought hadn't even occurred to her that she was carrying a personal tracking device everywhere she went.

She paid the taxi in cash and they approached the intercom to one side of the driveway. Amy pointed her phone through the bars, zooming in on the contemporary brick-and-glass house beyond. It looked like something out of a Hitchcock movie. Cold and austere. The perfect home for a haunted blond heroine.

"This place is sweet," Amy whispered. Her bag, slung over her shoulder, contained the paper fortune-teller and yellow dress. Evidence, in case they needed it. There was no way Laura would let it out of her sight.

She felt grateful for Amy all over again. She wasn't sure how many sisters would charge into battle so readily.

"Yes?" a voice crackled through the intercom.

"Hi, it's Laura Warren. We're here to see Kyle Williamson?"

Static blasted through the speaker, and then the gates glided open. Laura walked in, ignoring Amy as she filmed her, gaze set on the house. Something about it unnerved her. She couldn't picture a twenty-something living there. It felt wrong.

Driving down Sunset, she'd seen dozens of homeless people shuffling behind shopping carts or tucked into the shadows of deserted buildings, hiding from the sun like it could burn them up in seconds. This was only a few miles farther north, but it could be another world entirely.

"You get her talking," Amy said, "and then I'll excuse myself for a second, see what I can find."

"What? No. We're not snooping around—"

The door opened and Kyle appeared, a vision in a white bodysuit. Her blond hair lay in ringlets over her shoulders and her eyes were shock-blue, like perfect solitaires.

"Laura, hi, it's so great to see you again."

"Thanks for agreeing to talk to me. Oh, this is my sister, Amy, I hope it's okay she came along."

"It's a pleasure to meet you," Amy said. "Do you mind if I film this?"

Kyle's smile dimmed, doubt creeping into her face.

"You look gorgeous," Amy said, giving her a sincere look. "And we'll blur out any identifying features. Promise."

"It's for the investigation," Laura added, although she might as well have become invisible. She sensed the subtle buzz of tension between the two women, the kind that occurs when two unmistakably attractive people meet. A kind of mutual wariness and appreciation, like cats. They could be rivals or partners in crime, depending on the situation. Amy didn't back down, and Kyle finally blinked and looked at Laura.

"I guess it's okay," she said. "Please, come in."

She led them into an open-plan living room. Fresh magnolias filled a half-dozen vases, their delicate perfume lacing the air, and Kyle invited them to sit on a cream-colored sofa that curved beneath a chandelier. Patio doors gave a view of a crystalline infinity pool and, beyond it, the shimmering mirage of downtown L.A.

"Nice place," Laura said.

"Thanks, we just moved in. Leo traded up. Apparently, he's more into Malibu these days."

"Leonardo DiCaprio?" Amy asked. Her mouth snapped shut when Kyle nodded, and she appraised the room with renewed interest.

"I'm so sorry about Todd," Laura said, trying to get them on topic. Interviews usually had a structure, a formality imposed by hovering PRs and strict schedules. It felt strange talking without any of that. Unnatural.

Kyle toyed with her white-gold bracelets. "I'm still sort of in shock, I guess."

"He seemed like a nice guy," Laura said, even though she didn't entirely believe that. Kyle merely nodded, so Laura continued. "I heard there were meetings at the studio. Has anybody discovered anything new?"

"I'm just an actor, nobody tells me anything." She released her bracelets, focusing on Laura. "Speaking of, you did some pretty amazing acting of your own back there."

"Back where?"

"At the studio." Kyle leaned forward, her blue eyes sparkling. "I had no clue you were Polly Tremaine. You had everybody fooled!"

She had seen the Insta posts, then.

"You could have told me. I'm great at keeping secrets." Her grin widened. "Hey, we're both Tammy. How cool is that?"

Laura felt held in place by her gaze. Being around Kyle was like being shown a better version of herself. The oh-so-pristine Tammy of today, not the wrinkled, life-tired frump she'd become.

She jumped as a woman appeared, carrying a tray of green bottles.

"Oh, this is my assistant, Fiona," Kyle said as the woman set down the branded water. Laura saw that the tray also contained fresh apples, pears, and mangoes and a small knife, presumably for cutting and peeling. "Fiona's a godsend, I couldn't live without her."

"Thanks," Laura said, and the assistant smiled and retreated. To one side, Amy filmed Kyle, but her attention was on Laura. A slight frown crinkled the space between her eyebrows and Laura couldn't figure out what she was thinking.

"It just sucks for Todd," Kyle said, sipping through a metal straw. "He had such a vision for the show. It was going to turn out great. Now there's a chance the world won't get to see it."

"Do you think that's why somebody set the fire? They're trying to shut down the show?"

"I . . . well . . ." Kyle's gaze flicked at Amy's camera phone.

"We'll edit out anything you don't feel comfortable sharing," Laura said.

Kyle looked down at her drink, continued sipping.

"Can you think who might be responsible?" Laura asked.

Kyle clasped the bottle in both hands. "I really didn't want to say this, but . . . the psychic. I don't like her."

"I think Beverly enjoys making it difficult for people to like her."

"It's not just that." Kyle looked uneasy. "I heard something about her from one of the crew. One of them found out all this stuff about her. She made headlines a while back. They called her the 'Psycho Psychic.'"

"She has mental health problems?"

"Big-time," Kyle said. "She was arrested for murder."

Laura's hip creaked as she shifted on the sofa. "What? When?"

"Some girl died, I think it was around 2010. It was ruled a suicide, but it was hella suspicious."

"How did she die?"

"Her throat was cut." Kyle shuddered. "But even before I knew that, I got a weird feeling from Beverly. From the very first day, she was always there, in the shadows, watching. It was creepy."

Laura could relate.

"Did she ever give you any reason to suspect she was dangerous?"

Kyle thought about it. "I saw her near my trailer around the time it was broken into." She set down her water. "She was always doing weird things. Like, I saw her slip something into your bag that first day you were on set. I don't know why she'd do that."

Laura sat up. "You saw her put the fortune-teller in my bag?"

Kyle nodded. "She didn't see me looking. I told security and they said they'd look into it."

They hadn't.

"Sorry to interrupt," Amy said. "Would it be okay if I used the little girl's room?"

Laura gave her a warning look. "I'm sure you can wait—"

"Oh, no, it's fine," Kyle said. "It's just down the hall to the right."

"Thanks." Amy ignored Laura's glare as she left the living room.

As soon as she was gone, Kyle leaned in again, her voice low as she said, "Okay, let's talk showbiz. That's okay, right? This is too good. The original Tammy is right here in my house!"

Laura nodded stiffly and sipped her drink just to have something else to focus on. She blinked as light got in her eyes. Through the French doors, the pool reflected the sun, casting bright light into the room. She angled her body away from it.

"Why did you quit?" Kyle asked. "Like, no judgment. I started acting as a kid, too, and it's pretty intense."

"It just wasn't for me," Laura said.

"That's cool. I found it tough sometimes, too. Like, you're this little person and everybody expects something from you. It's a lot of pressure."

"Mm-hmm."

That quickly, Laura's head was full of her mother. She tried to think of something else, but the memories were like gossamer, slipping between her fingers as she tried to keep them away.

She remembered her mother pacing while slapping a script in her hand like a club.

"It's not difficult, Polly! Just say the lines after me."

The pressure of her mother's grip around her wrists.

The day Laura finally broke, she spat in her mother's face and ran.

"Laura?"

She blinked, saw Kyle looking at her.

"I really hope you know we weren't trying to rip off your movie," Kyle said. "My Tammy would've gone in a totally different direction from yours. I wanted to make you proud."

Laura's airway shrank as Kyle looked at her.

"Did you mean to play her innocent?" Kyle asked.

The sun got in Laura's eyes again. She tried to blink it away, but it persisted, making it difficult for her to focus on the other woman.

"I think so," Laura said.

She couldn't tell if Kyle suspected her of starting the fire. Was that the real reason she'd invited her to the house? Her excitement about their movie connection could be a front. Maybe the cops knew she was Polly, too. She imagined them sitting in a squad car down the street and felt the desperate need to count. She fought against it.

"So that's the key, right?" Kyle's voice echoed somewhere in the light. "Tammy seems so innocent, we can't tell if she's guilty of killing people."

Laura opened her mouth to speak but then glimpsed something beyond the patio doors.

A dark shape submerged in the pool, lingering beneath the still surface.

"Laura?" Kyle's voice sounded far away.

Laura couldn't look away from the pool. Sunlight flickered in her eyes, making it difficult for her to see, but then she saw the black shape move. Something broke the surface. Bright diamonds dripped from a black-clad arm and light flashed off steel.

Claws.

Needle-thin and glinting.

"It was me," Laura heard herself say.

"You?" Kyle asked. "I don't understand."

The light divided, sparkling like white fire, and Laura could only just make out Kyle's outline.

Beyond her, the shape crawled out of the pool onto the flagstones. It stood, glittering with water, and even though she couldn't see its face in the shadow of the hat, she knew it saw her.

It watched her from the other side of the patio doors.

"I was there," Laura murmured.

"What do you mean? You were where?"

Laura couldn't think.

She couldn't see.

Heat pressed in around her and it was the heat of the Cricklewood set, returning to claim her.

The light from the pool flickered and danced, filling her vision.

And the Needle Man wasn't outside anymore.

He was in the room with them. His rubber boots creaked with water as he came up behind Kyle. His black eyes were fixed on Laura. Black as oil.

And now Laura saw that it wasn't the Needle Man from the movie or the TV show. He was taller, more solid, and the claws were too long. They were so rusted, she could practically feel the ache of tetanus in her jaw. And she smelled him. Something dank and dead, like rotten leaves.

"*pollllyyyyyyyshhhhh . . .*"

"Kyle," Laura said, trying to get up, but her body was frozen.

The Needle Man raised his arms, as if preparing to pincer them around Kyle. Talons pointed down, toward Kyle's skull.

"No, don't," Laura said.

"Laura?" Kyle frowned.

The talons descended.

And with them darkness.

Screaming.

Laura came to with the sound of screaming in her ears.

She was still in the living room, standing even though she had no idea how her legs were supporting her. She looked at the woman gripping the back of the sofa. Kyle's assistant.

"What have you done?" the assistant screamed. "What have you done?"

Laura looked down at the knife in her hand. It dripped red. She felt cold. Freezing. Her body shuddered as if trying to get warm.

Not again, she thought, the words a desperate echo. *Not again not again not again.*

There was no fire this time, just blood. A lot of it. The sofa was red and Kyle was spread out on it, her white bodysuit no longer white. Her eyes were open, fixed on the ceiling, her face spattered with red.

"What happened?" Laura whispered.

"What did you do?" the assistant screamed again, and Laura wished she'd shut up so she could think of an answer. She remembered talking, the light in her eyes, then nothing.

Nothing at all.

Why couldn't she remember?

"Laura?" Amy skidded into the room and took in the scene. Her shocked expression hardened when she saw the knife in Laura's hand. "We have to go."

"I think—" Laura began, but then she was being dragged away from the body, past the screaming assistant and out the front door into the blinding sunlight.

Caption from the last Instagram post by Kyle Williamson

Liked by lalaliving2020 and 27,430 others

kylewilliamson Here's a little secret: when I was a kid, I wanted to be an Olympic gymnast. My bedroom was covered in posters of Shannon Miller and Dominique Dawes and I practiced three times a week at the local club. The thing is, I wasn't any good. I loved it—my GOD I loved it—but I was never the best. Nowhere near good enough to make it to state champion, let alone the Olympics. I was distraught. Inconsolable. Now I look back and I remember the heartbreak, the pain, and I wish I could tell my younger self: it's going to be OK. You're going to find a new dream. A new direction that will fit you like the best pair of Jimmy Choos. I'd tell that angry little girl that sometimes you end up right where you're supposed to be, and I really hope she'd believe me. She'd better believe me.

View all 256 comments

22 hours ago

FOURTEEN

We have to go back," Laura said, but Amy wasn't listening.

"Keep moving," she said, pulling Laura along.

Laura felt weightless, like a balloon bobbing in Amy's wake. She looked down at her hand and saw she was still holding the knife. It was glued to her, red and smiling.

"Stop!" she cried, yanking her arm free. She tossed the knife, which clattered into the gutter. She stared at it, trying to remember picking it up, attacking Kyle, but a black wall met her. There was nothing to remember.

"Here," Amy said, taking off her shirt and revealing a gray tank top underneath. She used the shirt to clean Laura's hands, but the blood didn't want to be cleaned. It stuck fast.

"We have to go back," Laura said. "We have to find out what happened."

"Not a chance in hell." Amy rubbed harder and Laura let her, even though it hurt. The pain was good. The pain was real. It rooted her in the present moment.

"Amy, I killed—"

"Stop."

As she looked down at her hands, Laura's mind spat out a distressing tidbit of information. Yvonne Lincoln, writer of *The Guesthouse*, stabbed her husband to death in '97.

She claimed the Needle Man made her do it.

Laura opened her mouth, but Amy gripped her hands tightly and stared into her face.

"Somebody made it look like you did it, that's all," she said. "You didn't kill her."

A siren whooped nearby. Laura looked around but didn't see a cop car.

"Quickly," Amy urged. She retrieved the knife, wrapped it in the shirt, and stowed it in her bag. Then she led Laura away from the street and down a walkway that ran between two houses. At the end, they turned left down a path behind the house, then stopped so Laura could be sick.

When she'd finished, she stood weakly, trying to breathe.

"It's just like before," she said. "The blackouts."

"She called the police," Amy said. "The assistant. We have to get back to the motel."

Laura didn't react. She was thinking about all the times she blacked out as a kid after making *The Guesthouse*. Her parents took her to doctors, she had scans in a machine, they talked about her brain, finally confirming after weeks that it was normal.

The blackouts were stress related. An aftershock of trauma.

They started a few months after the supermarket incident. She'd find herself on the floor of the classroom, kids gathered around her, or in the movie theater or a coffee shop. Sometimes nobody noticed; other times it was a hot topic. Kids were cruel and adults were critical.

She'd never killed anybody, though.

Until today.

"Laura? Are you listening?"

She looked at her sister. "The blackouts are happening again."

"You haven't had them in years."

"I'm having them now. And both times I've woken up to a dead body."

Amy opened her mouth to say something, but Laura spoke over her.

"What if this is some latent trauma from *The Guesthouse*? What if the person trying to shut down production is me?"

They looked at each other for a moment, and even though Laura didn't want to believe it, she knew that the obvious solution was often the most logical one.

"I have to turn myself in," she said.

"Stop."

"Somebody else could get hurt. At least if I'm in police custody—"

Amy took her hand and spoke softly.

"My sister isn't a murderer."

Something moved in her eyes as she said it, and Laura wondered if Amy believed her own words. Somewhere in there, she saw doubt.

"The water," Amy said. "Kyle's assistant brought us water. What if she spiked it? What if the assistant killed her?"

Laura found the thought oddly reassuring. Calming. Yes, that was logical. That made sense. More sense than her blacking out and stabbing a woman to death.

More sirens sounded nearby, and Amy took out her phone, opening the maps app.

"We have to figure out a way out of this neighborhood," she said. "This way."

Laura followed her down the path and they emerged onto a suburban street. At the far end, red and blue lights winked, approaching fast, and they ducked back, waiting for the cars to pass. Laura fought the urge to vomit again as the vehicles screamed by.

She could still turn herself in.

If the cops had her in custody, it might stop whoever was killing people.

"Okay, go," Amy said, tugging Laura across the street. They turned a corner, then another, and saw two more cop cars approaching.

"Shit," Amy said.

Laura watched the cars approach and considered stepping out into the road. Letting them arrest her. She was the common denominator in both deaths. She could be the reason people were dying. The thought of a jail cell filled her with terror, but so did the idea of regaining consciousness next to another corpse.

My sister isn't a murderer.

Amy couldn't know that. Beside her, Amy looked around for somewhere to hide, but the houses were all gated. There was nowhere. And maybe that was okay. Maybe Laura should be behind bars.

If nothing else, she had to keep her sister safe.

She was about to step off the curb when a female voice shouted to their right.

"Laura!"

A vehicle sat with its motor running. The passenger window was rolled down and, through it, Laura saw Beverly.

"Get in!" Beverly called.

"Who is that?" Amy asked.

"The psychic," Laura said, not believing it herself.

"The Psycho Psychic?"

"Get in now!" Beverly shouted, her face pulled tight with urgency.

"We're not getting in the car with *her*," Amy said.

Laura heard the sirens, saw the cop cars speeding toward them, and knew that she wasn't ready to face them yet. If there was even a small chance at clearing her name, she had to take it.

"We don't have a choice," she said.

They got into the back of the car and had only just closed the door when Beverly floored it.

Beverly's apartment was part of a gated complex with sun-bleached walls and an empty, grime-encrusted pool. Laura had never heard of Hawthorne, and there was probably a reason. A greased-up guy in a tank top worked on a motorbike outside one of the apartments. On the upper level, a dog barked and a woman leaned against the railing as she smoked.

The place felt tired. Forgotten. As far removed from the glamor of Kyle's neighborhood as it was possible to be.

As Beverly led them up the stairs to the upper level, Laura might have felt bad for her, or at least a modicum of surprise, but she couldn't feel anything. Her body was cold, her ears ringing. Her senses seemed to have shut down.

"Come in," Beverly said, giving the front door a shove.

Laura looked around a neat, unremarkable apartment. It was cleaner than the rest of the complex, so clean it was almost as if nobody lived there. The kitchenette and living room were functional, a coffee maker and toaster on the counter and a single Frida Kahlo print hung on the wall, the one depicting two Kahlos holding hands, their hearts exposed. The only other personal item was a knee-high sculpture of a cobra that faced the door, fangs bared.

Laura sat at the kitchen table, her hands still sticky with blood, but she couldn't wash them yet. She needed the reminder that what had happened was real. Not something she dreamed.

While Beverly took a pitcher of water from the refrigerator, Amy raised her camera phone.

"You can't film in here," Beverly said.

"I'm filming everything."

"Not in here."

Amy raised an eyebrow. "Got something to hide?"

"Turn it off. Now."

"Amy," Laura said, and her sister blinked, then lowered her phone.

"Nice place you've got," she said, the sarcasm unmistakable in her tone.

Beverly didn't respond. She set out three glass tumblers and Amy remained standing, watching. She had begrudgingly told Beverly about Kyle during the drive, though she left out the part where Laura thought she'd killed her. Beverly barely responded to the information. She seemed to be thinking, intensely, as if trying to work out a math equation that refused to cooperate.

"Drink," Beverly told Laura, pouring water.

"Don't," Amy said, stepping forward.

Laura looked at the ice-cold glass, which dripped with condensation.

"She didn't rescue us just to kill us," she said, and drank, even though she kept hearing "Psycho Psychic" in her head and thinking about what Kyle had said before she died. That Beverly had spent time in a psych unit. Had killed a girl.

The water felt good, though, cooling her insides and bringing the apartment slightly more into focus.

"It's probably time we were honest with each other, don't you think?" Beverly said, sitting opposite Laura.

"How did you know we were there? On the street?" Laura asked.

Beverly looked like she'd had this conversation many times before. "There's no way to explain it without sounding drunk or crazy, but I assure you I'm neither. Sometimes I feel a pull, like a hunger, deep in my belly. It pulled me to that spot an hour ago, and I had a feeling I'd find you there, even though I couldn't say why."

Laura didn't know how to reply to that.

"I went back to the hotel yesterday after I talked to the cops at the studio," Beverly continued, "like we agreed. But you weren't there."

"We left. Somebody trashed my room."

Beverly frowned. "When?"

"Sometime between us going to the studio and me getting back." Laura picked at the congealed blood around her nails. "We visited Kyle this morning. I blacked out, and then—"

She pushed against the wall in her mind, but it was no use.

She tried to order her thoughts. Stick to what she knew.

"You put the fortune-teller in my bag," she said.

Beverly blinked. "Who told you that?"

"Kyle."

"She lied." Beverly sounded so sure.

"Why would she lie about something like that?"

"Maybe *she* put the fortune-teller in your bag."

Laura's head felt like it was underwater, the pressure cooking her brain.

"You're the girl from the movie," Beverly said. She stated it so matter-of-factly, Laura almost couldn't believe she'd hidden it from everybody in her life for so long. The way Beverly said it, it seemed almost insignificant.

"How did you know that?" Amy asked, her voice sharp.

"Some things are obvious."

"Like not accepting help from strangers."

"Did you know Kyle was dead?" Laura asked, ignoring her sister.

"I suspected."

"How long have you known who I am?"

Beverly sipped her drink. "I knew the moment we met in the studio restroom."

Laura didn't doubt it. At the time, she'd found Beverly's gaze unsettling, felt her studying her reflection in that same, equation-puzzling way, like Laura was a riddle she wanted to solve.

For the first time, Laura wondered if she had been wrong.

What if Beverly really was psychic?

"You said you wanted to help me," she said. "Why?"

Beverly contemplated her glass. "I used to help people a lot."

"Kyle said you stayed in a psychiatric hospital," Amy cut in.

A pained expression crossed Beverly's face. She looked at Laura, as if weighing something. Finally, she spoke, her voice calm and emotionless. "It was seven years ago. I went through something and it took a toll. I wasn't myself. I didn't go to the psych ward willingly, but believe me when I say it saved my life."

"Was it because of the girl?" Laura asked.

Beverly nodded fractionally. "When I was a child, I realized I could sense things, not just from those who had passed on, but from the living, too. Extreme emotions: pain, suffering, joy. Mostly pain." Her gaze rested on the tabletop, though she didn't seem to see it.

"When I moved to Los Angeles, I did so for selfish reasons. The constant noise here helped drown out the noise of the living and the dead. Suppress it. I'd trained as a nurse, but hospitals are overwhelming for people like me. So I got a job as an assistant at a soda company. On the side, I worked as a psychic medium.

"A couple came to me for help. Their daughter was showing symptoms of possession. She was sixteen. I spent a couple of weeks with her, talking to her, chipping away at the thing inside her, before finally performing an exorcism. It seemed successful. I thought I had done my job."

Beverly's eyes were red-rimmed, although her expression remained stoic.

"A week later, the girl killed her family, then herself. She had suffered some kind of mental break. I learned she had been obsessed with a cult that advocated some pretty extreme practices, information her parents kept from me. They were devout Christians. Perhaps they believed in God more than Western medicine. I'll never know. But I should've seen the signs. I should have sensed something was wrong. It took me a long time to get over it."

The memory was etched into Beverly's face and Laura realized it was in every gesture the woman made. Every word she spoke was coated in the memory of that time. Laura knew what it was like to have something in your past that refused to let go. She understood her pain more than she could say.

"I'm sorry," she said.

"Me too," Beverly said.

Amy went to Laura's side. "We should go. Thanks for the getaway car and everything, but we can handle this."

Somehow, Laura managed to stand. Amy was already at the door.

"Laura." Beverly's voice was strained. "That film isn't cursed. It never was. But there's something around you. I sense it, and you're running toward it instead of away. Let me help you."

Laura didn't move. She stood between Beverly and her sister, feeling torn.

"Thanks for the intel, Zelda Rubinstein," Amy said. "We'll be sure to look into that. Pill?"

"If you go out there, it'll happen again," Beverly said. "And the authorities will pin it on you."

"We're not trusting somebody who thinks they can see auras," Amy said.

Laura looked at her sister. Amy had always been there for her, always believed her. But this wasn't going away. She'd outrun it for thirty years and she was tiring. She felt it closing in. One day soon, she'd have to face it.

And she couldn't explain what was happening to her. Maybe it was a mental break, or maybe it was something else. Something unnatural.

She had to know.

"Can you really help?" she asked Beverly.

Beverly firmed her jaw. "Yes, I can."

"Then we're staying."

A my put up a fight. While Beverly went out to buy cigarettes, Amy tried to convince Laura to leave. She stood by the door, gripping her bag strap, white knuckled, and her arguments all made sense—*we don't know her; she's a potential murderer; how did she really know we'd be in Kyle's neighborhood?*—but Laura knew they didn't have a choice. Where would they go? If somebody had seen them at the motel, they couldn't go back there, and the Loft was out of the question. Nobody would guess they were holing up with the psychic from *It Feeds*. Even *she* had trouble believing it. For now, at least, they were safe.

When Amy finally relented, Laura left her in the living room and went into the bathroom. She showered and changed into jeans and a T-shirt Beverly had laid out for her. They were Laura's size, which made Laura wonder where they'd come from. An ex-roommate, maybe? Her brain could only hold so many thoughts, though, so she let it slide.

It was early afternoon, but it could have been the middle of the night for all that meant to Laura. Time usually dictated her life. There was always a deadline or a meeting or an event to build her day around. Now time had become a mere concept. She felt unmoored from her life. From her home. From herself. All she could do was keep moving forward in the vain hope that, simply by staying in motion, she'd eventually pick up the track she seemed to have wandered away from.

In the living room, she found Amy alone, sitting on the floor by the power outlet while her phone charged. The blinds were drawn but the sun forced its way inside regardless, giving the room a too-bright glow.

"You okay?" Laura asked.

"Kyle's all over the news," Amy said, scrolling.

The reality of the situation wrapped around Laura again and anxiety drummed the inside of her skull.

"Is there footage?" she asked, recalling the security cameras at Kyle's gate. "Of us?"

"Nothing that's been released yet."

Laura knew it was only a matter of time before her own face was on the news. There was no way she hadn't been caught by Kyle's cameras, and she could picture with ease the blurry stills that would appear on CNN. The thought made her feel small, exposed. This was outside her control. The anonymous life she'd built for herself was imploding and there was no way the police would believe she was innocent. She was a material witness to two deaths.

She was almost grateful her mother wouldn't understand. The dementia had robbed her of the ability to grasp anything so complex and awful. It had also robbed her of the ability to judge. To sneer. To twist it around on Laura and tell her she'd thrown her life away years ago. This was just the encore.

And what was Laura doing to fix the situation?

She was relying on the help of a psychic she didn't necessarily believe in.

She just hoped she could keep Amy out of it as much as possible.

"I can't believe you want to stay here," Amy said. "With her."

"She could get us out of this mess."

"How? By summoning the Power of Three?"

Laura understood her reaction. She'd given Beverly the same one just a few days ago.

"What if we've been wrong all these years?" she said. "What if there really is something more? Something that can kill and never be caught?"

Amy said nothing for what felt like forever.

They'd always agreed the curse was bullshit and now, just by questioning that, Laura felt a gap widen between them. Amy got to her feet.

"We don't need her. Let's leave and figure this out together. Please, Pill."

It had always been them against the world.

Whenever their mother was particularly cruel, or Laura had nightmares, or Amy failed to get a callback, they'd eat ice cream, watch Winona movies, and tell each other the stories of their futures. How Laura would be an editor one day and Amy would have her own BBC drama.

It was just them.

They had each other.

Laura wanted to hug her. Tell her it was going to be okay. But she knew that if she did that, she'd break, and she'd be no use to anyone.

"I have to know," she said.

Amy considered her for a moment, a pleading expression on her face. Then she went back to her phone. "You should get some rest."

Laura got the message. Amy didn't believe in hocus-pocus. They were raised realists. *We ain't afraid of no ghosts*, because ghosts didn't exist. They'd been united in that belief.

Now, though, with her life teetering on a knife edge, Laura wasn't so sure.

She left Amy and went out for some fresh air. She found Beverly smoking, looking at the distant lights of L.A. Laura watched her for a moment, wondering what Beverly saw when she looked at the skyline. Not the City of Angels, but the opposite, perhaps. A place of pain and injustice.

"Thanks," Laura said, going to the railing. "For letting us crash."

Beverly blew a halo of smoke in answer.

"Amy will come around," Laura added. "She's sort of protective of me."

"Do you trust her?" Beverly asked.

The question caught her off guard. "She's my sister."

"Okay."

Laura didn't like her tone. "What is it?"

"Nothing. Only, I can't get a read on her. It's like something's blocking me."

Laura didn't know what to make of that. Psychic-speak always sounded made up.

"Before I found you on the street earlier, I saw something," Beverly continued. "You said the fortune-teller ended up in your bag? I saw somebody's memory, I think. It happens sometimes. It was like I was in their head, seeing through their eyes. I watched them plant the fortune-teller." She paused. "How long did you say Amy had been in L.A.?"

The question hung between them and Laura didn't like what Beverly was suggesting. There was no way Amy had anything to do with whatever the hell was going on.

"She's my sister," she said. "I trust her with my life."

"All right, then."

They stood in silence. Laura studied the smog hanging over the city.

"You said the *Guesthouse* curse doesn't exist," she said. "That a person set fire to the set. It must be the same person who trashed my room and left me the dress."

"Dress?"

Laura's mouth quirked in a humorless smile. "Somebody made me a dress just like Tammy's."

Even Beverly looked stumped by that.

"Who would do that?" Laura asked.

Beverly took a drag on the cigarette, kept her gaze on the horizon.

"'Curse' isn't the right word. 'Curse' is active. It means somebody damned a person or a place on purpose, with intent to harm. I think the people who died after *The Guesthouse* were victims of something else."

"Such as?"

"An entity, maybe. Something malevolent that attached itself to the production. There are all kinds of things out there, moving in the spaces between us. Seeking out opportunities."

"And how does that fit with this vision of somebody planting the fortune-teller?"

"Some entities can work through people."

Laura took a breath, tried to understand. "Assuming that's even possible, why them? Why is it killing movie people?"

"It's not just movie people. It's people with some connection to *The Guesthouse*. Maybe something happened back in 1993 that we don't know about. Something that attracted this entity."

Laura wrestled with the word. *An entity.* It went against everything she had ever believed in. But she had seen the Needle Man in her room the night of the fire. She had felt him peering over her shoulder ever since she read the press release on the plane. Maybe this was more than PTSD. Maybe he really was coming for her.

"You never sensed anything malevolent on the set of *It Feeds*, though?" she asked.

Beverly flicked ash over the railing. "Not a whisper."

"Maybe evil entities aren't interested in cheap rip-offs."

The psychic's mouth creased in the corner, a rare sign of amusement, but Laura gripped the rail as a question bubbled up from her gut, wanting to be spoken, even though she wasn't sure she could handle the answer.

"Is it me?" she asked. "Did I set the fire? Kill Kyle?"

Has something attached itself to me?

Am I losing my mind?

RIP Laura Warren?

"I can't say for certain either way," Beverly said. "I'm sorry." She turned to face Laura, and the sincerity in Beverly's dark eyes was startling. The psychic had held Laura at arm's length ever since they met, but something had changed between them. They weren't prowling around each other like wounded animals anymore.

Beverly stubbed out the cigarette, tossed it into an ashtray by the door. "There's a way to find out, though."

"What's that?"

"We're going to perform a séance."

INT. CRICKLEWOOD GUESTHOUSE--ROOM 205--EVENING

TAMMY sits in the dark, facing the corner of the room.

                    TAMMY
          Did you hurt the lady?

FOCUS ON: The SHADOWS in the corner.

Tammy appears to be listening. She absent-mindedly plays
with the paper fortune-teller.

                    TAMMY
          I'm sorry.
                         (pause)
          Uh-huh. Uh-huh.
                         (pause)
          Did it hurt?

TAMMY POV: The corner. The darkness there is THICK as
velvet.

Tammy LAUGHS.

                    TAMMY
          No, silly! Don't say that!
                    (pause, listening)
          Daddy's scared they're going to shut us down.

TAMMY POV: The corner. So dark. Solid with shadow.

And just maybe something tangible. Something dangerous.

                    TAMMY
          Okay, if you say so.

                         MOM'S VOICE
                           (o.s.)
          Girls! Dinner!

                           TAMMY
          I have to go now.

     She gets up and walks to the door, then STOPS as if she's
     heard something. She turns back to look at the corner,
     expression serious.

                           TAMMY
          Please don't hurt Mommy or Daddy or Melanie,
          okay?
                           (pause)
          You promise?
                           (smiles)
          All right, then. See ya later.

FIFTEEN

Beverly made them close the blinds in the bedroom and ordered Laura to lie on the bed.

The room was as basic as the rest of the apartment. Off-white walls, cream sheets, thin blinds that barely prevented the afternoon light from seeping in. Laura found it unsettling that there was so little of Beverly in her home. Most people couldn't help but mark their walls with their personality. Paintings and photos and mementos. But not Beverly.

Maybe she found such decoration as overwhelming as the voices she claimed to hear.

As Laura got comfy on the bed, Amy set up her phone on a mini-tripod.

"You can't do that," Beverly said.

"Watch me."

"I mean it. No recording."

Amy straightened, gave her a level stare. "Did you record the exorcism? The girl you helped?" Beverly said nothing, and Amy gestured at the phone. "If any of this goes south, the footage will be admissible as evidence in court. I'm not taking any risks."

The way Beverly looked, Laura expected her to call the whole thing off. When Amy didn't back down, though, she shook her head and turned away. "Fine."

Laura lay on the bed, trying not to let the tension between them affect her. She was only just holding herself together as it was. One tiny poke could send her over the edge.

"Breathe," Beverly said. "Focus on breathing. Four in, four out."

Laura shook nervous energy from her limbs and did as Beverly said, feeling faintly ridiculous.

"If you start masturbating with a crucifix, I'll run for coffee," Amy said.

Laura almost laughed, but then she saw Beverly approaching with a knife. It was sticky with blood, the blade flecked with bits of foreign matter that Laura didn't want to look at too closely. Her jaw tightened as she recognized the knife from Kyle's house.

"Where did you get that?" she asked.

"She took it from me when I was clearing out my bag," Amy said.

Beverly paused by the bedside. "If we're doing this, we're doing it right, right?" she said.

Laura eyed the knife, unable to subdue the icy tremor that ran through her. Beverly held it like an offering, balanced on her fingertips. She whispered something, then set the blade on a pillow beside Laura.

It all suddenly felt a little too real.

What if she blacked out again?

What if Amy got hurt?

What if something toxic and malevolent really did present itself?

She drew a shaky breath.

"Ready?" Beverly asked.

Laura nodded and closed her eyes, ignoring the knife.

"Breathe. Four in, four out. Listen to the sound of my voice. Don't worry about where you are. Acknowledge any thoughts that come up and quietly release them. You don't need them at the moment."

It sounded like some YouTube meditation spiel, but Laura tried to go with it.

Four in, four out.

Four in, four out.

After a few cycles of breath, she felt tingly and light-headed. She couldn't imagine this working. She'd seen Paul McKenna and Derren Brown on TV and she'd always thought people who were hypnotized must be faking it. Buying into the charade.

The scent of fabric softener entered her nostrils and she heard the faint snapping of a candle flame, even though she was sure Beverly didn't own candles.

"Four in, four out," Beverly said, her voice somewhere near Laura's feet. "You are safe. You are calm. You are safe. You are calm."

Laura felt the air on her body. It both pressed her down and cradled her. Her arms and legs were leaden. She couldn't move. Didn't want to move. She realized she hadn't felt this relaxed in weeks. Maybe months.

"Now," Beverly said, "begin to open yourself to the past few days. Picture yourself walking around L.A., wherever your feet take you. What do you see?"

Blood.

Fire.

She gripped the bedsheet so hard her knuckles hurt.

"Calm," Beverly said.

Laura released her clenched fists.

"You are safe. You are calm."

The images subsided and Laura saw only darkness. It filled her vision. Pooled into every pore. She was the darkness and it was her. There was no way to separate them.

A shape tumbled through the void.

The man falling from the bridge.

Falling from the roof.

"What do you see?" Beverly asked.

Falling, Laura said, but she wasn't sure she'd spoken.

The man fell away, leaving only a black wall.

No, not a black wall.

Laura felt a presence.

Every hair on her body bristled, became alert with warning, urging her to run, but she had no legs, couldn't move if she wanted to.

It was just her and the thing in the dark.

She heard a wet choking sound. Something gagging on blood and phlegm, coughing up bones, and she tasted hot metal. Hard objects lodged in her esophagus, sticking there, making it impossible to swallow or draw breath.

And the more she stared at the dark wall, the more certain she grew that something lingered there. Watching her.

Two eyes blinked open in the dark.

A grinning mouth cut itself into existence, filled with teeth, then razor claws flashed, making a sound like telegraph wires.

The darkness became solid. It became a figure, a black coat that shifted and rippled toward her.

"polllyyyyyyyy."

A voice like dead leaves blasted apart by a breeze.

Laura opened her eyes and choked.

She was back in Beverly's bedroom, back in her body, everything solid again, so solid it hurt.

And she wasn't alone.

A shape stood over her.

Its muddy boots were planted on either side of her torso and she was pinned to the mattress, unable to move.

It stooped to bring its bandaged face closer to hers, rusted claws cutting the air, always moving, never still.

"killerrrrrr," the Needle Man whispered. *"killll herrrrrrr."*

She sensed Amy by the door, but couldn't move her eyes to look at her.

"killl herrrrrrrr."

Laura felt its desire for death and pain, and she wanted it, too. She wanted to tear everything apart. Destroy and devour.

And then she remembered.

She remembered the Needle Man rising from Kyle's pool.

The rust-tarnished claws poised. Spearing. Tearing.

Killing Kyle right before her.

She remembered looking down and seeing the claws needling from her own fingernails.

"yessssss," the voice whispered.

"Stop!" Laura cried, and the sound of her voice freed something in her.

Sensation returned to her arms and legs and she launched herself at the figure, knocking it back off the bed and to the floor. Her fingers sank into the flesh of its throat and she squeezed, pinning it to the wardrobe.

The figure shook and gurgled, but not in pain.

It was laughing.

She grimaced at the stench of rotted flesh.

"Die!" she shouted, squeezing harder.

"Laura!"

Fingers gripped her shoulder.

She lost her hold on the Needle Man, felt herself being pulled back. Her vision wobbled.

She blinked and looked up at Amy, who looked terrified, her eyes showing too much white.

"Laura, stop," she said, sounding breathless.

"It was the—" Laura began, but then she turned to where the Needle Man had been, and she saw Beverly.

Beverly sat up against the wardrobe, massaging her throat, looking shaken.

"You flipped," Amy said. "Totally lost it."

"I thought—" Laura said, but she wasn't sure what she'd thought. The Needle Man had been in the room with them, had wanted her to kill, and she'd tried to stop him. Stop him, not help him. But Beverly . . .

"I'm fine," Beverly said, though her throat sounded sore.

The room looked the same as it had before the séance, aside from the rumpled bedsheets, but Laura felt like it had been turned upside down. She was so sure of what she'd seen. It had been real. The smell of putrefying flesh stuck in her nostrils and she felt the coarseness of the bandages on her fingertips.

Her eyes went to the phone resting in the tripod.

"Is that thing still recording?"

In the kitchen, Laura sat at the table replaying Amy's video.

"It wasn't the Needle Man from the movie," she said. "It was something else. Something worse."

"Something real," Beverly said, leaning against the counter. Her neck was still red from where Laura had held on to it and Laura had the feeling Beverly wanted to stay as far away from her as possible. She didn't blame her.

She felt a prickle between her shoulder blades at Beverly's words. *Something real.* That was exactly how she would describe it. She'd felt the rough fabric of his coat, smelled his rank odor. It had felt so real.

But the recording showed nothing.

No Needle Man.

Just Laura lying peacefully, then frowning and growing tense, then launching herself up and across the room to wrap her hands around Beverly's throat.

The sight unnerved her more than she could say.

Seeing herself on film was bad enough, let alone seeing herself acting like a possessed person.

Possessed.

It really did look like some force outside her body had invaded it.

"You hallucinated the villain from the movie you hate." Amy shrugged. "Seems pretty obvious, given what's been going on."

Laura couldn't deny that.

She scrubbed back through the recording again, replaying it frame by frame. It was just like the surveillance footage from the Loft Hotel, though. It only showed her.

"I saw him in my hotel room the night of the fire, too," she said.

"What?" Amy asked.

"And he was there when Kyle was killed. I remember what happened at Kyle's house. The Needle Man attacked us and killed her. I must have blocked it out before."

Amy said nothing, but her face was tense and she didn't blink. She looked at Laura like she was a stranger. Laura hated it, but what else could she say? It was what she'd seen.

"They never revealed who played the Needle Man in *The Guest-house*, right?" Amy said. "It was some big secret."

Laura nodded.

"Ever wonder what happened to him? What if he's in L.A. now and he's gone Method? What if he's a disgruntled actor who literally never got the credit he deserved, so it's payback time?"

"But I saw him in the bedroom just now."

Amy looked unmoved. "You've been jet-lagged and sleep-deprived for four days. I'm surprised you're not seeing yourself eating cheesecake with the cast of *The Golden Girls.*"

Laura's head hurt again. She focused on the video, fast-forwarding, then rewinding, scouring the frame for anything unusual.

"We should get rid of that," Amy said, nodding at the bloodied knife. It rested on the countertop beside Beverly. She must have brought it in from the bedroom. While Laura scrutinized the video, Beverly turned on the water and began cleaning the blade, washing the blood down the drain.

Laura stopped the playback and rewound it a couple seconds, then stared at the freeze-frame.

"What's that?" she asked.

Amy moved closer. Beverly set the knife on the counter and looked over Laura's shoulder as she held up the phone. It showed a static shot of the bedroom, Laura lying down, eyes closed.

"There, in the mirror." She pointed at the mirror by the window, in which a dark shape was discernible.

"It's my shadow on the wall," Amy said.

"No, look. You're off camera, over by the door. Beverly is by the wardrobe and I'm lying on the bed. None of us could cast a shadow there. And it's only in the mirror, not on the wall."

She pinched and zoomed in.

The shape in the mirror became clearer. Five lines of shadow, like claws.

Laura tried to contain a shiver.

"It's him," she said.

"Come on," Amy said.

"Beverly?"

Beverly stepped back, looking washed-out. She massaged her throat, then met Laura's gaze.

"You saw something in the bedroom. Something that looked like the Needle Man."

Laura nodded.

"You felt it, even though we heard and saw nothing."

"That's what I said. Do you know what it is?"

Beverly looked unwell. "I don't know. Maybe. I . . ." She stopped, looked at Amy, then the phone screen, then Laura again. "Have you ever heard of demonic parasites?"

"Like leeches?"

"Pretty much. Look, I know how it sounds, and it's a stretch, but the way you described it, and knowing who you are, what you mean in all of this . . . in a horrible way, it fits."

"Wow, vague that up for us?" Amy muttered.

"What *is* it?" Laura repeated.

"This thing, it seeks out trauma. It lives off it, moves from person to person feeding on them. And it found a lifetime's worth in you. I wouldn't be surprised if it got a hold of you the second you touched down in L.A."

"Jesus," Amy said. "Demons aren't real."

"They're not like the movies." The hollowness of Beverly's tone made Laura uneasy. "They don't exist in any physical form. They're not tangible like a person or an animal. They live around us. Invisible but alive."

"The Needle Man isn't real," Amy said. "It's a Hollywood creation."

"Sometimes that's enough." Beverly stopped massaging her throat. "This thing isn't really the Needle Man, it's just wearing its skin. That's how trauma works. The parasite finds the root of the trauma and uses it against the sufferer. For you, Laura, the Needle Man clearly represents everything you went through after *The Guesthouse* came out. This thing knows that."

Laura knew trauma.

There were things she hadn't told anybody.

She'd hoped that by ignoring the pain, pretending it didn't exist, it would fade away. Instead, the opposite seemed to be true. It seemed to have drawn something right to her.

"Assuming that's true," she said, "why is it killing people involved in *It Feeds?*"

Beverly shrugged. "It's keeping you in a permanently anxious state. It kills, you freak out, it feeds. The cycle goes on."

Laura didn't know what to think. Reality was muddying around her, becoming unfocused, as if she were still in the somnambulant state Beverly had put her in for the séance. All this talk of visions, trauma, and movie monsters made her feel tired and wired at the same time.

So far, though, Beverly's explanation was the only one they had.

"How do we stop it?" she asked.

"You can't seriously believe this," Amy said.

Laura didn't want to. Knew it sounded ludicrous. But a lot had happened since they were kids and she was running out of options. Not to mention time. She could only evade the police for so long.

"These things often draw from a power source," Beverly said. "Something linked to the origin of the trauma. It could be something obvious like a murder weapon, or it could be something more subtle like a piece of jewelry or a favorite book."

"What are you saying?" Laura asked.

Beverly crooked an eyebrow. "Destroy the object, destroy the parasite."

It sounded insane, like some *Poltergeist* shit. But Beverly looked so certain and Laura couldn't pry her gaze away from the shadow on the phone screen. Her only proof that something had been in the room with them.

Something posing as the Needle Man.

"The paper fortune-teller," she said. "I found it in my bag the first day I got here."

"Could be," Beverly said. "Do you associate that with any particular trauma?"

"Yes. Well, sort of." She shook her head. It didn't feel quite right. It wasn't the fortune-teller she hated, it was the movie itself.

But a movie was ephemeral. It existed in a hundred different forms, from the original VHS tapes and modern streaming files all the way to how it took root in a viewer's mind, became a part of their personality.

In the beginning, though, before it was copied and distributed around the world, a film was little more than a couple of reels spliced together by an editor.

"What about the original print?" Laura said. "Could that be a power source?"

"It could be."

Laura felt a surge of anticipation. "Todd Terror bought the original cut of *The Guesthouse* at an auction a couple of years ago. It's locked in his office."

"What exactly are you suggesting?" Amy asked.

Laura couldn't help a smile creeping onto her face.

"We're going to break into Todd's office and destroy the original film reels."

While Amy stared at her as if she'd finally joined Jack Nicholson in his cuckoo's nest, Laura thought about the advice her therapist had given her years ago.

Advice that helped her focus on the positive aspects in her life. Shrink the bad, feed the good.

Todd Terror had said he owned the Answer Print of *The Guesthouse*, not the negative, but in Laura's mind, her therapist's counsel remained wonderfully apt.

"*Sometimes, Laura,*" he said, "*all you need to do is burn the negative.*"

INTERVIEWER: People will kill me if I don't ask this.
The Needle Man is uncredited in the film, and so far
you've refused to reveal who played him. But given it's
been a couple years now, I'm hoping you'll finally tell
us? Pretty please with a severed finger on top?

CHRISTOPHER ROSENTHAL: There's a reason for that.
We wanted to keep a mystique about the villain, even
during filming. He never interacted with anybody on set,
none of the cast or crew. We shot a lot of his scenes in
isolation, separate from the other actors. The only
people who know his identity are me and the makeup guys.
I'm sorry, but that name goes with me to my grave.

SIXTEEN

The studio's on total lockdown since Kyle died," Beverly said. "Nobody except the big bosses are allowed in. It's going to be almost impossible to get inside."

"Not to mention this." Amy showed them an *L.A. Times* news story on her phone.

EX-CHILD STAR WANTED
IN CONNECTION TO HOLLYWOOD HILLS MURDER

The picture was Laura's *Zeppelin* magazine headshot.
She almost couldn't remember being that person.
The police must know everything.
That she was present when Kyle died.
That she was Polly Tremaine.
That she was a killer.
She felt the walls of Beverly's kitchen bowing around her, as if repelled, and she couldn't tell if it was just her imagination. Maybe the

world really was warping, attempting to keep its distance. Isolate her so she couldn't hurt anybody else.

She tried not to think about any of it. She had to focus on the plan, no matter how nuts it was.

There was only one way she could think of to get access to the studio.

"I'm turning myself in to the police," she said.

"Pill, no." Amy held on to her phone like it was giving her life.

"I'll tell them to meet me at the studio," Laura said. "It's the only way we'll get in."

"And when they arrest you?"

"They won't if I say I'm taking them to evidence inside the studio. Then all we have to do is give them the slip, raid Todd's office for the film, and we're home free."

"You hear how crazy that sounds, right?"

"Involving the police is risky," Beverly said. "They're not exactly known for their restraint. They could drop you on sight."

"Shit." Laura drummed the table with her fingertips. "There has to be some way to get into that studio."

"Pill," Amy said, "you can't seriously believe that destroying some old film reels will fix all of this."

"I don't know what I believe anymore. I just want this over." She stopped drumming. "Madeleine. The PR. She can get us in. She's not a big boss, but PRs are expert bullshitters. Plus, they're given pretty much unrestricted access."

"I have to ask," Amy said. "Why will she help us?"

"Because I'll make her."

"I shouldn't have asked."

"I know where she lives," Beverly said. "She threw some dreadful party a few weeks ago."

Laura jumped up. "Then let's go."

It took an hour to drive across town to the Beverly Hills apartment complex. Laura kept low in the back seat the whole way, jumpy with adrenaline and wound tight with anxiety whenever traffic backed up or lights forced them to stop. She tugged at the baseball cap Beverly had loaned her.

When they reached the lamplit complex, Laura asked Beverly to wait in the car. It earned her a glare but she needed somebody with her in case she had another blackout, and if a cop car passed by, Beverly was less suspicious than Amy.

She went with Amy up the brick steps to apartment 211 and knocked.

"I'm worried about you," Amy said.

"I know."

"I don't think I've ever been the voice of reason before."

"Keep it up. It suits you."

Amy nudged her with her elbow. "Moron."

Laura nudged her back. "Loser."

Madeleine answered the door, lightly perspiring in Lycra workout gear, her blond hair in a topknot.

As soon as she saw Laura, her smile vanished.

"Hi, Madeleine, can we talk?"

Madeleine looked terrified.

But she was too slow shutting the door.

Laura butted it open and stepped inside. The apartment was small but pretty, the peach-colored living room decorated with wrought-iron furnishings and potted plants. Madeleine retreated back across a purple yoga mat. An iPad on the coffee table played a prerecorded class.

"*—and when you're ready: Downward-Facing Dog—*"

"What do you want? What are you doing here?" Madeleine asked.

"Quiet. I'm not here to hurt you. I need your help."

168

"I don't have any money."

Laura almost laughed. People in L.A. were obsessed. She supposed seeing homeless people on every street corner had an effect on the general population. They were confronted with their worst fears five times a day.

Behind her, Amy shut the door. Madeleine's gaze didn't leave Laura's face.

"I don't need money," Laura said. "I need you to get us into the studio."

Madeleine didn't seem to hear her.

"Please, I won't tell anybody I saw you. Just don't hurt me."

"I'm not going to hurt you. Not if you come with us now."

"Did you really kill Kyle?"

"She's dialing," Amy said, and Laura saw that Madeleine had her right hand behind her thigh, her iPhone just visible. She must have had it tucked into her Lycra pants. Laura should've known better than to assume Madeleine would ever be without her phone, even during yoga.

Madeleine tensed, knowing she'd been caught. She didn't blink for what felt like forever. Laura realized she was going about this the wrong way. She'd assumed she could talk to Madeleine rationally, but nothing about this situation was rational—especially the part where the PR believed that Laura was a killer.

The only way to get what she wanted was to play into Madeleine's fear.

"*—now anchor your left foot to the floor and slide your right foot up to greet the sky—*"

Laura lunged. Madeleine yelped and spun sideways, but Laura was twice her size and impossible to outmaneuver. Laura only knew she'd forced the PR up against the wall when she felt Madeleine stiffening against her and smelled her coconut skin cream. The phone was in both their hands. Laura twisted it free and tossed it to Amy. In her other hand, she held an iron poker she'd somehow snatched from the artificial fireplace.

"Laura," Amy said, a note of warning in her voice, but Laura talked over her.

"Listen to me, and listen good," she said, raising the poker, her face so close to Madeleine's she could count every one of her perfect eyelashes. "Maybe I killed Kyle, maybe I didn't. Either way, I'm here and I'm desperate, and desperate people do desperate things. You want to find out how far I'm willing to go?"

Madeleine had stopped breathing. Her face was rigid, corpse-pale, and her eyes so wide Laura saw her own reflection in her irises.

"*—maybe you want to meet your edge today, but listen to what your beautiful body is telling you—*"

"You can call the cops if you want," Laura said, holding the pointy end of the poker to Madeleine's cheek. "*After.* You'll get your phone back. *After.* I'll even grant you an interview, get you the press coverage of your life. But *after.* Am I making myself clear?"

Madeleine nodded a fraction, looking confused.

"What happened to your voice?" she whispered.

Laura frowned, thrown by the question.

"She does that," Amy said. "She switches when she's stressed."

Laura swallowed. She hadn't noticed her accent changing. Her therapist first pointed out the habit when she was seventeen. Whenever she got angry or overly tired, she would slip into American, as if she had never left L.A. Laura shook herself, didn't have time to think about it. And she didn't ease up.

"We need to get into the studio, *tonight.* And you're going to help us. If you don't, you'll end up like Kyle, because nobody can know we were there until we're gone." She pressed the cold metal to Madeleine's cheek, the tips of their noses almost touching.

"By the time they find you," she whispered, articulating each word carefully in her British accent, "they'll only be able to identify you by the label in your overpriced yoga pants."

"Christ," Amy murmured, and Laura wondered if she'd gone too far, strayed into campy rather than creepy, but then Madeleine swallowed and her eyes pricked with tears.

"Whatever you want," she said.

Laura remained where she stood for a second longer, then nodded and stepped back. She held on to the poker. It made her feel powerful.

"Get whatever you need to access the studio and come with us."

Madeleine moved in a daze to the front door, Laura right behind her. Madeleine took her studio pass from a hook and nodded at Laura, her gaze heavy with fear.

"All right," Laura said, "after you."

She opened the door.

"*—hope you head into your day feeling rejuvenated and empowered. Now take a deep inhale and bow. Namaste.*"

They went out into the dying embers of the afternoon.

On the road again, Laura sat in the back of Beverly's Volvo with Madeleine, whose shoulders were rigid, her face turned to the window. Laura sensed Madeleine watching her out of the corner of her eye. The shock had worn off, but Laura sensed Madeleine's apprehension and realized she really had scared her.

She'd tapped into something inside herself that never got a chance to come out and play.

Maybe she was still an actor after all.

Or maybe that was the real her and the everyday journalist act was the fake.

She squeezed the poker, which rested in her lap, and wondered if she could use it if it came down to it.

Up front, Beverly drove, while Amy scrolled on her phone, either researching or blocking out the world. Probably a little bit of both. When they were kids, Amy was always the one with crackpot schemes, most of them involving doing the opposite of what their parents said, and Laura was glad she was around to help her in the worst few days of her life.

"Did Todd ever say anything about the print?" she asked Madeleine. At the PR's questioning look, she added, "The *Guesthouse* print he bought at auction. Did he ever say anything about it?"

"That's what this is about?" Madeleine's voice was different when it wasn't in "friendly PR" mode. Lower. Laura preferred it.

"Just answer the question," she said.

"But this is—"

"I really don't want to hurt you, Madeleine."

Madeleine eyed the poker.

"No, okay? He bragged about it and stuff but that was it."

"Nothing about hurting people?"

"Todd?" Madeleine briefly looked like her old self. "He could barely tie his own shoelaces, let alone butcher anybody." Maybe she remembered he was dead just then, because the humor left her eyes and she blinked away from Laura's gaze.

Laura turned her body toward the publicist, rested her arm along the back of the seat, and let the tip of the poker press into Madeleine's thigh.

"When we get to the studio, be cool," she said. "Tell them whatever you need to get us in, but if you attempt to alert the guard, I will hurt you. I'll hurt the guard, too, and it'll be your fault. Okay?"

Madeleine nodded.

Laura almost felt bad for her, but she couldn't drop the charade. She needed to see this through and that meant keeping Madeleine scared. Her hands were knotted in her lap and she had the rigid posture of a junkie desperate for a hit. She really was addicted to her phone.

The sky was pink and blue when they pulled up to the studio gate, the sun low. *Magic hour*, Laura remembered it being called. The brief window of time when the world looks mystical and even micro-budget directors can make their films look like a million bucks.

"Be cool," Laura warned again, closing her hand around the poker, and Madeleine fumbled with the window, forcing a smile as the guard approached from his security booth. He looked to be in his forties, solid.

"Hey, Rick," Madeleine said, "how's it going?"

"Maddy, what's up? Been a while since you worked this late."

"Yeah, you know, damage control. And to top it off, my car's in the shop. Crazy week."

The guard nodded. "You don't have to tell me."

"I won't be long," Madeleine said. "Just me and a couple of assistants. Thought it would be better if we did it after hours. Keep it out of the press."

The guard looked at Beverly and Amy, then gave Laura a cursory glance. She hoped that the baseball cap concealed her face, and kept the poker hidden to one side. She was glad it was a different guard than the one who had found her in the soundstage.

"I'll bring you some of those guilt-free brownies tomorrow as a thank-you," Madeleine said, her smile tightening. "Fresh batch."

The guard patted his belly. "Guilt-free? I wish."

Madeleine managed a laugh and the guard stepped back to raise the barrier. He waved them through, and Laura released a breath as they cleared the gates. Her palms ached where they'd gripped iron. They cruised into the deserted back lot.

"That was good," she said. "You'd make a good actor."

"So would half of Hollywood."

Spotlights lit the way to the production office. The back lot was eerie without anybody around. Silent, like a village of the damned. Laura reminded herself that the lack of people was a good thing. No witnesses, nobody to get hurt.

When they'd parked, Madeleine used her key card to get into the retro office building. They caught the elevator to the second floor and went down the hall. Amy's scintillated gaze ate up everything. Laura had seen that look all her life. Whenever Amy came across ads for auditions or saw an actor absolutely nailing a role, it was like a fever took her. She'd dreamed of Hollywood for so long, and now that she was inside one of its biggest studios, she looked oddly small in comparison.

Laura could never figure out if Amy only wanted to be an actor because their mom tried to turn her into one. Maybe Amy was naturally drawn to it, or maybe she was trying to prove something. That she was good enough. That their mom had been wrong to quit on her.

Either way, she was glad that Amy was getting something out of this, even if it was just a peek inside a real-life movie studio.

Too bad the reason for it was Laura having killed someone.

Todd's office wasn't locked, so Laura went straight in.

She immediately stopped as she spotted a dark shape in the corner.

The Needle Man.

"Jesus," Amy said right behind her.

"You see it?" Laura whispered.

"We all see it. It's just a model."

Amy went over and prodded the Needle Man. The figure wobbled on the spot, rocking a few times before going still. Laura eyed it distrustfully, but she had bigger concerns. She turned to examine the rest of the room.

The office was exactly as she had imagined. Movie posters, figurines, shelves lined with books and collector's edition Blu-rays. Aside from the fake plants that must have been added by a despairing interior designer, it was a film geek's paradise.

Laura set the poker on the desk and scoured the office. In a glass compartment of the bookcase, she found a row of flat, circular cans that looked a little like hubcaps. Eight of them in total. Two words were handwritten on the masking tape fixed to the frontmost canister.

THE GUESTHOUSE

The Guesthouse

© 1994 / Color / 1 Hr. 27 Mins. / R

CHECKING IN WAS THE EASY PART...

For decades, the **CRICKLEWOOD GUESTHOUSE** has lain empty. Deserted. That changes when the Manners family moves in, dead set on starting a new life away from the city.

When a guest tragically **CHECKS OUT EARLY**, dying under mysterious circumstances, the locals talk about the legend of the "**NEEDLE MAN**," a sinister figure with **CLAWS FOR FINGERS** who has **HAUNTED** the guesthouse for years.

But **WHO** is the Needle Man? **HOW** is seven-year-old Tammy (Polly Tremaine) able to predict the **FUTURE**? And WHY didn't anybody warn the guests that they were **MAKING A RESERVATION** . . . **TO DIE**?!

"THE GUESTHOUSE"
POLLY TREMAINE • TERRENCE HODGES • JULIA BARKER
ASHLEY YOUNG and ISABELLE PLUMMER
Written by YVONNE LINCOLN
Directed by CHRISTOPHER ROSENTHAL

SEVENTEEN

he Guesthouse sat behind the glass, so unremarkable in appearance that Laura almost couldn't believe that one can of film, one tiny piece of movie memorabilia, could be the cause of so much misery. She tried to slide open the compartment, but it was locked. Without hesitating, she picked up a Jason figurine and smashed the glass.

"Christ!" Madeleine cried.

Ignoring her, Laura reached in and took out the can.

She half expected it to resist her. It was surprisingly light, though, and now that she had it in her hands, it seemed even more insignificant. Mundane, almost. A reel only came to life when it was projected onto a screen. Right now, it was just a series of images printed on plastic and silver halide crystals.

She frowned. The second can in the row was also marked *THE GUESTHOUSE*, though it was followed with the number *2*. She shifted it forward and saw that the third can was marked *3*. For a horrible moment, she wondered if these were sequels, films that she'd failed to notice had been made, and her brain felt like it had split down the middle and was leaking hot lava.

But then she realized these were all *The Guesthouse*. She remembered that projectionists had to change reels while a film was showing because one reel only amounted to a fraction of a film's full run time. The can she held was only one piece of *The Guesthouse*.

One-eighth.

Eight cans.

Eight reels of film.

Eight people who died.

Eight pieces of *The Guesthouse*.

This was going to be a bigger job than she'd anticipated.

"Now what?" Amy said.

"We burn them," Laura said. "All of them."

Amy dragged a trash can from under the desk. "Here?"

"No, where it began. In the bathroom set."

The thought of returning there made her chest hurt, so she knew she was right.

She took down another can, then another, and they were heavy enough that she knew she couldn't carry all eight. Together, they must weigh over sixty pounds.

"Here," she said, passing two to Beverly, another two to Amy. She briefly considered Madeleine and decided she couldn't trust her not to bail on them. The job was too important to risk it. The four remaining canisters were heavy in Laura's arms, but that felt right, too. This was her load to bear.

Madeleine begrudgingly showed them where the keys to the soundstage were kept and went with them to stage five. It loomed over them in the dying light, monstrously large. Laura tore the police tape from the door and unlocked it, going inside.

The smell of smoke was still strong, and without any lights on, the warehouse felt even more enormous. A stomach waiting to digest her.

They switched on their phone flashlights, pointing them at the Cricklewood set. It was still standing. The firefighters must have gotten the blaze under control after Laura fled. Aside from a black hole in the roof, the guesthouse looked as sturdy as ever. It'd take more than fire to destroy it.

"Wow," Amy breathed. "Look at it."

Laura nearly turned around and left. The memory of waking up there, disoriented and scared, overwhelmed her and she gripped the film cans tightly, pressing them to her chest, forcing herself to breathe.

"Pill," Amy said, right behind her. "You don't have to do this."

Laura straightened and adjusted the cans, set her sights on the guesthouse. "I'm fine. Come on."

They approached the front steps, Laura leading the way. She stripped the police tape from the front door and went into the hall.

The house creaked and she was sure she heard things moving in the dark, fingernails dragging on varnished wood, but it must have been the set. Even empty buildings made noises, and sets were no different. She couldn't let her imagination get away from her.

She went up the stairs, the smell of smoke intensifying so that she almost felt it curdling in her lungs, and then stood outside the blackened bathroom. More police tape barred the way, a final warning, but Laura ignored it. She snapped it off and entered.

The shower cubicle was open and burned to a crisp. It resembled a wound, festering and angry.

Todd had died in this very spot. Lost his life in his very own playground. A wave of guilt crested in Laura's abdomen and she willed herself to remember what happened that night. Who set the fire? Was it her, or the Needle Man, or something else entirely? No memories surfaced, though, beyond that of the choking haze she had woken up to.

She reminded herself that the best way to honor Todd was by stopping his killer.

She went to the shower stall, focusing on the feel of the tiles under her shoes, and crouched down, her knees popping with the effort. She dumped the cans into the shower, then did the same with the other four from Beverly and Amy. Madeleine stood by the sink, watching with a look of disbelief and fear. Maybe she thought Laura really was crazy. Maybe that was a good thing.

Bent inside the cubicle, Laura popped open each can one at a time and dumped their contents into the shower, tugging out reels of film like glistening brown intestines. It felt like she had been waiting thirty years for this. Thirty years to rid herself of the film for good.

She bowed her head.

"I'm sorry, Todd," she whispered, quietly enough that the others wouldn't hear. Amy and Madeleine stood together, Madeleine hugging her arms. Amy's face was etched in shadow.

"Here," Beverly said, digging in her pocket. She handed over a lighter shaped like a cobra.

Laura sparked it up and considered the flame. Then she put it to the film and stepped back to stand beside Beverly.

The film didn't light the way she had expected. She'd had visions of it curling up like flypaper, burning bright and fast, the way it did in that Tarantino movie with all the Nazis.

Instead, a strong vinegar smell mushroomed into the bathroom and the film bubbled and clumped together. It writhed like a nest of snakes, not catching light, but melting, oozing, forming a monstrous brown pile that could be an excised tumor.

For a moment, light shone through the plastic folds, projecting an impossible image onto the back of the cubicle.

Seven-year-old Polly Tremaine.

Tammy. Standing in a doorway. Her eyes were black smudges, her mouth puckered in a half smile. The image strobed and swelled as if it were breathing. Tammy raised hands that contained the paper fortune-teller. Laura heard a rustling voice in the warping film.

"Pick a number, I dare you."

Tammy smiled as she opened and closed the fortune-teller.

The image vanished.

Beverly whispered. Maybe it hadn't been Tammy's voice after all. Laura couldn't hear what Beverly was saying, but it sounded like a prayer. Whatever it was, she hoped it helped. She'd use all the help she could get.

The malformed mass of film folded in on itself and what little light it had managed to emit faded.

They stood watching as dark returned.

The bathroom was cold.

Laura didn't feel any different. She didn't see anything escape in the smoke, no demonic face writhing in agony. The reels didn't scream as if they were in pain.

There was nothing.

Just quiet.

"I guess that's it," she said. She turned to face the others and froze. "Where's Madeleine?"

Madeleine wasn't in the bathroom. Laura hadn't heard her leave. They had been too fixated on the film to notice her slipping out.

"She was right there," Amy said. "I was watching her."

"We have to find her."

Beverly went into the hall.

"She can't have got—" Laura began, but then the room shook. The floor shifted beneath her feet and the walls juddered, pipes clanging behind plasterboard.

It felt like something angry. Something waking up.

"This place is going to collapse," Amy said, just as a piece of the ceiling fell. "We have to get out of here."

Laura jumped out of the way as another chunk of the ceiling collapsed. It crashed to the floor beside her and Laura coughed and got to her feet, then saw that she was alone.

Amy was gone.

"Amy?" Laura hurried for the shaking door. "Beverly?"

She went into the hall and something knocked her off her feet.

She winced in pain as her shoulder struck the floor.

No, not the floor. As she pressed her palms against it, she felt paper. Wallpaper.

She was lying on the wall.

Laura looked around her, feeling light-headed as she took in her surroundings.

The ceiling was on her right, the floor to her left.

The stairs plunged sideways.

Laura's nails dug into the wallpaper. Had she blacked out again?

Was she passed out on the bathroom floor, just like before?

She felt the wall shake and it felt real. Her body was heavy. She was chronically aware of the fact that she was kneeling on the wall, the house twisted and upside down, its center of gravity ruptured. Whether or not she was unconscious, the instinct to move gripped tight, refusing to let her remain still.

She tried to stand, feeling unbalanced at the sight of the doorframe by her foot. She held on to the ceiling for support, seeing the light hanging on its side. Beside her, the hall table seemed glued to the floor, its ornaments refusing to obey the same gravity that affected Laura.

"Amy? Beverly?"

She walked along the wall, resisting the panic that tugged at her, refusing to give in to it.

The house shook again and this time she knew she heard noises.

A gurgling hiss filled her ears.

Then a high giggle.

"Ready or not, here I come!"

Laura turned sharply at the sound of footsteps, seeing a little girl running up the stairs, dodging around something that got in her way, then vanishing down the hall.

Laura stared at the thing that had obstructed the girl and realized it was somebody swinging by their neck.

Beverly.

"Oh God." Laura rushed for her, clambering over the wall on her hands and knees. She kept expecting to slide down to the floor, expected the house to suddenly spin and send her flying, but it remained still.

Beverly had a rope around her neck. The other end was fastened to the banister. She hung sideways from it, away from Laura, her face bloated, eyes closed, lips bruising purple. Laura was sure she wasn't breathing.

She tried to reach her and realized she was shouting her name over and over, as if it would wake them all up. Her brain told her this was a dream, because what else could it be? Nothing made any sense. She felt movement beside her. She smelled rot and earth, and then something caressed her shoulder as it hissed.

"polllyyyyyyyy."

She ignored it, focused on the noose.

Sweating, she tugged at the rope, then withdrew quickly as scuttling shapes spilled across the backs of her hands.

Spiders.

Dozens of penny-sized red spiders scurried down the rope, swarming over Beverly's head. A number of them had diverted onto Laura's hands as she tried to free the noose, and she swept them off with a cry, her skin crawling.

The spiders kept coming, though, more of them every second, coating the rope so that it was almost invisible. They were all over Beverly's face.

Gritting her teeth, Laura seized the rope again, ignoring the sensation of the spiders being crushed under her grip. Beverly's dead weight pulled the rope taut, made it creak, and Laura feared she wasn't strong enough to free her. Drawing on all her strength, she gripped under Beverly's armpit and attempted to pull her up just enough to slacken the rope. Her other hand fumbled with the noose around Beverly's neck, praying, sweating, screaming. Somehow, she managed to inch the rope up and over Beverly's head, and Beverly slipped free.

The world spun on its axis and Laura's hands and knees left the wall.

She fell through the air, unable to tell what was up or down anymore, then landed painfully on the hard wood floor. The house kept spinning and bile seared her tonsils. She gasped for breath, attempting to bring the hall to a standstill. When the dizziness eased, she saw she had landed beside a writhing mass of spiders. They crawled all over something pale and twitching.

A body.

Laura only just made out purple Lycra beneath the swarm.

Not Beverly, but Madeleine.

Madeleine jerked and thrashed on the hall floor, foaming at the mouth, her eyes bulging at the ceiling, pinned open in terror. The movement seemed to be beyond her control. A nervous reaction. Laura scrambled forward to brush the spiders off her and noticed welts all over Madeleine's body. Bites. So many bites.

Madeleine stilled. She sighed, making bubbles pop around her mouth, and stopped breathing.

"No, Madeleine," Laura pleaded, brushing more spiders off her face, barely feeling them anymore, but it was no good. Madeleine's eyes were lifeless, her skin still blistering and swelling, distorting her features.

"Madeleine," Laura shouted again, shaking her, but then she noticed another body to her side.

Beverly lay on the floorboards, not moving. Groaning with effort, Laura clambered over and yanked the psychic's arms and legs out to lay her flat. She put an ear to her face.

No breath.

Laura dug her hands into her rib cage, tried to get her breathing.

"Come on, Beverly."

Spiders surrounded them, bright and fast as fire ants, and Laura batted them away, then pressed her weight into Beverly's chest once more.

Beverly gasped and opened her eyes. Then she coughed.

Relief flooded through Laura, but she knew they weren't safe until they got out.

"Can you get up?" she urged, helping Beverly sit upright. "We have to find Amy."

"I'm right here," Amy said, appearing at her side. Her gaze found Madeleine's slowly bloating body and she gasped, falling to her side. "Shit, Madeleine. She needs an EpiPen."

While Laura got Beverly on her feet, supporting her weight, she watched Amy search Madeleine's body with tears in her eyes.

"She doesn't have one." Amy looked at Laura. "Maybe there's a first-aid kit? Jesus, she's so cold."

"She's cold?"

Amy nodded, her face streaked with tears.

"I don't think we can help her," Laura said, even though the realization made her despair.

"Help me," she said. Beverly was heavy and too weak to hold herself up. Sniffing, Amy went to her other side and, together, she and Laura got Beverly out of the house and down the steps and hurried as fast as they could for the soundstage exit.

EIGHTEEN

everly, are you okay?" Laura asked.

They were back in the Volvo, Laura at the wheel, no clue where she was driving. She wanted to put as much distance between them and the guesthouse as possible. Find space to process what had happened after they burned the film. She still felt dizzy; untethered somehow. The most basic rules of reality had been distorted. The set had turned upside down.

And Madeleine was dead.

She had another body on her conscience.

A third person who would be alive if it weren't for her.

As they'd gotten into the car, she had made an anonymous call to emergency services, just in case a medic could save her, but in her heart Laura knew. Another victim of the guesthouse. The memory of Madeleine's puffy face and discolored skin made Laura's stomach contract and she fought to swallow a wave of bile.

Beverly slumped in the back, looking only half awake. She didn't answer Laura's question.

"Pill, are *you* all right?" Amy asked beside her, and Laura saw that her hands were shaking at the wheel. Her knees felt bruised and her shoulder ached from hitting the wall. She couldn't think about any of that, though. She had to keep it together.

"I'm fine."

"Want me to drive?"

"I've got it." She shifted to look in the rearview mirror. "Beverly?"

"Did you feel it?" Beverly's voice was hoarse.

"Feel what?" Amy said.

"The shift."

"Here we go again," Amy said, but her voice lacked power. She looked beaten up, too, even though she'd been spared the funfair aspects of the guesthouse. Laura supposed seeing a dead body did that to a person.

Beverly's gaze darkened. "Don't joke about things you don't understand."

"Why? Because I'll ask questions you can't answer?"

Laura wished she'd stop, but Amy hadn't seen Beverly strung up by her neck. She hadn't seen the world turn upside down, even though she'd been in the set with them. Why?

"I felt it," Laura said.

"It's so angry. Pure rage," Beverly said.

Laura sensed Amy tensing but said nothing.

"Did you see who attacked you?" she asked.

Beverly shook her head.

"We made it worse." The look of desolation in her eyes chilled Laura to the marrow. She got the feeling Beverly was trying to rewrite the past in the same way Laura had. But if Laura had learned anything, it was that the past was unchanging. All you could do was get as far away from it as time and space allowed.

"That poor girl," Amy said. "Madeleine. We killed her."

"It wasn't us, it was . . ." Laura trailed off.

"It was the house? The Needle Man? Laura, come on."

"Something was in there with us," Beverly said, which shut them both up.

Amy was right, though. Madeleine had died because of them—because Laura forced her to help. She felt unwell at the thought. For years, she had told herself she wasn't responsible for the *Guesthouse* deaths, but this was different.

"That guard saw all four of us together," Amy said, "which means the police will have added *us* to their manhunt. If they hadn't already, after looking at Kyle's surveillance footage."

Laura squeezed the wheel.

"We need to find somewhere to rest," she said. "But we can't go back to Beverly's now the cops know she's with us."

Or she could turn herself in. Surrender.

That would protect her sister, so long as the authorities believed Amy had nothing to do with the deaths. But if Laura was behind bars, she'd have no way of exposing the true threat. The cops were looking for a flesh-and-blood killer. They were looking for her.

More and more, though, it felt like this was something from Beverly's world. Something other. Something capable of burning and stabbing and hanging—then vanishing without a trace.

Amy straightened. "Are we done chasing ghosts?"

"It's not a ghost," Beverly said, her tone spiky.

"Sorry, I meant to say 'imaginary friend.'"

"Maybe you could call one of your fashion buddies to come help us," Beverly said.

"I don't see you helping. If anything, you're making it worse."

"Stop it," Laura said. "Both of you." Why couldn't they just get along? This was difficult enough without two-thirds of their trio constantly at each other's throats.

Amy ran her fingers through her hair, then picked up her phone.

"I have a suggestion," she said.

"Go on."

"I know somebody who's staying at the Dolphin Hotel. We can trust them."

"Who is it?" Laura asked.

"A friend. And those are in short supply at the moment."

Laura didn't like it, but she was out of ideas.

"Fine. Just tell me where I'm going."

Amy directed her across town, and the only thing that kept Laura focused was the thought that there could be a bed waiting for her. She'd do anything to get just a few hours' sleep. Maybe she'd wake up to a world that made sense again.

By the time she parked in the underground lot of the hotel, she realized she had no memory of the drive. Her brain must've switched to autopilot. It was in low-battery mode.

Together, they went into the building via a door that led from the lot into the lobby. Beverly moved in a daze, while Amy tapped on her phone, no doubt getting her friend's room number. Whoever they were, Laura hoped they wouldn't ask questions.

They went through a luxurious lobby and got into a gold-plated elevator. The whole place smelled rich, like black cherry and vodka.

It was so quiet on the fifth floor that Laura immediately felt on edge, and her unease grew as they approached one of doors. Amy knocked at room 502.

Laura stared at the number, not breathing.

In *The Guesthouse*, room 205 was where Tammy spoke to the Needle Man.

205. 502. Was the mirroring just a coincidence? Or was it trying to tell her something?

She forced herself not to go there.

The door opened, a man appeared, and Laura wondered if her tired eyes had finally failed her.

"Mike," she said, the name leaving her mouth involuntarily.

"Hey." Mike smiled, but the smile quivered with nerves, failing to reach his eyes. He moved forward as if to hug her, then stopped, his gaze switching between Laura, Amy, and Beverly. Stiffly, he hung back and rested his forearm on the doorframe, looking awkward and tall in a salmon-pink shirt that was unbuttoned to show a glimpse of his dark chest. Laura stared into his face, speechless.

Mike.

In L.A.

She turned on Amy. "*This* is the friend?"

Amy shrugged. "He texted me this afternoon to say he was in town. I wasn't sure you'd want to see him."

"You were right."

"It's good to see you, too," Mike said, a stab at bravado that was immediately undermined when he coughed to clear his throat.

"When did you get here?" Laura asked.

"This morning. I got on a plane last night, right after I spoke to the publicist, Madeleine. You'd know that if you answered your phone every once in a while."

"Sorry, I've been trying to stay out of jail."

"Touché."

The moment stretched and Laura wanted to tear his face off, make him feel even a tiny bit of the pain she'd been through. Pain he'd orchestrated, no matter how casually. She was still so furious with him that her vision blurred, tinged red at the edges.

But she saw the worry in his stance, the way he couldn't seem to stand still, constantly scratching his cheek or tugging at his shirt collar. She was glad, because he deserved to feel on edge, but she was also aware of the sight they must make in the hall.

"It's feeling kind of crowded out here," she said.

"By all means, come in." Mike eased away from the doorframe and disappeared into the room.

Laura ventured inside, checking the place over. The bathroom door was open, revealing a claw-footed tub and a polished marble floor. As far as she could tell, nobody was in there. In the large bedroom, the wardrobe doors were open and the forest-green curtains were drawn back, showing a large, vacant balcony, beyond which palm trees swayed. Unless somebody was secreted beneath one of the two queen-size beds, there was nowhere else to hide.

Mike was alone.

"Can I get you a drink?" he said, clinking ice at the mini-bar.

The little bottles of liquor looked good and Laura felt suddenly parched.

"Swish digs, Mikey. You always stay so upmarket?" Amy asked.

"Gotta grab those perks while you can." Mike handed Laura a glass of whiskey, avoiding her gaze. He offered the same to Amy and Beverly. Amy accepted but Beverly shook her head. She stood by the oak writing desk, her complexion devoid of color. She looked beaten-up and exhausted, her throat bruising.

"This is our spirit guide, Beverly," Amy said.

Laura shot her a look, but Amy was busy sipping her drink. Mike gave Beverly a curious stare. He hadn't poured himself a drink.

"You're the psychic?" he asked.

She nodded.

Mike's face was the picture of surprise. He must have imagined something a little different when Laura mentioned her to him on the phone. Laura felt bad for Beverly. The psychic must get sick of people looking at her like that. She returned Mike's stare without blinking.

"Look, this is all great and everything," Laura said, "but what exactly are you doing here?"

Mike leaned against the chest of drawers, giving her a small smile.

"I couldn't leave my best writer stranded in L.A. I'm here to help."

"Now I'm your best writer? What happened to *you're so tired and predictable?*"

Mike had the decency to look abashed. And Laura knew the truth. No editor in their right mind would fly out to the United States to contest a flight ban for one of their employees. Mike could pretend he was here in a professional capacity all he liked, but she knew better. This was personal.

"Have you spoken to the police?" she asked.

"Give me a chance. I've only just got here."

"Do you think you can talk them down?"

Beverly stumbled and held onto the desk.

"Shit, Beverly, are you okay?" Laura went over to her.

"I'm fine," Beverly said, though she looked anything but. Her hands trembled.

"You need to lie down."

"Here." Mike passed Amy a key card. "I booked another room down the hall. Why don't you settle Beverly in there while Laura and I catch up?"

Amy gave Laura a questioning look and Laura nodded. She watched her sister begrudgingly help Beverly from the room, the door shutting after them.

Now it was just Laura and Mike.

They remained silent for a moment. Eventually, it was Mike who spoke first.

"How are you?" he asked, his voice softening.

"Just great now that my boss is here to save me."

"Funny. And how are you really?" He sounded like he cared. Laura hated that he thought he had any right to show concern for her well-being.

"Tired. Pissed off. Constipated. A mixture of the above with a sprinkling of really fucking scared."

Mike nodded, released a breath. "I feel terrible. I'm so sorry. I should never have sent you out here. I was an idiot."

"I'd use a more colorful noun than that."

Mike took it.

He rubbed his head and Laura smelled Jean Paul Gaultier, the aftershave Mike had worn for as long as she'd known him. He was nothing if not a creature of habit. The scent conjured myriad emotions and Laura remembered the comfort of snuggling into his side at night, of breathing him in and feeling safe. She remembered the way he looked at her when she woke from a nightmare, nothing but breath and secrets between them. The way he cried when she ended it. She'd seen him more vulnerable than anybody, and she knew his macho act earlier was just that.

Laura leaned against the nightstand, grateful for the six feet between them.

"What happened?" Mike asked.

She sipped the whiskey, savoring its warmth. It buzzed on her tonsils and soothed her nerves. She told him the same thing she'd told Amy when she first showed up, starting with the talk of pranks on the *It Feeds* set, then the deaths.

"You have no memory of what happened?"

Laura shook her head. Couldn't get into it.

"You talked to Todd before he died, right? What did you think of him?"

"I thought he was a moron." Laura peered into her drink. "A harmless moron."

"And Kyle?"

Laura shrugged. "The same."

Except she had liked Kyle. In another life, she might have *been* Kyle.

"So, you wouldn't want to hurt them?"

Laura looked at Mike sharply. "What?"

"You heard me."

She nearly threw the glass at him. "I didn't kill them, Mike. How can you even think that?"

"A good journalist covers all bases."

"You're an editor, not a journalist."

"I'm just trying to establish the facts." Mike sighed. "If you didn't kill them, who did?"

"That's what I'm trying to figure the fuck out."

The quiet of the room was like a blanket and Laura felt heavy with exhaustion. Or maybe that was the whiskey. Now that she'd stopped moving, she felt tethered to the spot, gravity pulling her down, and the beds were right there, calling to her.

Mike eased away from the cabinet, taking a step closer. "I've spoken to a lawyer out here. We'll talk to her together in the morning."

"I'm not meeting anybody. Not until I've figured out what's going on."

"Laura, let me help you."

It was the least he could do, but Mike didn't know the full truth. All the strange things that had happened over the past few days. The fact that she'd stopped thinking about the perpetrator as a *who* but a *what*.

He was closer now, only a few feet of carpet separating them. He reached out, his fingers brushing her elbow. His touch was so unexpected, it sent a tingle up her arm, and his earnest expression was so soft it melted her gut.

She felt pressure in the back of her throat. Shit, was she going to cry? Goddamn the whiskey, it was tipping her over the edge. She hated that a tiny part of her wanted to let Mike wrap her in his arms. To take control, the way he had with the freelancer with the lawsuit. It would be so easy. She had pushed him away four years ago, killed their relationship when he started asking too many questions, but there were fewer secrets between them now. She was so tired. Maybe she could let him fight this for her.

Laura blinked, swallowed.

No. This was her fight. Her story. Mike would only confuse things even more.

"No lawyer can help," she said, moving her arm so that he lost his hold on her. "The police don't believe me. When I told them about being taken to the set, they made it seem like it was my fault. And the Needle—"

She stopped, closed her mouth.

Mike went still. "The Needle Man? Is that what you were about to say?"

Shit.

She sighed. "I saw somebody dressed as the Needle Man. I keep seeing them."

"Somebody in a costume?"

No.

"I don't know."

"Laura?" he pressed.

"I'm starting to think there's something to the whole curse thing."

Shit. Saying it out loud really did make her sound crazy.

More and more, Mike's presence unnerved her. Just a week ago, she knew who she was. She had her job, her apartment, her routine. She had her Winona Ryder pop art and her trusty desktop computer. But her life had been turned inside out like an old T-shirt, and having Mike there only reinforced the change. Her old life felt so far away, but a piece of it was here, looking at her. Mike rarely looked so serious, and the sight made her heart tighten.

Suddenly, Laura wanted to be anywhere but alone with Mike.

He studied her face. "Where did you see the Needle Man?"

"In my hotel room. At Kyle's house. At Beverly's apartment." She held out her phone, showing him the picture of the shadow on the wall, which Amy had forwarded to her. "We caught him on camera."

He looked at the photo, then at Laura.

He was so close, she could see his pupils dilating, then expanding. She smelled the whiskey on her breath, mingling with his cologne . . .

She didn't like the look he gave her.

It was almost the same way he'd looked at Beverly—

A knock at the door made Laura jump, but it was just Amy.

"Beverly's down for the count," she said, taking up her glass and swallowing a mouthful. "Maybe you should get some rest, too."

Laura nodded, pocketing her phone and stepping away from Mike.

"Sleep will do you good," he said. His voice was kind, but held a distant quality.

"G'night, Mike."

In the other room, the lights were off, but Laura made out two double beds. Beverly lay on one of them, on top of the duvet.

While Amy used the bathroom, Laura sat on the edge of the other bed. The urge to collapse into the pillows and surrender to sleep was huge, but she couldn't do that yet. Something was bothering her, a gnat in her ear.

"Are you asleep?" she asked the gloom.

"I was," Beverly said.

"How's your throat?"

"Ready to not be attacked again for a while."

"Right. Sorry." Laura looked at her hands. Her cuticles were ragged and torn. She'd picked one of them raw, but the pain was good. It kept her centered. She took a breath.

"Do you ever think about her? The girl you tried to help?"

A pause, then, "Every day."

"What was she like?"

"Stubborn, but kind. In the short periods when she was lucid, she talked about her favorite books. Why?"

Laura resisted picking her nails.

"Were there signs that she was slipping? Her mental stability?"

"You're not her, Laura."

Tension melted in Laura's shoulders.

She shouldn't be surprised the psychic had seen right through her.

Mike really had thrown her for a loop. Laura so badly wished she were still part of his world, the world of a week ago, but the events of the past few days had jettisoned her. She wasn't sure she'd ever be able to go back.

"What if—" she began.

"I'm sure this time," Beverly cut in. "I'm sure we're doing the right thing."

"Were you this sure with her?"

Silence.

Laura decided she didn't want to know.

"I've been thinking," she said. "Maybe Todd had something to do with this after all. You said you felt a shift, after we burned the film, like something changed. Maybe Todd did something before he died."

Beverly was quiet for a moment.

"I may have been wrong about the parasite," she said.

"What do you mean?"

"There are different kinds of demons. Parasites are just one kind. What happened on the set made me think we could be up against something else entirely."

"Like what?"

"Something could be controlling the thing that's posing as the Needle Man. Some kind of puppet master."

"Another demon?" Laura asked.

"No, a person."

A tremor went through Laura.

A person.

The words hung between them, ominous and heavy, and Laura couldn't begin to consider them. Weariness overcame her and she sank into the pillow, unable to process any more supernatural hokum. After a few seconds, she felt the darkness come.

The house reared up before her.

Laura stood on dusty ground, a breeze scooping dirt into the air and casting it at the façade.

Somebody stood in the doorway.

A little girl in a buttercup-yellow dress.

She raised a finger to her lips.

"*Shhhhh.*"

She curled her finger, beckoning Laura inside.

Laura couldn't stop herself from following. She moved up the front steps, moving closer and closer to that yawning front door, until it sucked her inside and she ceased to exist.

Horrorstory @h0rrorst0ry · 9h

This is a personal plea to Laura Warren/Polly Tremaine.
WE LOVE YOU & KNOW YOU'RE INNOCENT. Our
DMs are open if you want to talk.
#LeaveLauraAlone

💬 113   🔁 61   ♡ 1,548

NINETEEN

Three soft raps punctured the silence. Laura tensed at the knock. She twisted to look at Amy beside her in the bed. Her sister was already awake and frowning at the door, her blond sleep-hair doing a fair approximation of *True Blue*–era Madonna. Before Laura could stop her, Amy slipped from the bed, tiptoed across the room in a white T-shirt and gray sweatpants, put her eye to the peephole, then opened the door.

"Buenos dias, señoritas," Mike said, brandishing a large brown paper bag and a tray of coffees. "Figured you'd be hungry by now. You're all decent, right?"

"Unfortunately for you," Laura said, prying herself up. She'd slept in her clothes. Beverly's clothes, technically. Prepared, just in case.

Mike laughed as he set the bag on the desk. She was sure he looked embarrassed as she disentangled herself from the bedsheet, but then Amy elbowed past him to rummage in the bag.

"Nice, breakfast muffins. And coffee. Mikey, you're the best."

"I try."

Laura wasn't ready to see him smile. It would take more than contrition and condiments to remove his name from her shit list.

And she hated the fact that she'd forgive him in a heartbeat if he made all this go away.

"How's the psychic?" Mike asked. Laura followed his gaze to the balcony and saw that Beverly was outside smoking, her back to them as she stared out at the city.

"Her name's Beverly," Laura said. She went to the balcony door, slid it open, and stepped out into the warming air. The tiles were cool beneath her bare feet and, under a cloud of cigarette smoke, the day smelled dewy and crisp.

"Morning," she said.

"Yep." Beverly faced the street, her thin shoulders showing through a black tank top.

"Mike brought breakfast."

"Already had mine." Beverly tapped her cigarette on an ashtray.

"There's this rumor that nicotine contains negative nutrition."

Beverly shrugged. "I'm not a morning person."

"Me neither."

"Your sister snores."

"Family, right?" Laura paused, wondered if she dared try to puncture Beverly's outer shell. "You have any family?"

Beverly put the cigarette to her lips, inhaled. "A brother in Dallas. My parents are alive, biologically speaking, but they spend most of their time in church or playing backgammon."

"You're not close?"

Beverly seemed distracted. Beverly always did. Laura remembered what she'd said about finding the emotional noise of the city difficult and wondered how many people were currently living rent-free in her mind. Could Beverly feel every one of the hotel guests? Could she feel Laura?

Maybe she can tell me how I actually feel, because this numbness is giving nothing away.

Beverly exhaled. "So how are we ditching him?"

Story time was over.

"Mike?" Laura said.

"Seems like an unnecessary complication. Unless he knows something, he's either dangerous or in danger."

She had a point. The way Mike had looked at Laura last night suggested he wouldn't quit until he had her home, but he could die before that.

There was a time she'd have said Mike would do anything for her.

"What are you guys saying about me?" Amy asked at the door. She smiled sweetly, but the suspicion in her eyes was real.

"We were wondering if you're going to barf your breakfast now or in ten minutes," Beverly said.

Before Amy could respond, Laura tugged her sister onto the balcony and slid the door closed.

"We're ditching Mike," she said.

"The Mike who just paid for our hotel room and carbohydrates, no questions asked?"

"We can't trust him."

Amy frowned. "What do you think he's going to do?"

"At worst, call the cops. At best, get in the way." At Amy's look, she continued. "If we don't stop this thing, somebody else is going to die. Three people already have. We've had the shower, the stabbing, the spiders. Next could be falling or—"

"Bathtub," Amy said. "Yeah, I know. But Mike has the credit card. He could make our lives a lot easier. His lawyer friend might even get you off, so to speak."

Laura didn't laugh, not just because the joke was bad but because she was suddenly acutely aware that they were on a balcony, tempting whatever sick force was playing havoc with their lives.

"He cares about you," Amy said. *"A lot."*

Laura's jaw tightened. "What does that mean?"

Amy put her nose in her coffee and shrugged.

Great moment to be enigmatic for the first time in your life.

Laura drew a breath and released it.

"Let's get off this balcony."

She went into the bedroom, finding Mike leaning against the desk. He hopped up as she entered, giving her a hopeful smile.

"Muffin?" He raised the bag. When she didn't move, he added, "You should eat something."

Laura bristled. "The concerned ex-boyfriend thing is getting real old." At his pained look, she rubbed her forehead, tried to level herself off. "Look, you need to leave. If you're with us, you're in danger."

Mike dropped the take-out bag onto the desk, shoulders tense. "I get that you're angry with me. Trust me, I get it. But I'm trying to help you. If you weren't so stubborn—"

"You're the one who can't let anything go."

Mike's brows drew together. "This isn't about us."

"Isn't it?"

He didn't back down, his eyes shining at her.

"Is the 'cold thing' working for you? The detachment? Because it looks to me like it's getting you exactly where you've always wanted to be. Alone."

Laura wanted to argue back, but he was right. Damn him, he knew her too well.

"I'm sorry," she said. "But you need to leave."

He stepped forward, his gaze pleading.

"Laura." He took her hand. His grip found her wrist, and Laura's chest cramped painfully, forcing air from her lungs.

"Get off me!" She stumbled back, out of his reach.

"Laura," he said again, but she cut him off.

"I'm not somebody you need to save, Mike. You can't save me. Now, leave."

He didn't blink for a long time, and then he looked past her. She sensed Amy and Beverly behind her, watching them, and she knew that Mike wouldn't want to put on a show.

He shook his head. Then he reached into his pocket and took out a card, handing it to her. "This is the lawyer I mentioned. Look her up if you want to. She's shit hot on wrongful convictions and could really help you out. She's ready when you are." He released a breath. "In the meantime, I'll be in the other room."

When he'd gone, Laura pocketed the card without looking at it and felt her chest release. She paced the carpet, picking at her cuticles, her wrist still warm where he'd held it.

"Are you all right?" Amy asked, coming to her side. "Jesus, you're shaking. What happened?"

"Nothing, forget about it. Let's just figure out what we're going to do."

"There are bagels," Amy said.

Laura sank onto the bed and sat stiffly while Amy turned on the fifty-inch plasma TV. The coffee smelled amazing, but her stomach churned and she felt like half of her was in the hotel room, the other half in the past. A past she'd tried so hard to forget.

For once, she was glad her image was all over the news. The TV stations provided a morbid distraction from her own thoughts. News stories kept lining up her face alongside Kyle's, as if comparing their appearance. *Ladies and gentlemen, here's your beautiful Hollywood starlet, so young, so full of potential. And here's your bitter London hack—cynical, washed-up, and with a future behind bars. So tragic.*

"Damn," Amy said. "This is big."

"Not helping."

Amy muted the TV.

"Did Mike say anything about getting us out of this mess?"

"We're not relying on Mike."

"But—"

"I said no."

Laura's voice came out sharp and loud. Amy held up her hands.

"So, what's the plan?" she asked.

The truth was, Laura was fresh out of ideas.

She felt lost.

And angry. Angry that this was her life. She'd worked so hard to create something out of nothing and now it was being pried from her hands. Not only her career, but her life, too.

She was damned if she was going to let that happen.

There had to be something.

Beverly had talked about an entity and a puppet master. The very idea made Laura question her own sanity, but what if there was something to it? What if somebody had been there all along, watching her? Following her?

She took out her phone and loaded Instagram. Maybe Amy was right. Somebody on there could know something. They could be interacting with her the way serial killers often turn up at their own crime scene investigations.

Instagram was a minefield. She had been tagged in more posts. So many screen grabs of her as Tammy. People had made dolls and drawn art. There were too many comments to cope with. She went into her inbox and numbly scrolled.

Dozens of message requests. Laura scanned through them, feeling on edge. It was like searching for a single unbleached tooth in Beverly Hills.

She paused on one name—Brian Arenberg—and clicked through to his message.

Hi! It's been a while. Not sure if you remember me. You changed your name so I guess this might seem a bit creepy. Just wondering how you've been. The anniversary's coming up. Crazy, huh? Anyway, hit me up if you wanna catch up. ☺

"Brian Arenberg," Laura murmured. "Why is that name familiar?"

Amy looked up from her own phone. "Old boyfriend?"

"Funny."

On Brian Arenberg's profile, she examined his picture. Round face, black hair, some kind of movie T-shirt.

Her belly turned.

"This guy was outside the hotel a few days ago, with the paparazzi."

"What?" Amy turned toward her, watching as Laura flicked through the man's feed, seeing post after post about horror movies. His bio read: *I'm Brian, but you probably know me as Andy.*

Andy.

The name dislodged a memory of a little boy on the set of *The Guesthouse*. She remembered a goofy smile and a swagger that was endearing rather than annoying.

"Ready or not, here I come!"

"Shit, I know him," she said. "He was a bit player in *The Guesthouse*. He was one of the kids who came to stay at the Cricklewood. We were the same age, so we used to hang out. Shit."

"Block him," Amy said.

"What?"

"He could be dangerous. Like you said, don't feed the trolls."

Something about her expression made Laura pause. "But he could know something. He was there, too, at the beginning. I'm messaging him."

"Don't," Amy said, her voice strained. "Seriously. What if he calls the cops?"

"He won't be able to tell our location from Instagram."

"You don't know that."

"Why are you being weird?" Laura asked.

Amy opened her mouth to speak, but nothing came out. She looked flustered, which was unnerving in itself, and Laura couldn't tell if it really was because she was worried he'd call the cops, or if something else was going on.

"I'm messaging him," she said when Amy remained silent.

She felt the weight of her sister's gaze as she returned to her phone, but she ignored it. She'd completely forgotten about Brian Arenberg. When she'd left *The Guesthouse* behind, she left it behind completely. She figured everybody else involved with it had, too. But there he was.

What if Brian could help end this?

Or, what if he was Beverly's puppet master? That might explain why he was outside her hotel the day after she arrived.

She typed: Can we meet?

A green dot immediately appeared by Brian Arenberg's avatar. He was online, despite the early hour. An ellipsis hovered beneath her message; he was typing.

Holy shit you replied!!! Are you OK? I saw the news. They're saying another body was found at the studio. Are you OK?!

Laura steeled herself. She typed again, kept it simple.

Can we meet?

A few seconds, then: Yes!!! Where?

Your place. Safer.

Totally get it.

He sent his location. It was in an L.A. suburb near Echo Park that Laura had never visited.

She lowered her phone. "He says he'll meet me." After a breath, she added, "I'll go alone."

"What?" Amy looked outraged. "There's no way."

"I can't keep risking your safety. It's not fair. You could get hurt, or worse."

"I'm going with you," Beverly said.

"Fine, but Amy, you stay here."

Amy's eyes widened. "You want the psychic to tag along but not me? We don't even know her! What is she still doing here?"

"I have my reasons."

"You hear how creepy that sounds, right?"

Briefly, Laura wondered if Beverly's reasons were still the same. From the start, it had seemed like she wanted to atone for her past mistakes, maybe prove something to herself. Was that still the case?

"Jesus," Laura said. "Fine, we'll all go. But we're going without Mike. And we're going now."

Comments on a TikTok posted by DemonFaerieXYZ titled
"GUESTHOUSE GRL GON WLD!"

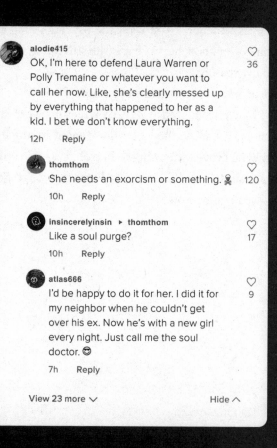

alodie415

OK, I'm here to defend Laura Warren or
Polly Tremaine or whatever you want to
call her now. Like, she's clearly messed up
by everything that happened to her as a
kid. I bet we don't know everything.

♡ 36

12h   Reply

thomthom

She needs an exorcism or something. ☠   ♡ 120

10h   Reply

insincerelyinsin ▸ thomthom

Like a soul purge?

♡ 17

10h   Reply

atlas666

I'd be happy to do it for her. I did it for
my neighbor when he couldn't get
over his ex. Now he's with a new girl
every night. Just call me the soul
doctor. 😎

♡ 9

7h   Reply

View 23 more ⌄   Hide ⌃

TWENTY

The house looked like any suburban American home. White, shuttered windows, sheer curtains, and a tree swing in the front yard. It could be something out of *The Brady Bunch* or *The Wonder Years*, timeless and unchanging, which in itself was unsettling. It was too perfect. Too much like a movie location. The all-American exterior could conceal any number of horrors.

Laura was out of the car the instant that Beverly parked. She approached the front door, felt her pulse throb. If Brian knew something, she was going to make him talk until it hurt.

She had decided force was the best approach.

There was an equal chance he was dangerous. The fact that he'd been outside her hotel with the paparazzi suggested as much. She couldn't trust anybody anymore, certainly not an ex–child actor who was one of the only other living cast members from *The Guesthouse*.

There had to be a reason he was still alive when hardly anybody else was.

It was midday and the air felt fresh. Charged.

This was what they'd been looking for. She knew it.

Behind her, Beverly looked like she'd stepped out of a bar brawl in her leather jacket and torn jeans. Amy hung back, her mind clearly on other things. She gripped her phone tightly and Laura didn't have time to worry about what was going on with her.

She rang the bell, heard it chime through unknown corridors and rooms.

A thumping came from inside the house and then the door opened to reveal Brian Arenberg, panting, his face flush. His black hair reached the shoulders of a baggy Nancy Thompson T-shirt.

"Polly," he said.

"Now!" Laura shouted, and she jumped him. Brian was a big guy but he wasn't strong. As Laura launched at him, he stumbled backward and his back struck the wall, knocking a frame to the floor. His arms went up, but Laura sprayed Mace in his eyes and Beverly kicked out the backs of his legs.

Brian collapsed onto his knees. Beverly forced him down onto his front. She dug her knee into his back and tugged his arms behind him. Amy hung back by the door, looking panic-stricken.

"What's going on? Why are you doing this?" Brian choked.

"I wanted to ask you the same thing," Laura said, squatting by his head.

"I think I'm blind. Oh God, it hurts so much."

"Quiet," Beverly said.

"What do you know about the Needle Man?" Laura demanded. She felt the same perverse thrill as when she'd confronted Madeleine. The sense that she was being herself for the first time in years.

"What?" Brian whimpered. "I don't know what you're talking about! Please, God! I can't see!"

Laura looked at Beverly. "Can you get a read on him?"

"Nothing that isn't obvious. Mace him again."

"No! Please! I didn't hurt anybody. *Please*, Amy!"

Laura froze. She thought she'd misheard, couldn't understand why Brian was saying her sister's name. But then she turned to look at Amy, who didn't blink, her face set in an unchanging mask of surprise, and Laura was certain she'd heard correctly.

"You know him?" she asked.

"Amy, please," Brian blubbered.

"Shit," Amy said. Her shoulders dropped, as if the fight had left them, and she gave Laura the same look she'd given her since they were kids. Guilt wrapped in an apology wrapped in fear of how Laura would respond. She sighed.

"I know him. He's why I'm in L.A. He's making a documentary and he asked me to be part of it. Flew me out here last week. I was going to tell you. Eventually. I'm sorry."

Laura couldn't process her words. She looked from her sister to Brian spluttering into the floorboards and even as her mind attempted to decipher what Amy had said, she shook her head. Either Brian Arenberg was one hell of an actor or he was innocent.

"Let him go," she told Beverly.

"Gladly. He's sweating like crazy." Wiping her hands on her jacket, Beverly got to her feet. They all watched as Brian pried himself up and sat against the wall, his eyes red raw, breathing heavy. Laura almost felt sorry for him.

"Pill," Amy said, but Laura interrupted.

"What's the documentary?" she demanded, even though she already knew the answer. There was only one thing it could be about.

Panic entered Amy's eyes.

"It's about *The Guesthouse*," Brian said. "Jesus, my eyes. I think I need water."

"You're making a documentary about *The Guesthouse*?"

"It's the thirtieth anniversary," Brian said, even though Laura had aimed the question at Amy. "I've been working on it for years, getting together as many of the old crew as possible. The ones who're still alive. I tried so hard to find you, but you did a great job on the disappearing act."

Laura felt weak. "You're helping him?" she asked Amy.

"He said he'd introduce me to agents. You know how difficult it is to get meetings out here. I had to. It's not a big deal, okay? You would never have agreed to be in the film." Her jaw tensed. "Somebody should take the spotlight you vacated."

A jag of anger cut through Laura's core.

It was like she was looking at an imposter who simply resembled her sister. She didn't recognize the woman before her. Selling her out to Mike at a drunken get-together was one thing, but appearing in a documentary about her? That was on another level.

And the scariest thing was that Amy seemed to feel entitled to it. She seemed to think she should benefit from Laura's unwanted fame—use it as a platform for her own career.

It made a horrible kind of sense.

"You didn't fly out here because you were worried about me," Laura said. "You were already here." Ice-cold realization hit her. "Is that why you've been filming me? For Brian's film?"

"No." Amy wouldn't look her in the eye.

"Amy—"

She threw up her arms. "Maybe, okay? I don't know. Brian wanted footage of you. I wasn't going to give it to him."

"What?" Brian said, sounding hurt.

"Christ." Laura felt unbalanced. Trapped. She couldn't handle any of this. It was too much. She saw Beverly observing the scene impassively, but she got the feeling Beverly had known all along that Amy was involved in something sketchy.

Laura turned on the spot, wanted to go out the front door and scream at the sky, but Amy was blocking her, so she went in the opposite direction, down the hall, not knowing where was she headed until she found a screen door and threw it open, charging out into the backyard.

She couldn't feel her body, she just had the vague sense of an autumn breeze whispering around her, cloaking her in damp and cold.

Amy was supposed to be on her side.

It was them against the world. Always had been, ever since they were little. The nights Amy cried herself to sleep over one of their mom's comments, Laura would curl around her like a wood louse, absorbing her pain. The days Laura had panic attacks so bad, only Amy could calm her with a joke so twisted it snapped the world back into focus.

When had that changed?

"Pill?"

Laura turned. Amy stood a few feet away, the knuckles of both hands white around her phone, which she clutched to her stomach.

"What did I do?" Laura demanded. "Just tell me what I did that pissed you off so much you have no problem throwing me under the bus. Repeatedly."

Amy's expression shifted between angry and upset. Her cheeks glowed red.

"I wasn't trying to hurt you." Her voice was velour-soft. "It wasn't about you. It's about me. L.A. Trying to do something with my life other than humiliating grunt work for an overcaffeinated fashion monster."

She's been there a while, their mom had said. Fresh anger pulsed in Laura's fingertips.

"You made it seem like Mom was having one of her turns. Do you realize how fucked up that is?"

"I didn't mean to. I was scared."

"Scared I'd strangle you to death?" Laura said.

"Yes."

Laura's fists tightened. Her teeth creaked as she clenched her jaw. She heard the singsong voice that had echoed in the guesthouse.

"Fool me once, shame on you.

"Fool me twice—"

"I was going to tell you," Amy said, "when the time was right. I *wanted* to tell you about the documentary, but—"

"But what?"

"I wanted to have something first. Brian said he'd help me, and I thought maybe if I had an audition or a job offer, something that said it was worth it, you'd understand. You'd forgive me."

"There's no—"

"I couldn't do it anymore," Amy broke in, and she was fighting back tears now. "Do you know how humiliating it is to stand in front of a room full of people and be told you're too old? Or stupid? Or fat? Not once, but dozens of times. *Hundreds* of times. Over and over."

"You could quit."

"Would you? Would you give up on something you really wanted? If it was *Zeppelin* magazine?"

Laura didn't speak. She knew she wouldn't.

Amy dropped her head. Her voice emerged small and defeated.

"I was going to quit. This was it." She waved her phone at the house. "This was my last attempt at making it, and then I was giving up. Burn the negative, right? If this didn't work out, I was going to quit as soon as I got back to the UK."

She stood with her back rounded and Laura suddenly saw what the years had done to her. Amy always smiled. Always joked or had a crackpot scheme at the ready. But not now. Now she was laid bare. The years had stripped something from her, and her pain was as bright as the sun striking the windows at her back.

Laura could see that Amy was haunted by the word she had heard more than any other when trying to make it as an actor.

No.

(You're not quite what we're looking for.)

No.

(Maybe in a couple years.)

No.

(Why don't you just quit already?)

Amy was planning on quitting. Usually, Laura would be ready with advice and encouragement. She'd convince her to keep at it, reassure her that it was only a matter of time, but this felt different. Words weren't enough anymore. Amy really was going to quit, and the sight of her so defeated made something creak in Laura's chest. It hurt, seeing her that way.

But it didn't excuse what Amy had done.

"I'm sorry," Amy said. "I really wasn't going to give Brian our footage. It was for us. For the case."

Laura wished she could believe her.

Wished she could just forget about the documentary.

But Amy had crossed a line and there was no going back.

"Did you hear what Brian said?" Amy said. "He's been interviewing everybody involved in *The Guesthouse*. There could be something in his documentary that'll help us."

Us.

Amy thought she was still part of the team.

As much as Laura wanted to scream at her some more, maybe say something she could never take back, something that would ruin them forever, she knew her sister was right. Laura was wanted for murder, they needed answers, and Brian could be the one who had them.

"Just don't talk to me," she said, heading for the door.

got the house when my folks died," Brian said as he led them down the upstairs hall, still rubbing his eyes. He'd cleaned off the Mace while Laura and Amy were in the yard, but his eyes were still red-rimmed. Laura felt a prick of guilt, but she'd had to be certain. The best defense was a good offense. She'd had no idea he'd be so fragile.

Behind her, Beverly and Amy followed, and Laura tried to ignore the emotion roiling through her. She might understand why Amy did what she did, but that didn't mean she was okay with it.

"The place is too big for one person," Brian continued, "but I figured it'll be good for parties someday. I was thinking of making them movie-themed. Like a frat-party murder mystery where we have to figure out who's Ghostface."

Laura got the sense that Brian wouldn't ever throw a wild party.

"I'm sorry if I freaked you out the other day, outside the hotel," Brian said, stopping outside a door at the end of the landing. "I guess it was sort of intense with all those paps hanging around."

Laura nodded. "How did you know I was there?"

"Internet. I've sort of been following the *It Feeds* production and I know Universal uses the Loft for their talent. When news broke about the fire and your involvement, I figured that's where you'd be. Had no idea so many paps would be there, too. Bunch of vultures. Anyway, check this out."

Brian opened the door and stepped aside so Laura could go in. His look of pride doubled her unease.

She found herself in a room meticulously curated with horror memorabilia. A *Nightmare on Elm Street* shower curtain hung at the window. An entire wall was lined with VHS tapes, a powder-pink TV-video combo set nestled among them. Mini Freddy, Chucky, and Needle Man figurines grinned at her, while Jason's mask, complete with machete gouge, rested on a shelf.

Her gaze stopped on a figure in the corner and she thought she'd finally gone mad.

Seven-year-old Tammy stared back at her.

A shiver spider-walked up Laura's spine.

It took her a second to realize it was a life-size cardboard cutout of her younger self. Young Polly wore her sunny dress, standing with her white buckle shoes pressed together. She held out the paper fortune-teller, face tipped forward so that shadows played under her eyes.

"That is creepy as hell," Beverly said.

Laura had a memory of posing with one of these cutouts at the film's premiere, but she hadn't given them a second thought since then. It was unnerving to be in the same room as one now. She kept waiting for the cardboard to creak and move as Tammy counted with the fortune-teller. Predicted how they would die.

"They're hella rare," Brian said. "Mom found this in a Blockbuster a year after the movie hit VHS. She tried to throw it in the trash every year after that, but I never let her. It's my pièce de horror résistance. Hey, check this out."

He reached behind the cutout and Laura heard the click of a switch. Red LEDs ignited in Tammy's eyes and a voice came from the cutout.

"One for sorrow, two for mirth, three for a funeral, four for birth—"

Laura felt woozy. The sound of her child voice caused hair to bristle across her neck and she felt herself coming unstuck, as if her insides were disconnecting from her outsides.

Brian chuckled. "Neat, huh? She still works!"

"Turn it off," Laura said as the chant began again. Brian fumbled with the cutout and the voice silenced, though Laura still heard the words, an echo in her skull.

"Sorry, I guess that was sort of weird for you," Brian said.

Laura tried to focus. "This stuff must've taken years to find."

"Oh, yeah! The podcast helped. I'm a podcaster now, maybe you've heard of *Horrorstory*? I do movie makeup, too. Y'know, prosthetics like fake noses and burns and stuff. I've made a bunch of shorts. I tried to get a part in *It Feeds*. I thought I would be a neat throwback to the movie, but they told me maybe next season." He shook his head. "So sad about those folks who died. I guess they thought they were safe because it was a different story."

"You believe the curse stuff?" Laura said.

"You don't?" Brian looked confused. "I figured that's why you went underground. I guess I avoided it all these years because I was only a minor role in the movie."

Laura couldn't get into the debate again. Didn't know what she thought anymore. At the door, Beverly peered around the room, taking it all in with an unreadable expression. Her gaze stopped on the cardboard cutout and remained there, and Laura wondered what she saw.

"This really is some collection, Bri-bear," Amy breathed, and Laura knew that tone. Amy knew how to turn men to putty. Men had always looked at her, and she let them, so long as they had something to offer. Mostly it was harmless, but it made Laura worry. People didn't like being used. Would Amy really stroke Brian's ego in return for an agency hookup? She had always thought Amy had more pride than that.

Amy noticed her look. "You should see his footage, Pill. It's actually pretty good."

Laura ignored her.

"You're still involved in the *Guesthouse* community," she said to Brian. "Have you met anybody who could help figure this thing out? For real?"

"There must be a ton of horror fans into curses and occult stuff," Amy added.

Brian rubbed his eyes. "Horror fans are some of the sweetest people you'd ever meet. They're more likely to help you change a tire than kill you."

Something about the way he said it sounded rehearsed, like this wasn't the first time he'd defended horror fans.

"Where's the footage?" Laura asked.

Brian crossed to a set of wardrobe doors and opened them to reveal a computer workstation. A monitor and keyboard sat on the desktop. Above them were shelves of mini-videocassettes, each meticulously labeled.

"I have around three hundred hours of material," Brian said, sitting in the desk chair and spinning. "But I have a rough three-hour edit of the best stuff. Let me load it up."

He turned to the computer and started opening files.

"What are these?" Beverly asked. She stood by an open drawer full of envelopes.

"Oh!" Brian jumped up. "That's fan mail from over the years. It's nuts how much stuff still comes to the house. Almost as nuts as the stuff people write."

Beverly shared a look with Laura.

"Why don't you take a look at them while I check out the documentary footage?" Laura said.

"I'll help," her sister said. Laura didn't respond. She knew Amy was only playing nice with Beverly out of guilt.

While they set the drawer on the floor and began going through the letters, Laura sat by Brian as he loaded up the video editor.

"Man, it's so awesome that you're here," he said, beaming. "And now you're the first person to watch *Checking In: The Secret Story of The Guesthouse*. Do you like the title? I'm so psyched."

Laura pinched the back of her hand and managed to smile.

She kept seeing two versions of Brian. The seven-year-old she'd hung out with during filming, and the nerdy man-child reclined in the chair. One of the only other survivors. Another one of her.

"How did you find me on Instagram?" she asked.

"I read one of your articles, the one about the gay porn star who got kidnapped and held in that guy's basement. Killer piece, by the way. I kept it. Anyway, there was an author photo. You look sort of different now, but I still recognized you."

Somebody had to eventually, she supposed.

And now that she was sitting next to another cast member of *The Guesthouse*, she had to know if she was the only one being tormented by its villain.

"Have you seen anything?" she asked. "Anything . . . strange?"

"Strange?"

"Like the Needle Man."

Brian stopped clicking the computer mouse. "Sometimes when I'm asleep. But I figure that's normal. People dream about movie killers all the time. That's sort of the point. They're supposed to freak you out. You ever notice it's all about the silhouette? They're designed to be memorable: all the easier to get under your skin and stay there."

Laura nodded.

"Why? Have you seen him?" Brian's voice was quiet.

"Sometimes."

"Yvonne said the same."

Yvonne Lincoln, writer of *The Guesthouse*. She'd been in prison since 1997, found guilty of stabbing her husband to death in the kitchen one sunny July morning.

"You've spoken to Yvonne?" Laura asked.

Brian nodded. After a second, he said, "I have to ask, why *Laura*? I mean, ever since I found out your new name, I sort of wondered . . . why did you change it to Laura?"

"It's Winona Ryder's middle name."

"No shit."

She smiled. "No shit."

"Sweet choice! Man, that bit in *Heathers* when she lights a cigarette on Christian Slater's corpse? It's the bomb."

Laura laughed for what felt like the first time in years. It felt good. It felt like *her.* Whoever had been running around L.A., waking up to dead bodies, wasn't Laura Warren. It was somebody else. The feeling lingered for a few seconds before it was flattened by reality, but it was good to know she was still in there somewhere. She could find herself again when this was over.

After a few more mouse clicks, Brian took a breath and looked from the computer screen to her.

"Ready?" he asked, chewing on his hair. She nodded and he hit play on his movie. Laura surrendered.

To Brian's credit, he'd done a decent job. The footage was neatly edited, the interviews staged in a dark room with the outline of a door artfully stretching behind the interviewee. It looked professional. She was sure he'd sell it to Prime or Shudder, no problem.

The faces of the people from her past gave her a double jolt of déjà vu and dread. Most she'd not seen in three decades, and when they appeared on-screen, she found herself tensing up, swamped by too many emotions to make sense of.

"I got the archive stuff from some dark web hacker," Brian said as old interview footage of director Christopher Rosenthal and writer Yvonne Lincoln played. "The studio refused to release it. But the more recent stuff is mine." He'd talked to the families of the deceased, who discussed their on-screen family, all of whom died years ago. Some of the faces were familiar, others not.

"You got Yvonne's son," Laura said as a twenty-something guy wearing eyeliner appeared.

"Yeah, nice guy. He made us mojitos and played Elvis on the stereo. Tragic about what happened to his folks."

"*Do I believe in the curse?*" Yvonne Lincoln asked on-screen, footage from 1996, just a year before her life sentence. She was red-haired, had a smoker's husk, and wore a military jacket. "*I'm probably the wrong person to ask. I'm a cynic. Ask me again when something gets me in my sleep.*"

"She changed her tune after the murder," Brian said. "Blamed the curse for her husband's death, claimed self-defense."

"I remember."

Laura knew the details of every death. She'd avoided the news feeds as a kid, too young to have access to them. But, over the years, she'd caved late at night and binged the stories. Yvonne's was the most troubling, because she was an attacker who claimed to be the victim.

Christopher Rosenthal appeared and Laura felt a twinge of affection. He looked just as she remembered, his easy smile the same. The footage was from 1998, a few months before he was found hanged in his home.

"I still love the movie," Christopher said, *"even though it's tarnished by the tragedy of the past few years. I think we accomplished something pretty fun and scary that will stand the test of time."*

"I still can't believe they're all gone," Brian said.

Melancholy stole through Laura and she felt renewed contempt for whatever force was behind all the pain and loss. Horror movies reveled in death. She'd been to theater showings where audiences clapped and cheered as characters were slashed and gutted. They cried out for more blood, more guts. She didn't begrudge them. It was theater. Pantomime. A safe place for them to vent their deepest fears.

But the thought of Christopher Rosenthal hanging from a noose made the back of her throat swell and throb.

Finally, Amy appeared on-screen. She looked somber, dressed in a black shirt, her blond hair tied up. When she spoke, her voice was threaded with emotion.

"Polly was so afraid, it really affected us as a family. I cried myself to sleep a lot as a kid. I worried about her. I was only little when the movie was made, but I read all about it, I saw all the things people said. And every time somebody died, I was relieved it wasn't Polly. I felt horrible about that, because it meant I was glad that somebody else had died, not her. I couldn't lose my sister. I'd rather die than have that happen."

Laura sensed the stillness in the room. She felt Amy's eyes on her, but she refused to turn around. This didn't change anything.

The footage went on to discuss the building of the set at Universal, archive photographs showing the Cricklewood Guesthouse in all its creaky, faded glory.

"Remember we used to play hide-and-seek around the set?" Brian said. "It was fun. Like the best playground ever."

Laura didn't want to remember.

"Listen, if this curse thing is real, it could come for us," Brian said.

"According to the media, it already has."

Brian looked deadly serious. "We should stick together. Just in case."

"Hey, Bri-bear, who's Ivan Rothschild?" Amy asked, looking up from a letter.

"Oh man." Brian got to his feet and went over, peering down at the email printout in Amy's hands. "I haven't spoken to him in years. We messaged a while back. Funny guy. Real old-school. He wrote a bunch of movies back in the seventies, big studio stuff like *Fatal Femme* and *Linger with Me*. And he worked on *The Guesthouse*."

"As a writer?" Laura asked.

Brian nodded. "He wrote the original draft. Not a lot of people know that. The story was his idea from the start, his concept, but he got sort of mad with the direction Christopher Rosenthal took the film. Long story short, Ivan got booted off production, the script was given a big rewrite by Yvonne, and Ivan never received a credit."

Something cold and sharp moved through Laura. She'd never heard of Ivan Rothschild, let alone the story of his dismissal from the film.

A writer with a grudge who got removed from the very film he created? That positively screamed curse.

"Beverly, have you read this?" she asked, and Beverly seemed to understand her meaning. She took the email from Amy and looked at it for a long moment. Nobody said anything. Finally, Beverly shook her head.

"I'm not getting anything from it, but that doesn't mean he's not involved."

"What are you, some kind of psychic?" Brian laughed, then noticed nobody else did. "Wait, *are* you a psychic?"

"Psychic medium," Laura said. She took the letter. "How did I not know about this guy?"

Brian shrugged. "He sort of got wiped from existence when he fell out with Chris. I've been trying to get a hold of him for the past year, but he stopped answering my emails. Yvonne knew him, but she won't tell me where to find him. I guess she likes having some kind of power, being in prison and all."

"Yvonne knows where he lives?" Laura asked.

"I doubt it."

"But you've visited her in prison?"

A proud look crossed Brian's face. "I'm the only one she'll see. The only one who believes her."

"We have to talk to her," Laura said. "Today."

"Didn't you hear what I said? She'll never tell us where Ivan lives."

Laura smiled. "She's never had a visit from Polly Tremaine before."

Horror Movie Writer on Trial for Murder

■ The trial of Hollywood screenwriter Yvonne Lincoln begins today.

By ATLAS FUELL
TODAY STAFF WRITER

The 42-year-old Los Angeles resident, best known for penning cult horror movie "The Guesthouse," stands accused of killing her husband, Kenny Lincoln, also a writer.

Mrs. Lincoln was apprehended by police in the early hours of Sunday, July 13, after she dialed 911, stating she had been attacked. First responders reported finding a deceased male in the kitchen, later confirmed as Mr. Lincoln. He had suffered fatal stab wounds to the neck and torso. Though distressed, Mrs. Lincoln appeared unharmed.

Mrs. Lincoln entered a not-guilty plea at her arraignment in July, stating that she acted in self-defense.

The trial is expected to last into the new year.

TWENTY-ONE

Laura tugged down the sun visor and checked her reflection in the car mirror. She felt ridiculous, but had to admit that she was impressed by Brian's ingenuity. Apparently, a lifetime of working in horror movies had served him well, because she looked nothing like herself.

The blond wig prickled her scalp and the layers of makeup felt heavy, like a mask, which was entirely the point. Brian had used prosthetics to subtly alter her appearance, giving her brown contacts and a wider nose. Only Amy would be able to tell that, beneath it all, she was Laura Warren, and even she might have trouble.

Beside her, Beverly drove, the others sitting in the back. Brian drummed the doorframe in what must be a nervous habit, and Laura wished he'd stop. She tried not to think about where they were headed, even though every mile of highway only brought them closer to the California Institution for Women.

Brian had been right about his privileged access to Yvonne Lincoln. He requested a visit via the online Vpass portal, and while they waited for the confirmation to come through, they killed time. Amy showered, Beverly smoked in the yard, and Brian sat Laura in a chair in the kitchen and began applying the prosthetics. He had just finished when the confirmation arrived. Now they were on their way to Chino, another place Laura had never heard of much less wanted to visit.

She wondered what Yvonne would be like. She'd been incarcerated for over twenty years. That changed a person. Especially when they swore they were innocent.

"Hey, Bri-bear," Amy said. "How many horror movies have happy endings?"

Brian cleared his throat. "Oh, tons. Well, dozens, minimum."

"But most of them are downers?"

"I guess in the art house world. You know, mainstream prefers the good guy to win."

"If this was turned into a movie, which do you reckon we'd be?"

Brian laughed, but it sounded strained. "I'm pulling for mainstream studio gloss, you know?"

Laura felt sorry for him. Amy was bored, or scared, and Brian was her plaything. He had no idea.

Laura sensed that what Amy really wanted was to tell her how crazy this was, that the authorities were after her and Laura was relying on makeup and a wig to get her in and out of a hornet's nest.

Amy said nothing, though, and Laura was glad. One word from her and Laura knew she'd regret the things that came out of her mouth.

The prison complex emerged out of nowhere before she was ready for it. The first Laura knew of it, Beverly was pulling off the road into a parking lot. Aside from a small sign stating *CALIFORNIA INSTITUTION FOR WOMEN*, they could be anywhere. The prison didn't loom over them like some kind of Shawshank. It was a flat collection of buildings that could be a school or a medical facility. Somehow, that only made it more ominous. The cool exterior masked the darkness within.

"Last call for getting out of here," Amy said.

Eyeing the prison entrance, Laura pressed her lips together and fumbled for the door handle.

"Let's go, Brian."

She left Amy and Beverly in the car and got out into the bright, arid lot. A lone water tower watched from a field a mile over, and Laura checked her reflection in the car window, telling herself she wasn't Laura. Or Polly. She was the name on the fake ID Brian had given her. *Callie Turner.*

She was an innocent woman on a day visit.

Nobody was waiting to arrest her. Not here. Not yet.

"Man, I hate this place," Brian said as he walked with her into the shadow of the facility, then through the sliding doors.

The reception was cool and gray. As sparse and impersonal as a morgue. They went up to the window, where a guard sat at a computer.

"Hey, Brian, how's it going?" the guard asked. She smiled through the glass at them, and Laura realized Brian really was a regular. That could only be a good thing.

"Oh, you know, working hard," Brian said.

"Or hardly working," the officer said.

Brian laughed too hard. "You got it."

Laura barely noticed the joke. She looked past the guard at the office interior, scanning the beige walls for wanted posters or computer-created images of her face. Anything that told her to run.

"Do you have your visitor confirmation?" the guard asked.

Brian palmed perspiration from his forehead. "Sure, it's right here." He dug in his pockets, looked confused, grinned, kept searching. "I swear I had it in here." He tugged out a piece of paper, which he dropped. When he picked it up, his face had turned tomato-red.

"Ha ha ha," he said, feeding the paper through. "I can be such a klutz sometimes. Is it hot in here or what?"

He tugged at his shirt, fanning himself.

"Everything okay, Brian?" the guard asked.

Brian took a couple of shallow inhales.

Christ, he's going to pass out.

"Brian?" the guard repeated.

"I, uh." Brian audibly swallowed, sweat trickling freely down his temple. He made a guttural sound as if something was stuck in his throat.

Fuck fuck fuck.

Laura had counted on Brian to get her inside. She'd hoped she could hang back and be as inconspicuous as possible while he made the small talk, got chummy with the staff. But they weren't even going to make it past the lobby. He was crumbling.

As she watched him tug at his collar, something switched in Laura's brain, and she felt herself step forward to rest a hand on his shoulder.

"He had too much coffee this morning," she said in an L.A. drawl. "Makes him as jittery as a virgin on prom night."

This time, she was entirely conscious of the fact that she was speaking with an American accent. Unlike the encounter with Madeleine, when the slip had happened subconsciously, this was on purpose. All part of her cover.

The guard blinked at her.

Laura raised an eyebrow. "Men, right? They're all big with the macho talk, but give them anything stronger than a cranberry juice and they're a mess."

"Yeah." Brian coughed and found his voice. "It tastes so good, though."

Laura rolled her eyes at the guard, who finally stopped frowning.

"Time to cut back, I'd say." She looked down at Brian's form. "So, we have Brian Arenberg and Callie Turner to see Yvonne Lincoln."

"Just hope she's in a good mood," Laura said. "I don't need any more attitude; I've already got kids at home."

"Truth," the guard said. She checked their IDs and Laura kept her gaze steady as the guard looked between her face and her fake ID. She logged her details into the computer, then reached under the desk and a mechanical buzzing sounded as a red light blinked on above a solid-looking door.

"You all have a nice visit," the guard said.

"Thank you, Officer. I'll keep an eye on this one." Laura nudged Brian toward the door and only allowed herself to take a breath when they had passed through it.

"I'm sorry," Brian began, but Laura pressed her fist into the small of his back.

"Just keep moving."

Her mouth felt chalk dry, her knees hollow as they went down a white corridor.

I'm Callie Turner. I'm a badass motherfucker who eats cop soup for breakfast.

Her palms were clammy and she wanted more than anything to scratch her scalp, which was starting to burn under the wig. She dug her fingernails into her palms.

A guard scanned them with a metal detector, then patted them down, and Laura kept expecting to have her arms wrenched behind her back, cold steel at her wrists, but nobody recognized her.

By the time they sat in the hard, mushroom-colored chairs at one of the dozen visitor tables, Laura felt dizzy with adrenaline. She'd sweated through her shirt, which clung to her back, and she couldn't remember how they'd reached the drab visitors' room. If she had to make a break for it now, she'd never find her way out.

A dozen doors stood between her and the outside world, between her and Amy, and even though she was still angry and hurt, Laura suddenly wished her sister were with her.

Just make it count.

Beside her, Brian wheezed, parchment-pale, seemingly even more on edge than Laura.

"Relax," she told him, and he nodded, wiping his upper lip.

Movement came across the room and Laura straightened. She watched as a woman wearing cream prison overalls was escorted over by an unsmiling guard. Her bushy copper hair was brown at the roots. Laura was surprised when the woman sat opposite them, thought maybe there had been a mix-up. Yvonne Lincoln looked nothing like the woman in Brian's film.

"Thirty minutes," the guard said, giving them a stare before turning.

"Thanks, Gus," Yvonne said. Her voice had a drawling quality. Lazy and dismissive. She reclined in her chair, not looking at Laura, and Laura was grateful because she couldn't help staring.

Yvonne had put on at least twenty pounds since the archive interview in Brian's film. Her skin was sallow, sunlight-deprived, and she looked older than her sixty-eight years. Her gaze remained sharp, though.

"Hey, Yvonne," Brian said. "How's it going?"

"Great. Got a manicure this morning and this afternoon I'm hitting the lanes with the girls."

Brian's laugh was tight and Laura winced. She cleared her throat.

"Right, uh, this is Callie," Brian said.

Yvonne's gaze didn't leave his face. "You found a girlfriend. Good for you."

Brian blushed. "Actually, she's a friend."

"Frozen out again. Poor Brian. Did you bring my stuff?"

Brian nodded and moved his hands under the table. Laura glimpsed what looked like a small bottle of hair dye, but then it was gone. She didn't see Yvonne take it, but the next moment, Brian's hands were back resting on the tabletop.

Finally, Yvonne looked at Laura.

"So, what are you doing here, honey? Do murderers get you hot or what?"

Laura remembered sitting in Yvonne's office when she was a kid, just before filming started. Yvonne had seemed so grown-up. She smoked nonstop and her room was covered in script pages and hand-written notes, and when she looked at you, you felt the power of her mind like a blade between the eyes.

"You're the star of this story," she'd told her, jabbing her finger into the desktop. *"Don't let anybody tell you any different, okay, sweetie?"*

She was direct in a similar way to Laura's mother, but the similarities ended there. Laura always got the sense that beneath the hard exterior, Yvonne cared.

Yvonne had brought that same directness into prison. Perhaps it was how she'd survived.

Laura knew how to be direct, too.

"We're trying to track down Ivan Rothschild," she said, dropping back into her British accent and holding Yvonne's gaze. She watched for a reaction while Brian laughed again, sitting on his hands.

"Callie—" he began, but Yvonne cut him off with an indolent drawl.

"Is that so?" Her eyes narrowed and Laura had the feeling of some-body looking right through her, like she was made of glass. "Who did you say you were, honey?"

Laura instinctually thought to lie, then remembered that this time the truth was the point.

"We met a long time ago," she said. "When I was a kid. You said I was the sweetest thing you'd ever seen. A star."

Yvonne's expression didn't change, but Laura saw the shift in her eyes. They became razors, edged with sudden interest.

"Polly," she said, and Laura shot a look at the guard standing twenty feet away.

"Don't worry about Gus," Yvonne said, "he couldn't find his baton with both hands." Her gaze remained on Laura. "You got some guts coming here. Nice disguise, though."

She must have seen the news.

"I just want to find the truth," Laura said.

Yvonne hacked something akin to a laugh.

"Oh, you want the truth? Good luck, sugar. Far as I can figure, there's no such thing, and the American legal system sure doesn't care about it. Go looking for the truth, you better bring a butterfly net, 'cause that's all you're gonna catch."

"Spoken like a convicted criminal," Laura said.

For a moment, she thought she'd blown it. Yvonne would close up like a clam. But then Yvonne threw her head back and laughed so loudly the sound echoed around the visitors' room.

"Wow, kid, who'd have thought you'd grow up to be such a ball-buster? Good for you. I guess some of your mom rubbed off on you."

Laura's shoulders stiffened.

"How is she? Your mom?" Yvonne asked. "Still chasing that Hollywood dream?"

"I'm not here to talk about her," Laura said, and Yvonne looked amused.

"Can't blame you. She always was a pain in the ass."

She knew. They must all have known what her mother was like. Laura took some small comfort in that, although it stirred anger, too. If the *Guesthouse* cast and crew could see what her mother was like, why didn't they do something to stop her? To help Polly? Why didn't her father? He waited until the kidnapping attempt to finally move them to London. What took him so long?

Maybe that was her mother's power. She was scary enough to silence anybody who tried to oppose her, even her family.

When Yvonne spoke next, all humor had left her tone.

"You're alive," she said, her expression giving way to something frailer, more vulnerable. "So many dead, but not you. How?"

"I don't know. We moved. Got out of Hollywood."

Yvonne's hands shifted and Laura saw she was picking her nails. She tried not to look.

"Takes more than moving," Yvonne said. "I'm guessing he has bigger things planned for you. Have you seen him?"

She let the question hang, unblinking, her hands still.

He.

"The Needle Man," Laura said.

Yvonne's expression soured. "You've seen him. Shit."

"You saw him, too?"

Yvonne nodded. "In my dreams at first, then he started coming through in the daytime. That was a treat, lemme tell you." Her gaze darkened. "He poisoned Kenny against me. The morning it happened, the Needle Man took control of Kenny. Made him attack me. I had to protect myself."

Laura frowned. That wasn't her experience. Yvonne's encounter sounded nothing like her own.

"I'm sorry," she said. "I'm sorry you went through that."

Yvonne looked vulnerable for a second, the corners of her mouth downturned, and Laura wondered if she'd cry. Then Yvonne blinked and leaned back in her chair, the drawl returning. "You know, I think about Vince a lot. The first of us to die. Maybe he was the luckiest, too. He had no idea what happened to him. The rest of us? We knew it was only a matter of time."

"Why? What do you know?"

Yvonne leaned forward and rested her forearms on the tabletop.

"So many stories out there. So many puff-piece theories. Some people blamed the soundstage for the curse, some of them our director." Her handcuffs rattled. "Hell, most of them would love to think *I* created the curse, that I'm some kind of witch who hexed the script, and dammit, I wish I was. I could make it all go away."

She went still. Her voice emerged raw as onions. "Everybody knows Hollywood creates monsters. You stick around Hollywood long enough, you see monsters everywhere. Seems to me, this is just one of 'em."

"You're saying the movie made a real monster."

"I hear the way it sounds, sugar, don't you worry. But here's some advice for free: never underestimate the power of a movie."

Laura's scalp itched and she felt the truth hovering just beyond her reach. Maybe Yvonne was right. Maybe the Needle Man had crossed into reality. Beverly had said something similar. Or maybe they were all crazy.

We all go a little mad sometimes.

Laura straightened. Focused.

"You want it to go away," she said. "Tell us where we can find Ivan Rothschild, and I think I can make that happen. Stop anybody else dying."

She realized she believed it, even though she had no proof that tracking down Ivan would end anything.

But it was all they had. She had no choice but to believe it.

Brian inched closer to the table, as if in anticipation of an answer, and Laura cursed him when she saw the wariness return to Yvonne's expression.

"What do you want with that creep?"

"He wrote the original script, right? What if he's the one behind it all? It all goes back to him."

Yvonne looked down at Laura's hands, and Laura realized she was picking her own nails. She gripped her fingers tightly, forcing herself to stop.

"Yvonne?" she said.

The other woman looked like she'd chipped a tooth. "I never liked that man. Never trust anybody who won't give you a straight answer."

"Please. Will you tell us where to find him?"

Yvonne raised a hand and sucked blood from her fingertip. She'd picked her nail raw.

"Better off not knowing," she said.

"We don't have a choice."

Yvonne sighed.

She lowered her hand, and Laura understood what Brian meant about her savoring the tiny scrap of power she had left. The power of somebody who would spend the rest of her life having every bowel movement and sip of fresh air controlled by other people.

"He's out east of L.A.," Yvonne said finally. "Got a place in Victorville, 1428 Woodgreen Avenue."

Laura felt as if a window had been opened. She breathed a fraction easier as she committed the address to memory.

"If you go see that freaky fuck, though," Yvonne added, "and by God, I hope you don't, do it in the daytime. It's the best way. Safer."

"We will. Thank you."

"Oh, you're welcome, honey." Yvonne's gaze swept her face, a smile playing on her lips, and for a brief moment, they were back in that office thirty years ago, a screenwriter and her lead actor about to embark on a terrible journey together.

"You're still the star, all these years later," Yvonne said. She leaned forward and Laura smelled cigarettes and perspiration. She feared Yvonne would try to touch her, to grab her hands, but the reality was worse. The older woman's voice emerged light as smoke, thick with foreboding.

"You be careful, honey. You know, these days, even the star can die. *Especially* the star."

The weirdest thing about one of the most haunted films of all time is that, on the surface, it isn't weird at all. *Bachelor Pad* (1989) follows three buddies in their early thirties living together in a New York apartment. Their cheap-'n'-easy party lifestyle is interrupted when one of the guys' ex-wives shows up with the kids, leaving the roommates with two middle-graders to look after—forever. High jinks and warm-hearted messages about family and responsibility ensue. Easy peasy, right?

Wrong. *Bachelor Pad* never made it in front of cameras because its leading men had a horrible habit of dying. Steve Fox was up for a role first, but he died in his sleep, choked on his own vomit after a night of partying. Second was Bill Curtis, who made it as far as the dress rehearsal before he was killed in a car accident. And, finally, Glen Moore wanted a slice of the *Bachelor Pad* pie, only to have a heart attack at a restaurant just around the corner from the studio. Which just goes to show that movies can kill you even when you haven't shot a single reel of film.

TWENTY-TWO

Beverly drove. Brian sat in the front passenger seat, where he returned to drumming the car door, which left Laura to sit in the back with Amy.

Out of the corner of her eye, she caught her sister looking at her. She focused on the neighborhoods that flashed by in quick succession. Tired, sun-fried houses on arid, dirt-brown streets. The sun struggled through a layer of smog that refused to shift.

It felt like they were driving headlong into the apocalypse.

"This guy better have answers," Laura said.

"Assuming he doesn't trap us in the basement," Amy said, "then try to wear our skin."

Laura fell silent. If she uttered even one word, it would give Amy the impression that she was okay with the terrible choices she'd made, when really she wanted to call her a spoiled brat who only ever thought about herself.

A month was the longest they had ever gone without speaking. Laura was eighteen, Amy fifteen. Amy wanted to go to a rock concert with a bunch of friends, and their parents said she could only go if

Laura went, too. Laura refused. She knew Amy's friends would want to get loaded and she'd rather jet salt water into her eyes than party with them. Besides, it was the season finale of *The O.C.* Amy threw a tantrum, screamed that Laura was a selfish bitch, and refused to look at her for a month.

The stalemate only broke when Amy drunk-called Laura a month later to pick her up from a house party. She begged her not to tell their parents, and Laura felt so sorry for her, she agreed. They'd driven home without saying anything and their parents were still none the wiser.

"We're running low on gas," Beverly said.

Laura saw the gauge quivering. "We'll stop somewhere on the way."

"You look good as a blond again," Amy said, and Laura realized she was still wearing the wig. She'd gotten used to it, but now that she was aware of it, it scratched her scalp all over again.

"Pill?"

Laura shifted to look out the window.

"Can we please talk about this?"

Laura's eyes stung as she tried not to blink. Not to show any reaction whatsoever.

"I don't want to die with you angry at me," Amy said.

"You're not going to die."

"Track record says otherwise."

"Can we stop with the drama?" Laura said.

"I'm not being dramatic, I'm being real. Three people are dead and the odds aren't in our favor. I need you to know I'm sorry. I didn't mean to hurt you. That's the last thing I wanted to do."

Laura firmed her lips together. She watched houses shoot by.

"It's not so easy for the rest of us," Amy said, her voice smaller. "You had *The Guesthouse* handed to you, and when that didn't work out, you moved into journalism. Just like that. Some of us don't get those breaks, not even after years."

"It wasn't *just like that* and you know it," Laura said. "I was seven when the movie came about! And I worked really fucking hard at becoming a journalist."

"Please. You barely broke a sweat and you were qualified."

"You don't know what you're talking about."

"Don't I?"

Anger throbbed in Laura's sternum. Amy knew how difficult Laura found growing up in the shadow of *The Guesthouse*, how hard she worked at establishing herself as a journalist, at the cost of just about everything else in her life. Amy was just trying to make herself feel better.

"Judi Dench was sixty-one when she made *GoldenEye*," Brian said.

Amy looked at him. "What?"

"Y'know, it's never too late? The business isn't quite as ageist as it used to be."

Amy sighed. "Thanks, Bri." She returned her attention to Laura, reached out to touch her arm. "Pill, please—"

"Don't," Laura said, pulling away. "The Gypsy Rose Lee thing is getting really old."

Amy's face screwed up. "What the fu—"

The car screeched to a stop.

Up front, Beverly stared out the windshield at the road. They were the only car in sight, a gas station ahead. It was the only building visible in acres of barren land.

"Beverly?" Laura asked. "Are you okay?" She shifted forward in her seat, touching Beverly's shoulder.

Beverly jumped and turned wide eyes on her, face pinched.

"Are you okay?" Laura repeated.

Beverly swallowed, then faced forward again.

"I'm pulling into that gas station," she said. "And only partly because we need gas."

Nobody spoke while Beverly filled up the tank.

When she was done, she went and stood by the road to smoke a cigarette. Laura unclipped her seat belt and joined her. She knew a guy at college with misophonia. If things got too loud, he freaked out.

Was that how it felt for Beverly? Only, there wasn't any escaping the noise when it was in her head. She noticed the shadows under Beverly's eyes, the faint bruising around her neck, and saw her hand shake as she dragged on the cigarette. She looked strung out.

"You don't have to do this," Laura said.

"I do."

"We can get by."

Beverly stared out at the land. "Trust me, you can't."

"What does that mean?"

Beverly inhaled, hugging herself with one arm. "I saw those things for a reason. The person trashing your room, planting the fortune-teller. I wouldn't have seen it if I couldn't help. I'm a part of this."

"You almost died," Laura said.

"There are worse things than dying."

Laura couldn't help smiling. Beverly had really nailed the tortured-psychic schtick. And Laura realized that Yvonne Lincoln had said something similar about Vince. He died years ago. Laura was the one still kicking around, a growing pile of bodies at her back.

"Just let me know if you need a time-out," Laura said. "I don't want you to get hurt again."

Beverly pursed her lips, kept her gaze on the horizon. Finally, she exhaled a halo of smoke and looked at Laura. She winked.

"I'm not going anywhere."

Laura had to admit she was relieved.

They drove in silence for the final few miles to Woodgreen Avenue. Laura spent most of that time trying to puzzle out what was going on with Beverly. She understood her wanting to prove that she could still help people, but she'd been hanged, almost died. Laura wouldn't blame her if she bailed.

By the time they pulled up outside a large suburban house, Laura's head ached. Her energy reserves were spent, but she couldn't give up now.

This is on you. Get it together.

Laura went first, getting out of the car and pausing momentarily as she approached the house. She couldn't help wondering what lay within. Couldn't help thinking the place looked like it belonged on Elm Street. The austere porch curved like an inverted jawbone, while the half-dozen sash windows crammed together in toothlike rows, jostling for space.

She knew it was cliché to feel like a house was looking at you, but that didn't stop goose bumps crawling over her forearms. She gritted her teeth, forced herself toward the yellow door. And knocked.

The woman who answered looked dead on her feet. Brown hair framed a pale face, and her green eyes flicked from Laura to the three people at her back.

"Yes?"

"Hi, my name's Laura Warren. I was hoping to talk to Ivan."

The woman's gaze sharpened and Laura wondered if this was going to be a difficult negotiation, but then she realized the look wasn't annoyance or suspicion. It was a sad kind of surprise.

"You haven't heard." The woman sighed. "Ivan died this week. I'm Ruth, his daughter."

"Oh, I'm sorry."

"Thanks. How did you know him?"

"We worked on a movie a while back," Laura said. "We haven't seen each other in years. I was in town, so I thought I'd surprise him. I'm so sorry for your loss."

"Thank you."

She had to know. She had to ask.

"How did he—" Laura began, but the woman cut in before she could complete the question.

"Suicide. He jumped off a bridge near LAX a few days ago."

Laura felt the energy drain out of her, like a plug had been pulled. She remembered the man falling. The rag-doll limbs and the silent impact as he hit the pavement. She'd only been in L.A. for an hour when she saw the jumper. It had felt like a bad omen. A horrible tragedy. A man had lost his life.

And now here she was at the dead man's house.

Her legs felt like tissue paper, but she managed to take a breath and continue.

"I'm sorry," she said. "I had no idea."

Concern flashed across Ruth's face.

"Do you want to come in? I'm only here another hour before I start my work shift. There's so much to sort through. But if you need to sit down . . ."

Laura resisted the urge to jump in the car and drive away. Drive until she ran out of road. But she knew they might still find answers here. Ivan was dead, but his daughter was inviting her into his home, no questions asked. It was more than she could have hoped for.

"Yes, thank you," she said.

She went inside, introducing Beverly, Brian, and Amy. They all nodded, looking uneasy. They let Laura ask the questions.

"Dad was sort of a pack rat," Ruth said by way of an apology, leading them through a winding maze of rooms. "He never threw anything out. It's going to take weeks to go through everything."

Bookcases filled every available space, their shelves loaded with faded volumes. The atmosphere felt oppressive, like the house was holding its breath, and Laura tried to focus. Tried to stop seeing the man on the bridge.

The living room was filled with cardboard boxes. Ruth started to load books into them, resuming the job she must have been doing when the doorbell rang. No wonder she looked tired. Laura noticed a framed photo of what must be Ivan with his grandkids. He looked stern even though he was smiling, as if his face wasn't accustomed to laughter.

Laura found herself staring at the hollow cheeks and bushy eyebrows, willing herself to recognize him, but he was a stranger.

"Which movie did you work on with him?" Ruth asked.

"What?" Laura tried to pull herself together. "*The Guesthouse.*"

Ruth stopped moving. "Oh."

"Did he ever talk about it?" Amy asked.

"You mean the movie that ruined his life?" Ruth said it like a joke, but her voice held an edge. "Hardly ever. If one of us brought it up, he got real quiet, and we knew we were in trouble."

"Even years later?" Laura asked.

Ruth nodded. "More than ever. It's like it grew in his mind. I don't think he ever got over them stealing his idea."

"I'm sorry," Laura said again, feeling foolish because "sorry" never cut it. "Sorry" was a comfort blanket embroidered with thorns.

"Were you close?" she asked. Laura noticed Beverly standing with her head slightly tilted, as if she were listening to something other than the conversation. The sight unnerved her, and she was glad when Ruth spoke.

"Not particularly. He spent most of his time writing, and even when he wasn't, it was obvious he was thinking about it. It made having any kind of a relationship with him pretty difficult." She paused, looking at a copy of *We Have Always Lived in the Castle.*

"Jesus, he loved this one." She seemed to realize everybody was looking at her. "Sorry. It's only been four days, but it feels like months. He behaved strangely for so long, but it got worse this year. We should've seen it coming."

"Strangely how?" Laura asked.

Ruth considered her. "Paranoid, I guess. He said people were trying to break into his home. He talked about seeing them in the house at night. Hearing voices. He refused to see a doctor. When we suggested that, he stopped talking about the things he saw. Became distant."

Laura thought of her own parents. After the supermarket incident, her father became hypervigilant, borderline paranoid. He wouldn't let her out of his sight. Things only improved when they moved and Laura quit acting.

She looked at Amy, wondering what it was like for her growing up. Nothing had seemed to faze her. She had appeared to be the typical second child, impervious to external forces.

Had Ivan been losing his mind? Or had people really been in his house?

She tried not to think about the man standing in the corner of her hotel room, but he was there in her memory, a black smudge, a nest of festering mold.

She refocused on Ruth.

"Have you come across any of his film stuff?" she asked. "I loaned him a script a while back."

A lie for a truth. It would all balance in the end.

"Dad's office is full of scripts," Ruth said. "It might be in there. I'll show you."

The office was in the back of the house, a small room filled with yet more books and files. The desk was heaped with papers, the blinds drawn at the window so that the room marinated in the scent of cigars and age.

"I haven't had the energy to sort through this room yet," Ruth said.

Somewhere in the house, a phone rang. Ruth excused herself and Laura looked around the room, wondering where to begin.

Beverly touched a box file.

"Here," she said, wiping dust from it. While Brian examined the books, Laura cleared a space on the desk and opened the file, revealing a stockpile of crinkled yellow paper. Articles and newspaper clippings. A notebook that was moldy with age. Laura felt a pang of longing for her missing journal.

"What is all of this?" Amy asked.

"Occult research," Beverly said, picking through the box. Laura leafed through the articles. Images and words jumped out at her. Woodcut prints of horned beasts with serpentine tongues. The words "demonic possession" and "orgiastic evil."

"He was into the occult?" Brian asked. "He never said."

"It's just movie research," Beverly said. "For some script he was writing, I guess. None of these sources are reputable." She went through the pages. "*Wiccan Web*, the *Journal of Paranormal Occurrences & Tragedies*, *Spirits R Us*. This is layman stuff."

"Who's this?" Laura took out a black-and-white headshot of a bearded man wearing Coke-bottle glasses and a Mona Lisa smile.

"Reggie Whitstaff," Beverly said. "He was an old-school paranormal investigator in the early 1900s. He was famous for investigating the case of a little girl who predicted how people would die. She predicted Whitstaff would be killed by lightning."

"Was he?" Amy asked.

Beverly shrugged. "In a manner of speaking. He died during surgery. There was a malfunction in the operating room, an electrical fault, he took ten thousand volts. Died on the table."

Laura turned the photo over and tensed.

On the back of the photo, a mess of rough, black lines had been scrawled. They joined to form the shape of a shadowy figure wearing a long coat. Its fingers were sharp blades.

The Needle Man.

It wasn't the Needle Man from the movie or the TV show, though.

It was the one Laura had seen in her nightmares.

The doodle appeared to be Ivan's work. Perhaps something he sketched on the fly while writing the movie. She pictured him grabbing the first piece of paper he could find and feverishly scratching lines into the back of the photograph.

Or had he drawn it while looking at the Needle Man?

A sketch of a monster leering at him in the dark?

Laura shivered and replaced the picture. She sifted through a couple more documents, then stopped as she came to a black-and-white photograph of a wind-beaten house. It was part of a newspaper clipping, but she didn't register the headline or the copy text. All she saw was the house.

A house she had never visited, but recognized as if she had lived a lifetime there.

It was the house from her dreams.

With a feeling of encroaching panic, she took in the headline.

"HAUNTED" HOTEL CONDEMNED
AFTER LATEST DEATH

The article talked about a hotel called Gimlet Point that closed in 1964 amid rumors it was cursed.

Laura examined the grainy picture. The house stood alone, set far back from the road, a stark wooden structure that was all sharp angles.

She couldn't help the cold that stole through her.

"What's that?" Amy asked.

"Rothschild didn't invent the guesthouse, he based it on a true story. A real place." Laura was so stunned, she forgot she was angry with her sister.

"Seriously?" Brian said. "Where?"

"The Gimlet Point Guesthouse in Craven, California."

"I've heard of Craven. It's a railroad ghost town that boomed with Route 66. It became abandoned in the 1970s when new highways were built. It's one of, like, hundreds of ghost towns out in the Mojave area."

"Sounds like the perfect creepy place to inspire a horror movie," Amy said.

"Hell, yeah." Brian came over to look at the article. "That's wild. I had no clue."

"Me neither," Laura said. "Listen: *The closure comes after a series of unexplained deaths on the premises. The most recent person to die was Anne Stackhouse, 32, who fell from the balcony last month.'"*

She couldn't believe it. All these years and she had never heard of Gimlet Point or the deaths that plagued it.

"What else?" Beverly asked. Damn her, she was good. She could tell Laura was holding back.

"I've seen Gimlet Point before."

"You have?" Amy said. "Where?"

"It's the house I see when I'm asleep. The one I've seen ever since I was a kid."

"Are you sure?"

Laura nodded. She had never been more sure of anything.

"Shit." Brian looked like he couldn't decide if he was excited or terrified.

Laura took out her phone and opened the maps app. She typed *Gimlet Point Guesthouse* into the search field and watched a pin drop in the middle of the Mojave, two hours east of their current location in Victorville. She switched the map to satellite view and held her breath as a rocky, pixelated gold-and-brown landscape revealed itself. It looked like another planet.

Pinching the screen, she zoomed in to the point where the pin rested, waiting for the pixels to fill in.

One by painful one, they began to appear. First the sun-scarred earth, then the slate-gray beginnings of a building.

The guesthouse began to reveal itself.

She glimpsed a bird's-eye view of a dilapidated roof sitting in the middle of nowhere, surrounded by dried-out terrain and—

The screen turned black.

The battery had died.

"Shit."

Laura stared at her bug-eyed reflection in the screen, her mind wheeling.

Just before the battery died, she had caught sight of something dark and solid, and she knew with absolute certainty that the guest-house was still out there. Just a couple of hours away. So close they could be there by nightfall.

It was just there.

Waiting.

THE CRAVEN BUL

"HAUNTED" HOTEL CONDEMNED AFTER LATEST DEATH

—— June 1964. Craven, CA. ——

Gimlet Point Guesthouse has permanently closed its doors after nearly fifty years.

The closure comes after a series of unexplained deaths on the premises. The most recent person to die was Anne Stackhouse, 32, who fell from the balcony last month. A year ago, a chef died after suffering severe burns in a kitchen fire.

Owner Harold Cusick, who immigrated to the United States in the 1940s and styled his hotel after British "guesthouses," maintains that the building is safe. "They say the place is cursed, but I've lived here for years with no bother," he told us. "Nobody wants to stay here anymore, though. I had no choice but to close. I'm heartbroken."

Gimlet Point Guesthouse is just the latest closure in Craven, which has struggled to attract visitors.

TWENTY-THREE

The diner felt like it was perched at the end of the world, gathering dust while it watched America burn. But at least it had AC.

Goose bumps prickled Laura's forearms as she stepped in from the desert heat, taking in the gleaming metal counter, the red booths, and the checkered floor. The jukebox looked like an original from the '50s, as did the neon signs flashing *VERONICA'S DINER* and *ELVIS LIVES*.

Laura scanned for cops but didn't see any, only a couple of patrons who must've been regulars since the turn of the century. Stopping off at the diner was risky, but they all needed a break from the car, and even Brian was getting hangry. Laura just hoped her disguise held.

"There's one free in the back," Amy said, brushing past Laura and heading to a corner booth. Laura followed and slid in to sit by the window, twisting the blind closed against the endless empty land. She kept her shades on, ball cap jammed over the blond wig.

"I could eat a horse," Brian said, picking up a laminated menu. "Or a cow, whichever comes with a side of fries."

"You big hungry nerd hunk, you," Amy teased.

"Heh, this sort of feels like a double date?" Brian said, nodding at Beverly opposite him.

"Oh sure," Amy said, "if hunting a supernatural murderer floats your boat."

"I'm taking it."

Laura set down her menu. The words wouldn't stop moving on the page and she couldn't think over the ache of tension in her neck.

The guesthouse was real.

She didn't need the newspaper article to remember every detail of it. All she had to do was close her eyes. She'd dreamed about it for years, never knowing what it was. What it meant. And without even really looking, she'd found the answer in a decaying file in a dead stranger's office.

Far from resolving themselves, the questions in her mind were dividing and multiplying like cells. Like a virus. Infecting every part of her. And now she was a slave to them.

After leaving Ivan Rothschild's house, they'd sat and argued for a while before everybody accepted that they had to drive out to Craven. It seemed impossible not to, especially when Brian discovered that the road from Victorville to Craven was named the Needles Freeway.

Laura got chills when she heard that. The kind that rushed to her crown and made her dizzy. She shouldn't have expected it to be called anything else—reality had taken on a fuzzy quality, like the time she took codeine for a pinched nerve in her back. Now it was as if she were following a predestined course, like plot beats, mapped out by somebody else but impossible to deny.

What did she hope to find out there in Craven? Somebody waiting with a smile and a confession? Somebody who revealed they had been messing with her life? Somebody who looked like the Needle Man?

"You should eat," Amy said, noticing Laura's discarded menu when the waitress came over. "I'll order for you. We'll take a couple burgers and fries, and a couple Diet Cokes."

"Same for me," Brian said.

"Just coffee," Beverly said, handing back the menu. "Black."

"You got it, hon."

When the waitress returned to the counter, they sat in silence. Laura's belly groaned, a sound like that of a dying animal. She wasn't sure she'd be able to keep anything down.

"Man, I wish I'd brought my camera," Brian said, tapping the tabletop. "This is exactly what the documentary is missing, a bona fide investigation into the origins of *The Guesthouse*."

"I still have my phone," Amy said, waving it. "Although I'm going to have to buy more cloud space. Video files aren't small."

Brian looked at Laura. "Are you sure you won't sit for an interview for the doc? The fans would go wild. They're desperate to find out what you've been doing all these years."

"They'll just be disappointed."

"Nah, they'll love you. Horror fans are for life."

"People don't want the truth. They want a beginning, middle, and end, with some kind of poignant coda to top it all off. The truth doesn't matter to them."

"Give it to them anyway," Amy said.

Laura looked down at her hands, her knuckles knotted together. She'd been dancing around the truth for so long, it seemed somehow vulnerable now. Something ailing, in need of protection.

"I saw Ivan die," she said.

"What?" Amy frowned at her.

"When we were driving from the airport, right after I landed at LAX. I saw a man jump from a bridge over the highway. Well, he fell."

Amy and Brian stared at her.

"That's . . ." Amy began.

"One hell of a coincidence," Laura finished for her. "Except what if it wasn't? What if he knew I was coming?"

Nobody said anything.

"You heard what his daughter said. Rothschild was obsessed with how he got screwed over by *The Guesthouse*. And we all saw the occult stuff in his office. What if he cursed the film, back in the nineties, caused all the deaths? And then the reboot streaming series came along; another piece of a pie he'd never get to taste."

"Why kill himself, though?" Amy said.

"He could be—" Laura began.

"A sacrifice," Beverly cut in. They all looked at her. "He offered himself up. His death for the deaths of everybody involved in *It Feeds*."

"Like the tourists in *Midsommar*," Brian murmured. "And, well, everybody in *Cabin in the Woods*."

"This isn't a movie," Laura said, a little harsher than she intended, because she had just realized that Ivan brought the death tally up to four.

Halfway through, her mind whispered, and she inwardly recoiled.

Eight people died after *The Guesthouse*.

Would another eight end up in the ground thanks to *It Feeds*?

She couldn't let that happen. The need filled her like a different kind of hunger. One that would only be sated by her keeping people alive.

Brian blushed and took a straw from the holder.

Amy leaned back. "If Rothschild's the one behind this, shouldn't we be ransacking his office for a way to stop him?"

"Yeah or, like, we could consecrate his grave," Brian added, twirling the straw in one hand.

Laura took off her shades and set them on the table. "We're going to Craven. The Gimlet Point Guesthouse is where it all started, I'm sure of it. It's the place that inspired Rothschild to write *The Guesthouse*. It's the place I've seen all these years. It feels right."

She gave Beverly a questioning look. Beverly nodded.

Amy's gaze hovered on Laura. "There's one big thing we still don't know."

"What?"

"Why you and Brian survived when nobody else did."

Brian dropped his straw.

"Think about it," Amy continued. "If Rothschild is killing every-body involved in the movie and, now, the series, why has he left you, its star, alive all these years? What's so special about you? No offense."

"You're trying to rationalize the irrational," Laura said.

"Maybe because you were kids back then," Amy mused.

"Or Laura's the Final Girl," Brian said. "The one person who gets to survive. Which doesn't bode well for me."

"Didn't somebody already make that movie?" Amy said.

Laura felt the past clutching for her once more, remembered what they were running from, and the booth suddenly felt too small. She felt trapped the way she had on the plane.

"I have to get out," she said. Brian stumbled to his feet and let her pass, and she tugged at her wig as she crossed the diner floor to the ladies' bathroom. She shouldered the blood-red door and went into one of the stalls, sitting on the toilet and breathing.

One, five, seven, nine . . .

Counting helped.

Counting made space for air.

She'd lost track of how many times she'd freaked out on a toilet seat in the United States. Maybe this was her new thing. A new ritual to accompany the numbers. Hide in a cubicle until the world got less scary.

Her brain struggled to contain everything they'd learned: a writer she'd never heard of, who was into the occult; Yvonne's theory about movies having a life of their own; Beverly's talk of entities and puppet masters. And then there were the things Beverly had seen. The visions of somebody trashing her hotel, planting the dress, scratching *She's here* in Kyle's trailer.

Gimlet Point Guesthouse.

It felt like they were overlooking something vital that would tie it all together, but what?

She tensed at the soft creak of the door.

A shadow rippled across the floor, long and narrow.

"Pill?"

Laura flinched at Amy's voice.

"Pill, are you okay?"

Laura's chest unclenched. For a second, the shadow had looked like the Needle Man, but it had changed after Amy spoke.

"I just need a minute," Laura said, her voice hoarse. She sat and listened to the AC, trying to calm her breathing. Trying to get a grip. But the hallucinations seemed so real, and no matter what she did, she felt herself being sucked toward the inevitable. Everything that had happened since she touched down in L.A. felt part of something larger.

She'd seen Ivan Rothschild fall before she knew it was him.

She'd been there when Todd Terror burned alive in the shower.

When the Needle Man came for Kyle.

Dark vines tightened around her, smooth and strong as electrical wire.

The dark vines of fate.

"Pill?"

She jumped. Amy was still there.

"You could have told me," Amy said softly through the door. "About the guy on the bridge."

"You could have told me about the documentary."

Amy's shadow didn't move.

"I'm sorry. I wanted to." Amy paused, as if in thought. "But I have the right to talk about my own life. *The Guesthouse* is part of my past, too. I can't remember anything before it."

Laura supposed that was true. Amy was four when the movie was made. It had been there for more of her life than Laura's. How had she never realized that?

"Just leave me alone for a minute, will you?"

"Now you sound like Mom," Amy said.

Laura was up and opening the stall door before she knew it.

"Seriously?" she said.

Amy stepped back and leaned against the basin, an innocent look on her face.

"Thought that might get you out of there."

"Take it back."

"Take what back?"

"I'm nothing like her."

"Okay," Amy said, meaning the opposite.

Christ.

She couldn't listen to this. Laura started for the door that led back into the restaurant.

"Right, walk away as usual," Amy said lightly, though there was a dark undercurrent to her tone.

Laura stopped. Faced her. "What do you want me to say?" she said.

"I don't want to argue."

"Then stop pissing me off."

"It's just . . ." Amy's shoulders cranked up and then she let out a sigh, as if giving in to whatever was digging at her. "Our entire lives it's been about you. You know that, right? How *you* turned your back on a superstar career. How *you* had the potential for so much more. How *you* think you broke Mom—"

She stopped as if she'd bitten her tongue.

"I think what?" Laura said. When Amy didn't reply, she added, "I don't think I broke Mom."

"Okay."

"I *don't*," Laura said, but Amy didn't look pissed anymore. She looked like she felt sorry for her. As if Laura couldn't see what was right in front of her. Laura shook her head, opened her mouth to deny it again, but her thoughts flooded with the stare her mom had given her that day she came home for her dad's birthday five years ago. The first day Pamela Tremaine didn't recognize her own daughter. The first sign of her fragmenting mind.

And before that, when Laura was eight and they'd moved to London, there were days her mom didn't leave her bedroom. There were days she didn't eat or bathe or speak, let alone look at her. She pined for her L.A. life. And it only got worse when her mother finally took a secretarial job at a local business, because it meant the fight had left her. It had curdled into spite.

Laura knew she was the reason her mom's life was ruined. She'd had it all, and then she had nothing, to hell with the awful circumstances that set it in motion.

She heard her mother's voice, low and hissing.

"Pull yourself together!"

She looked down at her wrists. They burned as if held in an iron grip.

One, five, nine . . .

"Fuck," Laura said, pacing, her boots loud on the tiles. It was there, buried amid the anger and resentment, poking into the light like a shard of metal. Guilt. Overwhelming guilt about her mom.

"You didn't," Amy said. "Break her. Just for the record. But she sure made us feel that way. Do you remember the way she reacted when you got a place in Manchester?"

Laura nodded. It was difficult to forget the fact that their mom nearly burned down the house when she put a greasy pan in the oven.

"Don't you wish you could tell her how much she fucked us up?" Amy said.

Laura's throat clamped tight. Her chest was on fire. Part of her wanted to defend their mom, to tell Amy to shut up, some primal instinct, but the rest of her wanted nothing more than to scream and howl three decades' worth of fury and hurt.

"I wish I could tell her how *angry* I am," Amy said. "How *afraid* I was. How dogshit I felt when she gave up on me ever landing a commercial or a TV gig."

Laura saw their old front door opening.

Five-year-old Amy entering. Sobbing quietly.

Their mother behind her, face like stone.

She saw her mother as she was now, smiling and soft and vacant.

"We can't," Laura said. "It would be cruel."

"As cruel as putting a six-year-old on a diet plan?"

The truth hummed between them, and Laura felt her body shaking. Emotion filled every atom of her, hot and bright.

"She loved us," she said. "But she hated us, too."

They stood looking at each other, tears tracking their cheeks, and they could be children. They could be old women. Age was meaningless in the face of their pain. It never went away.

"I'm sorry I didn't tell you about Brian's movie," Amy said, and she sounded sincere. Her voice crackled when she said, "I don't want to lose you, Pill."

Laura frowned. "You're not going to lose me."

Amy swatted a tear from her face. "You're never around."

"We talk all the time."

"We *text* all the time. You push people away, Pill. It's what you do. Look at Mike. He's in love with you and you've kept him at arm's length for years."

"Mike's in love with the idea of me."

"Well, I'm in love with the reality of you. And I can't live without you, okay? I can't."

Laura started to speak, but it was as if something had clicked into place. A piece that had been rattling around in her brain for years without finding the right slot.

The whiskey incident when they were teenagers. The boyfriends with tattoos and the time Amy declared she was vegan, but they all knew she was sneaking meat from the fridge. The reason she hated

Beverly without reason and flirted with Brian despite her less-than-zero interest in him.

Amy had been crying out for attention her whole life.

And the person whose attention she really wanted was Laura's.

How had she never seen that? Sourly, Laura wondered if she was more like her mom than she wanted to admit.

She stepped forward and put her arms around her sister. Squeezed her. Tried to show her she did care, even if she couldn't always say it. Amy was shaking.

"I'm in love with the reality of you, too," Laura said firmly.

"Even the blabbermouth part that never knows when to shut up?"

"Even the blabbermouth part." Laura released her, raising a weary smile. "And who knows, maybe all this press will be good for you. 'Sister of notorious murderer dazzles Hollywood'? Stranger things have happened."

Amy grinned through tears. "You do owe me." The grin faded. "Do you really think this is all some kind of supernatural revenge game set up by Ivan Rothschild?"

"I wish I didn't."

"If you believe it, so do I."

"Thanks."

Amy cleared her throat. "But I still don't trust Beverly."

"I can live with that."

An hour later, they pulled into the lot of the Twilight Sun motel. They needed time to regroup, figure out a plan of action. They couldn't just bowl up to Gimlet Point like a bunch of teenagers with a death wish. Not when they had no clue what they'd find. The motel would make a decent base, somewhere to retreat to if it all went south.

The Twilight Sun was tired and sun-faded, but there was only one other car in the lot, which was exactly what they needed. No witnesses. Nobody to squint at Laura and decide she looked a bit like the psycho on the news.

"Why do all motels in America look like they're run by some guy with mommy issues?" Amy asked.

"Because they probably are," Laura said.

They got a couple of rooms with a connecting door and gathered in the room taken by Brian and Beverly. Laura perched on the edge of a threadbare couch, while Beverly sat at the table by the window. She seemed lost in thought and Laura felt sure she hadn't looked at her since the diner.

"All right!" Brian cried, flicking through TV stations. "*The Omen*! I love this one."

"It's all for you, Brian," Amy said, sitting on one of the beds.

"Oh, man, they're showing the remake right after."

"*Aw*, Bri. The remake sucks."

"No, it's actually pretty solid. Remakes aren't always bad. There's *The Thing, The Hills Have Eyes, The Fly, The Crazies* . . . Even Hitchcock remade his own stuff. I bet the *Guesthouse* remake would've been awesome."

"Don't you love it when he talks dirty?" Amy wiggled her eyebrows at Laura.

"I always liked the new *Parent Trap*," Beverly said. "The one with the mean girl." At their looks, she said, "What?"

Brian chuckled. "I took you more as a horror fan."

"Those films always kill the psychic. Besides, 'remake' is a redundant term. It's impossible to make something twice. Lightning never strikes the same place twice because the same place is never there a second time."

Nobody said anything.

"What were we talking about again?" Brian said.

Amy laughed, but Laura's mind was elsewhere. It was fixed on their destination. The real guesthouse.

Something about it felt right in a way that was wrong. She imagined the house tugging at her, as if an invisible cord ran from her solar plexus to its front door. The connection had been there her whole life, she'd just failed to notice it before.

What if Ivan was there waiting for them?

As Brian chattered about movies and Beverly pondered the grooves in the tabletop, Laura came to a cold realization.

Whatever happened at the guesthouse, she probably wouldn't survive.

She was going to Gimlet Point and she was certain she'd never leave it.

Like the movie's tagline said, *Checking in was the easy part.*

Checking out could be the end of her.

She wondered what they'd write about her when she was dead. When she wasn't there to force a fact-check or a retraction. The way things were going, she'd be branded a murderer just like Yvonne Lincoln. They'd continue to mythologize her life the way they always had—and there wasn't a thing she could do about it.

But she wasn't dead yet.

This was still her story.

She stood, picked up Amy's bag, and went into the bathroom. With the door closed, she peeled off the wig, scratching her scalp with her fingernails and sighing with relief. She shirked out of the T-shirt Beverly had loaned her, then tugged yellow fabric from Amy's bag. The dress she'd found in her suitcase days ago. Without hesitating, she pulled it over her head and assessed her reflection.

She'd been so scared when she found it in her suitcase, terrified she was losing her mind or that somebody knew her true identity. She was sick of the worry. It was exhausting.

She was Laura Warren and Polly Tremaine and Tammy Manners.

It was time she owned her past, once and forever.

She took a breath and opened the bathroom door.

"Why are you wearing that?" Amy asked, staring at her like she'd cut holes in a trash bag.

Laura smoothed the buttercup-yellow folds. She wore it over her jeans, like a punk rock princess.

"Don't you like it?"

"It's creepy."

Laura shrugged. "Somebody made this for me, so I'm going to wear it."

Amy looked at her as if she'd finally lost it. Laura didn't blink.

"Well, all right, then," her sister said. "Whatever gets you through this."

"Is your phone charged?" Laura asked.

Amy nodded. "What's up?"

Laura's gaze switched between her and Brian, her mind already decided.

"I'm ready to do the interview."

If it's ghosts hiding in plain sight that tickle your tulip, look no further than *Kangaroo* (1985), an Australian mockumentary about a killer marsupial attacking travelers in the Outback. Check out the scene in which star Dani Vallance goes to sleep in her tent. If you look to the right of the screen, you can clearly see a face pushing through the fabric to watch her. But here's the thing: nobody else was on location that day. It was a weekend shoot and only a skeleton crew of four people was working, all of them inside the tent with Vallance. I don't know about you, but this one definitely gives me the willies Down Under.

TWENTY-FOUR

Laura tried to settle into the couch, but the springs dug into her thighs and she was painfully aware of everybody looking at her. She had removed the wig and prosthetics and the effect was exposing. There was nothing left to hide behind. Brian moved the table over to use as a makeshift camera stand. He balanced Amy's phone on top, rested it sideways widescreen-style, and held it in place with a couple of dog-eared motel paperbacks.

Beverly stood by the bathroom door, arms crossed. Even from across the room, Laura felt her gaze, like a contracting of the air between them. She wasn't sure when she'd started to find the psychic's presence reassuring, but she did now. Beverly had stuck with her through every twist and turn, her mind open, her guidance brisk but honest. Laura found she desperately wanted to provide Beverly with the closure she so obviously craved.

Mike couldn't save Laura, but maybe Beverly could.

She focused on Amy, who sat in a chair beside the table.

It had been Laura's one request—that Amy ask the questions. She could only do this if they pretended it was casual. Just a chat. She could forget about the phone passively recording her, if only she could look at her sister and feel safe.

"Ready?" Amy asked.

Laura took a settling breath and tried to ease her grip on her hands. She nodded.

Brian touched the phone screen, gave Amy a thumbs-up, and retreated to the bed, where he perched with his fingers bunching the bedspread.

"Can you start by telling us who you are?" Amy asked.

"My name's Laura Warren, but you probably know me as Polly Tremaine. When I was a kid, I starred in a movie called *The Guesthouse.*"

"You changed your name from Polly to Laura."

Laura almost smiled. "Wouldn't you? If you were known for the kind of things Polly Tremaine was known for?"

"And what was that?"

Laura opened her mouth to speak, but nothing came out.

"Let's come back to that," Amy said. "How did you get into show business?"

Laura looked down, then forced herself to look up again. "My mom. She took me to auditions when I was a baby. It sort of grew from there. She . . ." Laura swallowed. She'd almost started talking about how much she hated it, how much her mother pressured her, but the need to protect her mom overpowered her, even now, despite the way she'd been treated.

"She wanted to be a singer, my mom, when she was younger. Her family forbade it, forced her to enroll in secretary classes. She took a job at a record label in L.A. and by the time she was eighteen, she was married to my dad and pregnant with me. I guess she felt sort of trapped. I guess the acting thing seemed like a decent substitute."

Amy had gone very still. She cleared her throat.

"What's your earliest memory of *The Guesthouse?*"

Laura felt a surge of affection for her. The segue had been seamless. Amy would make a good journalist if she ever gave up on Hollywood.

"Meeting Christopher," Laura said after a moment. Her director was the first thing that came to mind. Her first and only movie director. "He made it so easy. He said that making a movie was like playing a game. He came over on the first day of filming and I wasn't scared because he had this big, genuine smile."

"Did he give you any advice?"

"He told me a director was far less important than an actor. '*So you get to boss me around as much as you like.*' I told him to stand on one leg, just to check. And he did."

Her mouth crinkled at the memory.

"After that, he told me that I could order him around as much as I liked, but when he said 'action' he was in charge. It seemed like a fair trade."

It was weird to think he wasn't around anymore. Hadn't been for a very long time.

"Did you speak to him?" Amy asked. "Afterward?"

"No. Nothing after the premiere."

"Do you miss him?"

The question caught her off guard. Was it possible to miss somebody she'd only known briefly, and as a seven-year-old?

"I suppose I miss the friendship we could've had, if it wasn't for what happened after the movie came out. We could've been friends if it had just been a movie. But when people died, it changed everything."

"What was it like when the movie hit?" Amy asked.

The curiosity in her tone made Laura realize her sister was getting something out of this, too. Amy must have years of questions stored up. They'd only talked about *The Guesthouse* a couple of times in their lives, and it had never been for more than minutes at a time. Little bites. Then Laura shut it down.

"It was intense," she said, and that was the truth.

Strangers knew her name. They yelled it when she walked down the black carpet for the film's premiere at Mann's Chinese Theatre, wearing the frilly yellow dress she'd picked out with her mother. So similar to the one she wore in the movie.

"You look so pretty, Polly!"

"Can we get a picture, Polly?"

"Hey, Polly, will you sign this?"

She'd viewed it as part of the game.

"It was fun, but overwhelming," she said. "The premiere was the last time it was fun. After that, I went back to school, and, well, kids can be mean. Adults can be worse."

"The kidnapping attempt," Amy said.

Laura had already braced herself for that topic. "Yes. A woman tried to take me while I was shopping with my mom. That's when I quit acting for good. Mom fired my agent and we moved to England, escaped L.A. and everything that goes with it. When I left school, I changed my name."

"Did that help? Did anybody ever find out your real name?"

Amy had the decency to look guilty when she asked.

"Only a handful of people over the years."

"How did they react?"

Laura thought about the few people at college who had found out during a drunken game of Two Truths and a Lie. "Some people wanted to protect me, like I was fragile. A victim. Others didn't care. I preferred the latter."

"Did they believe in the curse?"

"Possibly."

"Do you?"

Laura hesitated. She wanted to say no. It was her stock response. But she found the words didn't come as easily as they used to. She released a breath.

"Honestly, if you'd asked me four days ago, I'd have said no. But now, I'm not so sure. Things happened while I was in L.A. Terrible things. They reminded me about..." She trailed off, unsure if she could go where her thoughts wanted her to.

But she felt the barrier weakening. A part of her wanted to talk. To let go of the truth. Toss it like a grenade.

The expectant looks of everybody in the room told her she had their undivided attention. She focused on Amy.

"I remember him," she said at last.

"Who?" Amy asked.

"Vince Madsen." The name felt heavy in her mouth. "The crew member who died on set in the nineties. The one who fell from the roof. He was my friend. He made me laugh during downtime. Played tricks on me. He was so funny."

She forced herself to take a breath, wasn't sure she could say it, but then the words pushed past her teeth.

"I saw him fall," she said. Quieter, like a prayer, she repeated to herself, "I saw him fall."

The first to die.

Amy frowned. "I thought he was found by the director."

"Christopher," Brian said from the bed.

Laura kept her gaze on Amy. Her body felt lit up with anxiety. It crackled down her neck and into her fingers.

"We were playing hide-and-seek, me and Brian," she said, hating that she was trembling. "I ran into the soundstage looking for a hiding place, and I saw Vince working on the roof. He had no idea I was there, but then I saw him lose his footing and fall. I saw the whole thing."

"Oh my God." Amy's eyes shone at her from across the room.

A memory of childhood fear buzzed in Laura's teeth. The elemental horror of watching somebody die.

She'd kept it under wraps for so long, the memory of that day, the sight of the body, it almost felt like she'd dreamed it. So many of her childhood memories felt distant, somehow at a remove from her, like picture frames on a long corridor. But certain memories were lit in screaming Technicolor when you found them, and this one was etched into her brain like scar tissue.

It felt good to say it out loud.

"You never said anything," Amy murmured.

"I knew I'd get in trouble for being there. We weren't allowed on the stage unsupervised. When Christopher came in and found the body, I hid. Nobody knew I was there."

She remembered the red around the body, so dark, nothing like the fake blood they used during filming.

And the angle of his neck, purple flesh contorted by ruptured bone.

"Man," Brian said. He seemed to have forgotten they were filming. "I'm so sorry."

"It's okay," Laura said.

But it wasn't. As much as she'd suppressed the memory, it never stayed buried for long. The trauma leaked out in pieces.

The night terrors.

The dreams.

A grief counselor was brought to set to talk to the kids about what happened to Vince, but Polly hadn't liked the experience. His questions set her on edge and she refused to see him more than once. Nobody seemed particularly bothered after that. It was the '90s and they had a movie to finish.

Even when she got older, she couldn't ever talk about it—not with her sister, not with Mike—because trying to say the words always brought on a panic attack. Made it impossible to breathe. That childhood fear was paralyzing. Impossible to reason with or rationalize.

So she decided to forget.

Forget and move on.

"It's the reason I never believed in the curse," she said. "I figured the deaths were all accidents, just like Vince. But—" She stopped. "But what if I was wrong? What if something invisible was at work even then? And it killed Vince first?"

Nobody spoke.

Amy had turned paler than Laura had ever seen her, and her eyes were darker than pitch.

Laura felt numb. She looked at Beverly and saw that she was silently crying. From where Laura sat, she could see tears flowing freely, and rather than being unnerved, Laura felt comforted. Beverly understood in a way that few could. She felt what Laura felt. Laura wasn't alone.

Amy leaned in. "Are you okay to keep going?"

"Yes."

Amy nodded and took a second, clearly shaken by what she'd heard.

Finally, she said, "Can you talk about what happened in L.A. over the past couple days?"

Laura did. She started with waking up in the burning set, then what happened at Kyle's house. She went into as much detail as she could, imagining she was being interviewed for an article. Or a trial.

She was innocent.

Whoever ended up watching this, if anybody, they had to believe her.

By the time she finished, her hands shook in her lap. She thought she might throw up, but another sensation stopped her. Relief. It felt good to get it out.

"So you didn't set the fire? Or kill Kyle?" Amy asked.

"No. Absolutely not."

"Do you know who did?"

The Needle Man.

Ivan Rothschild.

Me.

"No," Laura said. "I wish I did."

Silence settled over the room.

Laura felt exhausted.

"I think we're done," Amy said.

Brian stood. "What about the making of the movie? Can we go into some behind-the-scenes detail? Get more about what it was like to star in *The Guesthouse?*"

"No," Amy said. "We're done."

Laura got up and Amy moved toward her, but Laura smiled weakly, touched her shoulder, and went into the bathroom. She shut the door and pressed her weight against it. Gravity seemed to have abandoned her. She felt too light.

Her wrists burned and she saw Vince's broken neck.

She went to the sink and put her hands under the cold faucet, but the burning sensation only intensified. Her fingers felt like ice, but her wrists were on fire.

A wheeze sounded behind her, just over her shoulder, and she slowly raised her head to look in the mirror.

The Needle Man stood at her back, facing her. His presence filled the bathroom with the smell of sickness and decay. The bandages around his face were stained and the black hat he wore was singed the color of coal.

"You're not real," Laura whispered.

The Needle Man said nothing.

He raised his rusted claws and they moved in a rippling wave.

Laura closed her eyes. Counted to ten. When she opened them again, she was alone.

She shut off the water and dried her hands, then left the bathroom.

"Pill?" Amy said.

"I need some air."

She went outside, barely feeling the ground beneath her feet. She didn't stop until she was at the road. Mountains loomed in the distance, rust red and silent, and there was peace in their stillness. She took a breath, smelling cooling pavement and dust, the trembling in her body subsiding. She'd exposed old wounds, but the air soothed them. She felt better than she did in the bathroom. If she could only stop thinking about the body on the soundstage floor.

"You did good," Amy said behind her.

"You too."

Amy moved to stand at her side, a breeze tousling her blond hair as she considered the mountains.

"Let's walk," Laura said, wanting to keep moving. They walked by the side of the road, powdered dirt puffing up from the ground. There were no cars, no people. Wherever they were, they were alone with America.

"That must've been awful," Amy said. "Finding that man. Why didn't you say anything?"

"I couldn't. I was a kid."

"All my life, you've been right there with me one moment, then miles away the next."

"I know."

"You know the weirdest thing, though? I've never seen you more alive than in the past few days."

"Maybe that's what happens when you face your shit."

"Maybe."

"The only thing that matters now is stopping this," she said.

Amy peered up at the flaking *Twilight Sun Motel* sign. "You really think we'll find answers at the old guesthouse?"

"I know it."

"Come on, let's go back in. Brian's probably talking Beverly's ear off about some obscure giallo."

As soon as she opened the door, Laura knew something was wrong. The lights were off and the room was bathed in the light from the TV. The images on-screen caused the hair to shiver on her arms.

The Guesthouse.

It was playing on the motel TV.

Her scalp prickled as her younger self walked down a dark hallway, moving toward a door at the very end. Room 205. Violins shivered on the soundtrack and the on-screen door was edged in yellow light that twitched over the motel room.

Beverly and Brian were nowhere to be seen.

"Guys?" Amy said.

The bathroom door was shut and Laura heard running water from the other side.

"Beverly?" she said. No reply.

She looked down. "Shit."

Beverly was on the floor beside the bed. She lay on her back, eyes rolled so that the whites shone. Foam bubbled from her mouth and her entire body was rigid, her hands clenched, her back arched, as if attempting to contain an electric charge.

"She's seizing," Laura said, hurrying over and kneeling beside her.

"Here." Amy took a pillow from the bed and set it under Beverly's head. She held her arms down, keeping her in place. Beverly emitted a strangled groan, something tortured. Animalistic. She looked like she was in agony.

"Is she epileptic?" Amy asked.

"I don't know."

"Pass me her bag."

Laura stepped back to look for it and the carpet squelched beneath her.

Water seeped through from beneath the bathroom door, soaking the carpet.

"Laura!" Amy said, and Laura shook herself. She took Beverly's bag from the bed and passed it to her sister. While Amy searched through it, Laura went to the bathroom door and knocked.

"Brian?"

No answer.

She turned the handle. Locked.

"Brian?"

When he didn't answer, dread settled heavy in her stomach. She kicked the door. She kicked it again and again, growing more desperate with each second, afraid of what lay on the other side. Finally, the door splintered and gave, inching open. She pushed it all the way.

The light was so bright it hurt her eyes. She blinked, tried to bring the room into focus. She saw the mirror first. It was cracked, as if it had been dealt a blow, and lines of splintered glass spelled three words.

YOU'RE MINE POLLY

Laura turned to the bath and felt a cry lodge in her throat.

"Pill? Is he okay?"

Amy appeared at her side, still holding Beverly's bag, and Laura pushed her back, preventing her from seeing. She fought for breath.

"He's not okay," she said.

INT. CRICKLEWOOD GUESTHOUSE BASEMENT--MORNING

ANDY, 7, steps down into the DARK BASEMENT. He trembles, looks around.

                    ANDY
     Tammy?

He HEARS something, turns, spots a TALL DARK SHAPE standing by the washer-dryer.

                    ANDY
     Tammy?

He ventures toward the shape, terrified.

                    TAMMY
     BOO!

TAMMY JUMPS OUT from behind the shape. We see it's JUST A MANNEQUIN.

                    ANDY
     Hey!

                    TAMMY
     Scared you!

                    ANDY
     Did not!

                    TAMMY
     You peed your pants.
              (Andy looks down)
     Made you look!

                    ANDY
                 (shivering)
        It's creepy down here.

                    TAMMY
        I like it.
             (She holds up the paper fortune-teller)
        Wanna play?

                    ANDY
        What does it do?

                    TAMMY
        It tells you how you'll die.

Andy eyes the fortune-teller, unsettled.

His head turns toward the stairs.

                    ANDY
        I heard my mom calling. See ya later, Tammy.

He races up the basement steps and disappears.

                    TAMMY
                 (calling after him)
        'Fraidy cat!

TWENTY-FIVE

Brian was gone.

The tub overflowed, slopping the bathroom floor with water, but it did little to dilute the blood.

Red liquid shone everywhere she looked. Cherry red on the walls, almost black on the ceiling, swirling thickly in the sink as it crept down the drain. At the center of the floor, the blood congealed in an immovable lump that even the water couldn't penetrate.

But there was no body.

The bathroom was empty.

It was as if Brian had been sucked out the window or into the floor, but the window and tiles remained intact. There was no sign of a struggle, nothing out of place or broken, aside from the mirror.

He was just . . . gone.

And the message in the mirror was all for her.

Laura backed out of the room, seeing that Beverly had recovered enough to sit on the edge of the bed. Her back was rounded, dark semi-circles under her eyes.

"What happened?" Laura asked.

Beverly stared at the carpet, and then her gaze went to the door.

"I heard voices in there. Brian said he needed to use the bathroom. I heard voices, then the TV station changed . . . and I blacked out."

She dropped her head.

Voices.

Goose bumps crawled up Laura's arms at the memory of the Needle Man reflected in the mirror not ten minutes ago. It had seemed as real then as it did during their séance. Nothing had shown up on the phone footage, but that didn't mean nothing was there.

"You didn't hear Brian getting attacked?" she asked.

"No."

"Did you see anything? Did you see the Needle Man?"

"No. Nothing. The pain was too much."

"What the fuck happened to him?" Amy demanded.

"There's no body," Laura said.

Amy hugged herself. "He could be alive, then."

"There's so much blood."

"Then he's injured somewhere. Right?"

Laura couldn't believe what she was about to say. "I think he's in the floor. I think the Needle Man got him."

They both knew Mrs. Manners died in the film by being dragged into the packed-dirt basement floor. Buried alive.

"Nobody else came in here," Amy said. "We'd have seen them from the road."

"The Needle—" Laura began, but Amy cut her off by pointing at Beverly with a shaking finger.

"It was you," she said.

"I told you, I blacked out."

"Has that happened before?" Laura asked. "Seizures?"

Beverly nodded. "Fifth time this week."

"Are you epileptic or . . . ?"

Speaking seemed to pain her, but Beverly said, "First time it happened was the same day Ivan jumped, though I didn't know it then. The second time, I woke up to the news about the studio fire. The third, I was driving to a 7-Eleven. I managed to pull over, and when I came to, you were by the road, covered in blood. Then it happened on the guesthouse set . . ."

Laura tried to process what she was saying. "You've had a seizure every time somebody died?"

"Seems that way."

Laura hadn't blacked out this time, but she had seen the monster from *The Guesthouse* right before Brian vanished. She opened her mouth to speak, but then she spotted a book on the bed next to Beverly.

Her journal.

The one that went missing from her hotel room two days ago.

At first, she thought she was imagining things. It didn't make sense that it was there on the bed, as if she'd placed it there herself. But then she saw the guilty look on Beverly's face and knew she wasn't seeing things.

"Where did you get that?" she asked.

Amy crossed her arms again, looked cold and defiant. "It was in her bag."

"I can explain," Beverly said.

"So explain." Laura's whole body was rigid with tension.

Beverly stood, then put a hand to her head and sat back down. She closed her eyes.

"I need water."

"Answer the question," Laura said.

Beverly gave her a pleading look. "I took it from your room."

"You trashed my hotel room?"

"What? No." The color bled from Beverly's face. "I wanted to help you. When I saw you go into the security guy's office with the detective, I broke in and took your diary. I saw you writing in it on set and thought it might contain something to help me connect with you."

The room felt hazy and Laura tried to remember that morning. Beverly had found her in the hotel lobby right after Detective Fernandez left. She must have just taken the journal, then gone outside in order to double back in again. Pretend she had just arrived.

"You thought that taking my journal would help you help me?"

"I needed you to trust me."

"So you stole my personal belongings."

"I'm telling you, she's played us from the start," Amy said.

"No." Beverly looked like her head was killing her. "Please, listen to me—"

"You destroyed Laura's clothes, too, didn't you? And put that fortune-teller in her bag? You've been fucking with us."

"Amy." Laura tried to think logically. Beverly had blackouts, just like her. Beverly had gaps in her memory, just like her. They'd both woken up with somebody dead nearby. Something else was going on. It wasn't Beverly. It couldn't be Beverly.

The Needle Man had been right there.

Why hadn't she done something?

Why hadn't she confronted whatever he was, rather than pushing him away?

Pushing him toward Brian?

"Let's talk about this," Laura said.

"Pill, seriously." Amy threw her arms wide. "She had access to the studio—to you and Kyle and Todd." She clenched her fists. "And Brian. What did you have against him? Was he a threat? Did he figure you out?"

"I told you, I blacked out."

"You killed him," Amy said. "And you've convinced Laura some evil spirit summoned by a disgruntled writer was responsible. Why? Do you *like* killing people?"

"Laura, please." Beverly stood, but Laura backed up. She couldn't deny that it made a horrible kind of sense. Beverly had been there the whole time. She'd known which hotel Laura was staying at. She seemed to know where Laura was no matter how erratic her movements.

But she'd done nothing but help Laura.

She believed in her innocence.

And Laura had seen too many things she couldn't explain away.

"Let's just calm down," she said, but Amy was at the door. She took the car keys from the table.

"We need to get out of here," she said. "Away from her."

"Laura, if you go, it *will* win." Beverly leaned against the night-stand. Her legs barely held her up.

"Thanks, Mystic Meg," Amy said.

Laura stood between them, betrayal and uncertainty crackling in her chest.

"It's why I've stayed with you," Beverly said. "To protect you. Look, I think maybe it *was* me who trashed your room and planted the dress and the fortune-teller." She looked at Laura with pleading eyes. "But it wasn't me. It was something working through me. I don't know how. I just know I have the memories of it happening."

"She admits it was her!" Amy cried. "Let's *go!*"

Laura looked from the psychic to her sister. Amy stood by the door, hand outstretched toward her, and Laura's mind was in overdrive.

"If you leave, you'll be defenseless," Beverly said. "You have to believe me."

"Pill, please."

Amy had kept secrets. Lied to her. Exploited her past for her own gain. But she was her sister. Laura couldn't choose anybody over her sister. If Amy was leaving, so was she.

She grabbed her journal from the bed and went to Amy's side.

"I'm sorry," she told Beverly.

Before Beverly could say another word, they left the motel room and got into the Volvo. Amy started the engine and hit reverse, puffing dirt as they pulled out of the lot onto the main road.

In the rearview mirror, Laura saw Beverly leaning against the doorframe. Her face was expressionless, but her mouth moved rapidly, her dark eyes fixed on the car. Laura couldn't make out what she was saying, whether Beverly was cursing them or sending up a prayer, and then Amy hit the accelerator and the motel faded from view, darkness folding around them.

Lyrics for radio jingle of Sparkleshine washing detergent, circa 1987

Laundry day got you down in the dumps?
Need a detergent that comes up trumps?
Kick those tough stains into line.
It's soft,
It's shiny,
It's *Sparkleshine*!

TWENTY-SIX

It was dark and Laura wasn't accustomed to being on the wrong side of the road. The world seemed even more back-to-front than ever, like she was living in a broken simulation. Any second now they could drive up into the sky, get pulled into the vacuum of space.

"Do you really think she killed Brian?" she asked.

Amy squeezed the wheel.

"They don't call somebody the 'Psycho Psychic' for nothing."

"But it doesn't make any sense."

"*That's* what doesn't make sense?"

She had to give Amy that one. Right from the start, Laura had asked her sister to suspend her disbelief, but she hadn't done the same herself. She'd always been a realist. The real monsters weren't goblins or ghosts, but the people who did awful things to other people. Human beings. They were the things people should fear in the dark.

Now, though, Laura wasn't so sure.

She'd lived enough strangeness in the past few days alone to believe there was more out there.

Monsters had many faces.

She just couldn't see Beverly as one of them.

The engine groaned and she watched the speedometer creep higher and higher.

"Hey, slow down, we don't want to get pulled over."

"If we do, we can tell the cops exactly where to find their psycho."

Laura sensed that Amy's anger wasn't entirely about Beverly.

"I'm sorry about Brian."

Amy frowned. "Why are you saying that to me?"

"You liked him."

"He was fun to flirt with." A second later, her voice broke. "He didn't deserve to die."

"I know."

"Fuck!" Amy hammered the wheel.

Five, Laura thought.

Brian was the fifth victim.

Guilt cored her out when she realized that a part of her was relieved. Not that Brian was dead, but that there was no way she could've done it. She hadn't blacked out. Hadn't awoken to find his corpse beside her. She hadn't even been in the room when it happened.

But she had seen the Needle Man.

What if she'd unwittingly summoned him? Released him into the motel room, ready for Brian?

The relief drained away and she felt like she could cry, but her eyes were too dry.

Five down, a voice whispered. *Three to go.*

While Amy drove, Laura held on to her journal. She flicked through the pages, seeing entry after neatly penned entry. She barely missed a day until she came to L.A., and she missed the soul-purging of it. Her head always felt lighter after she got her thoughts down on paper.

She stopped on one of the pages, reading the handful of ordered sentences.

Met Todd Terror today. What a loser.
I wouldn't be surprised if his own crew killed him
just to get away from him. Burn, baby, burn!

"What is this?" She turned to the next page.

Kyle Williamson is such a fraud. The whole interview,
I wanted to jam my pen into her eye. That'd give her
a new perspective. It might make her a better person.

"What are you looking at?" Amy asked.

"My journal. These entries . . . It's my handwriting, but I didn't write any of this."

"What do they say?"

"They're horrible." Laura's jaw tensed. "They make me sound like a monster."

"Wow, Beverly's full of surprises. She was setting you up. That's the only explanation. She killed the others, and she was going to pin it on you with the journal."

Yellow markings flashed and vanished under the hood, as if the car consumed them.

Laura's upper back ached.

She'd been so sure Beverly was helping them. But Beverly had admitted to taking the journal and, as far as Laura knew, she'd had it in her possession the whole time. Nobody else could have written the entries.

Laura kicked the car floor, resisting the urge to hurl the journal out the window.

How could she have gotten it so wrong?

"What if she reports the car stolen?" Amy said.

"Fuck." Laura thought for a second. "If she does that, she'll have to explain the bloody bathroom. I don't think she'll turn us in unless she has to."

Amy looked out the windshield at a sign by the highway. "There's another motel ten miles from here."

"We're not going there."

"Then where are we going?"

Laura tightened her grip on the journal.

"The guesthouse. We just need to pick up a few things on the way."

Five minutes later, they pulled into a gas station. It looked deserted, but it was open.

The pimple-faced guy behind the counter looked around twelve and seemed more interested in the movie playing on TV than the two women who came in wearing shades and baseball caps at nine p.m.

While Amy went to the refrigerators, Laura found the car supplies section. She scanned the rows of driving gloves, scented pine trees, spark plugs, and comedy bumper stickers, then grabbed two gallon bottles of fuel.

They were heavy, but that was only right. Nothing about what she was going to do should be easy.

She hefted them across the store and set them on the counter. The attendant stood transfixed by the TV, which showed an old horror movie in which a woman clambered across a roof to escape bandaged pirates.

"You weren't kidding about this," Amy said, eyeing the fuel as she joined Laura at the counter. She added a couple of bottles of Mountain Dew and a family pack of M&M's.

"Hey, Kurt," Laura said to the attendant, reading his name tag. "Can we exchange wares for cash here?"

Kurt broke away from the screen.

"You ladies planning on setting fire to an ex-boyfriend's car?" he drawled.

"Ex-*girlfriend's*," Laura said, enjoying the guy's face turning stop-sign red.

"Yeah, we caught her cheating with her aerobics instructor," Amy said. "I don't care how hot a chick looks in skintight spandex, *nobody* cheats on my best friend."

Kurt looked like he wanted to slip out of his skin and crawl out the back of the store.

Laura gave her sister a brief look. They still had it.

Amy paid with the last of her cash and Laura reached for the fuel, but then felt clammy pressure at her wrist.

Kurt had grabbed hold of her.

"Hey!" She looked into a face that had gone slack. The kid's mouth hung open and twitched at the corner. His eyes clouded over, but his attention was entirely on her.

"What the fuck," Laura said, tugging back, but the guy's grip was unyielding. She saw his Adam's apple move up and down, and a sound like a blissful sigh leaked from wet lips.

"polllyyyy . . ."

"Get off her!" Amy yelled, attempting to pry the attendant's hand away. It was no good, though. His fingers were fixed tight.

"he wants youuuu . . ."

". . . polllyyy . . ."

Drool escaped from Kurt's mouth, elongating from his chin and oozing onto Laura's hand.

"Get the fuck off her!" Amy shouted, and she was clawing at his hand now, drawing blood, but he didn't notice.

Laura's skin burned where he gripped it, the pressure intensifying, heat coursing up her arm.

And she wasn't in the gas station any longer. Her mind spiraled back to her dressing room at Universal Studios. She wore her yellow dress and threw her script pages at the wall, screaming at her mom that she didn't want to run scenes anymore.

Her mom seized her wrists in both hands, got down on her level, and hissed with a voice that sent snakes snapping at her stomach.

"Pull yourself together, for God's sake!"

"You're hurting me—"

"Stop being such a spoiled brat—"

"you've been his from the start . . ." the attendant whispered, snapping Laura back to the present. She saw his knuckles around her wrist and anger boiled up from the pit of her stomach.

"so clooooossssee . . ."

She sank her teeth into the attendant's hand, biting hard. He yelled and released her, staggering backward. She did the same, massaging her wrist, relieved to be free. The skin was bright pink, almost blistered by his touch, and she remembered the way her wrists hurt that day on set. A vague memory stirred. A memory she couldn't quite get at.

On the other side of the counter, Kurt had snapped from his stupor.

"Why'd you bite me, man?" He wiped his mouth and stared fearfully at Laura.

Laura caught movement out of the corner of her eye.

A car had pulled into the gas station. It stopped at the in-road, facing the store, and two people sat in front.

Even from here, she recognized the driver.

It was Detective Fernandez.

And beside her, in the passenger seat, sat Mike.

INT. GAS STATION STORE--NIGHT

TAMMY looks dog-tired and scared as she enters the store and goes
to the coffee machine. Fixes herself a large cup of joe. Takes it to
the cash register where the MALE ATTENDANT looks her up and down.

                          ATTENDANT
          Late for coffee. Trying to stay awake?

Tammy smiles warily.

                          ATTENDANT
          You driving far?

                          TAMMY
          As far as a tank of gas will get me.

She roots around in her purse. The attendant considers her.

                          ATTENDANT
          You in trouble, miss?

                          TAMMY
          Nothing I can't handle.

                          ATTENDANT
          A shame about your mom. The shower. Such a tragedy,
          burning up like that.

Tammy stops going through her purse. Looks at him fearfully.

                          TAMMY
          What did you say?

The attendant LUNGES OVER THE COUNTER, KNOCKS Tammy over, and PINS
her to the floor.

                          ATTENDANT
                      (rasping voice)
          Tammmyyyyyyyyy . . .

Tammy STRUGGLES to get free. Green drool oozes from the attendant's
mouth onto her face.

His EYES are ALL BLACK.

                          ATTENDANT
          You're ours now, Tammmyyyyyyyyy . . .

TWENTY-SEVEN

M ove," Laura said. *"Now!"*

The Volvo was parked near the store entrance. They had a clear route to it. For now. In ten seconds, Fernandez would block them and it would be too late.

Laura grabbed the fuel and hurried out of the store as fast as her trembling body would allow her. She saw Fernandez's car door open and didn't stop, throwing herself toward the Volvo. She opened the driver's door, hefted the bottles onto the back seat, and moved sideways so Amy could get in. As Amy clambered across to the passenger seat, Laura went to get in and—

"Ms. Warren, freeze!"

She stopped moving.

One hand curled around the doorframe, the other the car roof.

A desert breeze whispered across the nape of her neck, tugging the ruffles of her yellow dress.

"Okay, Ms. Warren, let's not do anything stupid." Fernandez's voice echoed across the concrete of the gas station. Somewhere in the fog of her brain, Laura thought Fernandez could do better than yelling movie-cop clichés.

She turned her head fractionally and saw that the detective was already out of the car, standing behind the open door and using the roof to support the gun, which was aimed right at her. Laura remembered the look Fernandez had given her in the hotel. A look loaded with suspicion but tempered with restraint.

She didn't look that way now.

She looked like she'd pull the trigger.

"Aren't you a little way out of your jurisdiction?" Laura said.

"Hands up!"

"I didn't kill anybody."

"Come with me and we'll talk about it."

"You know I can't do that."

"Laura," Mike said. He got out of the car and stood with his hands above his head, even though the gun was pointed at Laura.

"Back in the vehicle," Fernandez said, but Mike ignored her.

"Laura, please. She wants to help. Just listen to her."

He was begging. Mike never begged. He ordered.

He had listened to her in the hotel. He had wanted to help her, even though she'd started talking about the Needle Man and movie curses. She remembered the way he'd looked at her like she was talking gibberish.

"Tell me you believe me and I'll come with you," Laura said. Inside the car, Amy began to protest, but Laura shushed her.

Mike looked desperate.

"I want—"

"Back in the vehicle!" the detective repeated.

Laura's gaze switched between them. Would Fernandez shoot her? Or did she really want to help?

Mike took a step toward the Volvo, which was all the distraction

Laura needed. As Fernandez's attention slipped to Mike, Laura ducked into the front seat, hearing a tinny sound like popcorn ricocheting above her head.

"Jesus, she's shooting at us," Amy said.

"Buckle up," Laura told her.

She got the engine going, put the car in reverse, and floored the accelerator. The car jolted backward, traveling a couple of feet before slamming into the detective's vehicle behind it. The other car's hood crumpled on impact and Laura was thrown forward, narrowly avoiding busting her face on the wheel.

"Christ," Amy said, but Laura didn't waste a second.

She put the car into gear, jumped forward a few feet, then stopped, put it into reverse, and accelerated again. The same smashing *crunch* threw them forward in their seats, and Fernandez's vehicle made an awful groaning squeal.

In the rearview mirror, Laura saw that the detective was already on her feet, the surprise wearing off. She ran for the Volvo, shouting.

"Laura, stop!"

Just as the detective reached her window, Laura put her foot down and tore away from the gas station.

On the road, she looked in her side mirror and saw Mike running into the road behind her. Fernandez jogged back to her car, tried to get it started, but the vehicle remained stationary. Smoke belched from the hood. Whatever damage Laura had done, it was enough.

Her arms shook as she sped up, welcoming the darkness of the highway as it folded around the Volvo. She tried to forget the pleading look in Mike's eyes, focused on slowing her breathing and getting the shakes under control.

Three, nine, seventeen . . .

Mike wasn't important. This wasn't his story.

"I guess that rules out asking the cops for help," Amy said a few minutes later, when the road behind them remained empty.

"How did they find us?" Laura said.

The fact that Fernandez had tailed her out of L.A. and into the Mojave was unsettling. Just what kind of a cop was she? Was it the glory she wanted? A front-page picture of her bringing Laura in?

Amy shrugged. "Beverly must have called them."

"Why?"

"Because she's Beverly."

Laura wasn't so sure. Her wrist still hurt, and the memory of Kurt the attendant's slack jaw made her more uneasy than anything else.

"He," she said. "The attendant said *he* wanted me."

"Rothschild?"

A part of Laura wanted to turn the car around and drive back to Beverly, find out once and for all if she was the one behind everything.

What if Laura had been wrong about her?

Was she just angry at the psychic for taking her journal?

She couldn't take the risk.

"How far is it?" she asked.

Amy checked her phone. "Fifteen miles."

So close. They'd be there before she'd have time to prepare for it. She felt so conflicted about the guesthouse, it was like five different voices were screaming in her skull. Some urged her to pick up speed and get there as fast as possible; others begged her to turn around.

Laura focused on driving. The sky was overcast, not a single star breaking through, and the effect was suffocating. Darkness surrounded them on all sides. The only thing she could see was the segment of road lit up by the high beams. A rectangle of road that never changed. Kept going. Endless and immense.

A flash of white shot past her window.

In the side mirror, Laura saw a pale shape standing by the side of the road.

It vanished as she kept driving.

"Did you see that?" she asked.

"See what?"

"The woman."

"I didn't see anybody."

Laura was sure she'd seen a woman in white. The car's taillights had momentarily bathed her in red as they passed, and she almost looked like their mother. It had to be a trick of the light.

She shifted in the seat, adjusting her grip on the wheel.

Keep it together.

They drove on and Laura tried not to think about the gas station attendant, nor the circle of pink flesh around her wrist where he had gripped her, nor Mike's pleading eyes.

The memory was still worming up from the depths of her mind. Arguing with her mom, spitting in her face, running. She felt an echo of the anger she had felt that day, heavy and loud and wild.

What had happened that day?

What was her brain trying to tell her?

She couldn't bear the sound of the wheels on the road anymore, so she switched on the radio.

Elvis's "Suspicious Minds" came through the speakers, tinny and distant. A ghost of a song. Signal must be weak out here in the desert.

Laura hit the search button and listened to the crackle of static as the radio sought other stations. Various tunes intermittently burst through, single words flaring, then fading.

"Caught—"

"You're—"

"Running—"

"polllyyyyy . . ."

She tensed at the whisper. The radio stopped searching. The number *2.05* flickered on the ancient display.

Beside her, Amy leaned closer to the radio.

"kill herrrrr . . ."

Laura looked at her hands. Metal spikes sprouted from her fingertips. She raised a hand in front of her face, seeing how sharp the spikes were, how weathered her skin looked. Bandages snaked up her forearms.

"Laura."

She turned to look at Amy and saw purple bone, a neck bent like a U-bend, and a man's face staring back at her.

"Falling," he wheezed, his lips as dry as cracked earth. *"Fallliiiiing…"*

"Laura!"

Amy's voice was like a hammer to the skull. Laura jerked in her seat and saw that the car was veering off-road. She brought it back into the right-hand lane and tried to breathe. Her hands were back to normal and Amy sat beside her. The radio was off.

"It knows I'm coming," Laura said.

"We can still turn around."

A part of Laura wanted to. The small, scared part that had kept her away from L.A. for decades. The part that kept secrets and ran. But she wasn't running anymore. They'd come too far for that. There was no road back.

"I can drop you off here if you want," she said. "But I'm going to that house."

"I'm not standing in the middle of the desert with a dying phone battery. Have you seen *The Hills Have Eyes?*"

"Not recently."

"I'd rather take my chances with a haunted house."

"All right, then."

Laura kept driving. The farther they went, the more she became aware of a dull purr in her temple. It was more than unease. More than muscular tension. It was a presence. Something pressing against the car windows, watching her, knowing her. She kept feeling her consciousness slipping, as if the presence was trying to pacify her. Seduce her.

"Turn right," Amy said, studying her phone.

"Where?"

"Back there," Amy said. They had overshot it.

Laura turned the car around and found the off-road, trundling down a dirt track. Stones spat at the car like vipers and Laura searched ahead, both excited by and fearful of what she would see.

Finally, the headlights illuminated a house made of bones.

At least, that was her first thought.

Gimlet Point Guesthouse absorbed the car's headlights, sucked all light into the bleached, flaking panels of its wooden exterior. The house was angular in a way that reminded Laura of the paper fortune-teller. It had four pitched roofs, one above the porch, another capping the right wing, both clad with decorative milled panels. There were double-hung windows, ornate sunburst panels, and a couple of steps leading up to a solid, peeling door.

Laura eased to a stop a dozen yards away and sat looking at the guesthouse.

"Jesus," Amy whispered. "It's not even boarded up."

"People only board up houses they want to protect."

Laura had expected to be terrified. She'd expected to lose her mind.

Instead, a stillness settled over her. Quiet acceptance of her fate. After everything that had happened, all those years attempting to forget *The Guesthouse* and the people who died, this felt right. This was where she was meant to be.

"Are you ready?" she asked.

Amy didn't take her eyes off the house. "To have our souls torn apart? Oh yeah, born ready."

Nothing lived out here. Nothing breathed. The land was hard and barren.

Laura and Amy approached the front steps, Amy filming on her phone, Laura clutching the fuel cans but barely feeling their weight. She half expected the front door to creak open in welcome, or her younger self to appear, smiling with clawed fingers concealed behind her back.

But the house was quiet.

Amy tried the door. It was locked.

"I guess that's it," she said with a shrug, but Laura reached for the handle and turned.

The door opened.

"Must've been stuck," Laura said, even though she didn't believe that. The house wanted her, not Amy. It was too dark to see inside, even with Amy's phone light. They looked at each other, a wordless agreement passing between them. Whatever happened next, they were in this together.

Their hands interlinked and they went inside.

It took a moment for Laura's eyes to adjust. When they did, she struggled to comprehend what they found.

The interior of Gimlet Point Guesthouse was immaculate. Dark wood and floral wallpaper was everywhere she looked, the ceiling glossed tree-bark brown, the plush carpet sucking at her boots.

The place looked Victorian, but too big, too ornate. It looked like something out of the '70s, with kitschy light fixtures and picture frames.

It looked identical to the *It Feeds* set.

"What the hell is this?" Amy said, looking around warily.

Laura turned to look out the front door, half expecting to see the cavernous interior of the soundstage, but all she saw was the dark of the desert, which was broken only by the Volvo's headlights.

"This is messed up," Amy said. "I thought the place was abandoned."

Laura went to a doorless archway and looked at a lounge she had already visited. She'd interviewed Todd Terror on that couch. She'd been unsettled by the faces in the wallpaper and the brass furnishings.

She peered up the stairs, seeing where Beverly had hung by her neck, and then beyond that, the bathroom door, where she knew she'd find a blackened shower stall.

"It's messing with us," Laura said.

"It?"

"The house."

"Or the psycho behind all of this," Amy said.

Laura raised her hand, signaling for her to listen. All she heard was silence.

"There's nobody here," Amy said.

"Let's make sure."

Despite Amy's protesting, they searched the first floor, finding a lived-in kitchen.

The atmosphere felt expectant.

Waiting.

Anticipating.

Upstairs was the same. Each room looked lived-in but abandoned. Bedrooms made up for guests who never came. Mints on pillows, wine coolers and champagne flutes on side tables. She caught sight of yellow fabric and froze, but it was just her reflection in an en suite mirror, wide-eyed and tense. She almost laughed because she looked nothing like those women in horror movies who entered the minotaur's labyrinth. She was too old. Too tired. Too large. This wasn't a movie. But it wasn't reality, either.

As they searched, Laura felt a growing razor's edge of panic cutting into her. She thought about Beverly talking about demonic parasites and Yvonne shrugging off her witch reputation.

Everybody knows Hollywood makes monsters.

Where was it, then? Where was the thing that had targeted *The Guesthouse* and *It Feeds?*

Where was Ivan Rothschild's unquiet spirit?

Where was the Needle Man?

She'd pinned everything on this, but there was nobody at Gimlet Point. The place was abandoned, just like everybody said.

Finally, she stood at the top of the stairs and shouted, "I'm here!"

"Laura!" Amy stage-whispered behind her, but Laura didn't listen.

"I'm right here, Ivan! Show yourself, you fucking coward!"

Her chest was painfully tight, her head pounding.

Nobody answered.

"Fine," she said. She went down to the hall and uncapped the fuel cans.

"You're seriously torching the place?" Amy asked.

"I'm making sure."

Laura went into the living room and slopped the gasoline across the floor. She swung the can so it splashed up the walls. As she went into the hall, she was already hot and she hadn't even struck a match yet. Sweat beaded her forehead and trickled down her spine.

She went through all the first-floor rooms, enjoying the splashing sounds of gasoline following her through the house. She was careful not to get any on her dress. That would be just her luck.

When she was back at the front door with Amy, she took the lighter from her pocket.

Beverly's cobra lighter.

It had failed her the last time when she set the film alight. The set had turned upside down, tried to kill them. What would it do this time?

"Are you sure you want to do this?" Amy asked.

Laura flipped the lid of the lighter. A flame danced to life.

Maybe it was the house. Not an entity. Not Ivan. But the house itself.

"Burn the negative, right?" she said. "I think this place has caused enough misery. Nobody will miss it. Besides, it's the only way to be sure."

They stood near the doorway together. Laura checked that the door was open, ready for them to make a quick escape, and then she tossed the lighter into the lounge. She heard a low *whoomp* and felt a surge of heat as the gasoline caught.

"Let's get out of here," Laura said.

"Oh, Laura," a woman's voice said behind her. "If only it were that simple."

A shape had appeared on the porch just outside the front door, blocking their exit.

Laura felt nothing but heat as Beverly stepped inside and shut the door, locking them in with the fire.

Dialogue from the Beetlejuice *(1988) screenplay by Michael McDowell and Warren Skaaren*

"My whole life is a darkroom.
One big, dark room."

—Lydia Deetz
(played by Winona Ryder)

TWENTY-EIGHT

Beverly's expression was hard. She stood with her back to the door, dark eyes unblinking, reflecting the firelight. She barely seemed to notice the house or the sound of the lounge being eaten up by flames. She barred their only way out, her gaze fixed on Laura, heavy and liquid, and Laura's insides shrank.

"What are you doing?" Laura asked. "We have to get out of here."

"We're not going anywhere."

"Beverly—" Laura began, but the psychic shook her head.

"You can't keep running." Her voice was firm, but frayed with emotion. Her jaw was set. "You've run long enough. It ends now."

"She's lost it," Amy said, coughing. "She's finally fucking lost it."

"Nobody leaves."

Amy looked at Laura, then at Beverly, then stepped forward.

"Fucking *move*," she said, attempting to push past Beverly, but Beverly shoved her back, stood firm. Amy grabbed her shoulder and tried to force her out of the way, but Beverly barely blinked as she hooked her boot behind Amy's knee and swept her legs out from under her.

Amy hit the floor, only just kept her head from cracking on the wall. She remained there, stunned.

"Amy!" Laura broke forward. She didn't get the chance to consider what she was going to do—punch Beverly? Throw her against the wall the way she had Madeleine?—because she felt something curl around her ankle and pull, and then she was on the floor, too, beside Amy. Pain flared in Laura's hip and she half sat, half slumped with Beverly standing over them.

"For Christ's sake, Beverly—" Laura began, but Beverly broke in.

"Stop."

"Beverly," Amy said, as if she were talking to a person with a concussion, "try to understand what I'm telling you. The place is on fire. We have to—"

"*Shut up!* Just for once, shut. Up!"

Laura had never heard Beverly shout. She felt the force of it in her bones. The psychic's eyes shone and her skin shimmered, the same look she'd worn on her face the day she found Laura in the hotel lobby and said she wanted to help her. That felt so long ago now.

And Beverly had a knife in her hand.

She must have slipped it from the back of her pants. It was small and vicious-looking, gleaming with reflected fire. Despite the heat, an icy ribbon of fear looped around Laura's neck.

It was the knife from Kyle's house.

What was Beverly doing?

What was she *planning* on doing?

She pictured Beverly slitting the throat of the girl she'd attempted to exorcise almost a decade ago. She heard the words "Psycho Psychic" over and over, saw her flushed complexion, but Beverly was supposed to be on their side. That was what she'd claimed all along, and Laura had believed her.

Had it been an act? A cover for something else?

Maybe Beverly *was* behind all of this.

"I told you it's her," Amy choked into the crook of her elbow. "It's been her the whole time."

Beverly looked like she would shout again, her grip tightening around the knife, but then she focused on Laura.

"Laura. *Polly.* Please hear me."

Laura swallowed thickly.

"Whatever Ivan did," she said, "it'll be over soon. You told us to find the source of the curse and destroy it. In an hour, this place'll be nothing but ash."

"You still think some disgruntled writer did this?"

"Yes. No. I don't fucking know! We left reality behind three bodies ago!"

Beverly shook her head and she seemed almost sorry. "It takes more than a grudge to wreak the kind of chaos we've seen. It takes hurt. Pain. Trauma. We're not going anywhere. Not until you face what you've been running from."

Crackling filled Laura's ears.

The crackling of the ceiling being devoured above them.

The crackling of her ruptured nerve ends.

What you've been running from.

Beverly's gaze was too much. Too intense. Too probing.

"I don't . . ." Laura began.

"I've been trying to get a read on it ever since we first met," Beverly said, waving the knife. "It's good at hiding. But you're the eye of the storm, Laura. You can end this if you just confront it."

"Is that what you said to the girl you killed, too?" Amy said.

Beverly flinched. A muscle twitched above her left eye. "That was different."

"Was it?" Laura murmured. "Or is this exactly what happened with her, too?"

The knife slashed up and down as if it had a mind of its own.

"I'm trying to help you," Beverly said, her voice verging on plead-ing. "Maybe you don't remember. Maybe you've buried it so deep you convinced yourself it never happened. But it's there, the root of the pain. You just have to find it."

Laura felt too warm, her skin feverish, and every sinew in her body was alert to the building creaking around them. Fire spread across the hall ceiling above them, escaping the lounge, and the pressure of heat throbbed at the back of her skull. It pressed all around her. She tried to think through the panic lighting up her insides.

The front door was aflame now, too, offering no chance of escape. She remembered Beverly talking about parasites and puppet masters, thought of Yvonne Lincoln blaming Hollywood for creating monsters, and didn't know what to believe.

She frowned. By the staircase rested a collection of camera and lighting equipment. It hadn't been there a moment ago, she was sure of it. She struggled to swallow, her mind sluggish, either from the fire or from Beverly's words.

"Just repeat after me," her mom's voice said in the way that meant her teeth were clenched, and Laura remembered being in her dressing room in 1993, the lights around the mirror, the Funshine Care Bear smiling at her from the couch.

"'There's something in the attic,'" her mom said, reading one of Tammy's lines, and Laura shoved her fingers in her ears, didn't want to hear that voice. Hadn't been able to bear it then and couldn't bear it now, either.

"Laura!"

Beverly was shouting her name. Laura jerked back to the present and looked up, seeing the blade hovering inches from her face, the hall an inferno of spitting wood and blackening wallpaper.

"You have to remember," Beverly said, and there was fear in her face. Urgent, desperate fear.

"There's nothing to remember," Laura said, struggling to breathe.

Firelight flashed in Beverly's eyes.

"*You have to*," she said. "It's the only way."

Her frenzied expression set off firecrackers in Laura's chest. She felt the past clutching for her. Nausea flooded her mouth and she remembered the dressing room, her mother shouting, grabbing her. She couldn't bear it. She didn't want to remember.

"No fucking way," Laura said, and before she even knew what she was doing, she lurched upward, seizing the hand holding the knife in both of her own. She held tight, the blade between them, pointed at her chest, and found herself staring into Beverly's face.

"Please," Beverly said, and she was coughing now, too. "*Please,* Polly. It'll kill you."

Laura wavered, her arms screaming with effort.

"Laura!"

A man's voice broke into the hall. The shock of it caused Laura's grip to slacken and Beverly yanked her hand back, taking the knife with her. Laura twisted to look down the hall, where a figure appeared in the kitchen door. Surprise and relief flooded through her.

Mike looked even more haggard than Beverly, his shirt soaked through with sweat, his face gaunt with fear. He must have run to get there, though surely not all the way from the gas station. Detective Fernandez was nowhere to be seen.

"The house is on fire!" Mike yelled, starting toward them in the clumsy way people did when their brain was on autopilot, but then he spotted the knife in Beverly's hand, Laura on her knees, and he stopped.

"What's going on?"

"Stay where you are," Beverly said.

"Laura?"

"She's trying to kill us!" Amy shouted.

"*Shut up.*" Beverly jabbed the knife at her. "Just stop!"

"Where's Fernandez?" Laura asked.

"On her way," Mike said, his gaze on Beverly. "Right behind me."

Beverly smiled, her lips dry. Laura could always tell when Mike was lying and it seemed Beverly could, too. Mike glanced up as a flaming piece of the ceiling broke away and hit the floor, only just missing him.

"We have to get out of here," he urged, and his words kick-started something in Laura. She struggled to her feet, coughing, helping Amy up, her eyes beginning to stream. The air was so thick with smoke, it was all she could taste, and her body felt heavy. Too heavy. The urge to sit and gather her strength was enormous.

It'll kill you.

"Stay back," Beverly warned Mike as he took slow steps toward them.

"We're getting out of here," he said, "before the whole place collapses."

"No."

Mike was only five feet away. Four. Three.

"You don't want to do this," Mike said, and Beverly's focus was entirely on him. She seemed to have forgotten that Laura stood only a couple of feet away from her. Laura looked at the knife, then at Beverly. She screwed up what energy remained and threw herself at the psychic. Her fingers wrapped around the hand holding the knife and she shoved Beverly backward, right off her feet.

The knife came away and Laura clutched it tightly as Mike leaped forward. He seized Beverly's forearms, wrenching them behind her back. She was on her knees, hair spilling onto her face as Mike held her wrists tight. The front door was fully ablaze behind them. There was no way they could leave through it.

"I've got her," Mike grunted. "Now go. Get out! Through the kitchen!"

Laura wanted to move, but she kept hearing Beverly's words.

Remember.

It'll kill you.

She looked over her shoulder and saw another figure in the kitchen door.

Young Polly in her yellow dress, her expression blank, eyes big and round, fixed on Laura.

Beverly raised her head to look at Laura.

"Please," she said, her face pained.

"I can't," Laura said. She took Amy's arm and they pushed their way down the hall, heading for the kitchen, the little girl gone. Behind them, Mike hauled Beverly to her feet and shoved her forward, following close behind.

Laura went into the kitchen, which was already ablaze, though the air was clear enough for her to see the curtains flapping with flames, the table blistering black. The back door was open, revealing the desert.

"Come on," Amy said, starting toward it.

An almighty *crunch* shook the room. Laura dropped the knife to grab Amy's shoulders just in time to pull her back as the ceiling collapsed.

Laura coughed and blinked, struggling to see through the flurry of embers and ash. A hole had appeared above them. Only a part of the ceiling had come down, right in front of the door.

The house doesn't want us to leave.

The thought made her giddy. She almost laughed.

"Back," she said, and they moved back into the hall, where Mike still held Beverly's arms behind her back.

"I'm trying to help you," Beverly said. Her face was beaded with perspiration, and she seemed to understand now that the house really was on fire. Ash danced in the air like dandelion seeds.

What you've been running from.

What had she been running from?

Laura felt the truth hovering just beyond her reach, and it was paralyzing. Her chest hurt so much. Her lungs felt bound in wire.

"Up," Amy said, looking at the stairs. "We go up and out one of the upstairs windows. One that isn't on fire."

Laura nodded and, together, they climbed.

"Move," Mike said, shoving Beverly up ahead of him.

Fresh urgency filled the psychic's voice as she called to Laura.

"It started that day on set, didn't it? In 1993?"

Laura tried to ignore her as she reached the top of the stairs, where the smoke was thinner, making it easier to breathe, but Beverly's words stirred something in her.

"It's been inside you for so long, you don't even feel it anymore. But I do. I did. After you left the motel, I went into the bathroom. I saw what you saw, felt what you felt. The Needle Man, right there, waiting. Real and deadly and relentless. But you can stop him. Only you."

Laura clutched her chest, feeling her heartbeat as well as something else. A weight.

What had she done?

What happened that day?

She paused on the landing, which was thick with smoke, the floorboards aglow, but at least the fire hadn't yet penetrated the walls. Her vision swam and she saw more filming equipment, stacked against the walls, untouched by the fire. It was there one second, gone the next. Time was taking on a fuzzy, distant quality. Coming unstuck.

Beverly had seen the Needle Man in the motel?

"You saw it?" she asked, facing the psychic. Behind her, Mike looked both terrified and confused.

"Yes."

Laura's legs felt weak and sweat fused the fabric of the dress to her torso. Something probed the back of her mind. Something so awful she'd banished it to the darkest corner. She wouldn't think about what she'd done, not even if it needled her so hard her guts spilled out.

"What's she talking about?" Mike asked.

Beverly only had eyes for Laura.

"It's time," she said. Her gaze was steady and entreating. Calm had settled over her. The kind of calm that comes with perfect clarity. "You can make it stop, Laura. You just have to tell your story. Aren't you tired of carrying it?"

"I'm so tired," her mom had said. *"So tired of raising a spoiled, ungrateful brat."*

Pressure built behind Laura's eyes. The threat of tears. The pain in her chest was unrelenting, a midnight frost that paralyzed her rib cage.

No.

No.

In the dressing room, her mother had taken her Funshine bear and held it in her grip.

"Do you want Funshine back, Polly?"

She had nodded, tasting tears, hating her mother with every fiber of her being.

"Then say your lines and say them correctly."

She eyed the Care Bear, then her mother, her lips fusing together. No matter what, she wouldn't say the lines. If she did, that would make her Tammy, and she didn't *want* to be Tammy. She didn't want to be Polly, either. She wanted to get as far away from the studio and her mother as possible.

"Say. The. Lines."

Tears stung her throat, her whole body quivering with hatred. She wished she could knock her mother off her feet just by thinking it.

"You're making me do this."

Her mother gripped the bear tight in both hands, her gaze fixed on Polly as she twisted, wrenching, and Funshine's head tore away with a sound that filled Polly with horror. Stuffing oozed out, littering the floor. Funshine's smile now looked tortured. In denial.

"I hate you!" Polly shouted. *"I hate you, you bitch!"*

Her mother's face dropped. She looked stunned. Then her cheeks flooded with color and she tossed aside the bear, lunging for Polly so quickly she had no time to react. Her mother's face was so close, she saw her irises shrink, and her grip on Polly's wrists burned.

"What did you call me?"

Polly could barely see through the tears.

"Everything I do," her mother hissed, *"I do for you, and this is how you treat me?"*

It hurts. It hurts.

Her wrists were on fire, her mother's grasp like steel.

And Polly wished she'd drop dead. Wished for her mother's heart to stop.

But it didn't. And she'd never let go. She'd never let Polly go.

She spat in her mother's face.

The grip on her wrists vanished and Polly was free. She shoved past her mother, running for the door and then out into the hall.

On the landing, Laura's vision blurred at the edges, pain overwhelming her.

She didn't want to give in, but she was so tired. Years of guilt weighed down her limbs, made her heartsick. She searched Beverly's face for a sign this was a trick, but what she found was even worse.

Compassion.

Maybe Beverly had known all along. Or maybe she had only just fitted it together.

And now Laura understood.

Beverly hadn't trapped them in the house to kill them.

She'd trapped them so that Laura had nowhere left to run.

She had no choice but to face the truth.

Run. She'd run from the dressing room, down the corridor and into the set. She'd been so full of rage and fear and hatred, it filled her with an unquenchable fire.

Laura weakened. She felt the barriers crumbling, exposing her to the world.

And she couldn't contain it anymore.

The thing that happened that day.

"It's my fault," she said. "All of it."

The moment the words left her mouth, she knew something was wrong.

Pain exploded in her chest and she doubled over, feeling as if she'd been punched. Her stomach clenched, spasming.

"Laura!" Amy clung to her. She stared at Beverly. "What did you do to her?"

Laura choked, felt movement in her abdomen, her internal organs being squeezed. She gagged on something lodged in her throat. Something solid and alien. She felt it moving, sinking tiny claws into her esophagus. She retched and tasted blood. She couldn't focus on anything other than the pain.

The same pain she'd endured ever since she touched down in L.A., but worse. So much worse.

The pain of a trapped child.

The pain of what she'd done.

No air entered her lungs.

She coughed and tried to free the thing in her throat.

She was on her hands and knees outside the bathroom, vaguely aware of Amy rocking her, shouting, but all she heard was screaming. The scream of her own body in agony.

Black spots clouded her vision. She retched some more and then it moved. The thing in her throat dislodged and filled her mouth, wet and earthy and rancid. She gagged, wasn't sure she could get it past her teeth, then finally spat it to the floor and gasped in a breath. She sat back, coughing uncontrollably, because the air entering her lungs was toxic.

The house was still on fire.

Mike had released Beverly and stood with his mouth open, gaping at the thing on the carpet. Beverly massaged her wrists, watching.

Watching the thing that was now in the house with them.

It writhed and contorted, a black knot of flesh that glistened with bile. Laura remained on the floor, numb with shock, holding on to Amy. She watched in horror as the knot grew. It pulsed and twisted, thickening as if filling up with blood. It grew to the size of a curled-up child, then a teenager. It unfolded bit by agonizing bit, twitching, as if in pain, its tortured squirming first revealing a black-clad arm, then a slime-drenched bandage. Finally, it found its feet, straightened, unfurling into the unmistakable shape of an enormous man.

Laura felt his steamlike breath before she heard him.

A guttural rasp.

The Needle Man.

FILMING IS SUSPENDED FOR
THE REST OF THE WEEK WHILE
WE TAKE TIME TO PROCESS THE
TRAGIC EVENTS OF YESTERDAY
AFTERNOON. VINCE MADSEN
WAS A HARD WORKER, A GOOD
MAN, AND A GIFTED CREW
MEMBER.

HE WILL BE GREATLY MISSED.

- CR

TWENTY-NINE

The Needle Man unfolded from the floor, razor talons flashing as he stood. He was twice the size of a normal person, his back rounded, his head slung low as he fought for space. The fire creeping up the walls shied away from him, as if held back by an invisible force, and when the figure set his oily gaze on Laura, he released a blissful sigh.

"polllllyyyyyyyyyyy . . ."

"What the fuck?" Amy whispered, her hand on Laura's back. "What the actual *fuck?*"

Laura wanted to vomit again. Soot and who knew what else tarred her throat.

It had been inside her, but now it was out.

"What the hell is going on?" Mike said.

"We have to get out of here," Amy said, pacing side to side, scanning the ceiling and walls for a way out. "We have to *get out.*"

Laura was only vaguely aware of Amy moving around, her gaze riveted on the thing watching them.

"What is that thing?" she asked.

"A parasite," Beverly said. Behind her, the house blazed orange and white, the fire crawling up from the ground floor like a spider, its legs stretching in all directions. "A creature made of trauma and pain."

"It was in me. How the fuck was it in me?"

"I don't know. Only you can answer that."

"There has to be a way out," Amy said, her voice jumping an octave.

Laura faced the Needle Man, her vision foggy.

He filled the hall, immense and inescapable, his black coat and hat wreathed in smoke. The rag bandages around his face glistened, still wet. Rusted claws carved the air.

The logical part of Laura's mind told her he was a result of lack of oxygen, that her brain cells were dying one at a time, conjuring phantoms, but she felt the burn in her rib cage, tasted rancid flesh, and she knew the smoke-wreathed figure was as real as the fire consuming the house.

Needle claws lifted into the air.

"you're miiiiine . . . polllyyyyy . . ."

The figure lunged. Laura fell backward, braced for spearing pain, but the blow never came. It took her a moment to see that Mike had blocked the figure's path. He absorbed the monster's attack, emitting a low grunt as he shielded Laura from the thing she had birthed. Thin spikes emerged from Mike's lower back, the fabric around it darkening with blood. The Needle Man had driven a claw into his gut.

"Mike," Laura choked.

"Oh God," Amy whimpered, "oh Jesus. That thing's real. It's *really real.*"

"Fucking . . . run . . ." Mike grunted, bent double but holding on to the monster's shoulders. The Needle Man made a slurping sound, blood dripping from his claws.

The sight of Mike's blood unfroze Laura. While Amy took out her phone, murmuring, "No signal, there's no fucking signal out here,"

Laura clambered to her feet. She scanned her surroundings for something to use as a weapon, but she'd dropped the knife in the kitchen and she saw only fire. Beverly remained motionless by the stairs, staring at the thing skewering Mike.

"This is insane," Amy whispered. "How is this happening? *How is this happening?*"

In desperation, Laura slammed her palm into one of the banister uprights, not flinching as splinters bit her flesh, thinking only about Mike. She broke free the wooden baton, which was aflame at one end.

The Needle Man released Mike, who lowered to his knees, clutching his stomach, and Laura thrust the torch into the monster's torso. This time, the fire didn't shy away. The figure made a shrieking sound like a colony of bats as he staggered backward down the landing, thrashing his arms as the fire consumed him.

"Mike," Laura said, going to him. "Are you okay?"

"Only a flesh wound," he said, but his voice was thin, and he cradled his belly with both hands, failing to stem the flow.

Laura dragged him up from the floor, looping one of his arms around her shoulders, feeling him tense as she took his weight.

"Why did you do that?" she panted.

Mike winced. "I'm saving you?"

"You almost died."

"Better than watching you die."

He looked semiconscious, his shirt soaked red, and Laura hated to think what those five claws had done to his insides. She hated that he'd been hurt because of her. Hurt again. All she seemed to have done since she met him was hurt him. She felt the final remnants of anger evaporate.

"I'm sorry," she began, but a screech down the hall drew their attention. The Needle Man had become a flailing column of fire, his movements spreading the blaze, torching the walls and ceiling until he became lost amid the flames.

"You think it's dead?" Amy asked, eyeing the blaze.

"I hope so," Laura said. "Help me, will you?"

Amy didn't move, didn't seem able, but Beverly stepped away from the stairs, toward the place where the Needle Man had vanished.

"It'll take more than fire," she said.

"Little miss freakin' optimist," Amy said, her eyes wide, sweat coating her face. She was breathing hard, losing it. Laura didn't blame her, but she needed her. No way she could do this alone.

"Amy. Get it together. And help me."

Amy appeared to notice Mike for the first time since he'd been stabbed. She pocketed her phone and grunted as she put Mike's other arm around her shoulders. The weight eased on Laura, but they still had to get out. She cast about for an escape, but every one of the guest room doors was ablaze or leaking fumes. Opening one would only spread the fire.

"There's a door back there," Amy said, teeth gritted.

Laura spotted a flicker of movement at the end of the hall. A wrinkle of yellow fabric disappeared through a miraculously undamaged door. Beyond the door, a staircase led up.

"The attic," she said.

She knew that only stupid people went up rather than down in a life-or-death situation, but they had no choice. The first floor was a roaring inferno and the air was so poisonous she felt her consciousness slipping, blurred black at the edges.

Stay awake. Stay the fuck awake.

"It won't stop," Beverly said, her voice raw with smoke. "Not until you stop it."

As if on cue, a dark shape erupted from the fire.

The Needle Man landed, crouched like an insect on the carpet. He was man-sized now, and the flames that had consumed him dwindled to leave only a few flickers across his pant legs and boots. His clawed fingers slammed into the floorboards. A bandaged face tipped in Laura's direction.

"one for sorrow, two for mirth . . ." he whispered.

"Oh God, oh God, oh God," Amy cried. "It's not dead. *It's not dead.*"

"Come on," Laura said, struggling to maneuver Mike and her sister back toward the attic door. They moved clumsily, Mike an almost dead weight between them. He was getting heavier, and Laura couldn't tell if that was because of her own failing strength or his.

"I tried," Mike murmured, bloodstained drool escaping his lips. "I tried to be a good man . . . for you . . ."

Laura focused on the attic.

She got him through the door and stepped back to let Amy and Beverly half drag, half hoist Mike up the stairs. As they went, Laura turned to look at the Needle Man, still not fully understanding what he was, how long she'd had that thing inside her.

The Needle Man rose to stand, kicking a boot to extinguish the final flame. He surged toward her.

"three for a funeral, four for birth . . ."

She slammed the attic door and turned the key.

Five claws broke through the wood, narrowly missing her face.

"five for heaven, six for hell . . ."

"You go to hell," Laura spat, turning to run up the stairs into the attic. She was relieved to be able to breathe easier up there, though now that they were away from the flames, she heard her own labored wheezing and coughed to clear her lungs. Couldn't stop coughing. In the end, the only thing that stopped her was the sight of Polly standing by a rocking horse.

She looked just like Brian's cardboard cutout, but she was moving, swaying side to side, her face in shadow as she watched Laura enter.

"Can that thing climb stairs?" Amy said, lowering Mike onto a worn sofa, where he clutched his stomach and groaned, his eyes closing.

"Do you see her?" Laura asked.

Amy scanned the attic. "What? Who?"

"Me."

Amy shook her head and went back to searching for a way out. "There must be a hidden staircase or something around here. Old houses always have hidden staircases."

Laura surveyed the attic, trying to ignore the younger version of herself standing in the corner. The room was furnished as a child's playroom, and a toy chest scattered its contents across the floor. Ancient dolls and stuffed animals were dotted everywhere.

Beverly stood at the top of the stairs, looking down as the sound of crunching and smashing echoed up to them. The Needle Man was attempting to break in.

"We don't have much time," she said.

Mike groaned, the sound involuntary, something from deep in his gut, perhaps around the place he'd been impaled. Laura went to his side.

"Stay with us, Mike," she said, wiping perspiration from his forehead.

"I messed it up," he said, his words slurred. "All of it. I'm sorry."

"Stop talking like that."

"I wanted to keep you safe. You have to believe me. I only want good things for you. The best things."

"Mike, listen to me," she said. "Aside from sending me on the worst assignment of my life, you've been there for me. You have. And I need you to fucking stay with me, because we're going to get out of here, some-fucking-how."

Mike laughed, then curled up in pain. "You know you make swearing sound like poetry."

His hand was in hers, slippery with blood, and she held on to it, didn't want to let go.

"I always liked that," Mike whispered, his eyes closing.

"There's a way down!" Amy said. She was leaning out a window. "If we move fast, we can get down to the balcony below, then jump."

Laura squeezed Mike's hand. "Hear that? We're getting out of here."

He didn't respond.

"Mike?"

His chest was still.

"Mike!"

She shook him. His head rolled to one side. She peeled up the bottom of his shirt and saw the mashed flesh of his stomach, oozing blood so dark it was almost black. Already his skin was changing color. Becoming yellow.

"Mike!" She tipped his head back, pressed her lips to his, tried to breathe, but coughed, her own lungs failing.

"He's gone," Beverly said.

Laura didn't want to give up, but she saw it. The lack of life. The lack of anything.

Mike was dead.

"Fuck!"

Pounding echoed up from the attic door. The sound of wood being assaulted over and over. Laura turned to see Beverly looking down the stairs, whispering something under her breath.

"What are you doing?" she asked.

"Trying to slow it down," Beverly said.

Laura rose, her hand slipping from Mike's. She backed away from the sofa, unable to comprehend that Mike was gone. Whatever problems they'd had, whatever love or anger existed between them, it was gone now. Dead on the sofa.

The Needle Man had claimed a sixth victim.

"Mike's dead?" Amy asked, crossing the attic, tears streaking her face. She went to Mike, pressed a palm to his cheek, made a quiet sobbing sound when he failed to respond.

"What did you do?" Laura asked Beverly, her voice husky with grief. "How did that thing come out of me?"

Beverly blinked, looked both weary and defiant. "I've been trying to protect you. I *have* been protecting you, ever since we met. But too many people have suffered. Too many have died."

She shook her head. "I didn't want to believe it was you. But then I saw the figure in the bathroom, the imprint you left behind there, and I realized it was in you. Feeding on your trauma. It wants you to be Polly again. That's why it used me, too, to keep you scared. Somehow, it made me do all those things with the fortune-teller and the dress. We've been connected ever since that day in the studio restroom."

She took a breath. "But the only way out is through. Your monster is here, and the only way to destroy it is to confront whatever trauma created it."

For the first time, Laura noticed that blue tarp covered one of the walls. She felt a lethal prick of pain in her temple at the sight of it.

"Pill, what did you mean?" Amy said softly, turning a tear-tracked face to her. "When you said it was your fault?"

The tarp shifted slightly, and Laura felt new heat course through her. Not the heat of the fire but the heat of a memory forcing its way to the surface.

The attic door gave a splintering, cracking scream, then fell silent.

The Needle Man was inside.

"Oh God, he's coming," Amy said, stepping backward toward the window. "That thing . . . Pill, we have to get out of here."

The stairs creaked and the Needle Man emerged, talons wet with Mike's blood, mucus bubbling from arid lips. Beverly stood firm at the top of the stairs, hand held out toward him. She murmured words Laura couldn't hear, while Amy pressed against the window frame, her gaze riveted on the monster.

"youuuuu're miiiine . . ." the Needle Man hissed, pointing a claw at Laura.

"Stop!" Beverly shouted, and the monster remained on the top step. It seemed held in place by whatever Beverly began to whisper.

Laura looked at the psychic, then her sister, then her ex-boyfriend. She felt something crack and break inside her.

And out of the wreckage, fresh defiance bloomed.

"This ends now," she said.

She turned and walked into the center of the attic, facing Polly in the corner. The little girl stepped forward, into the light, though neither Amy nor Beverly appeared to be able to see her. The vision was Laura's alone. A living memory. She was dressed in the same yellow dress Laura wore now, a distorted reflection. Past and present reunited.

Laura felt words that had stabbed at her for years clamoring to take control of her tongue. She bit down. She'd do this her way.

She turned to Amy.

"Start recording."

Amy frowned, wide-eyed, but did as Laura said. She took out her phone and pointed it at her sister.

Laura took a breath and looked at her younger self.

"It started with Mom," she said, and the words came with the ease of an article she'd been itching to write but couldn't find the right opening line for, until now. "I wasn't playing hide-and-seek with Brian that day. I was with Mom. We were running lines during the final week of *The Guesthouse* and I was sick of it. I never wanted to be Tammy. I didn't want to be a part of the movie. But she forced me, said this was our big break. *Ours*, not mine."

She forced herself to take a breath. "We had a fight in my dressing room, and I ran out. I ran all the way to the guesthouse set. I was so angry, I just wanted to get away."

In the dark of the attic, Laura watched young Polly stomp across the floor, clenching and releasing her hands, rubbing her sore wrists. She couldn't stand still. Kept moving. Fired up by the argument in the dressing room. Searching for an outlet that satisfied the rage smoldering through her. She tore a doll from a shelf and stomped on its head. When that wasn't enough, she seized a framed picture and smashed it on the floor, scattering glass splinters all around.

"I made it to the attic," Laura said, "but then I saw something."

Polly's gaze went to the tarp rippling against the wall. She bit her lip as she approached it.

Laura stepped aside as Polly tugged back the tarp to reveal a hole in the wall. Beyond it was the roof and, beyond that, the night sky. Laura glimpsed a ghostly outline of the studio roof against a scattering of stars.

Polly ducked through. She began to move across the pitched roof. Laura followed, Amy right behind her. Beverly remained facing the Needle Man, her face showing strain but determination. Laura kept going, knew this was what Beverly had wanted since the moment she trapped them in the guesthouse.

"I went out onto the roof," Laura said, stopping at a juncture where two peaked roofs joined. Polly was a lot nimbler, and she was already on another section of the roof, near the edge of the building. Laura stood and watched Polly taking in the view. The desert glowed, bathed in the light of the fire, and above her head, she glimpsed the faint lines of the soundstage. She was both there and nowhere. In the present and in the past.

"The soundstage was so far below," Laura said as Amy filmed her, phone twitching in her grasp. "I felt free. Above it all."

Free of her mother and the movie and everything that went with it. She felt like a bird, desperate to fly.

"It didn't last. Something else was up there with me."

Laura watched a dark shape emerge behind Polly, pitch-black

against the dark blue sky. Polly heard movement and spun to face the Needle Man, eyes wide with fear. It wasn't the monster Laura had coughed up on the guesthouse landing. It was the movie monster from 1993, crouched atop the set, not a foot away from Polly, who stood transfixed as the figure loomed over her.

"Polly . . ." a muffled voice whispered, and Polly was trembling now, her face bleached of color, her body stiff with fear. The Needle Man reached out and seized her wrists, and Laura felt the pressure at the base of her own hands, kneading flesh into bone. It sparked something primal in her. Lit something wild and furious.

She'd been gripped that way before, too many times.

She saw her mother's face, too close, her fingers pincering her wrists, dragging her into the white fire of her eyes.

Always demanding.

Never smiling.

Never giving.

Only taking.

Leaching the life from her.

Polly only ever wanted to make her happy.

But nothing ever did.

Laura's heart hammered. She wanted to stop what was about to happen, but she knew she couldn't. Thirty years stood in the way.

"Polly," the Needle Man said, *"you can't be up here,"* and Polly's face screwed up with rage and rebellion. She tore her wrists free and charged the Needle Man, shoving him with the outsized strength of a person consumed by emotion.

The Needle Man let out a cry.

His hands went up, seeking something to grab hold of, but there was nothing but air. He made a strangled sound as he went over the side of the roof.

"I pushed him," Laura said, her rib cage juddering. "I pushed the Needle Man off the roof. It was all my fault."

Amy said nothing. She looked stunned, barely holding up her phone. It shook in her grasp.

"I don't remember climbing down. I was so scared. The next thing I remember was being on the soundstage floor, by the body. He was so still, but I heard the final breaths leave him, and I wondered if he really was a monster, or if he was something else."

A low hiss sounded behind her and Laura turned to see that her Needle Man had risen from the attic. Somehow, he had gotten past Beverly. Laura prayed she was still alive.

The Needle Man emitted a dank, rattling rasp and she felt the malevolence it contained. The pain it felt vibrated in her skin but, for the first time, she wasn't afraid.

She felt the weight of the thing she'd been carrying for three decades.

Now that it stood in front of her, she couldn't believe how heavy it had been. How she'd grown accustomed to the weight of it.

As Beverly clambered up to join them, Laura stepped forward and reached for the creature's face.

"Laura," Amy said, sounding afraid, but she fell silent as Laura tugged away the bandages, revealing a face she knew so well. A face she hadn't seen in thirty years.

The first victim.

Vince.

He looked just as she remembered him. Dimpled cheeks, stubble shadowing his jaw and hair falling into his eyes, which were the only things that were different. His eyes were pitch-black. Inhuman. Filled with nightmare.

She saw the source of the gargling. His broken neck.

"I'd forgotten it was you," she said.

"What's going on?" Amy asked, her hands shaking around the phone.

"Vince was the Needle Man," Laura said, keeping her gaze on him, wary that he could snap and attack at any moment. He remained motionless, though, as if entranced by her words.

"He played him in the movie," Laura continued, "but nobody knew that, not even me. Not until I killed him."

She'd thought it was the monster.

She'd thought it was her mother.

When Vince appeared on the roof behind her, dressed in his Needle Man costume, Polly had felt in her core that he was there to kill her.

But she'd wanted to kill, too.

She'd wanted to purge the ache of hurt and misery from her body, push it onto something else.

So that was what she did.

As she knelt by the Needle Man's prone form on the dusty soundstage floor, tugging away the bandages, she was horrified to discover that she hadn't slain a monster, but a man. And as she crouched there, watching the life leave Vince Madsen's eyes, pain and fear swelled through her, became too big for her body, so big she was afraid it would tear her apart.

Instead, she felt a lump form in her throat and she swallowed it down, and she forgot.

For the first time in decades, Laura remembered hearing a sound at the stage door and running to hide under the craft services table. From there, she watched her director, Christopher Rosenthal, enter the space. She watched as he found the body, went to it, crouched over, and stifled a cry.

Then he began removing the costume. Carefully, he lifted away the hat and gloves, unbuttoned the trench coat, leaving Vince in his T-shirt and jeans. No longer the Needle Man. Just a man.

And the knowledge of who was really behind the mask died with Christopher.

In the days and weeks that followed Vince's death, Polly told herself different versions of the story.

That she hadn't meant to kill him.

That he tripped.

That she hadn't been anywhere near Vince when he died.

"If I hadn't pushed him," Laura said, staring into the dead face as she stood on the rooftop, "he'd still be alive. They all would."

Tears filled Beverly's eyes as she stood by Amy, but Amy's jaw was set, as if she were holding back whatever emotion ran through her.

"How could you forget that?" she murmured.

"If you try hard enough, you can forget anything."

Laura looked up into Vince's face. Not Vince, but an echo, something forged out of her own pain. The darkest corner of her mind had created him.

"I killed all of them," Laura said. "Todd, too. And Kyle, Madeleine, Brian." Her voice hitched. "Mike."

"You're not a killer, Laura," Beverly said. "But you've been carrying a killer around with you. It poisoned that set, infected your co-stars and coworkers. Whatever was birthed in that moment, it killed them. Not you."

Laura wanted to believe it. She wished she could pin the blame on the thing that her own anger had birthed. Because she was just a kid. A kid in a world that took from her without ever stopping to wonder if she was okay. She had been so scared, so trapped and stifled and powerless, and a part of her had wanted the chaos, had wanted the blood. It was that part of her that created the Needle Man.

"I'm sorry," she said to the Needle Man. "I'm sorry for what I did. And I'm sorry for what I made you into."

He opened his mouth, tried to speak, but only a wet sound emerged, the fragments of his broken neck moving under the skin.

Laura swallowed down the lump in her throat, wanting to say more but knowing that the words wouldn't be for him, they'd be for her. To soothe her guilt.

She looked over Vince's shoulder at Beverly. The psychic looked exhausted, dark shadows beneath her eyes. But there was triumph in her expression, too. She had accomplished what she came here to do. Proved she could help when it counted.

"Thank you," Laura said, holding Beverly's gaze.

"I need a cigarette," Beverly replied.

Laura gestured down at the burning house. "I'm sure I can find you a light."

Beverly smiled. "I guess the psychic doesn't always die."

Laura felt the corners of her mouth twitch, but then Vince jerked into action, as if waking up from the spell Laura's story had cast. He raised an arm, and the needle claws flashed. His black gaze shone with renewed malevolence, his face twisted into a grimace, and Laura knew the monster wasn't done yet.

Purging something wasn't the same as stopping it.

"puuhh . . . leee," he gurgled, and the claws descended.

Laura raised her hands to protect herself, only just catching hold of his arm in time. He was so strong, her body shook with the effort of holding him off.

"Vince, please," she said, the needles clacking centimeters from her nose.

"It isn't Vince anymore," Beverly said.

There was no expression on the Needle Man's face, only a dead-eyed stare. An emptiness. He was made to kill and that was all he knew.

But Laura had made him.

He was *her* monster.

She must have some power over him.

With a cry, Laura threw him off her, and the Needle Man whirled around, claws biting the air as he turned. At the same time, Beverly leaped forward to help.

She stopped suddenly. Gasped.

The psychic's hand went to her throat, and Laura watched blood well between her fingers.

The Needle Man's blades had caught her as he flailed.

"Beverly!" Laura cried, leaping forward to catch her as she dropped to the tiles. She cradled Beverly in her arms as blood pumped from her neck, pouring over her leather jacket. She stared up at Laura.

No. This wasn't the way it was supposed to end.

Beverly had done what nobody else could.

She had saved Laura.

She couldn't die.

"Hang on," Laura said, searching the folds of her dress for something to fasten around Beverly's neck.

Beverly's hand rested on hers, pressed firmly. Caused Laura to stop.

"End it," she said, coughing up blood.

The Needle Man's focus swung to Laura and Amy.

Gently, Laura eased Beverly to the tiled roof and got up. She pushed Amy behind her, facing the thing that had once been Vince. His claws raked the air, narrowly missing her, and she no longer feared him. Any power he had, that power came from her. Beverly had been right all along. Only Laura could defeat him. This was her story to end.

"You're not Vince," she said. "Not anymore. Your time is over. We're fucking done here."

The Needle Man jolted forward and Laura grabbed his clawed hand, surprised that she was able to stop him. Grunting, she twisted the claw, drew on every cell in her body, and drove the needle points into the Needle Man's chest.

His eyes snapped wide, his mouth opening and closing. Black blood frothed between parched lips. He staggered back, dark veins forking across his face as blood pumped from his chest, slicking his black coat.

"Time to move on," Laura told him. She stepped forward and pushed.

The Needle Man fell.

She watched him topple off the roof, sail through the air, and strike a pitched roof on the first floor. It buckled beneath him and he vanished through it, into a wall of fire.

The flames consumed him.

Laura stood and watched the spot where he had disappeared, not breathing, her nails cutting into her palms as she waited. But the Needle Man didn't emerge. This felt different. She remembered Vince as he was in the '90s, goofing around with her and Brian between takes. Before he was the Needle Man. Before any of this.

She had created the Needle Man and she had stopped him.

She took a breath, tension easing from her neck, her shoulders lowering.

It was over.

The Needle Man was gone.

A hand touched her arm and she jumped, but it was just Amy.

"Is it over?" Amy asked.

"I think so."

Laura gave the broken roof one last look, then turned and went to Beverly. She rolled her over, but knew immediately that she was dead. She tried to ignore the leaking slash in her neck and closed her eyelids. Despite the blood, Beverly looked peaceful, a ghost of a smile on her lips.

"Thank you," Laura said, bowing her head.

Who knew, maybe there was life after death. She hoped Beverly had found quiet from the voices at last.

"It's about time we got the fuck out of here, don't you think?" Amy said.

Excerpt from the article "The Haunting of Polly Tremaine" by Laura Warren, published in Zeppelin *magazine*

It used to be that when I thought about *The Guesthouse*, I thought of all the things I could've done differently. The people I could've helped. The stories we could have told. But here's the thing people often forget when they talk about *The Guesthouse*: I was just a kid. A seven-year-old child. And the people who died weren't characters in a movie being stalked by a mythological monster. They were real people. They were my coworkers. My contemporaries. My friends. And their deaths were all very real, very human tragedies.

There never was a curse.

I know that might be difficult for fans of *The Guesthouse* to accept. The idea of a movie curse is exciting. It's thrilling. It makes us wonder and analyze and feel horrified all over again. At some point, though, we have to confront reality. The true horrors that lie outside of the cinema.

When I go to bed at night, it's not *The Guesthouse* or the Needle Man that haunts me. It's the thought that my friends died and nobody really cared. Not for the right reasons, anyway.

(continued on next page)

THIRTY

One Year Later

The studio lots were smaller in England. This one felt quainter, less threatening, more like an airfield than a place where movies were made. The two-story main building was a checkerboard of windows. Beyond it rested cube-like soundstages, accessible only via a flimsy security gate.

Sitting in her car in the lot, Laura checked herself in the rearview mirror, brushing her fingers through her newly styled hair, lighter than it had been in years, and noted the lack of shadows under her eyes. Thirteen months after the guesthouse burned, she felt lighter in herself, too, like all the cobwebs of too many years had blown away. There was a word for that feeling.

Freedom.

She had imagined pining for freedom from a California prison cell while serving multiple life sentences for the deaths of the *It Feeds* cast and crew. The authorities certainly seemed intent on pinning them on her. She was remanded in custody without bail for a month. But Mike had come through for her from beyond the grave. Laura still had the card he gave her that day in the hotel, and the lawyer turned out to be perfect. Felicity Jackson was indomitable, experienced, *terrifying*, and, somehow, she ensured that the case never made it to trial. When it was presented to a judge, the circumstantial evidence buried it quicker than her co-stars.

It helped that Amy had covered their tracks.

After defeating the Needle Man, they had climbed out of the attic window to the balcony below, and when Laura's feet finally touched the ground, she couldn't remember how she had scrambled down the side of the house, but the relief of solid earth beneath her feet almost caused her legs to crumple.

Then she noticed Amy tapping at her phone, her face dirty with soot, blood, and tears.

"What are you doing?" Laura had asked.

"Deleting the recording. Deleting all of it."

Laura tried to convince her not to. She had to own the truth. She'd killed Vince. It had to end there. But Amy hadn't wavered, trashing everything they'd recorded over the course of those frantic five days in L.A.

"You don't owe the internet any kind of truth."

Months later, Laura barely heard the ruling when it was called out in court, her brain fizzing with anxiety.

When her lawyer took her arm and repeated that she was free to go, she felt numb.

She was free.

Free.

It took her seven months to stop looking over her shoulder, waiting for the ruling to be revoked.

Because she knew she was guilty. Even though she hadn't killed anybody with her own hands—except Vince, once upon a time—they died because of her.

Ivan. Todd. Kyle. Madeleine. Brian. Mike. Beverly.

Seven new victims of the Needle Man.

Laura took small comfort in the fact that she'd saved one life. Seven victims instead of eight this time.

But that didn't bring back her '90s co-stars.

They were dead because of the thing she had created.

Now she carried around a new kind of weight in her chest.

One that she was still learning to live with.

Laura checked the time on her phone, drawing strength from her Winona Ryder background. Winona had survived her thirties. She survived all the Hollywood crap: the bad press, the toxic relationships, the gremlins of her mind. She was in her fifties now and the happiest she'd ever been, according to most sources. Maybe Laura could be, too.

She got out of the car and approached the security gate. The guard took her name, checked it off a list, and handed her a visitors' badge, which Laura pinned to the front of her yellow shirt.

"Welcome to the movies," he said with a wink.

She followed the directions down the blacktop avenue between soundstages, ignoring the tremor in her jaw as she pictured Madeleine the PR skipping ahead of her, talking about *It Feeds* and horror history. She took a left and arrived at a row of trailers lined up outside one of the soundstages. She knocked at the first door.

"Come in," a female voice called.

Laura stepped up into the trailer. In a whirl of black hair, Amy turned from a dresser mirror, swaddled in a silk robe. Her face was made up with more product than Laura had ever seen on her sister. Eyes thickly outlined, cheekbones darkly contoured. The kind of makeup that only looked good on camera.

When she saw Laura, Amy leaped up and threw her arms around her.

"You made it."

"Wouldn't miss it for the world," Laura said, taking in the rest of the trailer. Magazines were heaped on the sofa, makeup and handbags on the coffee table, an overstuffed rack of clothes by a door that must be the bathroom. The only thing that surprised her was the *Muppets Most Wanted* poster on the wall, signed by the cast. It must have come with the room.

Amy released her. "How are you?"

"I'm good. And I'm loving the new look."

Amy patted her hair, beaming. "It's different, right? We were thinking Uma in *Pulp Fiction.*"

"You know blondes have more fun."

"So *Kill Bill?* Just tell me I look like a spy."

Laura smiled, happy for her. "You look like a star."

Amy grinned and went back to the mirror, checking her makeup. A script lay open on the dresser, an episode of the BBC series *Knock Twice.* After everything that had happened in L.A., Amy got a callback from the show over a year after she'd auditioned. One of their actors got a Hollywood offer and quit, and the casting director remembered Amy's audition. Now she was a series regular.

Laura was glad. Amy had worked hard to get here. So what if Laura's court case was the reason casting remembered her? In this business, you used what you had. Even controversy. *Especially* controversy.

Now Laura was the one drifting in search of a direction. But she was okay with that. Sometimes drifting was good for the soul.

"Are you enjoying the show?" she asked.

"Are you here to interview me?"

"Once a journalist, always a journalist." Amy knew Laura had quit. She was done telling stories. Nobody tried to convince her to stay at *Zeppelin* magazine, not even her coworkers. They knew the industry was struggling and, frankly, they could do without the competition.

Laura hadn't written a word in months. Not even in her journal. She visited her mom every weekend. She took her out in her wheelchair. Went for walks in the park. Bought her ice cream. Tried to focus on forgiveness.

It was painful at first, looking into the face of the person who had terrorized her for the better part of three decades. But that person was gone now, and Laura finally felt ready to grieve her. The hurt remained, a shadow in her heart, but it was time to move on. Mindfulness helped quiet the noise in her brain, although she wasn't sure if that was just because mindfulness was so boring; she often passed out while meditating.

Either way, she hadn't counted in months.

"Listen," Amy said, "why don't we take a seat?"

She swept the magazines onto the floor and they sat. Amy played with the hem of her shirt. She suddenly looked nervous.

"What's up?" Laura asked.

"There's something I have to tell you, but I'm trying to figure out how. It's such an amazing opportunity, but the last thing I want to do is hurt you."

Laura's chest cramped.

"Okay," she said.

Amy pressed her hands together in her lap. "Last week, my agent got a call from Netflix. They're resurrecting *It Feeds* now that things have died down and . . . well, the thing is . . . they want me to play Tammy."

All feeling left Laura's body.

Her brain struggled to process what her sister had said.

"They want me to play Tammy."

That was the reason Amy invited her to the studio? To break this news to her?

"Pill?"

Laura blinked, looked into her sister's face. She tried to pull herself together.

"That's . . . great," she said.

Amy's expression lifted. "Really? Because I can turn them down if you have any reservations. Any at all. Honestly."

She took Laura's hands, and Laura realized she had been picking her thumbnail, easing a strip of skin away from the cuticle. It stung.

"I'm happy for you," Laura said, her tongue sluggish. "Really."

Amy squealed and dragged her into a hug. "Thank you thank you thank you. I hoped you wouldn't mind. That's why I already accepted the part. This is going to be so good for us, I just know it."

Us.

Not *you.*

Not *good for you.*

"It's our big break!" she heard her mom say.

Ours. Not hers.

Laura swallowed, her mouth dry.

"Can I use the bathroom?" She tried to sound upbeat. "I drank too much gas station coffee on the way here."

"Oh, sure, it's right through there."

Laura stood and went to the door by the clothes rack.

"Pill," Amy said, and she paused, turned. "I love you."

Laura managed a smile and went into the bathroom. It was just big enough to hold a shower cubicle, sink, and toilet. She stared at her reflection in the mirror above the sink, her mouth downturned at the corners, her eyes large and dark. The yellow fabric of her shirt turned the underside of her face a sickly pallor.

She noticed a shadow behind her, stretched across the wall. She moved and the shadow moved. It was her own. Nothing else was in there with her.

Turning on the faucet, she ran cold water over her wrists, then scooped it up into her face. She barely felt it.

She hadn't told anybody that she still dreamed about the Needle Man.

Even though she had purged him from her body, vanquished him at Gimlet Point Guesthouse, he lingered in her dreams. Sometimes she wondered if she really had killed him.

"They want me to play Tammy."

Laura choked on the water, coughed as it flooded her nostrils. Her sinuses stung and she remembered fighting for air in the burning guesthouse.

She wanted Amy to be happy, God knew she'd been through enough. And Amy had been there for her when the world turned inside out. When her nightmares became flesh, Amy had protected her. She'd deleted the videos. She'd kept Laura's secret.

Now she wanted her blessing to play Tammy?

Laura's fingernails scraped the porcelain sink.

She felt like she'd been split down the middle, her insides spilling out black and charred.

How could Amy be so stupid? So blind? She wanted to play *Tammy?* After everything that had happened?

They had ended it in Craven.

Buried the past.

Laura had found peace. Or as close to it as she had ever known.

Now Amy was digging it up again. Taking that peace away from her. Laura wanted to scream *no.*

No-no-*no!*

"No! You can't have him, he's mine!"

Last week, her mom had one of her bad days. She wouldn't change out of her nightgown and cradled one of Laura's old Care Bears as if it were her newborn. When Laura tried to ease it out of her grasp, her mother started screaming.

"He's mine! You can't have him!"

"Be good," Laura told her, *"or the Needle Man will get you."*

"Be good," Laura murmured now, raising her head to look in the mirror.

Darkness flickered in her eyes.

And she felt a lump in her throat. Swallowed. Swallowed down the hurt and rage until it became a pulsing ember in her chest.

She heard movement in the other room and braced herself against the sink.

She heard a strangled cry, something being knocked over, then a grunting sound, a pounding like legs against the floor.

Grunting, writhing. Gasped, choking breaths.

A gurgling sigh.

Then silence.

A few seconds later, footsteps. Then a sound at the door.

Tap, tap, tap.

Something metal against the wood.

A whisper, low and rasping. A voice that crept up her spine into the base of her skull.

"polllyyyy ..."

Laura gripped the sink, closed her eyes, and started counting.

NEWS   CULTURE   REVIEWS   HOT TAKES   OUTTAKES   SUBSCRIBE

"THAT'S MY MAN!" STAR TO LEAD HORROR SERIES "IT FEEDS"

Reality TV star Rose Simpson has signed on to lead the cast of Netflix streaming series *It Feeds*.

Best known for reality show *That's My Man!*, Simpson will make her acting debut playing sexy student Tammy Manners, the daughter of a hotelier who runs a cursed B&B.

It Feeds is already famous for its many false starts and behind-the-scenes problems. The show shut down for over a year before a whole new cast and crew signed on under the direction of Jesse Doyle (*Night Fear*).

The role of Tammy Manners was originally set to be played by Kyle Williamson, before her death saw the role pass to Amy Tremaine. Tremaine also tragically died a month ago, after an attack at a British studio where she was filming the BBC series *Knock Twice*.

"I'm so excited to be joining the show," Simpson said in a statement. "I love being scared. Bring it on!"

SEARCH

The studio looked deserted. Beyond the gates, lamplight pooled in the vacant parking lot, and the windows were as dark as the night sky. Laura tugged her coat collar up against the chill as she stood outside the gate. The collar shielded her from the wind, but it also hid her face from anybody who might appear without warning. It was a face that was in the papers again and she could do without the hassle.

Few people came out here, though. The studio had been built in isolation, away from populated areas. There was little chance that anybody would interrupt her.

Laura looked down at the collection of cards and flowers to the side of the gate. They clustered in a sizable lump of browning petals and rain-wilted cards that screamed empty sentiment, placed there by people who had never met Amy and, now, never would.

WE MISS YOU!

SORRY FOR YOUR LOSS

YOU'LL ALWAYS BE OUR STAR

Among the offerings, Amy smiled up at Laura. Her brown eyes were bright beneath blond bangs. The sight of the photograph was too much. Laura felt a prick at the back of her throat and averted her gaze to take in the wilted flowers.

It was strange how the loss seemed more profound now. She supposed reality took time settling in. Amy had always filled a room, and it was difficult to imagine her six feet under, lying in a coffin in a cemetery Laura dared not visit. It was risky enough coming to the studio, but the place was shuttered for the night. There was less chance she'd be spotted here than at her sister's grave.

The thought of Amy in the ground made it difficult for Laura to breathe and she forced herself to think about Amy when she was alive, vital and opinionated and funny.

She'd never given up. Despite all the setbacks and rejections, she'd kept at it.

Laura had thought she was setting herself up for a fall.

Now, though, she understood Amy's efforts for what they were.

Cultivation.

Perfection.

Evolution.

Amy had strived to become the best version of herself, and she finally got there.

Laura was evolving now, too.

She felt it beneath her ribs. Not a weight anymore, but more of a presence. Warm and glowing.

For thirty years, she had lived unaware of the power inside her, blind to her own potential. Now she knew the truth. The thing beneath her ribs would always be there, even after what happened at Gimlet Point. Maybe it had changed, too. Evolved. It no longer felt like something separate sharing her body, a parasite or a haunting. It had become an essential part of her. Something primal. Powerful.

She was meant for more.

Journalism was bush-league. Inconsequential. Today's trauma became yesterday's news, and the cycle was never-ending. She could do better.

A thorn pricked Laura's heart as she looked again at the rain-spattered photo.

Amy.

She chewed the inside of her cheek as she remembered leaving the trailer bathroom a month ago, keeping her gaze from the body on the floor. It took all her willpower not to look—she knew she'd never make it out of the studio if she did—but she couldn't ignore the blood. It seeped through the carpet, moving as if with purpose. As if seeking Laura out.

She could still smell it, the bitter tang of her sister's blood, and she wished it hadn't come to that.

She wished her sister had chosen differently.

If she had just turned down *It Feeds*, she'd still be alive.

Their father would have been devastated. It was a small blessing that he was already gone.

Laura sniffed, almost surrendering to the sting in her throat, her eyes tingling with tears. She thought of gummy bear cuddles, the movie nights watching *Clue*, the times they made up stories about their futures.

"I'm in love with the reality of you."

She bit down on her bottom lip, tasted metal.

Amy had allowed herself to be seduced by Hollywood. She had given in to the allure. She had been weak. In the end, the decision had been Amy's to make, and Laura wasn't responsible for the fallout.

It had to end somewhere.

Still, the loss hurt. A voice in her head told her she'd done something terrible. It sounded like her mother. Laura bit down harder. Their mother wouldn't understand what had happened. She'd be spared the pain of losing Amy. Just another reason to despise her.

As much as she tried to forgive her mother, Laura knew it was futile. The damage was done. The voice was always there. And knowing that her mother was alive, could always pick up the phone or drop by whenever she liked, left Laura feeling unsafe. As unsafe as she had as a kid. Aware that any second the monster could reach out and grab her. Maybe force her to hold a match.

Laura surveyed the offerings, wrinkling her nose at the gaudiness of it all.

It was affection adjacent. Sentiment without sense.

There had been no cards or flowers when Hollywood spat Laura out. Nobody besides herself to mourn the childhood she missed out on. Nobody to take responsibility for what she endured.

It was only fair that when her coworkers died in the '90s, she told herself she wasn't responsible.

Even though she knew that everybody involved in *The Guesthouse* who died had, at some point during production, seen Polly suffering at the hands of her mother . . . and done nothing to help her.

Her on-screen mom would laugh and joke with Pamela at craft services, shaking her head as she said, *"Kids, right? Who needs them?"*

Her on-screen sister told Polly to stop being a crybaby diva.

Even Yvonne Lincoln was complicit. Of them all, she'd had the fearless spirit required to stand up to somebody like Pamela Tremaine. Instead, she chose to focus on the movie.

And Christopher Rosenthal? Well, he'd cast Polly in the first place, hadn't he?

Laura put a hand in her pocket and felt the object resting there. It gave her something to focus on. Carefully, she removed it, pinching the folds in the paper to sharpen them. Then she bent down and set the paper fortune-teller in amid the cards and flowers.

It rocked slightly in the breeze.

She hadn't been able to tell Amy how she'd die, but that didn't matter. The fortune-teller was more of an emblem. A symbol. A reminder that Laura was the one in control now, perhaps for the first time in her life.

It was all coming together.

Yvonne had been right.

In the end, Hollywood really had made her.

It had made Laura the person she was today, and she finally knew why.

She had to stop the cycle. Stop the people who capitalized on tragedy. The ones getting fat off other people's pain. That was how nature worked.

It required checks and balances. Positive and negative. Forest fires cleansed the soil.

When something got out of hand, it had to be brought back in line.

Laura couldn't wuss out now. She couldn't afford to be selective. She had work to do.

She took a breath, filled with relief and regret and hope, because she had found her purpose.

The wind slipped inside her collar and caressed her neck with cold fingers.

"yesssss, pollyyyyyshhhhhhh," a voice whispered, and Laura shivered, feeling the power beneath her skin. She wasn't afraid of it anymore. She felt unshackled. Strong. Driven.

"I have to go," she told the photo. "I don't think I'll be back, at least not for a while. I have a lot of work to do." She stood, her thoughts on the days ahead. "I just have to make one stop on the way."

As she approached the car, she took out an object that rattled as she absent-mindedly shook it. A box of matches. She rattled it some more, a full pack just waiting to be used, and she remembered the line from *The Guesthouse.*

"Fire is always hungry and it doesn't care what it eats."
That was the thing about fire.
It didn't take much.
Just a single flame.
And the whole world could burn.

Acknowledgments

I love horror movies. I was raised by the many fantastic films and film-makers homaged in this book. *Candyman, A Nightmare on Elm Street, Poltergeist,* and *Scream* are just a few of the VHS tapes I watched on repeat as a young adult, huddled under the covers in my bedroom, terrified and enthralled by equal measure. I hope that *Burn the Negative* stands as a fitting tribute to those stories and their tellers.

I must thank my agent, Kristina Pérez. It's scary how good an editor you are, and I'm so grateful to have you championing my work. (Not gonna lie, it helps that you dig *Scream* as much as I do.)

Everybody at G. P. Putnam's Sons has been a dream. Special thanks to my editor, Mark Tavani, for loving Laura from the start, and for believing in the value of "fun horror." Thank you for helping me to sharpen this book until it drew blood. Thank you, Aranya Jain, for your expert insight and editorial guidance—this book is so much better thanks to you. I'm so grateful to designer Laura Corless for turning this book into a work of art—your attention to detail in the creation of over thirty (yes, *thirty*) documents is simply staggering. Sincere thanks, also, to copyeditor Amy Schneider and proofreaders Rob Sternitzky and

ACKNOWLEDGMENTS

Katrina Alonso, who caught my mistakes and put a match to them. And on the production side, thank you Erin Byrne, Emily Mileham, and Claire Sullivan for aiding Laura on her journey to publication.

I've been overwhelmed with support from friends, family, and fellow writers—too many to mention here, but you know who you are. In particular, thank you, Kat Ellis, Polly Glass, and Troy Gardner for your early advice and encouragement. For phone calls/texts/pub chats, thank you, Matt Glasby, Rosie Fletcher, Lydia Gittins, William Hussey, and Paul Cunliffe. You keep me writing.

So many bloggers, vloggers, reviewers, and podcasters have shown me enormous kindness. A massive thank-you to my spooky Tales of Point Horror sisters Chelley Toy and Emma Pullar.

Thank you to the lovely authors who took the time to read and blurb *Burn the Negative*.

Thank you, Winona Ryder, for being really freaking cool.

Thank you, Penny, for putting all other monsters to shame.

And Thom. Thank you for being the positive to my negative.